ATLANTIAN MAGIC

ADVENTURE

By

Pd Michel

Pd MICHEL

This is the second edition of the Book Atlantian Magic –Adventure Through Four Realms

It is being rereleased in a smaller format. There have been no significant changes in the book.

Cover art taken from publicly available photographs, modified with a graphics program by the author.

Second Edition Copywrite   © 2019 by Pat Michel

ISBN-9781796696141

ATLANTIAN MAGIC

To my mother and father.

I know they are keeping a chair open at the family table for me in their mansion in heaven.

Acknowledgements

I wish to and thank Sheri, Dave, Rich, Christopher, Ayla, Lizzy, and Sam for their honest criticism of my writing. I also want to thank Melanie, Thom and the rest of the Friday Night Writes group at Dogeared Pages Bookstore in Phoenix Arizona. I owe much of what is good in this book to their friendship, encouragement, and what we learned together as writers.

I consider myself privileged to have attended talks and seminars given by many knowledgeable authors, some well-known and some yet to be discovered. There are too many over several years for me to thank individually. They have my heartfelt thanks for sharpening my pen and helping me develop my writing style.

Pd Michel

Chapter 1

Marvin couldn't remember ever having a worse headache. He was lying on the ground on the edge of the hiking trail. He sat up. The rough rock and vegetation of the desert trail had left bruises and scrapes. His whole body tingled, like when an arm falls asleep and blood flow was returning. He felt the back of his head. Pain from a wound made its presence known as he pulled the dried matted blood off his hair. He grabbed a bottle of water from his day pack and drank most of it. Maybe it was dehydration.

He felt confused, but it was coming back to him. He was hiking a desert mountain trail he had walked on countless times, and he saw the woman. She had a hooded cloak and brown hair. A strange glow outlined her. She was twenty feet off the ground with no visible support and moving towards him. Two hooded figures whose face he couldn't see were behind her. She pointed a staff towards him, and a bright beam of light shot out. The light hit him, and for just a second, he saw a large circular mouth with tentacles and thousands of teeth. She was riding on top of it. It became visible as her flash hit him and knocked him backward. It was all he remembered until he woke up.

He slowly stood up, making sure he had his balance. The doctor said the new medications might make him tired for a few days. But he didn't say anything about passing out and hallucinating. The dried blood on the back of his head told him he had hit it when he fell. Maybe he had lost his balance and hit his head. Maybe that's where his hallucination had come from.

In times past, Marvin had run up this trail. He did it to get faster and gain some cardio. He had lettered in swimming, wrestling, and track in high school. But four years of college had taken some of his strength away, at least some of the cardio. He still hit the gym and rode the exercise bike a couple of times a week.

In the original plan, he would have married Carol, and they would be attending grad school. But their plans had come crashing down just weeks before the wedding.

She had met his parents a couple of times before when they visited them at college but had never spent any time with them. So, a month before the wedding, she had flown down to spend a few days with them. His parents wanted to get to know her better before the confusion of the wedding.

They took her out to lunch without him; the better to get to know her. He found out later they were giving them a special honeymoon as a wedding gift. They had found three honeymoon packages they were sure Marvin would like, so they decided to give her the final pick to make sure she would like it. They talked to the travel agent after lunch and started driving home.

Marvin never did find out which package she had chosen. The driver of a construction truck going the opposite direction hit them head-on. It didn't matter to Marvin that a burst artery in his brain had killed the driver and caused the vehicle to veer. All that mattered to him was his family was dead.

That was a year ago. Grad-school without Carol no longer had an appeal. He had inherited his parent's house. His dad's old boss had offered Marvin a job near the home. So, he took the job. The people were friendly. It paid the bills and utilized his college degree.

Then he found out he had cancer. He must have had it for a while. It had metastasized and spread. He had six months to live. Maybe three or four good months before his cancer sapped his strength and he needed to go into hospice or a hospital. The side effects of treatment were almost as bad as his cancer. It might extend his life to a year, but after the operations and chemotherapy; his quality of life wouldn't be high. He would never be able to do the things he had wanted to do in life.

So, he was hiking on his favorite trail through the Desert Mountains of Phoenix. He was trying to decide on whether to undergo chemotherapy to live a degraded life for a little longer, or to live life for a few months before his cancer started taking away his strength. But he had nothing to live for, so why extend his life? His mom and dad were dead. His bride was dead. All his friends from college had moved out of town. Maybe he could travel and do a few things he had planned to do. But he wouldn't enjoy his life without Carol. All the places he wanted to visit, he wanted to visit with Carol. Maybe this hike would help settle what he should do.

He continued his hike down the trail. He still had the tingling sensation, but it was going away, and his head had cleared. His thinking was back to normal. It must have been dehydration, he rationalized. It would have been faster to go back the other direction, but he was afraid his doctor would tell him he shouldn't hike anymore. More hiking, in places he had never been to, was one item he wanted to do before he died. He wasn't ready to give it up yet.

Marvin put his thoughts behind him so he could enjoy the rest of the hike. He took a deep breath. It was a beautiful spring day by Phoenix standards but would be warm to most people. The sun was shining, and the sky was blue and clear. He saw a lizard run under some brush on the side of the trail. Wildlife hid well in the desert, so he had learned to appreciate whatever he saw.

He hiked the trail up and over the saddle between two peaks. The trail ran along the side of the mountain and occasionally passed between peaks on a saddle. Below was a bowl surrounded by hills containing cactus, brush and a couple Palo Verde trees.

Marvin looked down into the bowl and saw a flash and then a large glowing ring of light. Four people exited the ring of light, and two large creatures waited for them. The creatures must have been the same as the ones that the woman in his previous hallucination was riding. They had large, round, teeth-filled mouths surrounded by tentacles. Other than the mouths, the creatures appeared to be giant levitating worms.

The group of four faced the creatures. They whirled or swung their weapons, and different colors of light came from each of them. The light knocked back the creatures, but only for a moment. The worms attacked again twice as fast.

The battle looked even at first. Marvin watched. He had never heard of a hallucination being this vivid and colorful. But this couldn't be real. Maybe he was dreaming.

There was a man dressed in metallic armor and breastplate which reflected the sunlight. Beams of blue light came from the end of a sword and were striking one of the creatures. Another man wearing armor was firing arrows from a bow. The arrows left the bow and became bright blue bolts of light. They hit and penetrated deep into the creature. The third man was wearing a cloak covering his armor. He was spinning a spear in a defensive maneuver.

The spinning of the spear distorted the background, as a heat wave distorts an image. Then there was a sudden loud popping noise, and the distortion traveled towards a worm. It knocked the creature back. The creature recoiled in pain for several seconds before renewing its attack. The fourth person was a woman about his age. She wore a hooded cloak and held a sword with a blue sheen. She slashed, and the sword emitted a beam of light that cut through the worm. The worm withered in pain but reformed around the slash.

The creatures were wiping their tentacles around, attacking the people.

Then he saw the woman swing her sword again, but no light came out from the sword. The creature hit her with a tentacle and knocked her back. He heard her scream, and the hood of her cloak flew off. He saw her hair, hair the color of Carol's.

Marvin could no longer just stand and watch. Whether it was a hallucination or a dream, he had to help her. He half ran, half slid down the side of the mountain into the bowl, haphazardly trying to avoid the cactus and bushes on the slope of the rugged hillside. What could he use as a weapon? How could he help? Maybe he could distract the creature.

Rocks covered the hillside, hard, heavy, black volcanic rocks. He picked up a rock and threw it. It missed the worm. The rock was heavier than a baseball and passed underneath the levitating monster. His day pack had impeded his throw, so he dropped it and grabbed another rock.

He saw a tentacle hit the person with the bow. It knocked him backward and down.

Marvin threw his rock. It hit the worm, and it bounced off. The worm didn't even notice it. He needed to throw it harder.

He grabbed another rock. He felt the tingling sensation in his body grow. He set his feet as he had in baseball and threw with all his strength. Like electricity, the tingling rushed through his body, down his arm, and into the rock. The rock flew at the first creature. This time, it penetrated into the monster's body. The creature stopped its attack on the woman and recoiled back in pain. Marvin grabbed another rock and threw it. It bounced off the creature.

He found a rock, set his feet, and focused on the tingling. He felt the sensation go into the rock and threw it with all his strength. He felt an electric jolt race through his body as he released it. It hit and penetrated deep into the worm.

Marvin's legs became like rubber. He fell down into a squat and caught his fall with his outstretched hands. He looked up. Through the transparent body of the creature, he could see the rocks giving off a blue glow. The slug was thrashing about wildly. Suddenly the creature exploded. Parts flew in several directions, sizzled, and evaporated like ice in a hot pan when they hit the ground.

The two remaining men hit the other creature with a burst of energy from their weapons, and it fell apart, melting like an ice cube on a hot day. It hit the ground and dissolved.

Marvin collapsed down onto his knees. Whatever the tingling was, it had drained him of energy. He felt faint, and he passed out.

Chapter 2

Marvin woke up feeling tired and thirsty. Crouched over him was a beautiful woman. She looked to be in her young or mid-twenties. Her golden blond hair reminded him of Carol, which was why he was compelled to save her, even if she was a hallucination. Marvin sat up and slowly rose to his feet.

She was talking to him in a language he didn't understand and had never heard before. He said hello. She turned and said something to the three men. They said something back. She made a strange motion in the air, turned his head to the side and kissed his left ear. She then kissed his right ear. Then she lightly touched her lips to his. He felt a tingle that connected his ears and his mouth. He said, "Hello. Who are you, and what happened? What language do you speak?"

The woman commanded, "Speak language."

Marvin once again asked her who she was, and what had happened. She said, "Speak language." So, Marvin started to tell her why he was hiking, and about his family. Every time he stopped talking, she would tell him to continue speaking. Only it was different every time. It was more refined. "Speak language," became, "Continue speaking," then "Continue talking." Marvin had run out of good topics to talk about when he heard her say, "You're talking to me is enough."

She walked away and started to speak with the men. He had never heard a language like it before. They were far enough away that he didn't hear everything they said. But somehow, he understood the words he did hear. Most of what they said made no sense to him. They were talking about portals, magic, obligations, the thief, and the king.

Soon they finished talking. The woman bowed her head towards the man carrying the sword. He grabbed her hand, hugged her and kissed her. He pointed his hand and then made a circular motion of his arm. A circle of light formed and a portal opened. The men and the rest of her party stepped through. The circle closed down and vanished.

Marvin stood up and watched the men leave through the portal.

The woman turned towards him and asked Marvin a question. "Do you want to die with honor or do you want to live with honor?"

She saw the confused look on Marvin's face. She said, "I owe you a life debt. I can honor your body and join you on a difficult journey to end the sickness to your body. Or I can honor your body and give you a hero's death."

Marvin was quiet. It took him a second to figure out what she was saying. She was offering him a quick death or a difficult journey and a chance to live. He quickly replied, "I want to live. I chose the journey."

The woman touched him. He felt a tingle coming from her flow into his body. She said, "I have slowed the sickness in your body and given your body strength. Do you have a place we can stay for the night?"

Marvin replied, "Yes, my house is half an hour's walk away."

She asked, "Do you have provisions at your home or do we need to hunt?"

Marvin thought for a second, still thinking he might be hallucinating. "I have food at my home. If it's not what you would like, we can buy food from a store."

She said, "Good, let's go to your house and prepare for our journey in the morning."

The woman's self-confidence and the way she took command reminded him of a military officer. Marvin started to hike up the side of the bowl towards the trail. He was out of breath when he finished climbing the hill to the trail. His wind came back as he started walking on the flat area of the trail.

He said, "I'm Marvin, what's your name?"

She replied, "My name is Princess Shandria of Atlantis. We need to be quiet for now. I am trying to hear the desert. We can talk more at your house."

She motioned with her hand that he should continue to lead, so he kept hiking.

The Atlantian Council had sent Shandria and her group on a mission to find the stolen arch crystal, or at least to bring back information about where it was. It was the heart of Atlantis, and they would go to war to have it returned. Her brother, Prince Handrian, had been in charge of the mission. They had followed the thief through several realms, using the magical signature left over from the thief's portals to trace her. But the thief had traveled to this strange realm, and the portal trace had died while they had fought the narworms.

Shandria had never before been to such a backwater realm. At least she thought it was until she felt Marvin's cry of newborn magic. While he was recovering from his magical exertion, they looked at him and discovered he was Atlantian. Why was he here? How did he get here? She didn't know. The magic the thief had hit him with had ignited his magic. Magic should have befriended him when he was young, but this was a magic dead world. Earth, the original realm all the others had sprung from was magically dead. This must be Earth.

She was listening to the desert, and there was nothing to hear, no magic to talk with. At least her magic was still alive and growing happily in her body. But there was no magic coming from outside, and her magic was clinging tightly to her. Magic wasn't happy here. She wanted to get out of this realm quickly.

ATLANTIAN MAGIC

Marvin had saved her life and the lives of her companions when his newborn magic sprung to life. His baby cry of magic had energized the iron rocks and exploded them inside the narworm. Magic enhanced iron was toxic to most magic created life forms. It had killed the narworm.

Atlantian honor demanded life for life. He had saved their lives, so they owed him a debt. She must try to save his life since he was dying or give him an honorable death. If this realm was Atlantis she could have rewarded him, perhaps give him a servant to fulfill the debt, but this was Earth, and there were no servants.

They followed the trail and left the mountain area into a neighborhood of houses. They were too large to be peasant homes. Most of them were two-story, yet they had far too little land for an estate. The vegetation was ornamental, not for eating, although there were a few edible cacti among them. And what were the metal and glass houses on black wheels? Were they carriages or wagons? What pulled them? She didn't see any horses or harnesses. Perhaps they were like the vehicles the Dwarves used. It was a strange and curious realm.

They arrived at his home. Marvin used a key to unlock his door, and they entered. She was surprised to find it was much cooler inside than outside. A flattened, rock-like material cut into squares tiled the floor by the door. A form-fitting rug covered the rest of the floor from wall to wall. It was all the same color with no design. It looked clean, but she couldn't figure out how they took it outside to clean, and they didn't have magic in this realm to clean it in place.

He pressed a switch on the wall and the room filled with light. Shandria could sense the movement of lightning from the switch to the light fixture. It followed straight lines that bent at corners. And it flowed smoothly like water, not like the usual flash of lightning, how strange.

She was surprised he was the only person to live here. The rooms were far too large. Any of the bedrooms could fit an entire peasant family. But he wasn't a peasant; he wasn't a nobleman or a royal. He called himself a free man in a country of free men. If everyone was the same, how could you have order? If everyone had the same place in society, how could society function efficiently? It was all so confusing.

Marvin showed her around the house. Then he took her outside and showed her his backyard. Rocks covered the ground. There were bushes and a small tree, but no food. Not even an herb garden. There was a pool made of cement in the backyard.

Marvin pulled a device that made a buzzing noise from his pocket. He excused himself and walked back inside. It was a phone call from his doctor's nurse. They had sent a biopsy of his cancer. The lab found no markers for any of the new genetic targeted therapies. They would have to use the traditional treatment. It was expensive but covered by his health insurance. The doctor had sent the justification to his insurance company. It usually took a week for them to approve the treatment.

Marvin asked about his prognosis. The nurse said the doctor would talk to him at his appointment next week about the new prognosis. But Marvin had researched his cancer on the internet. He knew his chance of living was better if he had the genetic marker. His prognosis was now less optimistic. He talked to the nurse for a few minutes before he hung up.

He walked back outside and saw that Shandria had taken off her armor, all her clothing, and was bathing naked in his swimming pool.

Shandria said with a smile, "The water feels good to my body. Come join me."

Marvin wasn't sure what to do. He had lived here with his parents since before he left for college, and he had lived here on his own since they died, but he had never once gone swimming without a bathing suit. Now a beautiful, naked princess was asking him to join her. Many things passed through his mind. But what he heard his voice say was, "One minute, let me get us some towels."

He walked back inside and turned on the pump to the waterfall. He grabbed two large towels from a closet and headed out to the pool. Shandria was splashing in the water and playing under the waterfall like a child. He was feeling self-conscious about the thought of being naked outside, yet he took off all his clothing and joined her in the pool.

"This is wonderful," she said. "It reminds me of the palace pool back at Atlantis."

She started laughing and then splashed water at Marvin. Marvin was still getting used to the fact that he was naked in a swimming pool with the most beautiful woman he had ever met. But he knew how to play this game. He splashed her back. They started splashing each other for several minutes before they decided playtime was over.

Shandria climbed out of the pool and grabbed her clothing. Marvin thought she was going to get dressed, but she jumped back into the pool with her clothes in hand. She started to wash them. Marvin heard her humming a happy melody he had never heard before.

She hung her cleaned garments out on the chairs and the table around the pool to dry in the sun. She took various items from her pack and laid them on the pool deck. Last, she cleaned her pack. Pieces of equipment drying in the sun covered the pool deck. She placed a half-full bag in the shade without opening it. Marvin wondered if there was food inside.

Shandria took a comb that had been in her pack and jumped back into the pool. She once again submerged her hair and then started to comb it. She was smiling, humming, and enjoying herself. Marvin was trying unsuccessfully to watch her without staring.

He decided to leave the pool while she was distracted combing her hair. He grabbed his towel, dried off, and wrapped the towel around the lower half of his body. He would have liked to spend more time with her in the water, but he was afraid the sun would burn him in the parts of his body usually covered by a swimsuit. He still considered himself a stronger than average guy, but he hadn't worked out seriously since he left college. He was self-conscious, not only because she was a naked female, but because he had never seen anyone like her before. She was beautiful, athletic, and definitely out of his league.

He walked into the house and dressed. A month after his parents died he had donated all their bedroom furniture, bought new furniture, and moved into the master bedroom at his grandmother's insistence. He cried himself to sleep the first night. He realized it was the turning point in his grief and he had finally accepted their death as real.

Marvin realized all Shandria's clothing was wet and drying in the sun. He had donated his parent's clothing, but he didn't have the heart to donate Carol's clothing, the clothing she had packed for her visit. It was still in the closet of his old bedroom. He knew Carol had a nice white bathrobe her mom had given her as a gift. He pulled it out of the closet, thought about how much he missed Carol, and took the bathrobe outside to Princess Shandria.

Shandria was relaxing on the lounge outside, drying off in the sun. She was still naked. He put the bathrobe on the table near her. "This is a bathrobe. We use it after bathing to help dry off and stay warm. I thought you may want something to wear while your clothes dry."

She replied, "Thank you for the offer, but I am almost dry, and I am enjoying the sunshine."

Marvin looked at her uniformly lightly tanned body and asked her. "Aren't you worried about sunburn?"

Shandria thought for a moment then realized what he was saying, "The magic inside me talks to the sun and protects me from burning. I am trying to listen to what the sun and the wind and this realm are teaching me. But they are silent. There is no magic here.

"I sent out a few magic threads, which came back to me. They were weak and unhappy when they returned. This realm is not magic-friendly. There is an area a long distance north of here where I can open a portal to the realm we need to go to. We must head there. I will listen more. Maybe I can learn something."

Marvin said, "If I'm bothering you I will leave so you can listen."

She replied, "That's OK. I am still getting used to this realm and need to relax and learn from it. Tell me about the metal and glass carriages. Are they pulled by a beast or moved by magic?"

Marvin had to think for a second. He smiled. "We call the carriages cars. An internal combustion engine powered by a flammable liquid rotates the wheels. The rotating wheels cause the cars to move. Does that make any sense to you?"

She replied, "Internal combustion is not known to me, but it is said the Dwarves use engines powered by fire, so maybe it's the same."

"It may be, at least it sounds like a similar method."

Shandria said, "The closest realm with an arch is far away. It is easier to create a portal at a location two to three month's travel on foot towards the north. How fast can we get there in your car?"

"Let me think." Marvin figured foot travel was 10 to 15 miles a day times 30-days or 300 to 450 miles in a month of foot travel. That's between 600 and 900 miles, for two months, and 900 to 1350 for three months.

He said, "I'm not sure how many miles we would travel on foot per day, but we should be able to drive there in one or two days in my car. Some areas are further away from roads. It may take us another few days to hike there after we get close. Can you tell me more about where we are going? If you could, I might be able to tell you more."

She replied, "It's a place where the fires of the earth are near the surface. The active energy of the earth is good for magic."

Marvin replied, not fully understanding her explanation, "We don't have any volcanoes north of here. Let me go inside, and I can pull up a map on my computer."

Marvin walked inside, and Shandria followed him. He was both disappointed and glad that she had put on the bathrobe. She had tied the robe, so it didn't hang open. He walked into the room he used as his office. It used to be his gaming room, but he moved his game systems into the living room and hooked them up to his big television. He moved some paperwork off the guest chair. "You may want to sit down. This will take a few minutes."

Shandria watched as he logged onto his computer. She was fascinated watching the screen.

Marvin did a search and pulled up a map. "It looks like there are several inactive lava fields in southern Idaho. And here is Yellowstone National Park." He pulled up a picture of Old Faithful Geyser going off and the various thermal areas.

Shandria said, "That looks promising. If there are no other areas like it north of here, then that must be it."

Marvin said, "Oh, I forgot to offer you something to eat. I don't know what you would find tasty. Are you a vegetarian or do you eat meat?"

She replied. "Atlantis is an island nation. We eat mostly fish and seafood. But we find other meats as delicacies. We eat fruits and vegetables we grow on the island."

Marvin said, "It's almost lunchtime. Most of my meat is frozen. I have some hamburger patties I can grill without waiting for them to defrost. I also have some salad makings and some fruit. There is a good backpacking and camping store nearby. Since we may be hiking for a while, maybe I should buy us some supplies after lunch."

Marvin looked at Shandria and said. "Your clothing would make you conspicuous in our society. I still have some clothing from Carol that may fit you in the guest room. You can take a look at them and see what you are comfortable wearing."

Shandria said, "Trying on clothing can be fun. My sister and I were always trying on clothing. We would swap and wear each other's clothes."

He escorted her to the guest room and then downstairs. He grabbed some frozen hamburger patties from the freezer and threw them on the grill.

While he was flipping the burgers, Shandria came outside. It was all Marvin could do to keep his jaw from dropping. She was wearing tight fitting shorts and a shirt she had found upstairs. She was an eleven on a scale of ten.

Shandria said, "That was fun. It reminded me of when I use to play dress up with my sister. How do I look to your eyes?" She turned to the side, and then back to the other side, all the while keeping her head turned towards Marvin.

He was too self-conscious to get a good look at her in the pool but standing right next to her with her modeling the clothing he could see the strong arms and muscular shoulders he associated with the girl's gymnastics team. Marvin said, meaning every word, "You look fantastic. Seeing you made me realize a princess from Atlantis is far too beautiful to look inconspicuous anywhere. But the Earth clothes will help."

Shandria smiled.

Marvin asked. "Do you like the smell of the hamburgers?"

She replied, "They smell good to my nose, and will make my stomach happy."

He said, "Lunch will be finished soon."

She asked, "Is there anything I can do to help?"

Marvin thought for a second and said, "Let me know if you would rather eat outside or inside. And I will set the table while the meat finishes cooking."

She replied, "It's beautiful outside."

Marvin said, "Ok, let me set the table." He walked inside, sliced up a tomato and onion, and brought them out along with plates for the table. He placed two hamburger buns on the grill to brown and brought out some oranges and apples from the refrigerator on a plate. Not knowing what she liked he brought out ketchup, mustard, mayonnaise, and barbecue sauce for her to try.

He pulled the buns off the grill and placed one on each plate. Then he put the hamburgers on a plate between them.

They sat down. Shandria asked, "What are your eating customs?"

Marvin thought for a second and said. "We tend to be informal; many people ask God to bless the meal before eating."

"I would like to hear you talk to God," she said

Marvin wasn't much of a person to pray in public. And after everything that had happened to him in the past year, his prayers had become mostly emotional outbursts of anger and tears of "Why God, Why?" The anger had mostly gone away, but there was a big lonely empty spot in his heart.

He saw Shandria looking expectantly towards him. So, he bowed his head and said, "Father, thank you for this meal, and for my guest, amen."

He looked up and saw Shandria smiling. "Atlantians believe God is a father to us also."

Marvin thought about what she said. Then he replied, not wanting to get into religion, "That's interesting." He then shifted the conversation to the meal. He showed Shandria how the burger fit on the bun. He told her about the condiments and said she may want to try each of them and choose whether to put them on her bun. She tried several and decided to eat the burger without any condiments. They split one of the apples and one of the oranges. Shandria liked both the fruits.

Carol's old shoes didn't fit Shandria, so after Marvin cleaned up the plates from lunch, Shandria put on her boots. She repacked her pack and brought it and her weapons into the house. Then they entered into Marvin's car and drove to the store.

The speed of the car amazed Shandria. The amount of traffic, the road network, and the size of Phoenix surprised her.

The size of the big box hunting and camping store also amazed Shandria. She felt like a kid in a candy store. She looked closely at all the equipment. Most of it would just weigh down a backpack.

The fire starters were useful if you didn't have magic. She used magic to purify the water, so she didn't need any purification equipment. The various knives and machetes were of unusual design, but her sword served the same function for heavy work, and the dagger she carried she used for food preparation. Her sword and knives wouldn't break and were always magically sharp. And her sword was an ancient weapon of power.

She did like a couple of the backpack designs. She listened to the fabric and found one that she could perform some minor enchantments on to improve its durability and waterproofing. She suggested it for Marvin. Hers had magic woven into the fabric that would take several days to replace on a new pack, so she kept hers. She did like the lightweight aluminum cooking pot, but the handle seemed too flimsy for her, and it was dead to magic. Metal spoke only when softened by heat. Aluminum was a strange metal, and she didn't know whether it would hold an enchantment. She stuck with her own.

Hammocks, hydration packs, cots, camp pillows, utensils, camp stoves, and the whole array of bear, snake, and bug repellant seemed silly and added weight.

Sleeping bags made no sense to her. They trapped you if a wild animal attacked. She slept wrapped in her cloak. It allowed her to move and defend herself. Her magic protected her from cold or heat, so there was no use carrying a heavy, bulky sleeping bag. Then she remembered that Marvin's Magic would have to develop before it would protect him.

The sleeping bags were made of several different artificial materials, some materials spoke, and some didn't. Some materials wouldn't speak to each other and wouldn't hold an enchantment. Shandria found a sleeping bag that would hold an enchantment and was good for cold weather. She couldn't find a cloak but found a poncho she could enchant, which Marvin liked.

Air mattresses made no sense. They were bulky and unnecessary. A little magic made the inside of the tent or her tarp into a cushion. She did like the lighter weight tent design and the folding poles. The tent was made of the same magic friendly fabric as the outside of the sleeping bag. So, a little bit of magic weaving would keep out the rain, snow, and the wind. Some more weaving would make it harder to tear and more durable. She would add a little magic to it each day, and it would soon be as functional as her current tarp.

She saw a variety of guns. She was unfamiliar with them. They were heavy and metal, which wouldn't hold magic without a forge, so she wasn't interested. Then she saw the bows.

The compound bows were a strange, unique design to her. Many of the other hunting bows she liked. She wanted to shoot each one and was sad to find out the store didn't have a place where she could try out the bows, but her travel bow was all she needed. Marvin said he had only shot a bow once or twice at summer camp. They didn't have the time necessary to train him, so there was no sense getting him a bow.

Chapter 3

Marvin and Shandria did some more shopping but couldn't find Marvin an acceptable cloak. They just weren't in fashion. By the time they finished shopping, it was dinnertime, and they were hungry, so Marvin took Shandria to a seafood restaurant. The waitress walked them by the bar to their table. Shandria was holding Marvin's arm as they walked. Marvin had to admit the attention Shandria was drawing was amusing. He liked the looks on people's faces. They were staring at him as if they were trying to figure out if he was a movie star and Shandria was his escort, or if it was the other way around.

Shandria was surprised they served the meals individually, and not on a group platter or bowl. She had used a spoon before, but this was her first experience with a fork. Atlantians usually ate out of the same bowl and used their fingers for most foods.

He enjoyed his lemon pepper salmon, but he would have been better off if he had taken Shandria to a steakhouse. She didn't say anything, but she was unimpressed by the seafood. Marvin realized that having eaten all varieties of fresh seafood prepared by the best chefs of Atlantis, it must taste mediocre to her. She only ate half her fish, but she enjoyed the salad bar and returned several times to try the different vegetables, fruit, and dressings.

Drinking wine with meals was a custom in Atlantis, and she wanted to try them all. She had four glasses of four different wines. She enjoyed herself but was tipsy when they left the restaurant.

Marvin logged online when they returned to his house. He found a hotel near the entrance to Yellowstone Park and made a reservation. It was already dark outside, so they went to bed. They were planning to get up with the sun.

He had just closed his eyes when Shandria silently climbed into bed next to him. She spooned in behind him, put her arm around his waist, and fell right asleep. Marvin was tired but having Shandria naked in his bed made him wide-awake. He knew that other cultures on Earth often slept several people in one bed. But single American men and women only slept in the same bed together when they were intimate friends.

Marvin was uneasy for half an hour before the warmth of her body comforted him to sleep. He had to admit it was a good night's sleep.

The next morning, they dressed and put their equipment into his car. He set the map on his cell phone for West Yellowstone and started to drive. He wanted to talk to her about the cultural differences of nudity and sleeping together but didn't know how to go about it. Her bathing naked in the privacy of his pool and her sleeping in his bed with him were more his issue than hers. If he was going to spend the next chapter of his life on an adventure with her, he needed to get used to her culture and to be honest, he liked sleeping in the same bed as her.

So instead, he said, "Tell me about magic."

Shandria said, "Wow, that's a big topic. And it's a little like explaining ice or snow to someone who has never seen it."

He thought for a second and asked, "Well, then tell me what I can expect as I learn it."

Shandria said, "New magic bursts forth, like a newborn baby's cry. That's what happened to you when you killed the narworm. Magic is alive. It is growing inside you. Soon it will fill you and be part of you.

"Magic will start to talk to you, and you will start to feel the magic around you. But just as when a baby first opens its eyes, it will be blurry. It will take a while for you to focus, and a while for you to understand what it is telling you. Then you will be like a baby learning how to walk, learning how to use its legs."

Marvin asked, "How long until it starts?"

Shandria replied, "I don't know. It varies. I've never been anywhere like this realm. It is unfriendly to magic. Probably soon after we leave this realm, your magic will burst forth with a lot of power. Usually magic starts at a much younger age. Your magic may grow faster than a child's magic."

He asked, "Will I need to be taught?"

Shandria asked, "Do you teach a child to walk or do they learn on their own?"

Marvin thought for a second and replied, "We kind of hold their hands and help them walk, but they would learn on their own."

Shandria said, "Your magic will teach you to crawl and walk. And I will hold your hand. Then I will teach you how to run, jump, and climb. Does that make sense?

Marvin replied, "I understand the analogy. I guess I will just have to be patient."

After several hours of driving, he could tell that Shandria needed to move around. The car had climbed out of the Sonoran Desert of Phoenix. They were now at over six thousand feet of elevation, and the weather was brisk. It was springtime in Phoenix, but winter still had its last gasp farther north. The nighttime temperature would be dipping below freezing. Shandria left the car wearing the shorts and shirt he had given her yesterday. She didn't seem to notice the colder temperature.

Marvin was wearing blue jeans and a short sleeve shirt. He wanted to put on his jacket but didn't because of Shandria's clothing.

Marvin stretched out his back and legs by touching his toes but spent most of his time watching her stretch out. Shandria was flexible and touched the ground with her palms. She finished stretching and walked over to a large pine tree. She looked up at the top branches and put her hand on the tree. After a minute, she came back towards Marvin and said, "Even the trees don't talk here. I will send out a magic thread this evening when we are closer to the yellow rock."

Marvin smiled at her use of yellow rock rather than Yellowstone, but then he realized she was speaking in Atlantian, and the magic she had given him was translating. Marvin realized that he was speaking in English but discovered he could speak in Atlantian if he wanted to.

He asked her if she needed to use the bathroom. He had explained to her last night after dinner how a flush toilet worked. Atlantis used squat toilets and composted the waste for fertilizer.

She walked around for a few minutes then said, "I guess it's time for us to get back in the car. It's a lot faster than horse or wave travel. It's too bad there is no magic in this realm to talk to. There are many nice people, but it is so lonely here without magic."

They started driving, and soon it was time to stop for gas and have lunch. Shandria didn't like the smell of the gasoline station, but she thought it interesting how he paid for the gas by swiping his credit card and pressing a few buttons.

They drove to a diner for brunch. Shandria liked the pictures of food on the menu. She didn't understand the letters on the menu, so Marvin read the words. The names of the items made little sense. A hamburger was meat from a cow and not from a pig. Buffalo wings were chicken. A hot dog had every type of meat in it but dog meat. And what was a lumberjack breakfast, pine needles?

The waiter asked them if they were ready to order or still looking. They told him they were still thinking. He asked them what they wanted to drink. Marvin said, "Two glasses of water, and a large glass of lemonade and one of orange juice."

After discussing the menu, Marvin ordered a lumberjack breakfast with wheat toast, scrambled eggs, sausage, bacon, waffles, hash brown potatoes, and pancakes. He then ordered a basket of breaded chicken strips and fries. He told the waiter they were going to share the meals and asked him to bring an extra plate.

The eggs were familiar to Shandria, and she ate them with her spoon. Potatoes were rarer in Atlantis. She liked that that Earth custom allowed her to eat the breaded chicken and french fries with her hands. Then she discovered the maple syrup and put it on her French Fries. Shandria had fun spearing maple syrup covered french-fries with the fork and made a sort of game out of it.

She loved the strawberry syrup on the waffles. The bacon was too salty for her taste. But she wanted to take the salt shaker with them on their journey. Marvin told her salt was inexpensive. They would buy as much as she liked before they left at another store.

She put strawberry jam on a half slice of bread and blueberry jam on another. Marvin enjoyed the look on her face when she tried something new. If the taste made her mouth happy, it was a smile. If it made her mouth sad, it was a frown or a grimace. He enjoyed the way her emotions made her eyes change.

The lemonade, which was fresh squeezed, made her mouth sour, but she liked it and drank some more. She enjoyed the orange juice. Marvin ate what Shandria didn't. Soon they were both stuffed.

After brunch, they drove back on the road and headed north. Marvin showed her how the radio worked. She understood how vibrations of magic crystals carried sound but using lightning to cause invisible light to carry sound was strange to her.

Marvin was glad he had satellite radio since AM and FM radio stations were rare this far from a big city. Shandria would listen to one song for a while and then move to another satellite channel. She would skip past the stations where people were talking. After an hour of listening to her play part of a song and then changing channels, Marvin changed his mind and started wishing he didn't have satellite radio.

He was happy when she grew bored and turned off the music, but he was unprepared for her next question. "Why are most of the songs about sex and sexual desire, and some are violent?"

Marvin wasn't sure what to say. He answered, "I'm not sure why; maybe because sex is biologically driven desire. We do have a varied culture, and some parts are violent."

Shandria asked, "So, is violence part of you?"

He replied, "No, I'm not violent. I've never been in a fight, other than playing around with friends when I was young and competitive wrestling in high school which is a sport. You're the one with the big sword. How violent are you?"

"I'm a princess of Atlantis. I have been training in all the fighting arts, physical and magical since I was young, and I still have a lot to learn. We are not an expansive or a violent people, but other people are, so I train to protect my people. It's been many generations since we have had to fight a war. The battle you saw was the first military action for me.

"How violent are humans?"

He was quiet for a while. Then Marvin continued. "We have two hundred different countries on this planet. Some are more violent than others are. The last big war our country fought was over forty years ago. But we are fighting a smaller war right now. And several other wars are going on around the planet.

"We don't train our children for war as some countries do. Our soldiers chose to join the army when they are young adults. The military trains them. We are a large country and always seem to be in a war with someone. So even though I am not a violent person, I guess I live on a violent planet."

Shandria listened to his apologetic voice. She said. "Life is what it is. We just have to do our best to follow the part society gives us. Don't blame yourself, just do your best."

Marvin said, "Thank you. My life has changed so much in the last year, leaving college, my parents and fiancée dying, working at a professional job, and finding out I was dying of cancer. Now I don't have any idea what my part in society is. And to make life more confusing, I just agreed to spend what could be the rest of my life traveling with a beautiful, magic and sword-wielding Atlantian princess who offered to kill me if I wanted her too. I'm excited, intimidated, and scared. But what other choice do I have."

Shandria paused for a second and then replied. "There is always a choice. Sometimes the choice is to die or accept change. Sometimes we have to struggle to survive. It's the nature of life. It's not easy but necessary. I had no desire to end your life in the desert. The choice was yours. You chose, I respected your choice, and I have sworn to protect you and to teach you until something kills our bodies or healing comes to your body."

Marvin asked, "So what are Atlantian society sexual customs?"

"It varies. I am a princess. Once I prove myself, my family and I will discuss a suitable prince for me to marry. Until then, my mother's magic protects my chastity. It would cause me pain and kill anyone who tried to have sex with me. Other levels of our society are different, but the custom for a princess is to wait until marriage. My brother has concubines to take care of his sexual needs, at least until he gets married. What are your society's customs?"

Marvin said, "It's up to the individual adult. Most sexual relationships are monogamous. Many people wait until marriage to have sex, but some start having sex before they marry. My fiancée and I only started sleeping together after we had known each other for a while. Soon afterward, we became engaged. Some people have many sexual partners. Marriage is supposed to be to one partner for the rest of one's life. But there are many divorces."

Shandria said, "That's sad. A breakdown in families usually leads to a decline in society. You use sleeping together as a sexual term. Did my sleeping with you bother you?"

"Somewhat, so did your being naked in my swimming pool. A man and a woman together naked has sexual connotations in our society, but not in all societies. So, I accepted the freedoms of your customs. And after I figured out you weren't in my bed for sex, I had a good night's sleep. We will be sleeping together on this journey and will see each other naked. I am adapting, and I accept your custom."

Marvin continued, "I will do my best to be a good traveling companion to you. I know you have trained for combat and I haven't. I desire to protect you, but I might end up getting in your way until I learn more or my magic grows."

Shandria said, "That's fair enough. Sharing your resources with me, driving us towards our goals, and above all, sharing your heart with me speaks to mine. We will be good companions. My heart is happy that we are on this journey together."

They took another stop and stretched their legs again. Marvin said, "I was thinking about your clothes. I know you are warm in those clothes, but they are too lightweight for the weather and are now drawing as much attention as your traveling clothing would. If you like we can stop at a store and get you some warmer clothing, maybe some long pants before we get to the hotel."

Shandria said, "Based on a song my ear heard on your radio, girls like to shop, so it should be fun. Maybe we can get the salt now too."

They found a big box store with a large selection of women's clothing right off the freeway. Shandria looked at all the clothing, but few of the clothes were rugged enough for outdoor use. Marvin directed her towards the blue jeans. The cotton in the fabric was magic friendly. She had no clue what size she was. A saleswoman helped her find her size and a nice long sleeve shirt. The woman directed her to the changing room.

After a few minutes, she came out of the changing room and asked Marvin how she looked. Marvin liked how she looked and told her so. She tried touching the ground. She decided she didn't like the jeans. They were too tight. She couldn't move and fight. The saleswoman found her a different pair that used stretch fabric. Shandria did part of a stretching routine and liked it better.

They passed by the intimate apparel, and she asked Marvin about those. He told her they were undergarments, but he knew nothing about women's underwear. The saleswoman said she would help.

Marvin felt weird being around the ladies discussing underwear, so he left the immediate area. He returned when he saw them walking towards the changing room. Marvin sat down on the seat outside and waited. After a few minutes, Shandria came out again wearing only a pair of lace panties, a lacy bra, and her golden necklace. Marvin stood up, and his jaw dropped. He stuttered, "It looks great, but in our culture, undergarments aren't worn in public except under clothing."

Shandria walked back into the changing room. The saleswoman asked Marvin, "Where is she from?"

Marvin thought about making up a story but told her the truth. "She is a princess from Atlantis, and I am helping her get back home."

The woman gave him a strange look and then walked away. Marvin thought, "I wonder if that line would work on a pushy saleswoman."

Shandria walked out of the changing room wearing her new clothing and her boots.

Marvin said, "I think we have to pay for them before you wear them."

"The saleswoman took the tags off the clothing and said I could wear them, and we could pay for them at the front register."

The saleswoman, who was on commission and wanted to make sure they knew her name was Barbara, tried to talk her into buying more clothing and fashion accessories. Shandria said no several times. Finally, Marvin took Shandria's hand and had her walk with him up to the counter. When he arrived there, the woman tried getting them to sign up for a charge card. Marvin said no and pulled up a ten percent discount on his cell phone. He had found it on the store website while waiting for Shandria to change.

They exited and found a grocery store on his cell phone and drove there. Shandria found she liked the way the sea salt talked to her best. It was in a smaller container than the table salt. She took all four packages that were on the shelf. They walked down an aisle that had jerky and trail mix. She grabbed a dozen bags of both. She was excited about her find. Marvin thought the Jerky was expensive. But he didn't care about the cost. He had the money in his account, which automatically paid off his card each month. He doubted they would take his credit card in Atlantis. It just hit him, that he may never return to Earth.

It was dark when they checked into their hotel room. The hotel receptionist recommended a steakhouse a block from the hotel. Neither Shandria nor Marvin wanted to spend any more time driving. They walked there and ate dinner. The theme of the bar was country western. Again, Shandria enjoyed the wine, and soon she was asking or telling, he couldn't be sure, Marvin to take her out dancing.

Marvin was glad Carol had insisted he take a country western dance class their last semester at college. He took her out on the floor. He was amazed at how smooth a dancer she was. Especially, since she had never danced the two-step before. He found out later that dancing was a big part of the Atlantian culture and she had been dancing since she was young.

He convinced her to share a slice of cake with ice cream on top with him for dessert. She had never before eaten chocolate or ice cream. Marvin enjoyed watching her face as she tried it for the first time.

They walked arm in arm back to the hotel. They talked about food, dancing, the trip, and about life in general. He was starting to think of her more as a friend than as a beautiful woman. Her friendship was winning out over his hormonal attraction.

That evening he showed her how to adjust the shower temperature. She loved the novelty and stayed in it for almost an hour. She came out wearing a bathrobe. He watched her comb her hair and dry it with magic. There were two queen size beds. It was late when they arrived back at the hotel room, so he turned off the lights and slid into his bed. This time it didn't surprise him when Shandria took off her bathrobe and slipped naked into bed behind him. He fell asleep sooner, enjoying her body's warmth.

They repacked their gear in the morning, putting the salt and the trail snacks in their packs. Carol's old clothes ended up in a separate suitcase Marvin had brought for their drive. Shandria was wearing the outfit they had bought the night before. She said she would change at the park.

They ate another large breakfast, and then Marvin said goodbye to what may be his last meal on Earth, at least for a while.

They drove to the park, paid the entrance fee, and stopped at the visitor center. Marvin used the last flush toilet he may ever use and met up with Shandria. She was happy to be outdoors again, and away from the smell of the city. Marvin, on the other hand, was wrinkling his nose at the smell of sulfur from the volcanic vents

Shandria said she could open a portal almost anywhere on the west side of Yellowstone, but near the top of a mountain or ridge was closer to the sky. Portal magic was sky magic so it would be friendlier. They drove to a trailhead for Mount Washburn and parked their car.

Marvin was leaving his entire world behind. He knew his cell phone would be useless, so he put it in the glove compartment. But he couldn't bring himself to leave his wallet or car keys. He put on his pack and was ready to hike up the mountain. Shandria striped out of her Earth clothes next to the car and changed into her travel clothing. She put on her sword and sheath, her cloak, and her pack. They started hiking up the trail from the parking lot. It was a 1200-foot elevation gain to the top of the mountain at over 10,000-feet. Marvin's body was used to the lower elevation of Phoenix. He was breathing hard before they left the parking lot.

Shandria was obviously in better shape than Marvin was. She looked like she could run to the top. Marvin had to stop often to catch his breath and let his leg muscles recover. He could tell with every step that the high elevation was affecting him.

It took them a couple of hours to get to the top of the ridge. Shandria found a place she liked and asked Marvin if he was ready. Marvin looked around at the country he had grown up in, and said, "Goodbye." Then he said to Shandria, "I'm ready."

Shandria made a big circle with her hands, and a large portal appeared. Marvin could feel a tingling coming from Shandria and tingling from the portal. He felt the hair on his arms stand up as if they were near an electric field. Shandria said, "You first."

Marvin took a step and fell through the portal.

Chapter 4

Marvin had the wind knocked out of him when he landed hard on a sheet of ice. Something was wrong. It was cold, windy, and overcast. He stood up. White ice and snow surrounded him as far as he could see. The white clouds and the blowing snow made even finding the horizon difficult. He looked around and didn't see Shandria anywhere. He yelled and yelled her name, but all he heard was the howl of the wind. And he was getting colder with each breath.

He was wearing his winter jacket, which for a kid from Phoenix was warm enough to play in the snow once a year in Flagstaff before laughing and warming up with hot cocoa or coffee afterward. But this wasn't Flagstaff; this was Marvin's idea of Antarctica in a blizzard.

Marvin started to shiver. He needed to get out of the wind before he froze to death. He looked around and saw a rocky outcropping a few hundred yards away during a break in the blowing snow. He started to run. He hoped the outcropping would block the wind. The muscle action would warm him up, and it would get him to the outcropping faster.

He was out of breath before he ran halfway there. He must be at a high elevation. He slowed down his run to a slow jog, panting with each breath until he reached the outcropping. The outcropping blocked some of the wind, but not enough. It was blowing right through his blue jeans. His legs and unprotected face were starting to feel numb. Marvin had learned winter survival in boy scouts. But it was all theoretical, and he had never tried it. He knew he could get out of the wind by digging into the snow.

There was a large, deep, snow drift on the downwind side of the outcropping. The snow was compacted enough to be firm but not too hard to dig through. Marvin dug down into the snow, thankful for his thick cold weather gloves as he dug. He was breathing hard and had to stop several times to catch his breath while digging into the snow.

He dug down into the snowdrift until he had a hole that was waist deep. He crouched down into the hole. The wind chill factor dropped significantly, but it was still cold. At least the wind was no longer blowing through his blue jeans. A cracked and broken layer of ice from partially melted and refrozen snow now covered his jeans. He pulled the collar of his jacket up, trying to give his numb face some warmth, but the small collar provided little relief.

He once again yelled Shandria's name several times but didn't receive any reply. The hole he had dug had reduced the wind, but it was still below freezing. Snow was an insulator. He needed to completely dig in, or he would freeze to death. He took off his backpack and started to dig a tunnel into the snow bank with his hands. The snow was easy to dig, yet Marvin was breathing hard, exhausted by the altitude. Fifteen minutes later, he had a small tunnel large enough to crawl into, and long enough for his sleeping bag. He was shivering so hard that his neck and back muscles were starting to cramp up. Even his leg muscles hurt.

Marvin took out his poncho and pushed it into the snow tunnel. He laid it down flat. He rolled out his mattress pad and sleeping bag and slid them into the tunnel. Partially melted snow covered his blue jeans and the top of his socks. He took off his shoes and socks placing his bare feet onto the cold tarp. He quickly pulled off his off his wet snow and ice-covered jeans and slid the lower half of his body into the sleeping bag. The sleeping bag was cold, but there was no melting snow sucking away his body heat. The snow slid off his jacket, so he left it on.

He slid the rest of the way into the sleeping bag and used his pack to seal the hole of the tunnel behind him. The back of his pack was facing him. It allowed him to open up the compartments. He had a sweatshirt in the main compartment. He took it out and wrapped it around his face and head.

Marvin lay in his sleeping bag shivering and listening to the muffled howl of the wind outside the tent. The skin on his face started to burn as it warmed up and feeling returned. So, did the feeling of the skin on his thighs as they warmed up. Once Marvin started warming up, he slid out of his jacket and pulled it into the sleeping bag with him to keep it warm.

Taking off his coat was supposed to allow his upper body heat to fill the sleeping bag and warm up his legs and feet. His shivering slowly reduced and finally stopped. His snow cave wasn't warm, but it wasn't below freezing. It was definitely better than outside. His sleeping bag was insulated well enough that he was no longer in danger of hypothermia or frostbite. One thing he wasn't, being from Phoenix, was cold adapted.

"Now what?" thought Marvin? "I'm totally screwed. I'll freeze to death if I leave this tunnel. If I don't, I will run out of food and then freeze to death. Maybe the wind will die down, and the wind chill factor will warm up. But then where will I go? If this is Antarctica, there is no place to go. If this is a mountain, then maybe I can drop in elevation to where it is warmer."

Marvin reached into his pack and pulled out his water, some granola, and a spare pair of socks. He put them into his sleeping bag so they wouldn't freeze. It would take his body a lot of energy to thaw out ice. Having his water freeze would be a disaster.

All Marvin could do was hope for better weather. What had happened to Shandria? She should have exited the portal right by him. Marvin refused to believe she had abandoned him. The portal was supposed to be someplace near a city where she had friends. Unless her friends were snowmen, this wasn't it. Magic had gotten him into this, and he was sure magic was the only thing that could get him out.

Chapter 5

Shandria felt the portal unravel as she stepped through. She landed hard on an ice-covered flat area. Marvin should have been right next to her, but her portal had failed. She looked around at the snow-covered glacier. Marvin was nowhere she could see and had no magic to protect him. This weather would quickly freeze him to death.

Shandria stilled her heart and listened to the magic. She knew she was too far away to find Marvin, but the portal had generated a lot of magical noise when it unraveled. She looked, and then she saw it, the spot where the portal had dropped off Marvin. It was several miles away. Magical interference filled the area. Travel by a magic portal would be risky. And using any type of magic would disrupt any magical signature in the area and make it almost impossible to find Marvin. Shandria started to run and soon reached a rhythm in her running. She thought, "An hour, maybe two." He needed to hold on for an hour or two.

The Northern Jewel had a snow-covered mountain. The uniqueness made it a popular tourist spot, and the Sea Scouts trained there. They spent a week learning winter survival skills and frozen water magic. It was hard work and fun, but at the time she never dreamed she would have to go to a realm of snow and ice.

She ran at her long-distance pace and arrived where Marvin should be. She looked around. The blizzard had erased any tracks in the snow. Not too far away was a rocky outcropping. She closed her eyes and focused in that direction. She didn't see anything, but the rocky outcropping would keep her magical sight from seeing anything unless she spent more time looking. At least she didn't see his frozen body. Hopefully, he headed there to get out of the wind. It was her best bet. So, she started to run.

Chapter 6

Marvin's feet were still cold, but they had warmed up considerably. Suddenly his pack shifted. He heard Shandria ask, "Marvin, are you alright?"

He yelled, "Shandria, is that you?" He realized afterward that it couldn't be anyone else.

Marvin felt the cold air rush in as Shandria moved his pack. Then the tunnel started to expand in size. Marvin was sure it was Shandria's magic.

Shandria crawled in. She touched Marvin's sleeping bag, and he felt it grow warmer.

Marvin, said, "Thanks for warming up my sleeping bag. I'm so glad to see you. I was freezing cold. I knew I couldn't find you and was praying you could find me with magic."

Shandria said. "I'm so sorry. The portal unraveled. I saw where the portal had dumped you out. I knew you wouldn't last long without magic. I started running and hoped you had found a way to get out of the wind. I'm glad you were wise enough to dig this snow cave."

She continued, "You probably figured out, we are not where we intended to go. We are in the right realm, but high above the tree line on a glacier. Right now, our priority is to get you warm. Then tomorrow we will try to get down off this glacier and down from this mountain."

Shandria used magic to seal the entrance to the tunnel. Marvin could feel the air inside warming up.

Shandria crafted a light weave and the tunnel, which had grown dark with the setting sun, became bright.

She asked Marvin if he had eaten yet. Her two-hour run had left her starved.

The cave was now large enough and warm enough that Marvin could sit up in his sleeping bag. They ate some of the trail food from Earth. Shandria put her tarp down as a floor for her half of the snow tunnel. Marvin was amazed at how little the cold affected Shandria. He watched her curl up in her cloak. She ended the light weave, and the tunnel became dark. They were both exhausted. Shandria had expended a lot of energy running, and Marvin had spent a lot of energy shivering to stay warm. But now, the magical warmth of his sleeping bag and the thin high-altitude air put him quickly to sleep.

Chapter 7

The next morning it was cold, and the wind was howling. The overcast sky provided no warmth from the sun. Shandria exited the Ice cave, and Marvin followed. He could feel the bite of the cold on his exposed cheeks. Shandria had used her magic on his jacket and pants. He could still feel the cold air, but his body stayed warm. "Where are we?" he asked.

Shandria said, "Let me listen."

Marvin tried to be quiet. He looked for cover from the wind but didn't find any. He was wearing his winter jacket and his sweatshirt underneath. His poncho was draped over the top of his jacket.

The wind was blowing from a different direction than the day before, and the rocky outcropping wasn't stopping it. It was trying to blow away his poncho. Both sides of the poncho flapped like a pair of flags in a hurricane. He grabbed one edge of the poncho and spun, putting his back towards the wind. As he turned, the wind plastered the back side of the poncho against his back. It had bunched up, so he pulled it all the way down on his legs. The poncho was waterproof, windproof, and had a hood. The wind had been blowing through the fabric of his blue jeans, and the poncho helped. The front side of the poncho was still noisily flapping in the wind.

There were ties on the edge of the poncho. Marvin fumbled with one set at his waist. He entertained taking his gloves off for a second but decided against it. He was hoping for a bowknot, but the gloves made his hands too clumsy. He settled for a second overhand knot, creating a granny knot. He did the same thing with the other side.

The bottom half was still flapping in the wind, and the top half was catching the wind and puffing out like a parachute. There were a set of ties under his arm. He managed to tie those together by pulling one arm inside the poncho and bringing his other arm around on the outside. He tied the second knot. He completed tying off his poncho on one side, and then tied the other. But air entering in from the holes on the poncho caused it to balloon out. At least it wasn't flapping as much.

Shandria was busy listening, so he tried listening as Shandria told him to, but all he could hear was the howl of the wind and the flapping of the bottom part of his poncho. Maybe the magical feeling, the electrical tingling sensation, could help him. But all he felt was wind and cold.

Then his poncho stopped ballooning out in front of him. The wind had stopped blowing. No, the wind was still blowing. Only now, it no longer affected the poncho. One moment the poncho was outlining his body, plastered against it by the wind and ballooning out in front. The next moment it hung loosely about him, unaffected by the wind. He felt Shandria's hand on his shoulder.

She had put wind-blocking magic and warming magic on his poncho. Or as she would say, she wove magic. The howling wind was still there, yet the magic muffled the noise, and they no longer had to shout to talk. Marvin's face was starting to feel warmer.

Shandria said, "I'm sorry. I was worried about the glacier and forgot your magic wasn't developed enough to protect you. I should have woven more protective magic into your clothing last night or this morning."

Shandria continued. "We need to descend off this glacier. It looks like that way is the best direction." She pointed out a path and started walking. The sun was rising behind their back. The sun rises in the east, so they were heading west. Somehow having a name for the direction helped Marvin cope in this barren white land.

The altitude kept Marvin breathing deep and fast. He was glad they were heading downhill. Sometimes the path was straight and smooth, other times they ran into large crevasses that blocked their path and were forced to walk around them. Once they came to the edge where the glacier fell off at a snowy white cliff that dropped a hundred feet down. They followed along the edge and after a half hour of walking were at a gentler slope that they could climb down. They descended, only to find they had to climb an icy ridge on the other side. At least in the crevice, they were out of the wind.

Shandria decided it was time to eat. She gave Marvin a couple of strips of beef jerky and one of the packets of trail mix. He expected them to be freezing, but they were at body temperature. It must be Shandria's magic. He didn't realize how hungry he was until he took his first bite.

Shandria said while they were eating, "We've descended about a thousand feet. I hope we can get to the end of this glacier and drop another thousand feet before nightfall."

"Will that get us off the ice?"

"I don't know. But we will be closer to where it does. It's wiser to take the route the glacier offers us than to fight against it to head straight to our destination. As long as we travel down, we are doing well."

Marvin said, "Thanks for enchanting my poncho and clothing. I thought I was going to freeze to death."

"Technically your poncho isn't enchanted. I don't have the time to make the magic permanent. I wove temporary magic into it. It should last for a couple of days, maybe longer. The fabric is friendly and holds magic, but it is new to me.

"This cold, dry air and the altitude will quickly dehydrate your body. You should drink a bottle of water before we continue."

Marvin realized he was thirsty. He drank down a bottle of water. Then he sealed the empty bottle and placed it back in his pack.

They tried climbing the other side of the ravine. Marvin couldn't find any place where his boots wouldn't slide off.

Shandria touched his boots and his gloves. His boots and gloves stopped slipping on the ice of the glacier.

The glacier was steep for the first hundred feet. Marvin had to stop several times to catch his breath in the thin glacier air. Then the slope started to level off, and they were on another sheet of ice. Marvin looked backward. The glacier they had come from was noticeably higher, but when he looked forward, all he saw was a white expanse. They had to go around another crevice in the ice. Then the glacier started to slope downward again. They hiked around another crevice and continued.

The glow from the sun was low on the horizon. Based on his Boy Scout skills, Marvin could tell they were heading towards the southwest. It would soon be dark, and he was exhausted. He looked at Shandria and caught her eye.

She saw the exhausted look on his face and said, "Just a little farther."

After hiking for another fifteen minutes, they reached a spot where Marvin thought there was another block of ice. But he touched it and smiled when he realized it was an ice-covered rocky outcropping. Marvin was happy to see something that wasn't ice.

Shandria pulled out the tent they had bought and spent several minutes singing and holding it. Then she said another word and the tent unrolled and magically set up. It was a two-person tent designed for high wind conditions. It was tall enough that they could sit up in the tent, but not stand up. They crawled into the tent and took off their backpacks and cloaks.

Marvin took off his winter jacket and said, "Your heat spell sure made this tent warm."

Shandria laughed. "I crafted several weaves. None was a heat magic weave. I wove permanent repair magic on the tent. I will continue to enhance its magic over the next few days, and soon it will be able to withstand the puncture of almost anything that is non-magical, and it will repair itself if damaged.

"The rest of the magic I wove was temporary. Except for the packing magic. With a command, it will set up and repack itself in the morning.

"The magic you called a heat spell is a comfort weave. It contains several instructions that keep the cold out and your body heat in. It makes the floor more comfortable when we lay down. The light in the tent is a temporary weave into the air."

Shandria said, "I'm starved and want to try one of the hot meal pouches you bought for us at the camping store for dinner. And let's get some sleep. I know the altitude is making your body tired. We may have several long days of hiking until we can get off this glacier and off of this mountain."

They added water to the food pouches the salesman at the camping store sold them while telling them a long story of eating them on his last hunting trip, while he waiting in a blind for a deer. You could warm them on a camp stove or eat them cold out of the pouch. Shandria heated them with her magic in the pouch. They used their spoons and swapped their meals back and forth. Marvin thought both were okay; they were filling. One lacked flavor. The other meal had too much salt.

Shandria liked the second meal better, so Marvin let Shandria eat most of the second meal. They finished eating and cleaned up afterward. Marvin slid into his sleeping bag and fell right to sleep.

Shandria had spent many nights sleeping in her travel clothing. The permanent protective enchantments she had placed on the clothing were old friends. She released the magic that was giving them light, rolled up in her cloak, and spooned in behind Marvin.

But sleep didn't come quickly. Shandria was a princess of Atlantis, but maybe not for long. Her magic was starting to fail her body. It was starting to be intermittent. Her family loved her, especially after her older sister died, but if she couldn't regain her magic, if she couldn't regain her control, she would spend the rest of her life working in the temple. With intermittent magic, there was always a chance magic woven incorrectly would kill her. Her older sister was experimenting and had misweaved some fire magic, which killed her.

Shandria's magic was failing her body. The magic that would have stopped the narworm had refused to weave. She had never crafted a hazardous portal before, but it had started to unweave as they jumped through. They were lucky to be alive, but they should have landed far south of here, not on this glacier. She had to reweave the repair magic on the tent several times for it to stay. Temporary magic was simpler. She only used a temporary weave for the comfort-magic because she was afraid she might accidentally unweave the repair magic.

She thought of Marvin. She had a life debt to this non-royal, a peasant, a child in magic. She would be a faithful companion and would protect him with the last weave of her magic. She was a princess of Atlantis, and she would uphold her responsibility until her last breath.

Chapter 8

Marvin woke up stiff, sore, and tired from yesterday's hiking. He had a headache and wondered if it was altitude sickness. He was happy it wasn't severe, and hopefully, he would acclimate in a few days. But then again it might be a side effect of the magic that Shandria said was growing inside him. Time would tell. But all in all, he was feeling happy. This was one exciting adventure to go on during the last few months of his life, and there was a chance his cancer could be cured.

They removed everything from the tent. Shandria touched the tent and Marvin watched the flexible tent poles come out of the tent and fold themselves. The tent fabric repeatedly folded itself, each fold making it smaller. Then it rolled itself around the poles and packed itself into the tent bag.

Marvin thought he was starting to see the magic. It was fuzzy, but there was a glow around the tent pole as it came out of the tent. There was a small flash at each junction as the segments of the tent poles pulled away from each other and folded themselves. He saw sparks of light at each crease as the tent folded itself. Then his eyes blinked. His eyes felt tired like he had stayed up all night studying, and he no longer saw the magic.

They took out their empty water bottles. One by one, Shandria put them near the ice-covered rock. The ice melted and filled the bottles. His magic sight came back, and he saw the magic again as she filled the bottles.

He said to Shandria. "I think I can see the magic. Can I try one?"

Shandria smiled and stepped to the side. She handed him the last empty water bottle.

Marvin took the bottle and put it by the glacier. He focused and tried to direct the magic. Then he felt the ice and the magic inside him. Magic threads jumped out of him. A section of the glacier ice in front of him exploded. Freezing rain mixed with snow and ice blew towards him and rained down on him. Marvin tried covering his face with the arm that wasn't holding the bottle, but he was too late. A bucket of freezing water splashed into his face.

Shandria bent over and started laughing, loud laughter from her belly. Marvin stood there looking foolish, holding a water bottle with only a few drops of liquid inside. Shandria pointed at the almost empty bottle and kept laughing.

Marvin felt embarrassed. Then he realized he had performed magic. He had performed magic! Marvin started to laugh too. After a good laugh, Shandria took the bottle from him and filled it up. They put the bottles in their packs.

Shandria said. "That was one powerful baby kick of magic. When I was ten years old, my nanny was trying to get me to take a nap. I wanted to play with a doll, but my Nanna put it away into an antique wooden box that used to be my grandmothers. She was waiting by the door for me to fall asleep. I felt the magic, and I felt the box. I wanted my toy. The wooden box exploded, sending pieces of wood flying throughout the room. Nanna shrieked and ran from my room. I didn't understand what had happened and was afraid. I thought I had hurt her and was in big trouble for destroying the box my grandmother gave me.

"A few minutes later, my mom and dad ran into the room with Nanna. They were all excited, and I was scared. My mother grabbed me from my bed, picked me up into her arms, and gave me a big hug. She kissed me all over my face and gave me to my father. He hugged me and kissed me.

"I realized I wasn't in trouble. Everyone was excited my magic had come in with such power. They took me down to the palace kitchen, and we celebrated with sweet cakes and cookies. I was afraid when I saw my grandmother, but she gave me a big hug and kiss. She said she was proud of me, and my first magic occurring inside her box was like a special gift I had given her.

"The next day we had a party. At the party is where they gave me my princess necklace and my adult name Shandria. I had magic and was officially a princess. It was a fun party. It's funny when I look back at it now, but it was scary to start with."

Shandria came over, pulled back Marvin's hood, and kissed him. She put his hood back over his head and said, "Happy Magical Birthday!" Then she turned and started walking down the glacier.

Marvin wanted to talk to her more but knew he would have to wait until their next stop. He decided to spend time learning how to listen. He wondered, how do you listen to magic? He had seen magic. He had felt magic. Did magic speak, or was it just a term used to describe it? He would have to keep his senses open, to pay attention, and let his magic mature.

They were descending the glacier and soon came to an area strewn with large boulders cut from the mountain by ice and moved down by the expansion and contraction of the glacier. The terrain was becoming rough. They were repeatedly climbing through or walking around the boulders. Some were larger than a house, many were the size of a car, some were waist high, but they tended to clump together. Many times, they found themselves climbing over uneven patches of boulders. Marvin's legs were sore from yesterday, and he was feeling it with every step. Soon they stopped for their morning meal.

Shandria pulled a small package the size of a sandwich from the back of her pack. She broke it in half and handed half to Marvin. It was crunchy and had a sweet taste like honey. It didn't taste fishy but was salty, and somehow reminded him of the ocean. There must have been magic in the pastry. The soreness and tiredness in his muscles disappeared.

Marvin said, "This tastes great. What is it?"

She replied. "It's shalmara. It's composed of nuts, fish, honey, and various sea creatures. It's magically preserved and has some magical recovery properties. Usually, we eat it after a week of travel, but I wanted to celebrate your birthday, and I didn't have any birthday pastries or candy."

Marvin looked at Shandria and said, "Thank you. Is it okay for me to give you a hug?" Shandria reached out her arms and Marvin gave her a hug.

He took out a bottle of water and asked, "Is there any way you can turn water into wine?"

Shandria smiled and said, "That's easy. All I need is some grapes, some wine starter, and some time."

Marvin laughed. "Should I keep trying to use my magic? What should I do?"

"When you feel like using your magic, use it. It's powerful for baby magic. You may want to direct it away from anything that might break. You will learn how to control it naturally and improve with practice. A baby's legs kick where they will. Then over time, he will learn how to direct his kick and how to coordinate his kick with the rest of his body. Then he will learn how to walk. Magic is like that, but what takes several moons with a child happens in days with magic." She smiled. "You have a whole ice field to practice on."

They finished their water and started walking. Marvin took Shandria's advice. Every time he felt his magic nudge him, he released it. By lunchtime, he was getting good at blasting showers of snow, ice, and water out of the glaciers.

Marvin noticed that the magic he was using had a mix of vibrations or colors. And each one hummed a different tune, a different frequency or note. The next time he felt like using his magic, he tried controlling it. Then he tried humming the frequency of one of the vibrations. A thread responded and came forth. He directed it into a block of ice. The ice started melting into water, but then the other frequencies and colors joined the first one, and a shower of snow, ice, and freezing rain resulted.

Marvin barely noticed most of the journey past the boulder fields, through the ice planes, or around the crevasses that day. He was busy playing with his magic. All he talked about to Shandria during lunch and breaks was about magic. At the end of the day, they had walked a lot, but much of it was back and forth to avoid obstacles. They had covered little direct distance towards their goal. They were still in a boulder-strewn area filled with deep crevasses and covered with ice, but Marvin was too excited to care.

Chapter 9

Three nights later, Marvin lay down to sleep. He was sure they were at a lower elevation. There were fewer boulders, but deep fissures now gouged the ice. They were constantly going around the fissures, and he knew they weren't making good progress. At least his headache had gone away. How much from acclimatization, how much from the lower altitude, and how much from his magic helping his body to adapt, or maybe it was his body adapting to his magic, he didn't know.

He felt excited when his magic had come in. There was a new feeling inside his body. It was a mixture of excitement and warmth. But other than being able to blow up ice boulders, he felt like his magic hadn't improved much. Even blowing up ice chunks was getting to be a bore. He was starting to do it out of reflex, much like a baby's random kicking before they could walk.

His backpack was getting lighter from the food they had been eating. Shandria wouldn't talk about it, but their exertion and the cold had caused them to eat through food faster than they planned. It should have lasted them for three weeks. That evening they shared one trail meal. Neither said anything. They both knew they had to ration food.

Marvin felt guilty for getting Shandria into this jam. Without him, this would never have happened. She would have continued with her brother, and they wouldn't be in this predicament. He had initially slowed them down, but after almost a week of travel, his pace had picked up. He felt they were making a reasonable pace, but they spent most of their time backtracking around cracks and fissures. They were making slow progress towards getting off the glacier.

Shandria was acting more introspective. Marvin had only heard her laugh once in the last few days. And her smiles seem to be less real as if she was hiding her worry behind her smiles.

That night, after they lay down to sleep, Shandria was restless, so Marvin sat up.

"What's wrong?" she asked.

Marvin replied, "What's wrong is what we are avoiding saying. The first day you said we would be out of the ice by the end of the day if we were lucky. That was five days ago, and there is nothing but white on the horizon. We are hiking back and forth around the chasms, and we are making slow progress through the ice. We've started to ration our food. And you seem worried. I know I'm a baby when it comes to magic, but I am an adult, and I am your partner. If we don't talk about the truth, how can we work through it?"

Marvin looked at Shandria with a worried look on his face. Shandria looked at Marvin. She wasn't a liar. She didn't know how to lie, she had been hiding the truth by not talking about it. She felt like such a failure.

Tears filled her eyes, and she started to confess. "I didn't just offer this journey for your sake. I need healing too. My magic is starting to fail me. I'm having trouble controlling it. The portal unraveled and put us far off course. It's taking me more and more tries to weave magic. I've tried several times to weave some magic that would move us through this faster, and I'm having trouble talking to the ice. I know what direction we have to go, but not how to get past the obstacles. This morning I tried weaving a small portal to get us past the fissures, and I tried weaving an ice bridge over a chasm, but they wouldn't weave. I'm such a failure" She started crying again.

Marvin wasn't sure what to do so he put his hand on her shoulder while she cried. Then he said, "You're a princess, and I'm nothing. I'm the failure. It's my fault we are on this foolish journey. I had nothing to lose and allowed you to take me on this dangerous adventure. I'm out of shape, and I have been slowing you down. My blowing up ice blocks hasn't helped us one bit. After several days of trying, I still blow up more ice then I make water. I'm probably going to die anyway, and my foolishness is going to drag you to the grave with me."

Marvin started to cry. He didn't want to die. When he and Shandria met, he was on the verge of coming to grips with his death by cancer. He quickly grabbed onto the hope she offered. But the thought his decision could cause her to die was something he emotionally couldn't handle.

After several minutes, the crying subsided, and Shandria said. "We are both survivors, neither one of us is a quitter. We can't give up. We won't give up. We will work together and complete our journey."

They talked for several minutes before they lay back down to sleep.

The next morning, neither spoke of the previous night. Shandria started walking in the same direction until they came to another fissure, which they had to zigzag around again, but then they hiked for two hours and didn't encounter any more obstacles. The area was a flat icy plane.

The sun broke through the clouds just before lunchtime, a cold, light breeze blew down the glacier and cleared away the constant clouds that had covered the glacier valley. As they headed down the slope towards the southwest, they saw nothing but more ice, then they saw a ridge between a pair of mountains to the west.

Shandria knew they needed to get over the ridge. She said, "Glaciers form in mountain valleys. This Valley goes on for a long distance. The first day I was sure we needed to head that direction." Shandria pointed towards the ridge and continued, "I think it's our best path to get off this glacier. We also passed the last of the fissures. Now we can make better progress."

They hiked up a gentle slope that slowly became steeper towards the end of the day. Marvin was breathing hard and felt the exertion in his legs, but he didn't have to slow down and rest. They stopped early for the night near the base of the ridge. It was high enough to block the late evening light.

That night Marvin successfully melted a block of ice to water without an explosion. It was an uncontrolled flood of water, but it was water.

Shandria spent the extra time permanently enchanting Marvin's poncho. Marvin was starting to see the magic more clearly. It was like he just got a new pair of glasses. The magic consisted of vibrating, fine threads of different lengths, colors, and thickness. Shandria's magic weaving was selecting threads of various shapes, colors, and sizes, weaving them into the fabric of the tent, and into the fabric of his poncho. Sometimes her magic changed the color or size of the threads. Other times she left them as they were.

The next morning Marvin tried filling the empty water bottles. He filled them all, but he was melting large amounts of ice to fill each small bottle. Freezing water covered the ground. Marvin decided it was a win. It was messy, but it was the first time his magic had done something useful.

He spent all day trying to melt smaller amounts of snow. Towards the end of the day he realized, short magical strings wove small puddles of water. He also discovered he could slow down or speed up the vibrations on the threads that Shandria said were the words. Slower vibrations melted the snow and ice slower.

Weaving a long string was like tying a rope, easy to do even with gloves on. But weaving a small string was clumsy. It was like trying to thread a needle while wearing a pair of mittens. His magical hands were unsteady. But each time he tried, it became easier.

The slope of the ridge between the two peaks wasn't too steep. There were many places where they walked on top of the bare rock. Rather than head straight up the slope, Shandria set an angled path. Marvin was getting stronger, his pack was getting lighter, and he had tightened his belt by a notch. Shandria could go straight up the ridge, but she knew they would still spend more time stopping for Marvin then hiking if they had tried going straight up.

Soon they reached the saddle point at the top of the ridge and looked down the other side. A fog covered the valley below. But as Shandria would say later, "A friendly wind blew away the fog." They were at the edge of the mountain range, and the land sloped down for as far as they could see. Off in the distance, they could see the green of pine trees dotting the landscape.

They traveled into twilight, hoping to get to the tree line, but didn't quite make it. They stopped at a flat spot to camp for the night. Finally, they were traveling at a faster pace. Shandria was confident they would reach the trees before mid-morning.

ATLANTIAN MAGIC

The next day they set out at sunrise. They were on the west side of the mountain and were in its shadow for the first few hours. They reached the tree line at midmorning. Both Marvin and Shandria smiled and touched a tree. Marvin hadn't realized how much he had missed seeing color until he saw the green of the pine needles and the brown of the trunk. Marvin raised his hand up for a high-five. Then he had to explain what it meant to Shandria. She slapped his hand back and laughed.

Marvin found a dead branch and stuck it down into the snow. The snow was at least two feet deep. It was firm but not packed, yet he wasn't sinking into it. He asked Shandria if the grip magic she had woven into his boot kept him on top of the snow.

She smiled. "That was shoe magic, or more precisely foot covering magic. The magic is making your shoes an ideal covering for your feet. Different threads in the weave are different instructions. One thread or command in the magic added grip. Other threads keep your feet warm and dry. Another is keeping you from sinking into the snow."

Shandria started leading them further down the slope.

Marvin started watching his feet when he was taking a step. He could see a spider work of magical threads leaving his shoe and interacting with threads spreading out through the snowy surface. The threads were dispersing his weight and keeping him from sinking into the snow; just like magical snowshoes. There was far more variety of magic here than on the glacier. The threads were more colorful and varied. Marvin's eyes started to lose focus after a few minutes, so he let his magical vision rest, but each time he used it, it focused better, it came back sooner, and he could use it for longer.

By lunchtime, the sparse trees were becoming denser. By nightfall, a thick pine forest surrounded them. They set up camp at a flat spot under a tree.

It wasn't until Shandria mentioned it that Marvin noticed the smell of the pine forest. He knew he was on a different planet in a different realm, but the forest and the smell reminded him of camping on the rim near Flagstaff.

Shandria gave Marvin a new assignment. She wanted him to spend some time every day with his glove off and his hand touching a tree, while he listened to the tree.

Marvin put his hand on a tree. He felt the rough bark of the trunk. He heard the whistle of the wind through the branches. He heard the creak of the branches as they bent in the wind. He closed his eyes.

He wasn't sure what he was supposed to hear. He could hear his breathing and his heartbeat, but nothing that he could associate with magic. His concentration waned. He crawled back inside the tent.

That night, Marvin asked Shandria about her family. She smiled and replied, "My oldest brother is Prince Handrian. He was in a hurry and didn't introduce himself, but he was with me in your realm. My oldest sister, Princess Panoria died a few years ago. Then I have a younger brother, Prince Casparian, his magic came in last year. He is a high-energy rascal, always running around. He's a boy's boy and a lot of fun. You will really like him. And I have a baby sister. She talks up a storm and constantly asks questions. She won't get her princess name until her magic comes in. It should happen soon. I hope we are there when it happens. They are both so much fun. I miss them so much.

"There is my mother, Queen Isaria, my father, King Vandian, my grandfather, King Baracian, and my grandmother, Queen Elantria." She talked for several minutes more telling him more about her family and some close cousins.

Marvin asked her, "How can both your grandfather and your father be king? Do they both rule?"

Shandria said, "In our society, we have more than one ruling king. We had three kings when I was younger, and my great-grandfather was alive. Not long before that, we had four. And we will have three again when my brother gets married. They each rule on petitions and conduct routine business. They often work as a team. Both of them can rule on the law. Often they hold court together. My father says he is still learning from grandfather's wisdom.

"My mother and grandmother hold queen's court. Usually, they decide petitions on women's and family issues. Sometimes they combine courts. I hold Princess Court and Handrian holds Prince Court. Judges of the court resolve most petitions and assist us in our verdicts."

"When will your brother marry?"

Shandria replied, "He is looking for the right princess and will select one when he gets back, probably next year."

"When will you get married?"

"Sometime after their wedding, after we complete this journey, and my magic heals, my parents and I will select several good princes as suitors. I will meet them, and they will get a chance to court me. My suitors will indicate their desire to marry me, and my parents and I will agree on one, but probably I will have already chosen him."

"Where do the suitors come from?"

"Atlantis is the main island of an island nation. The suitors will come from the sons of the princes of one of the islands. Most likely I will marry a prince from one of the seven jewels of Atlantis, the seven largest islands."

Marvin asked, "Is there anyone in particular?"

Shandria replied, "I know all of the princes from the jewel islands, and some I consider friends, but there is no one who I am attracted to. But I'm not worried, they are all good princes from good families.

"My grandmother said she wasn't that interested in my grandfather at their introduction meeting. She said he seemed aloof and quiet. But then the second time they met, he started to open up. By the third time she realized he would be a wise and strong king, and then she saw him playing with some younger children and knew he would be a loving father. Soon she realized he would be a loving husband and friend and she wanted to be his wife.

Grandfather said he had his eye on my grandmother for years and was nervous during the first few formal meetings. Then my grandfather said, "Something clicked, and I became comfortable around her. And I grew happy every time I was going to see her."

Shandria yawned and released the light magic. Marvin saw the light magic weave for the first time. It was several magic threads woven together into a circle. She broke the pattern, the threads unraveled, and the light ended. The threads returned to the air with the other threads.

The next day, Shandria said she wanted to get further down the mountain, where there would be more game and less ice and snow. They would find a suitable place to camp and look for food. Marvin filled the water bottles again. He was getting better at it, melting far less ice and snow for each bottle he filled.

They started hiking towards lower elevation. Sometime after lunch, Shandria began to point out tracks in the snow. She obviously had a trained eye. Marvin had to walk over to see them. Many looked like random marks in the snow.

That evening, Marvin watched Shandria craft her light weave. It looked like she was creating threads from nothing, but as he watched more carefully, he saw she was getting most of them from the air itself. She wove them into a circle. The completed weave energized threads in the air around the tent, and the air itself created the light.

Marvin told Shandria he was starting to see the threads in the light spell. Shandria said, "It's good that you can see the light weave. Now you can start to understand why we call it magic weaving. Spells are a different type of magic, which Atlantians don't do."

Marvin asked, "Why not?"

"I'll explain it to you when you are better able to understand it, but for now, spells are evil. They destroy the magic threads. Magic weaving is magic friendly. The threads stay alive."

"Is light weaving something I can learn?"

"It's usually the first weave we teach our children. It's easy and nondestructive for a beginner. A flash of light or a flash of color is all that happens when you weave the magic wrong."

"I thought I was weaving magic when I was melting the ice?"

"It's part of weaving since its magic friendly, but currently you are only directing the magic and having it release magical energy. Soon you will start to see the threads vibrating, and you will learn to vibrate them and then to control them and to weave them with other threads."

Marvin asked, "You talk about vibrations, seeing, and hearing magic. Are they related?

Shandria said, "They are aspects of the same thing. Magic has vibrational energy, which we see, hear, feel, and sometimes taste and smell. It interacts with our senses. Sometimes we see the energy as a color. If I roll a boulder down a hill, you can see it with your eyes. You can hear it with your ears. And if it's large, you can feel the ground shaking. Magic is like that.

"How is your listening to trees going?"

Marvin replied, "I don't know. Occasionally, for a brief moment, I think I hear something other than the wind, but then I lose it."

"Next time try to stay real still, and not react at all when you hear her. Magic is shy, and you are as strange to her as she is to you."

"You called magic her? Is magic her or is that just a custom?"

"Magic is alive and has a personality. Everyone develops a relationship with her. Women usually refer to magic as her. Men usually call magic him. Some people refer to different types of magic or weaves with different genders. But it's rare that anyone calls magic it."

Marvin lay down and looked at the light weave. He was starting to see the magical threads in the air around him and was able to focus longer on the magic. But tonight, his eyes were tired, and he soon fell asleep.

Chapter 10

Shandria was surprised to discover Marvin had never gone hunting. He had never killed an animal for food, except for fishing with his father, so she told Marvin about her Sea Scout training.

Atlantian royalty and nobility learned seamanship, and survival, including how to catch, kill, and prepare their food during Sea Scout training. At the end of their training, their instructors dropped them off alone on an outer island with just a knife, where they had to survive. They prepared a shelter, purified their water from seawater, and fished, hunted and foraged for food. At the end of five days, they put together a skiff from island material, navigated, and crossed the sea to one of the inner islands.

After graduation, they spend a year as a teenager in the Sea Guard. Shandria was on a small naval vessel with a commanding officer and a dozen other Sea Scout graduates, a mixed group drawn from the different islands. They would visit the smaller uninhabited islands to ensure there were no lost ships and that no one was taking up residence without crown approval. They received minimal provisions when they docked every few months. They caught all their food and made all repairs to their ship and equipment. And they were constantly training. It was a test of both their skills and their practical magic.

Shandria took out two long, flat, curved pieces of beautifully polished wood from her backpack. She took out a handle. She inserted the wood pieces into the handle, added a string, and had a hunting bow. Shandria stroked it and sang to it. At first, Marvin was wondering what she was doing, but he saw the threads and realized she was weaving magic on her bow. He asked her about the bow.

"It's an Atlantian travel bow. I've had it for years, since before I was in the Sea Scouts."

She took out four smooth, round, wooden sticks. They were the shaft for four arrows. Then she took out several arrowheads and tailpieces from a small container. The arrowheads were metal like her sword. She attached them to the arrow shaft. Then she attached the tail pieces.

There was a flat outcropping near where they camped. It had a flat ledge at ground level covered with ice and snow. Shandria told Marvin to remove the snow from the ledge and to collect enough dead wood for a fire that would last for several hours. Marvin asked her about kindling. She asked what kindling was.

Marvin said, "Kindling is smaller sticks that you use to start the fire, then you put bigger and bigger sticks and build a larger fire."

Shandria at first didn't understand what he was saying. Then she laughed. "We can do it your way, or we can use magic to light the fire."

Marvin thought about it for a second and then started to laugh at himself. He brushed most of the snow off the ledge, then melted the rest of the snow off with magic until it was dry.

He collected wood while she was out hunting.

Shandria returned at midmorning. She was carrying a pair of rabbit-like animals that she called lopes. She demonstrated how to remove the skin of the first lope, and then she had Marvin skin the other lope. Shandria removed the skin from her lope in about a minute. Marvin was sure it would have taken her half as long if she weren't explaining the process to him. It took Marvin much longer to skin his lope.

She already had a fire going by the time Marvin was done. She then showed him how to field dress the lope, removing all the internal organs. She kept the liver and heart.

Shandria cooked most of the first lope on the bone, but the other lope and what was left of the first she cut into thin strips for processing into jerky.

She gave Marvin a cooked heart and liver and kept a set herself. She said a quick prayer of thanks to the Father of all and then thanked the lope for giving them strength. She popped her set, one at a time, into her mouth. Marvin had never eaten a heart or liver before, although his grandmother used them in her stuffing. He saw how much Shandria enjoyed eating them. He ate them and decided he much preferred them in his grandmother's stuffing.

Shandria prepared a wooden frame. She made a dry rub with the sea salt Marvin had purchased along with a few spices from Atlantis and rubbed it into the meat. She hung the meat strips on sticks over the coals. She covered the top of the frame with some pine boughs to keep the smoke in and to dry the Jerky.

Shandria wove some magic and then showed Marvin how to remove the last of the membrane from the skin by cleaning the fur using snow. She wove some more magic to clean, tan and softened the pelts.

The lope skin had peeled off in the shape of a cylinder. Shandria wove magic to seal up the bottom of the pelt, turning it into a sack. The lope sack stored the jerky for travel. Marvin watched and saw that it took Shandria three times to get the weave correct. He said nothing.

Lopes were the size of large rabbits. Each provided several pounds of Jerky. Shandria said it should last them for several days.

The fire mesmerized Marvin. He could occasionally see magic threads, weaving and bobbing with the flames. They were elusive, but he managed to grab one thread and sent it into a stick that was next to the fire. Much like the ice had the first time, the stick exploded, and pieces of burning wood flew in all directions. He was glad that none hit them or their tent.

Shandria's eyes became large, then went back to normal, and she said, "Good, you've discovered fire inside a fire. Now find it in the air around us and learn to control it on the outskirts of our camp where it is safer." It was already dark, and the fire was burning low. Shandria continued, "But maybe that needs to wait for another day."

Marvin had a good night's sleep, stuffed with the meat of Shandria's hunt.

The next morning, Shandria said, "I will take over filling the water bottles. The water from the glacier was pure, but lower down the mountain animal waste can contaminate the water. Once you advance to weaving magic, then I will teach you how to purify the water."

They broke camp, but rather than hiking right away, she had Marvin try to start a fire from threads in the air. The results were random. His first attempt did nothing. His second attempt produced a gust of wind, which scattered some branches and caused a sapling to bend. He produced a flash of light, melted some snow, and many times had no noticeable effect. After many tries, he created a small explosion of fire.

Shandria said, "I knew sooner or later you would do it. But every time you used a magic thread it was a victory."

Marvin asked, "How come it works with water and fire, but it was random with air?"

Shandria answered, "On the glacier, most of the magical threads are speaking water. Most of the magical threads from the campfire speak fire. Threads in the air speak air, but air transports many other types of threads. Threads in the air are more likely to speak something else. Next time you practice, hold the thread and listen before you use it. You will soon become sensitive to what the threads are saying."

It was time to go.

Shandria was carrying her bow in her left hand. Marvin didn't see any arrows. He mused on where her arrows were all morning long. She had them assembled, and he hadn't seen her break them down. They were too big to fit in her pack. He was sure she had them.

They took a break a few hours later. Shandria pulled a couple of strips of jerky from her pack and gave one to Marvin. He asked her where her arrows were. She pulled back the cloak from her left arm. All four sat aligned side by side, facing downward, and sticking to the outside of her arm where she could quickly grab them.

She said, "I have seen several good animal tracks. If I see or hear anything to hunt late in the afternoon, we will have fresh meat for dinner."

"Have you been listening to the air while we hiked?"

Marvin replied, "I've been looking at the threads in the snow and the trees." Marvin smiled and said, "And wondering where your arrows were."

Shandria laughed. "It's amazing how one unsolved puzzle can distract our minds

There was no fresh meat that evening, but there was fresh meat the following one. And Marvin was starting to hear the magic. Each magic string vibrated, like the vibrations of a speaker. Like a baby, magic crept along the ground, but like a bird, it flew through the air. Shandria told Marvin, "Magic contains information from all around us. You will quickly learn its speech. And then you will learn how to talk back, to change the magic to say what you want. Then you will be ready to weave your first magic."

The next day as they hiked, Marvin spent most of the day learning the names of the magic threads. He learned a few names like fire, light, earth, water, and wind. The language of magic was unique and could get complex, but for the most part, it was simple. He could already understand a few words. At least words were how he thought of them.

Soon after lunch, Shandria asked Marvin to listen and to stay close. A pack of large animals had started to follow them. There was a rocky outcropping with a small clearing ahead. She was hoping they could get there before they had to confront the animals.

They made it to the clearing and stood a few feet in front of the outcropping. It was at the base of a high drop off and formed a rock wall behind them. It prevented the animals from circling behind them and attacking them from their rear. It was a good place to defend.

Shandria wanted to start a fire, but there was no time to gather wood. The alpha male of the pack slowly entered the edge of the clearing. It was the largest wolf Marvin had ever seen, and the only one he had ever seen outside a zoo. It didn't look friendly.

Shandria drew her sword and pointed it in the direction of the wolf. But her magic didn't weave. A beam of energy should have come from the sword and killed the wolf, but nothing happened. It wasn't even weaving. It was directing magical energy through the sword. The wolf was ready to pounce towards Marvin. She took a step towards the wolf and looked him in the eyes. She had identified herself to the wolf as the alpha and had issued a challenge. The rest of the pack knew it too.

Shandria was now its target.

Chapter 11

One good thing about challenging the alpha wolf is the rest of the pack would let them fight in individual combat. The wolf leaped towards Shandria. It was fast, but her training, practice, and reflexes made her faster. The wolf jumped high, so she dropped low, and shifted her weight to her left foot, as she stepped behind her left foot with her right foot, further shifting her body away from the line of the pounce. She couldn't enhance her sword with her magic, but it was magically sharp. The wolf's fur and skin were hard, and her slash with her sword was weak since she was twisting away as she stepped. It would have cut deep on most animals, but it only left a gash on the side of the wolf, partially bouncing off its dense fur and its ribs.

Shandria had drawn first blood. She spun to face the direction of the wolf.

The growling of the wolf turned into a shrieking howl as it landed near the base of the cliff. The wolf spun around at the rock wall. Its tail hit Marvin with enough force to knock him into the wall.

The encounter was faster than anything Marvin believed was possible. He had heard that Hollywood slowed down martial arts moves for a movie or TV camera, but this was faster than he could have imagined. Then his adrenaline hit him, and everything seemed to move in slow motion. He watched the wolf bound to the side, circling away from Shandria. It was focused solely on her and paying no attention to him.

Shandria once again tried her magic with no results. She would have to depend on her combat training. She readied herself for the next time the wolf attacked. It could be another leap, but the wolf could rush her. She anticipated moves and angles, then she let go of them. All she could do was choose her distance, her stance, and her angle. This would be a fight of reflexes. To hold on to one defense would slow down her reflexes against a different attack. She continually shifted her feet, balance, distance, and angle in a deadly dance with the wolf.

The wolf pounced again.

This time Shandria shifted to the right and stepped behind her right foot with her left foot, going low again. The step sideways and back into a twisted her body and moved her out of the way. She spun with the twist. She was right-handed, and this time her sword was moving with the twist, giving her a strong strike. She thrust the point of her sword deep into the belly of the wolf, penetrating through its lower ribs. It was a mortal wound. But it would take a minute for it to kill the wolf. Her sword stuck in the side of the wolf long enough for the wolf's momentum to rip it out of her hand. Her sword flew out of her hand and rolled to the ground.

The wolf circled away to its right. It was dying, and it was in intense pain from its wounds. But it's rage, anger, and adrenaline helped mask its pain.

Shandria stepped towards the sword to get it, but it was too far away. The step was a tactical mistake. It put her out of position and in a poor stance. The wolf pounced one more time. Shandria held her left arm up and grabbed the dagger from the sheath on her leg with her right hand.

The wolf crunched down on her left arm with its teeth. Its weight and momentum knocked her to the ground as it landed on top of her. Shandria thrust the dagger between the ribs underneath its armpit. It slid deep into its side, and into its heart.

The wolf held onto her arm with its teeth. The weight of the wolf on Shandria trapped her as he went unconscious and died.

There was a loud howl from the rest of the pack. They smelled blood. It was the blood of their alpha. They knew their leader was severely wounded, and possibly dead. If it were a clear victory, they would have retreated, if only to regroup, but it wasn't. Their prey was vulnerable, and they were hungry. They slowly entered the clearing through the forest.

If Shandria had stayed upright, the pack would have temporarily left. She had bested their alpha. But she was pinned beneath his weight. She was now fair prey.

Marvin stood there without moving. He wasn't sure whether he was in shock, or just too scared to be scared. His mind kept saying, "What can I do? I need to do something. What can I do? What can I do?" Then he saw the magical threads illuminated by the fear-powered adrenaline in his system.

He grabbed a thread and directed it at a wolf with all his resolve. It hit the wolf in the face and exploded into fire. He grabbed another and targeted another wolf. This one energized the water in the wolf's head, and it exploded, spreading shards of ice. Light magic temporarily blinded another wolf. Marvin kept grabbing and throwing magic threads.

His newborn magic was helping him, eagerly offering itself into his control. He lost count of how many threads he threw. Many had no visible effect. But some released their magic with strong results. A tree near the clearing burst into flames from a thrown fire thread that had missed its target.

The wolf pack turned and ran away from the carnage.

Marvin stopped after the last of the wolves retreated into the forest. He was exhausted. He felt like he had run a marathon, but the encounter had taken less than a minute. He saw Shandria roll the wolf that was on top of her off to the side. She rose to her feet and quickly retrieved her sword.

There were three more dead wolves in the clearing, ripped apart by Marvin's exploding magic. Blood, tissue, and wolf fur covered the ground. Wolf blood covered Shandria. She was holding her left forearm where the wolf had bitten down. The wolf's sharp teeth hadn't penetrated the magic she wove into her shirt. But the force of the wolf's bite had crushed her forearm and done damage that would take time to heal.

Without thinking, Marvin ran over to Shandria and hugged her. He feared the wolf had killed or seriously injured her.

Shandria stood there for a few seconds returning the hug. She let her tears flow. Her magic had failed her, and she had almost let her duty and oath to protect Marvin fail.

She released her hug, grabbed her sword, and removed the dagger that was still sticking out of the side of the wolf. Suddenly, she tilted her head upward and gave a loud howl, similar to the one the wolves had made earlier. She said a prayer for the wolf and the pack. Marvin remembered part of what she said. "We both wanted to live, and today it was our turn."

She walked over to a snow bank and cleaned off her equipment and herself. The magic woven into her clothing made the blood come off quickly. She had Marvin clean himself off in the snow also.

Shandria, said, "The wolves were a worthy adversary, trying to survive. You should say words of respect to their bodies."

Marvin didn't know what to say, so he pretty much repeated what Shandria had said earlier. What she said was true. "The wolves were just trying to survive."

Shandria walked over to the first wolf Marvin had killed. She used her dagger to remove one of the wolf's large canine teeth. She quickly cleaned it off in the snow and put it in a pouch.

She said, "We need to get out of this area. The wolves will be back soon as well as other predators and scavengers. The smell of blood is in the air. Even now, the wolf pack is starting to gather. They will honor the bodies of their fallen by using them to nourish the pack."

Marvin and Shandria resumed their journey, quicker than their regular pace, and walked until late twilight before they set up their camp. That's when the emotions of the encounter with the wolf finally hit Marvin. He began to shake and cry.

Shandria saw him and watched to see if he wanted to be alone or with her. He seemed like he needed some space, so she left him alone. After a few minutes, he composed himself and said, "I'm going to get some firewood."

He returned after a while with a bundle of wood, still shaken from the encounter. This time she had Marvin start the campfire using his magic. It would help get his mind off the wolves. Shandria knew it would take some time for him to come to grips with the attack.

It was a clear cold night, and the stars were beautifully twinkling. They ate dinner outside the tent. Shandria was working with a piece of leather. She fastened the wolf tooth to it and tied it into a necklace.

Shandria said, "Killing that wolf is a significant point in your life. Whenever you think you can't accomplish something, look at this. I Princess Shandria, award you the Atlantian Order of the Wolf, and for once again saving my life, I award you the title of Sir Marvin of Atlantis."

She hugged him and kissed him briefly on the lips, as she placed the wolf tooth around his neck. Marvin explored the tooth with his fingers for most of the evening.

For the first time since they had come through the portal, it was a clear night. They looked at the sky for several minutes. The night sky shocked Marvin. The moon was somehow different, and the stars were somehow wrong. At least the Milky Way was still there. He found the first constellation he had learned in Boy Scouts. He identified the three stars in a row that was Orion's belt, but the rest of the constellation was somehow bent and crooked. Even the big and little dipper looked different than he had remembered them from Boy Scouts. He mentioned it to Shandria.

Shandria said, "This isn't Earth. It's a different realm. You can usually identify the major stars and constellations, but there are always differences."

Marvin went to bed that night thinking about all that had happened. The canine tooth against his chest was over an inch long, and sharp. The encounter had happened too fast for him to be afraid, but now he was feeling the fear. It was in self-defense, but he had never killed an animal before. Up until today, this had been an adventure, a good movie, a Boy Scout hike, a fast amusement park ride. But the wolves had almost killed Shandria and him. And only when he saw the night sky did he emotionally realize he wasn't on Earth. He wasn't even sure if he was in the same universe.

Marvin zipped open his sleeping bag. The magic of the tent and his clothing was keeping him warm. Rather than lay inside he lay on top, wrapped himself tightly in his poncho, spooned into Shandria, and held her like he had in the hotel bed so long ago. He needed the reassurance her physical touch gave him. His poncho felt warmer than normal. The magic of his poncho was holding him tightly, comforting him. His mind was racing, but his physical and emotional exhaustion won the battle, and he fell asleep.

Shandria was glad the bruises on her left arm were healing. They were more severe than she had told Marvin. There was a hairline fracture of one of her forearm bones, and there was enough tissue damage that she could barely open and close her hand. It had taken her several tries, but she finally managed to craft a healing weave. The swelling had come down quickly, and it would speed the healing.

She was starting to mistrust her magic. A more complex weave would have healed the tissue damage in a few minutes, and the bone would fully heal in about an hour. But if she wove the magic wrong, it would make the injury worse. At least her arm would be back to normal in a couple days rather than a couple weeks without magic.

Now that the encounter with the wolves was complete, she was feeling the fear also. She had vowed to protect the life of a peasant, no not a peasant, a brave scholar of Earth history, culture, and technology. And she had rewarded him by making him an Atlantian noble. He was a person with only baby magic, yet his baby magic had saved her twice, and hers was getting less reliable. It had almost cost them their lives again. It would have if Marvin didn't save them.

She knew he was working through his fears from the encounter. He had left his sleeping bag, spooned in behind her, and was holding her tight. She was an Atlantian princess and warrior. A master of Atlantian magic and someday a grandmaster. She had never before felt she needed anyone. But tonight, she was glad he was holding her tight.

Chapter 12

The next day both Marvin and Shandria were quiet and introspective.

Marvin was replacing the fantasy mindset of the previous days with the harshness and reality of survival.

Shandria also had her new reality. She could no longer trust her magic. She felt lost and almost betrayed. Her magic wasn't getting better. It was getting worse. And she was having trouble accepting it.

They were making better time since they left the glacier and dropped down in altitude. The forest was starting to change from a pine forest to deciduous forest. It would be another day before Shandria's arm healed enough to shoot her bow.

Shandria cheered up when she found a nut tree after lunch. The snow under the tree wasn't deep. She dug down into it and found what she was looking for. It looked to Marvin like a walnut. She told Marvin to help her find more.

Marvin thought for a second and said, "It would be good practice for me if I melted the snow around the tree. It will be easier to find the nuts."

Shandria knew it was a good idea, so she told him to go ahead. He used his magic to melt the snow for twenty feet around the tree.

Walnuts littered the base of the tree. They cleaned off the soft outer shell of the nut. Then they ate their fill, smashing them open on a rock with another rock. They collected and cleaned as many as would fit into a large side pocket on Marvin's backpack.

Shandria took a few extra nuts. As they traveled, she buried them one by one in the soil at spots that looked good to her. Spreading its seeds was her way of thanking the walnut tree for the nuts it had given her.

That evening's meal was a supplement to the nuts they had eaten. The next day they came upon a frozen-over stream. The water below the ice was flowing in the same direction they were walking. It wasn't surprising since they were walking downhill. They crossed over and followed it. Soon it joined with another stream, and then to a large lake. They needed to cross to the other side of the lake. It was the middle of the afternoon, and Shandria wanted to wait until the following morning.

ATLANTIAN MAGIC

Marvin had a survival kit he had made in Boy Scouts from a small aluminum box. It included a fishing kit with hooks, sinkers, and fishing line. He told Shandria.

Marvin tried to chop a hole in the ice with his large knife. It was slow going. Shandria pulled out her sword. It took her only a couple of swings to chop through and create a hole wide enough to fish through. Only afterward did Marvin consider that he should have tried to melt it with his magic.

Shandria found something to use as bait. They dropped their lines into the water. Shandria cut a few pine branches and placed them over the opening she had cut. She told Marvin the darker spot caused by the branches would attract the fish. Fifteen minutes later, she caught the first fish. Then Marvin caught one. Shandria said that was enough for the night. Marvin made another fire, and they ate fish for dinner.

He asked Shandria to show him how to weave light magic. He practiced for about an hour. At first, the weaves unraveled and produced no light, But Marvin kept at it. And soon his weaves would flash and then extinguish. He was starting to see spots from lights flashing in his eyes when he made his first successful weave. He called it a victory and decided to end the day on a high note. He left the light on outside the tent when they crawled in to go to bed. It was a good first weave, but it was unstable and disappeared by the time they crawled out of the tent the next morning.

The next morning, they woke up, packed the tent, and hiked across to the west side of the lake. Soon it narrowed back into a river. Around mid-afternoon, they found a small stone hut. Shandria read the writing outside and said, "The writing is Dwarvish. It says, 'Tired traveler, rest and be refreshed.'"

There was no lock on the metal door. They knocked, then they entered in.

Shandria let Marvin weave light for the hut. It took him several tries before he formed a working light weave.

It was a one-room stone hut. It had numerous metallic tools and a fireplace. It also had some chains and miscellaneous metallic parts that looked like they belonged to an old train. There were no provisions, but there was a stack of wood in the corner near a hearth and more chopped wood outside near the back door of the hut.

They were happy to see a map on the wall. It showed a road that ran north and south. At the top of the map was a drawing of a mountain. It had crossed pickaxes at what looked like an entrance. There were several small huts along the road. Farther south on the map was Iron Mountain. The symbols on the map showed a town.

There were several traveler stations on the map. Based on the closeness of the river, they figured they must be in the hut halfway between the mine and the town. There was another traveler station south of them. They had no idea how far it was between huts. Shandria said, "It might be one day's travel for a

Dwarven steam-powered wagon or a horse. That's several days of travel by foot."

There was plenty of game in the area. They decided to rest tomorrow and maybe for another day, to replenish their provisions.

Shandria took Marvin hunting the next morning. She had him look at the magical threads in the ground and on the snow. He had been looking for tracks in the snow when she tried to show him earlier, and she had been looking at the effects the animals had on the magical threads.

He was amazed at the information in the magical threads. Once he knew what to look for, it was easy to see where animals had walked and where they were hiding. He pointed out one place where there was something underground.

Shandria said, "It's a lope den. They are hibernating through the winter. We are looking for something that will give us enough meat for several days."

They saw a small deer-like creature in the forest. Shandria handed Marvin her bow and an arrow and told him to shoot at the deer. He was surprised at how much strength it took to pull back the string. It was far harder than the one he had used in Boy Scout summer camp. She said, "Think of the arrow and the animal."

He pointed the arrow at the animal and released the string. The arrow started to fly wide, but then the magic in the arrow took over. It curved and struck the deer in the chest. The deer bolted and ran several steps before it fell over dead. They hurried to the deer. Marvin tugged at the arrow and was surprised to see how easily it slid out, easier than the targets they had used at summer camp. It must have been the magic on the arrow.

Marvin looked at the beautiful creature he had just killed and felt sorrow. Shandria had Marvin thank the deer and to thank the creator. During the prayer for the animal, much of Marvin's remorse left him. They had to eat to survive, and today was their turn. Killing the deer was necessary for their survival.

They hung up the deer with a rope by its antlers in a tree, and Shandria walked Marvin through cutting open and field dressing the deer. She took the deer's heart and the liver.

They took the deer down from the tree and packed its insides with snow and ice. Shandria placed the heart and liver inside the deer with the snow. Together they dragged the deer back through the snow to the hut.

Snow covered and hid the Dwarven road. Marvin stopped when they crossed it, and noticed it was easy to see there was a straight, unobstructed path running north and south where there were no trees or bushes.

Shandria instructed Marvin and helped him skin the deer. Then Marvin brought in the wood and started the fire. Shandria cut the strips of meat from the animal and prepared the meal.

They had found plants hiding under the snow, which Shandria said were sweet potatoes. She asked Marvin to go back and dig up a couple of the tubers. It looked like a purple-skinned potato and was purple on the inside.

He brought the potatoes back to the hut, and Shandria sent him out with a large metal cooking pot to get some water from the river. Near the bank, the water was flowing fast enough that there was no ice on top the water. He filled the pot and brought it inside.

Shandria emptied some of the water out. She sent Marvin back to the river to clean the dirt off the potatoes. He had to take his gloves off. The water was freezing, so he cleaned each potato as fast as he could. Then he realized he could have tried using magic to remove the dirt, but he didn't really know how to do that yet. He put his gloves back on, and their magic weave warmed up his hands.

Shandria presented him with the heart and liver on a plate. "It's your kill, so this belongs to you. You can either cook and eat these or cut them up and share them with me. Or we can eat part and put the rest in the stew with the potatoes. Marvin cut the heart in half. He said, "This half is for the stew. Then he cut the other piece in half again. This part is to cook and share. There was a big smile on Shandria's face. He did the same thing with the liver. They cooked them separately.

Shandria worked hard preparing the food and salting the deer meat. She would have liked to make sausage out of some of the pieces, but she didn't have the spices. She had Marvin take the remaining parts out past the road. She said, "Some animal will get to eat because of us." They prepared the skin as a pack to carry the Jerky and built a small shoulder sling.

It was a good meal. But something was wrong with Shandria. She started to shiver. Then she collapsed.

Marvin put his hand on her. She was burning up with a fever. He looked at her. Dark magical strings were spreading through her body. His magic rebelled; he felt sick to his stomach; he knew they were evil. He tried to affect them but didn't know how.

Then the magic inside him showed him the source. It was her necklace. She had told him it had no magic. But it did. It was evil, destructive magic. It was what Shandria had called a dark magic spell. It was on her necklace, and it was killing her.

Chapter 13

The clasp on Shandria's necklace burned Marvin's fingers as he grabbed it to remove it. Instinctively he pulled his fingers away and put them in his mouth to cool them off. But he had to get the necklace off Shandria. He pulled his fingers from his mouth and quickly undid the clasp. Small blister started to form on his fingertips as the dark magic burned his fingers.

He tried to pull the necklace off, but it stuck to Shandria's neck and refused to come away. A series of various colored golden plates, an inch to two inches long, separated by beautiful small gemstones were hanging from Shandria's golden chain. They were sticking to her neck. He had reached the level of pain where he had to release the necklace and stuck his fingers again into his mouth. He had to get it off before it killed Shandria. He grabbed the necklace by one end, quickly yanked it free, and immediately dropped it, returning his burning fingers to his mouth. The necklace slid several feet across the room.

He saw the black threads of evil magic coming from the necklace and searching like tentacles of an octopus. He knew they were looking for Shandria.

The pain in Marvin's fingers kept him from grabbing the necklace again. He pulled out a small multi-tool from his survival box. It had a stainless-steel, needle-nosed pliers. He grabbed the necklace, threw it into an iron pot, and closed the lid. The metal of the pot blocked the magic. He couldn't see through the metal of the pot, but he could feel the evil magic inside the pot. He was sure he heard the dark magic hitting the sides of the container, and hissing like a snake, trying to get out.

He walked over to Shandria. On Shandria's neck were blisters in the shape of the golden plates of the necklace. When he removed the necklace, it pulled off the skin that was covering the blisters. She was now cold and shivering. She threw up the stew she had eaten for dinner. He wasn't sure whether she was having mild seizures or just shivering uncontrollably.

He wrapped her in her cloak, lay down by her, and held her tight, trying to comfort her. Inside her, he could sense the dark threads of magic. They were moving around like wiggling snakes or worms, and he was powerless to help. But they were shying away from where his hand was. His hand was still holding his metal multi-tool.

ATLANTIAN MAGIC

The dark threads didn't like metal and Dwarven metal filled this room. Marvin put every metal object in the room against her body, cooking utensils, pots, pans, parts that looked like they came from a steam engine, and several old chains. It was having an effect. He could see some of the dark strings dissipating like smoke. But many were still active in her body. He was sure they were doing damage.

He had one more piece of metal. The container he kept his survival kit in was aluminum. He grabbed it, hugged Shandria from behind, and placed it over her heart, between her breasts. He heard a loud shriek from the air around him. He saw the dark magic threads leave her body. The aluminum was a metal that magic didn't know, from a planet where there was no magic. Healthy threads of magic seemed to ignore the aluminum box. But to the dark magic threads, it was a deadly poison. They turned to dust and disappeared.

Marvin wrapped Shandria tighter in her cloak. She was sleeping restlessly, still shivering, and her skin was cold. Marvin threw his sleeping bag over her body, held her from behind, and held the aluminum box against her chest. The metal chain he was lying on was uncomfortable, but there was no way he was going to move it away from Shandria, and there was no way he was going to let the aluminum box slide off her chest.

Shandria's body normally had energetic lines of magic flowing through her, but it was now dark. Marvin tried to speak to the magic in the room. He called to it to enter and heal her body but was afraid to force it back into her. He pleaded with the magic. Slowly the magic responded. First, a thread from his body, and then magic from the room slowly flowed back into her body.

Chapter 14

Marvin had a sleepless, worried night, but he woke up with the sun anyway. Shandria was still sleeping. It was unlike her to sleep this late. At least she was sleeping soundly and her fever was gone.

Marvin paced around the hut all morning, groggy from lack of sleep, worried about Shandria, and afraid to let Shandria out of his sight. He grew hungry and ate lunch. Soon after, Shandria sat up. She yelled as if she was in pain and acted like she was going crazy. She touched her neck where her necklace was. Large blisters and sores outlined where her necklace had been. She yelled, "Where is my necklace. My body needs my necklace."

Marvin said, "It has a dark spell on it. It was killing you."

She yelled again, "Where is it? Tell me where it is."

He had seen that look before on a face in an area of town he shouldn't have been in. It was on the face of an addict who needed a fix.

"I threw it away."

"Where did you throw it? I command you as Princess of Atlantis to tell me."

"I threw it into the river."

She yelled, "You lie. You would never leave this room. It's somewhere in here."

He involuntarily looked over towards the pot. Shandria saw his eyes move and headed towards the pot. He took one-step to intercept her and suddenly found his legs swept out from under him. His body hit the floor hard.

She opened the pot, dropped the lid, and grabbed her necklace. She put it on.

Marvin stood up from off the ground.

Shandria looked at him with an angry, crazed look in her eyes. She yelled, "How dare you lie to a princess of Atlantis!"

Suddenly a blast of magic hit Marvin and threw him back towards the wall. He bounced off the wall but managed to stay on his feet. Then he heard Shandria's voice change and so did her eyes. In desperation, she weakly cried, "Help me," as she once again collapsed.

The dark magic of the necklace was once again in her body. He grabbed his multi-tool. This time he destroyed the clasp when he removed the chain. He ripped it from her neck where it was trying to attach itself, threw it back into the pot, and closed the lid. He picked Shandria up and laid her back where the chains and iron tools were. Then he once more held the aluminum box against her chest. The dark magic left her body as tendrils of black vanishing smoke. He held her until the convulsions stopped, and once again covered her in his sleeping bag.

This time he was going to throw the necklace away where she couldn't get it. He opened up his aluminum box and emptied out the fishing line, hooks, the fire-starter, needle and thread, and various small items he held in there. He opened up the pot and used the multi-tool to grab the necklace. He could see the dark threads once again searching for Shandria. He quickly put the necklace into the aluminum box. A shrieking noise filled the air.

The necklace tried to leap out of the box, but he held it firmly in the box with the multi-tool. He grabbed the lid of the box and snapped it closed, removing the multitool at the last minute. He held the lid shut for several more minutes until he was confident the dark magic inside had died. Then he put the box into the iron pot just to be sure.

Marvin paced back and forth. He realized he couldn't keep the box in the room. Shandria would wake up and grab it again. He had to get rid of it. He grabbed the box from the metal pot and marched outside, cutting a diagonal path through the snow downstream towards a spot on the river where the current kept the river free of ice. He dropped the box into the river, but then had second thoughts. The box sealed tight. It was water resistant and floated. He quickly ran two steps down the river and grabbed it back out. He realized the spell might have permanently damaged Shandria. They might need to know the spell to heal her, and they might need the necklace to find out.

There were stones piled up near the stairs by the door in the back of the cabin. He hid the aluminum box under them and disturbed the snow nearby so that it looked like he was going to the woodpile. He brought some wood into the hut just to cover his tracks.

Shandria slept through the night. Marvin was exhausted but still woke up several times to check on Shandria. The next morning Marvin once again nervously paced back and forth, playing with his light magic. Then he managed to push some air around the hut with air magic. But it was more to reduce his worry, and in response to the kicking of his baby magic, then to learn anything. He ate a piece of venison jerky for lunch. Shandria was sleeping soundly. Marvin walked outside to where they had pulled up the purple sweet potatoes, dug up two more, walked back to the hut, collected water from the stream, and cleaned the potatoes.

He put one of them into the pot, filled it with water, and started boiling it to complete his dinner.

Shandria woke up once more. She yelled at him. "Where is my necklace? My body needs my necklace!"

Marvin said. "I know it does. But it will kill you, and your need will go away. He went to hug her. She started banging on his chest with her fists. Marvin held her gently by her upper arms. She didn't try to get away.

Then suddenly she stopped hitting him and yelled. "Tell me where you put it!" She pushed him away and pulled out her sword.

Marvin looked at her sword and said, "If you promise as a princess of Atlantis not to hurt me, I will tell you."

"I promise," she said.

He stared at her sword. She sheathed it.

He said, "This time I did drop it in the river."

Shandria looked into his eyes and knew he was telling the truth. She ran out the back door and saw a path that led straight towards the river where he had filled the pot, and another, which headed diagonally downstream towards a spot clear of ice on the river. The stream curved at that point and the moving water kept the edge ice-free.

Marvin let her go. He couldn't stop her if he tried. He was glad that he had dropped it into the river so he could tell her he did convincingly.

Marvin finished cooking the potato and took it outside for Shandria to eat, but she refused, so he came back inside and ate it while he cooked the second potato.

He finished cooking the second potato, put it on a plate, and walked out the back door. It was starting to snow, and the wind was picking up. Marvin saw a packed down path by the river's edge where Shandria had been walking back and forth in the snow looking for her necklace. He walked over to her and handed her the potato.

She barely took her eyes off the river when she said, "My body isn't Hungry."

Marvin replied, "We both know your body still needs food, and I cooked this for you. You haven't eaten in two days. You can eat it here or come back with me to the hut and eat it."

Shandria grabbed the potato with her hand and started eating it. Soon it was gone. Marvin gave her a bottle of water that she drank. He began to head back inside.

After a few steps, Marvin stopped and turned back towards Shandria. He said, "It's about to storm. Come back with me to the hut and eat the rest of your meal.

Shandria said, "I need to find my necklace."

Marvin replied, "And you need to eat the rest of your meal."

Shandria was impossible to reason with, so Marvin walked back to the hut. An hour later, he came back outside with some jerky and some walnuts. He convinced her to eat, but she wouldn't come back into the hut.

It was storming outside, but Marvin found the potatoes again, happy that there were so many. He took several, cooked three, ate one, and then took one to Shandria.

He handed the potato to Shandria and insisted she eat it.

Then he said, "It's dark out and storming. You will never find it tonight. You need to come back with me to the hut to eat the rest of your dinner and get some sleep."

He turned around and started walking away.

Shandria yelled at him. "I need you to help me look."

He turned back around and said, "I know you need me and I need you, but neither of us should be out in this storm, so follow me to the hut." He turned around and stopped for a moment with his back towards Shandria to allow her time to decide.

Shandria looked once more longingly down the river and then headed back with Marvin towards the hut, her head hanging low.

That night Shandria ate several pieces of jerky and some nuts, as well as the potato Marvin had cooked. She said, "I'm sorry for hurting you, I know the necklace was trying to kill me, but I can control it now. My body needs my necklace."

Marvin replied, "You can't control it. When you say, your body needs your necklace, it's the necklace controlling you, and you are smart enough to know it."

Shandria said, "But I'm a princess of Atlantis, I need my necklace."

Marvin said, "You are a princess of Atlantis with or without that necklace. You can get a new one when we get to Atlantis. What you need to understand is you will never wear your cursed necklace again."

Marvin asked, "When did you get this necklace?"

"I told you I got it when I first started using magic."

He looked at her for a few seconds and asked, "When did you last take it off?"

Suddenly she confessed, "OK, it's my sister's necklace. My nanny gave it to me when my sister died to help me with my grief. It was our little secret."

Shandria's face changed as she realized the truth. She burst out, "Oh my god! Nanna put a spell on my sister's necklace and then gave it to me."

Marvin said, "This is the sister you said died from a bad weave."

Shandria's eyes became wide. She yelled, "She killed my sister too!"

Marvin said, "It's doubtful it was your nanny. More likely someone used your nanny to innocently swap necklaces."

Shandria's eyes opened wide again. She said, "We have a traitor in the palace."

Marvin asked, "Has anyone else died in the royal household recently?"

"Just before my sister, my great-grandfather became ill and died. Great grandma was found dead soon afterward. They said she died of grief."

Shandria's eyes grew wide again, and her mouth opened wide. She said, "Maybe they were poisoned! They were so young."

After Shandria had settled down, Marvin wondered about great-grandparents being young. He asked, "How old were they when they died?"

Shandria said, "They weren't even four hundred years old yet."

Marvin replied with surprise in his voice, "Four hundred is young? The life expectancy for humans is seventy to eighty years, and only a few live to a hundred."

Shandria replied. "Wow, Humans don't live very long. Most Atlantians live for eight or nine centuries. Some have lived as long as eleven, but that's rare."

Marvin thought for a few seconds, "How old is your father?"

"We just celebrated his One hundred and fiftieth birthday three years ago. It was a weeklong celebration, but with people coming and going and the special events, it lasted twice that long. All the single princes and princesses from the various islands attended. We laughed, sang, danced, ate, and drank spiced wine. We raced skiffs in the ocean and had games of skill with our bows and weapons. It was so much fun. My mother said the birthday was for my dad, but the rest of the celebration was for the princes and princesses to spend time together and get to know each other. We would spend the rest of our lives with one of them."

Shandria's mood picked up when she was talking, but then she became suddenly quiet. Marvin knew she was worried about her magic and suffering from withdrawal. Without her magic, she would no longer be a princess.

The storm outside raged on for the next three days, and so did Shandria's emotions. One minute she was thanking him for saving her life, the next she was angry at everything, then she was depressed. She sometimes cried. She unpacked and repacked her backpack several times. Several times, she spent time by the river in the snowstorm. Twice she accused Marvin of hiding the necklace. He allowed her to search through his pack and even took off all his clothes once to search them.

Finally, there was a break in the weather, but it wouldn't last for long. The snow had blown in from the west and blocked the front door. Marvin left through the back door and then used magic to blow away the snow at the front door.

Shandria took her bow and walked through the front door to go hunting. She said she needed time alone. Marvin agreed. After three days stuck in the same small hut together with her withdrawal caused irrational behavior, he needed some space also.

Marvin walked outside and along the ridge overlooking the stream. He found a small rise and listened to the wind. The wind may have blown from one direction, but it carried magic strings and information from all around. He focused his concentration down the road to the south, but he had no way of knowing how far he was observing. He could tell if something was farther than something else, but he had no way to calibrate his distance viewing. He swung his concentration northwards and found the lake they had crossed. It gave him an idea of the distance and range of his vision.

He then searched and found Shandria. He looked near her and saw a large predatory animal stalking her. Marvin knew Shandria's magic wasn't working. He started running.

Shandria was aware of the animal's presence. It was a solitary animal. But it was larger than the wolves. In the animal's mind, she was alone, hurt, and vulnerable. In other words, good prey. She faced it and readied her bow and her first arrow. One arrow would kill it, but she was sure one arrow wouldn't stop it right away.

The snow tiger crept up through waist deep snow. Its broad paws helped to spread its weight. It crouched down low, ready to spring. It saw Shandria looking at it and sprung, getting closer with each bound.

She let the first arrow fly, followed by a second, then a third, and then her last. She was fast, and all four arrows left the bow in less than two seconds. Shandria pulled out her sword, ready to move quickly to the side. The tiger took one more leap, took a step, stumbled, and fell dead a dozen yards from Shandria. She waited several minutes to be sure it was dead. Shandria looked into the sky and growled like a tiger. Then she said a few words of praise for its beauty and strength.

Shandria was cutting off its black-striped white-hide when Marvin arrived. Shandria said, "He attacked, so I had to kill him. The skin is beautiful and rare. It would be a dishonor to the tiger to leave it here to rot."

She once again cut out the heart and took a piece of the liver. She said, "The meat is too stringy to turn into jerky, but we will take some and boil it into a stew. The heart is tough and stringy, and the liver is too large for us to eat. We will show honor to the Tiger by boiling part of it in the stew."

Marvin asked, "How can I help?"

Shandria replied. "You can honor the tiger by carrying his hide to the hut. I will honor him by cooking the meal and preparing his fur."

After they got to the hut, Marvin went outside to dig up more potatoes. Shandria had found some onions and a bunch of yellow carrots. Shandria put the stew on the fire then spent the next hour outside scraping and cleaning the skin, as another storm started to blow. She took a break, ate, and then walked back outside. She taught Marvin a weave that she could no longer craft and had him help with preserving the skin. She worked on it the rest of the day until she was satisfied with the skin. She no longer had the magic to complete the process to turn it into a blanket. And the weaves were too complicated for Marvin's young magic.

The wood basket inside the hut was almost empty. Marvin refilled it with the wood from the pile outside the hut.

He walked back to the remains of the tiger, scaring away a pack of small scavengers. He broke off one of its teeth from its jaw by bashing it with a rock and prying with his knife. He cleaned it in the snow, and then returned to the hut.

After dinner, he gave it to Shandria and said, "You defeated this great animal without magic and without your necklace. It may be several weeks before your body heals. You've always had strong magic and worn your necklace. But your real strength is your heart. This is to help you remember."

He hugged and kissed Shandria on her forehead and saw a tear in her eye.

Marvin said, "I would turn it into a necklace, but I don't know how and I would just make a mess of it."

Shandria laughed. That evening Shandria made a pendant of the tooth with a thin strip of leather and then cuddled up in Marvin's sleeping bag. It was the first deep sleep she had since her necklace attacked her.

Marvin wanted to bring in some more wood. He quickly walked outside without putting on his coat or gloves and realized he was feeling strangely warm. He took off his shirt and stood outside for a while, watching his breath condense in the cold air. He could feel the cold, but his body wasn't cold. He walked around for several minutes before carrying his clothes back inside.

Shandria saw him. At first, she frowned, wondering what he was doing, then she realized what had happened. His magic was mature enough to protect his body from cold. She laughed and clapped her hands.

The next morning the second part of the storm was raging. Marvin walked outside again, this time wearing nothing. He cracked the thin layer of ice that was on the water by the shore of the river and stepped into it. The water was freezing, but even though he could feel its temperature, his magic kept it from pulling the warmth from his body. Marvin's body felt warm. He left the stream, laid down naked in the snow, moved his arms and legs back and forth, and made a snow angel. Then he walked back to the river and sat down in the hole, skinny-dipping, and washing in the ice-covered river.

Marvin had gotten the childishness out of his system. He laughed at his foolishness, walked back inside, dried off, and dressed. He felt foolish when he told Shandria, but it had been fun. And he enjoyed her laughter. Shandria knew it was a rite of passage for him and his magic.

Then she realized she liked the idea of cleaning up, so she walked outside naked to bath in the stream. She felt cold, but her magic once again had started to protect her body. She washed her body before she entered the hut. Later that day she had Marvin fill the largest pot with water. She heated it up until it was warm and hand washed her clothes in it.

Shandria had Marvin fill the pot with fresh water and taught Marvin how to handwash his clothes. They hung up their clothes, and she had Marvin blow them dry using magic before putting them back on.

Marvin had mastered light weaving. He proved it to Shandria by talking to the magic and creating lights of different colors. Shandria clapped, then started teaching him and having him practice different elementary weaves.

ATLANTIAN MAGIC

Shandria's had no magic for two days after the necklace attacked her. But then her magic slowly returned. She could now weave beginning magic. But intermediate weaving failed more than it worked. And she couldn't do any complicated weave or one that required a lot of magical energy. She talked about it to Marvin. They both were optimistic that it would return over time.

She finally thanked Marvin for getting rid of the necklace and said she couldn't believe how much it had controlled her after it had attacked. She pulled out the tiger tooth necklace and said, "You are right. The other necklace showed my status as a princess, but this tooth showed my actions as a princess. And I did it all with no magic or necklace." She kissed Marvin and thanked him once again.

Marvin said, "After I took the necklace off of you. I looked inside of you, and there were no magical threads. I didn't know what to do. I listened to the magic. I thought of forcing it into you, but I was afraid I could hurt you. I pleaded with the magic, which was reluctant to re-enter your body. Then the threads slowly returned to you while you were unconscious. There are areas inside you that are dark, scarred by the dark spell.

"I have been watching over you, afraid the dark spell will return, and most of those areas are still dark places where magic won't flow. I should have told you sooner, but I was worried that I was violating a taboo by looking into you. I'm sorry, but I was so worried."

Shandria said, "Looking at a stranger for no reason is frowned upon by adults, but children can't help but do it. It's more like how staring at someone can be awkward. I see those dark areas also. Maybe they will heal. But we are not strangers. You are my protector, and it is expected that you will be verifying my health and I yours."

Shandria held out her two hands and asked Marvin to select one. He did. She opened her hand and gave him a small stick. He gave her a questioning look. She laughed and said, "I guess you have never played sticks and stones. I'll have to teach you."

There was a board already laid out on the table which Marvin thought was a decoration. It was similar to checkers on a smaller board, but pieces moved forward and captured diagonally, much like a pawn in chess. But if they were passed an opponent's piece, then they could also move and capture diagonally backward.

Shandria won the first few games, but Marvin, having played chess and checkers, soon caught on. He didn't beat her in the last match, but he didn't lose as bad. It was an entertaining diversion. Shandria taught Marvin a few new weaves to work on.

The snowstorm broke, and the sky cleared the next day. They planned to leave the next morning, so Shandria went hunting, and Marvin refilled the woodpile inside the hut. Then he walked outside again and retrieved the box with Shandria's necklace in it. He hid it in the bottom of his pack, put away all the iron tools, and cleaned up the hut.

Shandria returned with what looked like a large rodent. She called it a river digger. They didn't have to eat the heart or the liver. The meat wasn't bad. It was a good meal for the day.

The tiger's fur was too big to put into a pack or to carry. Marvin said, "I don't think we need this," and left his sleeping bag in the corner of the hut. Shandria rolled up the pelt and put it into the container that had held Marvin's sleeping bag. It stuck part way out, but at least Marvin could strap it to his pack.

Marvin was glad to see Shandria cheer up, now that they were once again heading towards their objective.

A couple of times along the way they stopped and dug up plants near the road. Shandria dug up some wild onions, more potatoes, an herb that looked like garlic, and some ginger root. She said, "You should never dig up all the tubers, and you should replace the soil. If you leave some, they will regrow and replace the ones you took."

At a couple of locations, she planted a few of the tubers she had dug up. It thanked the plants and provided more for the next traveler or animal.

The road was smooth and flat. They hiked farther than on any other day but didn't hike all the way to the next way station. They camped in a grove of trees near the trail where they could observe the road, and the trees hid them. That night Marvin slept in his poncho, and Shandria slept with her arm around Marvin.

They saw no one on the road, and there were no marks in the snow indicating anyone had traveled on it recently. It took two more days to get to the next traveler's station. It was larger than the first one and showed recent use.

The map at the traveler's station showed they were close to Iron Mountain. It showed two roads heading out of Iron Mountain. One road headed east and had a sign to Silver Mountain. The other headed south towards Crystal Mountain. Shandria was excited. "That's it!" she said, "The portal arch is at Crystal Mountain."

Three days later, they reached the outskirts of Iron Mountain.

Chapter 15

They walked south on the road, which followed the river most of the way. The river then turned southwest and flowed under a bridge. On the far side of the bridge was a large stone gateway with a massive portcullis. On either side of the gate were towers designed for archers. There were no walls on either side of the towers.

As they approached the gatehouse, a man holding a crossbow stood up, pointed the weapon at them and yelled, "Who goes there?"

Shandria replied in Dwarvish, "Two weary travelers on our way to Crystal Mountain. Can we get by?"

The man asked, "What's your business in Iron Mountain?"

She replied, "We have no business at Iron Mountain. We are heading to Crystal Mountain."

"You have to pay the gate tax for me to raise the portcullis."

"How much is the tax?"

"Two copper croners."

Shandria replied, "We don't have any copper or any croners for that matter."

They argued back and forth. Even if they had a sack of gold, the guard wouldn't take it. The regulations said two copper croners were required to raise the gate; by regulation, that was all he could take.

Marvin yelled out, "Is the tax for going through the gate?"

The guard shouted back. "Northern Gate Regulation number 102.47 says. Two copper croners shall be received to raise the portcullis."

"Is there a tax for going around?"

The guard was silent.

Marvin yelled back, "Thank you."

Marvin walked over to the river and froze the top solid. Shandria laughed as the two of them walked across the river to the other side and then walked around the tower.

The guard picked up a loud horn and blew it two times, waited a few seconds, then blew it twice again. He kept blowing the horn. It was a loud, high-pitched, obnoxious sound.

A hurried looking Dwarf wearing an iron breastplate and carrying a crossbow walked out the door of a stone building, which stood near the tower and next to the road. He turned towards the gate and yelled up at the other man, "Private, stop that noise." He looked out through the portcullis, oblivious to Marvin and Shandria standing thirty feet away from him.

The man blew the horn twice more and yelled, "Look to your side corporal."

The corporal shouted once more, "Private, stop blowing that damn horn." He turned around. He looked shocked as he noticed Marvin and Shandria. He raised his crossbow up and pointed it at Marvin, then at Shandria. He wasn't sure what to do and kept pointing it back and forth between the two of them.

The private kept blowing the horn.

The corporal ordered Marvin and Shandria, "Wait right here." A large metal key ring, with one large metal key, was hanging from a peg on the wall. There was a door on the tower next to the peg. The corporal walked over, propped his crossbow up against the wall, and grabbed the key ring. He unlocked the door, put the key ring back on the peg, opened the door, and started to walk up a set of stairs. After a couple seconds, he ran back down and grabbed his crossbow. He entered in through the door again and headed back up the stairs. The private kept blowing the horn.

They heard the corporal yell, "I told you to stop blowing the horn. Why did you keep blowing it?"

The private replied, "Regulation 1132.47a says that if anyone refuses to pay the tax. I am to blow the horn."

The corporal responded, "And when does regulation 307. 02 say you are to stop blowing the horn."

The private answered, "Regulation 307.02a says when the situation is resolved. Regulation 307.02b says when relieved of duty. Regulation 307.02c says when the military response unit arrives. Regulation 307.02d says on orders from an officer or the senior enlisted person. Regulation 307.02e says…"

The corporal yelled, "That's enough private! It is winter. I am the military response unit. I am also the senior enlisted person, and I said to stop. Next time you disobey an order, I will write you up on my report. Do you understand?"

The private replied, "Yes, corporal."

The corporal said, "Now get back to your watch."

The corporal came back downstairs. He put down his crossbow, closed and locked the door, and rehung the key on the peg. He grabbed his crossbow, walked back to where he was standing before he pointed the weapon at Marvin, and said, "Why didn't you pay the gate tax?"

Shandria replied, "Because we didn't go through the gate. We walked around the tower."

The corporal lowered his weapon, removed the bolt, and released the tension on the bowstring. He said, "That idiot. I'm sorry for all this fuss. They keep sending me stupider and stupider recruits. Please join me out of the cold and the wind. And let me welcome you properly."

He opened the door of the barracks and invited them inside. Shandria and Marvin followed him in. She exchanged a smile with Marvin that showed she was trying not to laugh.

The Dwarves constructed the barracks out of stone. The roof of the barracks was tall enough to play basketball in, but the furniture was smaller than normal. He invited them to sit at the table. He excused himself and left the room.

He returned with a wooden barrel that looked too big for him to carry. He grabbed three large pewter mugs and filled them from a tap on the barrel. He gave them their mugs, sat down at the table, and raised his. He said, "To my weary travelers, may you have the blessings of the journey."

Shandria raised her glass, "And to our gracious host. May the comfort you give the weary be known by all."

Marvin was surprised at how large the mugs were and how potent the brew was. He had never drunk mead before. He was sure this was it. It tasted of honey and grapes.

Shandria leaned towards him and said in English, "Drink slowly."

The corporal said, "I apologize for pointing my weapon at you earlier. I thought you had skipped paying the tax. It's required by regulation 102.47."

Shandria knew he was curious about them but asking a weary traveler their business is improper in Dwarven culture. She said, "It's understandable, and I take no offense. I commend you for following your duty. I am Shandria, Princess of Atlantis, and this is Sir Marvin. He is my traveling companion and protector."

The eyes of the Dwarf grew wide, and he excitedly yelled, "A Princess of Atlantis! By regulation 215.3 I need to contact the duty officer."

He ran out of the building before anyone could say anything. They heard the sound of a noisy steam-powered motor starting up. Then a long blast of an air horn followed by two short blasts filled their ears. There was a five-second pause, and then the noise repeated. After several sets, the signal stopped. Then the sound of the engine stopped. The corporal returned a few seconds later.

"I am sorry I had to leave you. But regulation 1721.3 allows only the senior person to operate the engine unless he assigns the duty to a junior person. I would have assigned it to the private, but regulation 1721.3d requires the person to be trained and qualified to operate the engine, and the private isn't.

"The Lieutenant should be here soon. Until then you are my honored guest."

The corporal was excited to entertain a princess. She knew he had many questions, but custom didn't allow him to ask about their business. So, he started talking about his wife and their new child. They hadn't been married for very long, only about eighty-five years. Custom dictated that they were married at least a hundred years before having a child, but his wife's father was turning three thousand years old and they wanted to present him with a grandchild.

Shandria told him she was on a discovery journey, and it had taken her here. She was heading towards the arch at Crystal Mountain.

After several minutes, a horn sounded from outside the hut.

In walked another Dwarf wearing a similar uniform but with colorful shoulder-pieces, which Marvin figured must signify his rank. He yelled, "Corporal, why did you call me away from my duties? Who are these travelers?"

Shandria stood up and said. "I am Princess Shandria, from Atlantis, daughter of King Vandian, granddaughter of King Baracian. I am a weary traveler to Crystal Mountain, and the corporal has graciously given me and my traveling companion a moment of comfort."

Thanks to the language weave Marvin had received from Shandria when they first met, he could understand what the guards were saying, even though they had been speaking in Dwarvish. For each word of Dwarvish spoken, the magic taught him several more. He now knew Dwarvish well enough to speak a few short sentences. Soon he would know enough for a regular conversation. Inside a week, he would be able to talk like a native speaker.

The Lieutenant grew flustered. He said, "This is most unusual. We need to follow regulations 783 through 793.7, regulations 814.1, 814.2, and 814.7. We need to inform the king. He may want us to follow formal visit regulations 623, through 634.9. We aren't even in our midwinter ceremonial uniforms. This is most unusual."

Shandria said, "You don't have to go through any bother for us. This is an unofficial visit. We are on a journey of personal discovery, and a mission of compassion. But I have heard of the wisdom of the Dwarven King and would be honored to meet him."

Per regulation 225.1, the Lieutenant sent out a messenger on horseback, who carried a message marked URGENT back to the captain at company headquarters. The captain, per regulation 225.2, sent a messenger to the major, who per regulation 225.3, sent a messenger to the Colonel at Battalion Headquarters, who per regulation 225.4 sent a messenger to the general.

The major ordered, per regulation 286.7, his private carriage sent from company headquarters to accommodate the delegation from Atlantis. Per regulation 286.7b, he accompanied the carriage.

About an hour later, Marvin and Shandria heard the sound of a steam motor approach the building. A few minutes later, the door opened, and in stepped the major wearing his dress uniform.

He took a scroll from an old ornate leather case, and said, "Per regulation 934.1," then he read, "In the name of King Feldspar the third." He paused, put the scroll down on the table, took out a quill pen and some ink, made a modification to the manuscript, and said, "Sorry, it's an old scroll." He started over, "In the name of King Feldspar the fourth." He paused and once again marked up the scroll and started reading again. "Son of King Feldspar the third of the lineage of Feldspar the Great, Supreme Protector of all Dwarves,

ATLANTIAN MAGIC

Protector of the Eastern Lands, Protector of the Western Lands, Protector of the Southern Lands, and Protector of the Northern Lands. Recipient of the order of the geode, the order of the golden nugget, the order of the iron pickax, the order of the Vermillion circle, the order of the green delta, and order of the red square." He stopped again, wrote on the scroll, and continued, "And the order of the Iron Crossbow. I do hereby welcome the Atlantian delegation to our beloved land. I greet you with the handshake of eternal friendship."

The major rolled up and put the scroll back in its case, then walked closer to Shandria and stood almost at attention with his arm held out to shake her hand. Shandria stood up. She smiled, shook his hand, and thanked the Major in the name of Atlantis for his steadfast and loyal friendship of King Feldspar, and reaffirmed the friendship of Atlantis."

The major escorted Shandria and Marvin outside to his carriage. The front part of the carriage looked like a small old-fashioned steam locomotive. It had a large cylinder-shaped container, which Marvin thought might be carrying coal. He found out later that it contained water. The Dwarves heated the engine with magic. The carriage itself was a metal box with windows on the sides and the back. It reminded him of an old hippy van from the sixties, except it was metal colored. The smell of steam was in the air.

Two dozen soldiers riding short but stout looking horses accompanied the carriage. Marvin and Shandria entered the coach. The Major sat across from them and talked to them as if they were best friends who hadn't seen each other in a while. Shandria joined him in a conversation about their journey. After a while, Marvin felt comfortable enough to talk. Shandria told him earlier not to mention that he grew up on Earth. They need to settle his legal status first.

The Major had a battleax also, but it was more ornate, maybe it was his rank, or maybe it was ceremonial. He asked the Major about it. The Major said, "It's a functional battleax, but it has been decorated to be more ceremonial."

Shandria could see that the major was starting to wonder about Marvin. Marvin was obviously not dressed like an Atlantian. Shandria stepped in and said, "I've read the exploits of Feldspar the Great as a child, but it was translated into Atlantian, and I've always wanted to hear it in Dwarvish."

The major was all excited and asked which story she wanted to hear. Shandria said, "How can one choose a favorite? They are all wonderful, and I'm sure they lost something in the translation to Atlantian. Please tell me your favorite."

Just then, they heard the sound of the horn signaling they were nearing their destination.

The major looked sad and said, "We are almost at headquarters, I would hate to interrupt the story just as it started."

Shandria looked sad, "I understand. I know you are a busy man."

69

He excitedly replied, "Never too busy to tell a guest a saga of Feldspar the Great. We will soon arrive. I know it's hard to wait, but the anticipation will make the story more exciting."

Shandria smiled.

The carriage stopped. The major escorted Shandria and Marvin between two lines of Dwarven soldiers standing at attention and holding their ceremonial axes.

They entered a large hall at the military compound. The major escorted them to guest chairs at a table, which was closer to their size, and served them more mead.

Then the major started to tell the story of "Feldspar the Great and the Thousand Ogres." Soon soldiers filled the hall. They were all drinking from large metal mugs. It was an epic ballad, written in Dwarven prose, that all the Dwarves knew. There were several stanzas, which were Dwarvish songs, and everyone sang together.

Whenever Feldspar the Great raised his battle-ax and clashed with the ogres, people clanked their half-filled mugs with the person next to them. Soon, Shandria and Marvin knew the key phrase and started clanking their drinks together. Feldspar the Great had his Axmen of Might join him often in battle. They had their key phrase and banged the mugs twice on the table when the storyteller named the Axmen of Might. Soon Shandria and Marvin were joining in. The ballad took about half an hour to tell. There was a break and a line quickly formed at the bathroom.

It took Marvin a minute to figure out the squat toilets. He wondered how they handled the sanitation of the waste. Afterward, a line formed at the mead barrels, where being a guest of honor they insisted he go to the front.

In the Dwarvish army, men and women were at different posts and had different jobs. Only men had gate guard duty. But an occasional wife or child would visit. There was an empty guest bathroom for visiting women, so Shandria had privacy.

But no Dwarf could resist the "Sagas of Feldspar the Great." Soon a second Dwarf was telling a different tale.

It was the story of the powerful magic that Feldspar the Great had woven with the other races to transport the great races to their new homes. Marvin realized the tales of Feldspar the Great were from Earth. He guessed that the ogres were humans left on Earth.

Several thousand years ago, the magical races combined their power and moved their cities and population to their own realms.

The abuse of magic by a race called the Darfarin was depleting the Earth's magic. The great races used the last of Earth's natural magic to create the great unity weave and to leave the Earth for their own realms. They had expected the Earth to recover after they left since magic is alive. But they realized they had left Earth dead to magic, and it always would be.

ATLANTIAN MAGIC

"Tales of Feldspar the Great" continued for several hours until the Colonel arrived. He waited until the telling of the traditional ballad was complete. Marvin was amazed at how much the Dwarves could drink. They were guzzling, and he was sipping, yet he was fighting not to get so drunk he was socially undesirable.

The colonel gave a long welcome speech to Princess Shandria, per regulation 1722.03 of course, and per regulation 1827.23, he arranged accommodations for her and her traveling companion. Per regulation 1837.1, the colonel provided his private carriage to transport them to Crystal Mountain.

Following regulation 115.5, he had already sent ahead a messenger to the king.

And of course, the Colonel filled their mugs again from his personal barrel of mead. The Dwarves treated them to another saga of Feldspar the Great. Sometimes they stomped their feet, banged on the table, or waved arms. During a storm "In the Tale of Feldspar the Great on his ocean quest to Atlantis," they had to hold their mug in their right hand, put their left hand on the shoulder of the person next to them, then rock back and forth, taking drinks at the appropriate time. Then they did the same thing with the mug in the other hand on his journey back.

Marvin and Shandria had a lot of fun, but it was too much of a good thing.

The general and his aide escorted them to accommodations at a Bed and Breakfast on the outskirts of town for the night. Marvin was drunker than he had been since his college days, and he paid the price for all the drinking the next morning.

Chapter 16

There was a knock on their door half an hour before sunrise. Breakfast was cooking downstairs, and the inn owner would serve it in ten minutes. Their carriage would be waiting for them at sunrise.

Breakfast was delicious after their time on the road. The hostess served several exotic fruits, finger cakes, and some spiced diced potatoes. They both picked at their meal at first, but the meal calmed their stomachs, and they realized how hungry they were. Shandria said something to the hostess to keep her from serving them some of her homebrew breakfast mead.

The hostess gave them a basket of food for their lunch, which included a sealed glass bottle of her breakfast mead, which she was obviously proud of and wanted them to try.

The carriage, being the colonel's, was a little bigger, and a little nicer than the major's carriage. There was no one else traveling with them, so they spread out. The natural motion of the carriage helped rock them to sleep.

Every couple of hours the carriage would stop and let them step out and take a break. At midday, they had a formal break for lunch. The back of the carriage held provisions for the trip. The soldiers invited them to eat with them, so they joined them and shared the fruit from their bed and breakfast. They ate some of the hard-bread travel rations which the Dwarves washed down with their ration of mead. Shandria and Marvin stuck to water.

Dinnertime was more of the same.

The Dwarves set up tents where they slept for the night. Shandria and Marvin had a tent to themselves, set up by the Dwarven soldiers. It was larger than, but not as comfortable as, the small tent they had stayed in by themselves. Shandria had Marvin enchant the tent with a comfort weave. His magic was developing so fast that she taught him how to make it permanent. It took him several tries and half an hour to weave the magic into the tent.

The next day they were up with the sun again. Midway through the day, they arrived at small stone and metal hut which contained a large double-handle pump. A pipe rose up overhead. Two soldiers moved the handles up and down, pumping the water into the pipe. A third soldier made sure the water flowed down out of the pipe into the carriage's water holding tank. The soldiers filled their canteens.

ATLANTIAN MAGIC

Shandria and Marvin filled their water bottles also. Marvin wove the purification weave, which removed all impurities from the water. He realized that in the last couple of weeks, Shandria had taught him dozens of weaves. He discovered that many of the weaves were similar patterns; just changing a thread changed what you told the magic. The vibrations of the threads contained the magical instructions. The threads remembered and executed your instructions.

That night Shandria and Marvin wove comfort magic on the soldier's tents. It was cold outside, but the Dwarves slept snuggly. After a third day, they arrive at a traveler's way station. Shandria was tired of hard tack. She said she was going hunting, and half an hour later she came back with a deer. It took her only a few minutes to clean and prep the deer for cooking. Shandria and Marvin sliced up the deer into strips and hung them on wooden skewers to cook. The Lieutenant of the platoon asked her if she had prepared the meal in accordance with regulations: 147.1, 217.6 and 418.7.

Shandria replied, "All military operations between Dwarves and Atlantians are combined operations. Since Atlantians cooked and prepared the meal, we followed Atlantian regulations."

"What Atlantian regulation?"

Marvin had trouble keeping a straight face when Shandria replied in Atlantian, "You can either eat this or leave it to the wolves. I'm trying to be nice, and I don't care."

Then she said in Dwarvish, "That's what we call it in Atlantian."

The Lieutenant didn't understand a word and wasn't sure what to say, so he allowed it as not to cause a diplomatic incident. When the lieutenant left, Marvin broke out laughing.

The soldiers were obviously happy to be eating fresh venison for dinner and appreciative of the comfort weave on their tent.

The Lieutenant found out about the magic they had woven on the tents and was upset. They had violated several regulations. Weaving magic on Army equipment was against regulation 327.16. The magic effectively altered army equipment from its approved condition against regulation 427.2. He stated several more. Shandria thought, "He can freeze in his tent all night if he wants to."

She said, "We are under a permanent treaty of friendship that is thousands of years old. That treaty authorizes Atlantians and Dwarves to assist each other in areas of military operation, including troop movement and comfort. I don't answer to you. I answer to the royal family of Atlantis and King Feldspar. Wait. I am a member of the royal family of Atlantis. Here, I answer to myself. Under terms of our treaty, I have offered Atlantian assistance to you and your troops, including a fresh hot meal and a comfort weave for the shelter.

"Now if you disagree with the treaty of friendship, or my authority as a princess of Atlantis, then my companion and I will walk to Crystal Mountain. We will enjoy ourselves, hunting and fishing along the way, and when we get there a week from now, I will remember to mention your name to King Feldspar when I file my official protest. Of course, being Atlantian royalty, I could just take command of this joint operation and relieve you of command. But I have no desire to destroy your career.

"But if you don't want to be warm tonight, I will remove the comfort weave that kept you warm last night from your tent."

It would have taken two seconds. But Shandria was angry that she caused a magical white aura to surround her, then wove a pyrotechnic display of light and sound in the direction of his tent. There was a tree in the area she caused to catch on fire and burst apart. Shandria saw the lieutenant's eyes widen, so she stopped her tirade, and released the magic from his tent.

Dwarven magic was the magic of earth, metal, and fire. It was powerful, but slow magic. It was the magic of the forge, coaxed into reluctant metals by hammer, heat, and muscle. It was the magic of the builder, slowly shaped into stone during construction. It was slow, patient, dedicated magic, applied over hours or sometimes days.

Shandria's glow of light and her bursting the trees on fire were quick and easy magic, rarely seen by Dwarves. The magic she wove was beginning magic by Atlantian standards, it was showy magic, but the Lieutenant didn't know that. And she was glad. Her magic seemed to have stabilized, but it wasn't up to Atlantian normal levels, and it definitely wasn't powerful enough for an Atlantian princess.

The Lieutenant backed away. The men greeted her with a new sense of awe. Shandria was aware of Dwarven customs. She walked over to where the soldiers were camping and watching her. She turned to them and said, "That made me thirsty. Does anyone have a spare mug?" She knew it signified all is well and her display was over.

It was quiet for a second then one of the men came over with a mug filled with mead. She made a scene about taking a big drink, then sat down with the soldiers and asked, "Does anyone have a good story to share?"

One of the soldiers asked her if she could share a story with them.

Shandria thought for a second and said, "I will tell you a story of the great races."

She began, "The great races once lived in the same realm called Earth. Some of us can wield all types of magic at a beginning level, but each race has its specialty. We each excel in one or more branches of magic. Each race has advanced magic that no other race can use.

"Dwarves know the magic of solids like earth and metal. You are masters of forge and fire. And some are at a grandmaster level."

The Dwarves let out a cheer and mugs were clanked together.

"Atlantians know the magic of the fluids, air, water, and sky. A dedicated individual can reach a grandmaster level. Our nature is fluid so we can learn many types of magic to the intermediate level, and some to the master level.

"Alfarin are grandmasters of flexible magic, wood, nature, healing, and movement. Their flexibility means they can often work other magic.

"Olympians and Asgardians are giants, masters of strength and vigor, but each adult has a mastery of another type of magic, usually at a grandmaster level, and a few get to a level past grandmaster.

"The Anastasi are masters of sky and spirit, they can see through the veil and get wisdom from other times and other realms."

There are many races, but these races enchanted the arch crystals and split the realms.

"For millennium we lived on Elder Earth in peace, maybe not in complete harmony, but we respected each other, we traded with each other, we learned from each other, and some of us, like Dwarves and Atlantians, forged eternal bonds of friendship."

The Dwarves let out another cheer. Cups were raised and clanked together to acknowledge the bonds of friendship.

"There was a time of crisis, a time when magic itself was in peril, and we banded together. Dwarves and Atlantians working together as one, enchanted many great weapons, swords, Battle-axes, and a few ancient weapons."

Shandria pulled out the sword from her sheath and laid it on the table. "This is my ancient sword, created by friends in the forges of Elder Earth. Grandmasters of Dwarven and Atlantian magic enchanted it. It's one of the ancient swords of Atlantis. It was enchanted at the same forges and fought alongside the Ax of Feldspar the Great."

The Dwarves let out another cheer. Cups were raised and clanked together to acknowledge Feldspar the Great.

Shandria continued, "It was a troubled time, and our records are incomplete, but I believe Feldspar the Great helped forge this sword."

There was silence and awe as the Dwarves looked at the sword, which had started to glow a light blue color.

"When my body was young, soon after my magic befriended me, I convinced my older brother to take me to the magical armory of Atlantis. This sword called to me, and I called to her. My father, the king, at first was furious at my brother for taking me to the armory. I was too young. The queen was angry also. But then they realized the sword had chosen me, and even at my age we had bonded, and they understood."

"I was barely strong enough to pick up my sword. But I slept with her that night, much to the chagrin of my nanny. This sword has been my constant friend, my protector, and my teacher since my youth. No one has wielded her but me for centuries. But she is a friend to Atlantians and Dwarves. And she wishes to speak to each of you."

She held the sword out to the soldiers. They were both fascinated and scared. Then, one Dwarf stepped forward. He looked at the sword, reached towards, and took it from her hands. He held it for a few seconds then with a smile he handed it to a second soldier. The second soldier took it. After a few seconds, he passed it to a third. Each Dwarf held her sword. There were smiles on every face, and on a couple of faces, tears ran down their beards. The Lieutenant joined them when he heard his loud, boisterous Dwarves grow quiet.

The last soldier handed it to the lieutenant, who hesitantly took it. He held onto it for a few seconds. Then with a smile on his face and a tear in his eye, he handed it back to Shandria and said, "Thank you." He turned to walk away. Then he turned around, knelt down on one knee, bowed his head, and said to Shandria, "I'm sorry, princess. I didn't understand." He stood up and offered his hand.

Shandria would have none of that. She hugged him instead. She turned her head to the side and said, "Get mead for the lieutenant."

Shandria held her mug high. All the Dwarves lifted theirs. She said, "To the wisdom of the Dwarven and Atlantian kings of old."

The Dwarves clinked their mugs and drank deeply. Shandria did too.

Soon Shandria excused herself and headed to the tent to sleep. She asked Marvin to craft the comfort weave back on the lieutenant's tent. The magic and smell in the air told her it would be cold and windy that evening.

Marvin had watched Shandria pass her sword. He joined her when she walked back to their tent for the night. "So, what did the sword tell the soldiers?"

Shandria replied, "I don't know. The sword wanted to speak to the Dwarves. What it said was unique to each of them. It took decades to enchant all the ancient swords. During that time, the sword is in constant contact with its makers. It learns the wisdom of its makers and develops its unique personality. And it learns over time. Today it told each Dwarf something unique. Most likely it was personal and private."

"Is that how the sword talks to you?"

"On rare occasions, but usually she is teaching me the lessons of the sword, lessons from the women who have wielded her. She sat in the weapons vaults of Atlantis for many generations and then chose me. Even with my magic diminished, she is still my friend."

Chapter 17

The next day the soldiers were different. A few had become introspective, but most seemed happier, and they all accepted Shandria as a member of their family. Their friendship was carrying over to Marvin. If anyone was having trouble adapting, it was he. A few weeks ago, he was a human trying to figure out what to do with his remaining few good weeks before he died of cancer. Now he was using Atlantian magic and traveling towards a place that could cure him. And Shandria said he was Atlantian. But how could he be an Atlantian? His mother and father were human. He would have to have been adopted, but he wasn't, or was he?

That evening Marvin told Shandria he needed to think, to take a walk. Shandria knew he was Atlantian. He was fluid. He was seeking his level, and he needed to flow to find it. Shandria insisted he put on his pack, so he did, and started walking.

His parents always told Marvin he was of mixed European descent. He enjoyed that. He took a couple of years of German in high school and a couple of years of Spanish in college. He had fun at October Fest, Saint Patrick's Day, and Cinco de Mayo celebrations, but he had never been to Europe. What did he know about Europe? It was all play-acting to him. On the designated day, he met friends at a bar. He drank German beer, sang a few Irish songs, enjoyed some tequila, then he was back to being his self.

He knew far more about European culture than he did about being an Atlantian. Most evenings he would read a news report from Europe on the web. But what he knew about Atlantis was from the dreams of ancient philosophers warped by modern fantasy writers.

He had spent a month traveling and sleeping next to an Atlantian Princess, but he had never seen her interact with other Atlantians. After a few days with Dwarves, he now knew more about Dwarven culture than he did about Atlantian culture. He had never been to Atlantis. What did he know about being Atlantian?

It was a fascinating adventure, and he enjoyed his time with Shandria, but he was missing his home, good old suburb USA. Even with his family dead, it was still home. This was an exciting camping trip, but it had gone on too long. Tomorrow they would get to Crystal Mountain, and everyone was excited but him. He needed to do what he had always done when he was in turmoil. He took a hike.

It was well below freezing outside, and his enchanted poncho kept him warm. He stopped and took it off. He was glad he had brought his pack. It was a place to carry his poncho. He saw the last bag of trail mix in his pack. He opened it. It from home.

He turned off the comfort weave on his clothing. The crisp coldness of the air felt good.

It was a clear moonless night. All he saw was stars above, and the outline of a small ridge between mountains to the west. He munched on the trail mix as he hiked. Part of him wanted to devour it; part of him wanted to eat it slowly so it would last longer. He decided to eat it slowly. He wanted to enjoy the taste of home.

He arrived at the base of the ridge that was shading part of the sky. He started hiking up the side. It was steep, and the dim light made the climb more difficult. His magic kept trying to help him, to show him the terrain and to keep him warm, but he rejected it, holding it at bay, much like a person could choose to use one hand or to close one eye.

"I need to do this the Earth way," thought Marvin. "I need to conquer this as a man from Earth." He continued climbing the mountain, fighting against the slope, fighting against his heavy breathing and the beating of his heart. He fought against the lack of light, and against the magic yearning to help him. The climb was longer than he thought it would be. The length just caused him to harden his determination to get to the top. He continued, wishing the journey was over, refusing to think of himself as anything but an Earthman.

Who was he? He was dying slower, but he was still dying. Was this quest worth giving up his last few months as an Earthman to seek a cure he might not find in time? He needed to find out who he really was. He tried increasing his pace, but he realized the sickness inside him had stolen that last few percent, the few percent he had always drawn on when he needed to go the extra lap or to put on a burst of speed. He plodded along driven by his need to know.

It was close to midnight when he reached the top of the ridge, exhausted, tired, and breathing hard. The muscles of his legs and lower back were burning. His breath condensed as he exhaled into a fog that was almost invisible in the dim light, and his body was starting to shiver.

He saw a rock that was flat. He sat on it, the coldness of the stone crept through his pants, but he didn't care. He had done it; he had conquered the mountain without magic, like a man.

Then he started to cry. Why the hell was he on this crazy adventure? Rather than extend his life, this adventure had almost killed him. He almost froze to death, wolves attacked him, and he was entirely dependent on a woman who had gone insane and attacked him with magic and pulled a sword on him.

ATLANTIAN MAGIC

But none of the danger was Shandria's plan, and she had warned him it would be dangerous. His illness had caused him to choose this path. What else could he do? Was he an Atlantian? No human could perform real magic.

He had gotten part of the emotions out of his system and realized it was stupid to freeze on this rock. He stopped fighting against his magic. He let his magic warm him up while he looked out upon the ground.

He saw more through his magic in the dark than he ever had in full daylight without it. He didn't just see shapes and colors. Now, his non-magic vision was like watching low definition, static-filled, black and white TV. With magic, he saw not just the surface, but he saw the magic of the object. It wasn't only 3D vision; he saw the object and its recent history. It was like more like having 4-D x-ray vision.

He looked up at the stars. He saw an interlacing of magical lines between the stars that he had never seen on Earth. He and his father had gone camping and had slept out under the stars. His father had taught him Orion's belt and the hourglass shape of Orion. It was the first constellation his dad had taught him. He looked at the three stars of Orion's belt. The hourglass shape of the constellation was somehow different. He found the dog-star Sirius, the brightest star in the sky. It was out of place but not by much.

He wanted to see the familiar night sky of home. He needed to see it once more. Then something changed in his vision. His focus narrowed. He felt the magic inside him respond to his need. Then he saw the constellation as he remembered it, the stars of Earth.

If he could see the constellation of Earth, then he should be able to see the Earth. He changed his intent to see Earth, to be on Earth. Suddenly in front of him, he saw a spiral of magic spinning. There was a flash of light, and a glowing circle appeared. He looked through it and saw the desert mountain area where he had met Shandria, her brother, and his party. His magic had opened a portal.

The magic for this portal was beyond his knowledge level, a gift from the magic itself. He could feel the drain, the massive flow of magical energy. It was at the top of his power level.

He approached the portal. He felt and smelled the warm, dry air of Phoenix. If he stepped through, he would be on Earth. But he would die in a few months. He felt so out of place that it was almost worth it.

Then he thought of Shandria. She would never be able to weave magic at this level of power in her condition. She would never be able to weave a portal, and her magic would never get healed. He had given her his promise.

Marvin had asked the universe who he was. He still didn't know. But he knew who he wasn't. He wasn't a person that would die without a fight. He wasn't a person who would break his word. He wasn't a person who would abandon a friend who needed him, someone he could allow himself to love if her society allowed it. He released the portal and watched it collapse.

He closed his eyes and rested them for a minute. Then he looked up at his favorite constellation, bent as it was, and said, "Thanks, Dad."

He had found his answer. At least he had found part of it. He started the long walk back to the camp. He was glad it was downhill.

Shandria had lain down to sleep. She understood Marvin's need to get away. It was typical Atlantian behavior. He was water and needed to flow. They had been stuck together for several weeks. It was why she had gone hunting without him. When she was younger, she had often jumped into her shallod to flow away. It was a small boat usually paddled and similar to a kayak, but it had a parachute sail that she could blow with her magic.

It was freeing to weave the magic of the wind and the waves to move the shallod where she wanted. Other times she had hiked into the center of the island up to the top of a mountain and played with the magic of wind and air. Once she had dared herself and jumped off a cliff, weaving the magic of the wind to hold her up and to slow her descent. It worked until the last ten feet where there was too little air below her to hold her up. The landing hurt, but for a minute, she was flying.

She had fallen asleep. But she grew concerned when she woke up near midnight and Marvin wasn't there. She searched with her magic, saw his trail, and followed it, finding him miles away on top a ridge. Then she felt a portal open. It had opened to Marvin's home. It was his portal, it had his magic signature, yet he didn't know how to weave portal magic. The magic was too advanced for him. It must have been his great desire to go home that had helped him open the portal.

Few people could weave the advanced magic needed to open a portal between worlds without a portal arch, and most of them were either Princes and Princesses of Atlantis or high in the military or government. It was Atlantian magic, master level Atlantian magic. And he had done it without a weave. She knew from his magic and physiology that Marvin was an Atlantian, but now she was wondering, who was Marvin to have such strong magic?

Then after several seconds, she saw the portal close. She could no longer see Marvin. She had trusted him. She had confided in him. Just when she realized she needed him, he had left.

His powerful magic had flooded the area. It was noisy untrained magic, and like a flash of light in the eyes, it had disrupted the magical flow in the area. It had blinded her for a minute, but then she saw him.

ATLANTIAN MAGIC

Marvin was heading back to camp. He had stayed with her. She had thought she could trust him, but now she knew it. He had been tempted almost to the breaking point, and yet he had stayed. It would take him several hours to walk back. She thought about staying up and waiting for him, but she fell asleep secure in the trust that Marvin had just proved.

When the rising sun woke her, she found him curled up next to her, holding her from behind. She lay there for a few minutes, enjoying being with him. Something had changed since the cabin. For the first time since they had met, she felt like he was her companion and protector, and not just her charge.

They boarded the carriage and Marvin slept most of the way to the capital.

Chapter 18

They rode through the outskirts of Crystal Mountain right after lunch. It was urban sprawl, Dwarven style.

Uncountable numbers of small, Dwarven made mounds dotted the landscape. Snow covered fields of farmland surrounded the stone mounds. Out of the top of the mounds were chimneys, perhaps for ventilation or cooking. Upon closer inspection, the mounds were entrances to a below-ground tunnel system. The mounds had sturdy metal doors, which looked like they could resist an army. All the doors were open.

It was winter, and snow covered the ground. Few people were outside, but the guards waved at them as their carriage passed by. The soldiers surrounding them waved in return.

They travelled for several minutes before coming to a tall wall of stone. Marvin looked at the wall, which reminded him of pictures of the Great Wall of China. The noted exception was that rather than one set of battlements, the wall had three sets of battlements, each one higher than the one in front of it. It would allow each line of archers to shoot over the person in front of them. They traveled past the wall between two large towers. Between the towers were four open portcullises the guards could drop to seal the entrance at a moment's notice. Even if an army destroyed one, they still had to get through three more. The wall was not just tall. It was wider than a four-lane road.

Their caravan stopped inside the gate. A gentleman in court finery greeted them. Shandria turned towards Marvin and said, "Follow my lead. Officially you are Sir Marvin, my traveling companion and protector."

The official welcomed Princess Shandria and her party to the capital city. He bowed low, as Shandria walked towards him. Marvin thought it interesting how low the official bowed since Shandria was a head taller than he was. Then he stood upright, and Shandria extended her hand for him to shake. He said a few words of welcome, and then escorted her forward. She walked between hundreds of Dwarven troops lined up at attention in their military finery.

Marvin followed several paces behind her. At the end of the line was a stone ramp leading up to a large ornate carriage. There was a platform at the top with armed soldiers in their dress uniforms. A woman dressed in court finery stood on a raised platform near the carriage. The official escorting Shandria walked with her up the five steps of the platform, then released her hand and bowed low. He then came back down the ramp and indicated to Marvin that he should wait at the bottom.

He watched as Shandria curtsied and bowed her head to the woman at the top. The official told her she was Queen Olivine and had ridden out to welcome the princess. He watched them hold hands for several minutes, and then the queen hugged her and had her stand beside her. The official asked Marvin to hold his hand so he could escort him up, to kneel on one knee, and to bow his head to the Queen at the top, then stand up, and take the queen's hands if she offered them. The court procedure was new to Marvin, but he had watched many movies on television, and it was similar, so he had an idea what was required.

The official escorted him to the queen. He knelt down and bowed his head, and then stood up straight. He was nervous. He saw the Queen's infectious smile. His nervousness subsided, and he discovered he was returning her smile. She extended forward her hands. He extended his hands, and she gently held them.

She closed her eyes for several seconds. Marvin felt the warmth of her touch and saw the magical threads inside him intertwined with hers. It was as if their magic's were shaking hands and conversing. They stood there for over a minute, and then he felt her magic withdraw. Her magic left a warm feeling behind, and he was sad she stopped.

The queen said, "My precious child. You are very welcome here. I would not have expected to see you escorting an Atlantian princess until your magic had matured. You are young and conflicted. But you are faithful, fearless, and growing in knowledge and power. You carry exotic metals, dress in strange materials, and carry no real weapon. I can't wait until court formality allows us to have a long talk.

"But for now, I have court business to discuss with the princess. Please honor the princess and me by riding on top of the carriage as part of our honor guard."

Marvin said, "I am honored to meet you and by your warm welcome. I look forward to our next meeting." Marvin knelt and bowed again to the queen. He didn't know if it was part of the court ritual, but it seemed the right thing to do.

The queen turned and escorted Princess Shandria into the carriage. The official showed Marvin where the honor guard was sitting.

He walked down the stairs and then climbed up on top of the carriage, where the rest of the honor guard was. The carriage was another magic-fired, steam-powered vehicle. The engine was at the back of the carriage, and the honor guard was on top at the front, with the passenger area below them.

Marvin felt out of place with the ceremonially dressed Dwarves that were the Queen's honor guard. He definitely stood out, not just his height, but his forest-camouflage colored poncho with the hood, his blue Jeans sticking out below the bottom of his poncho, and the touch of white sweat socks, which disappeared into his brown hiking boots. But he had no sword at his side, just a general-purpose camping knife, larger than a kitchen knife and useful for chopping small limbs. It was made of an alloy this world had never seen.

The Dwarves around him wore bright red uniforms, covered with metal breastplates. The guards held polished and shined axes, and crossbows strapped to their backs. Their axes and breastplates glowed with a magical blue color.

The Dwarves around him looked at him, wondering why the Queen had interrupted their perfectly aligned and balanced honor guard by having him sit up top with them. But their Dwarvish courtesy and friendliness won out, and they greeted him and found him a seat towards the front. But as soon as the carriage started rolling, they became a silent lot. The Dwarves stared outward, keeping their military discipline, and looking for anything that would compromise the Queen's safety. But they were still Dwarves, and they waved back at the few farmers and children playing in the snow-covered fields around them. Marvin half wondered what regulation number they were following.

Soon they arrived at a second wall which was identical to the first. The terrain changed to hills inside the wall. Most of the hills had open metal doors sticking out of them, and bare grapevines covered them. Marvin had been probing the structures the best he could from a moving carriage with his magic. The doors led to tunnels where the Dwarves lived. Dwarves were a race that trusted in rock and stone more than open sky for their protection.

The glow of the battle-axes carried by the Dwarves captivated Marvin's eye. Then he realized the glow wasn't their color, it was a magical light, which appeared blue to his magical sight. His curiosity made him want to probe the magic, but the magic resisted him. It seemed unfriendly to him, but he was bored, so he kept at it. Then he realized the magic wasn't unfriendly, it was shy earth magic, and he wasn't Dwarven.

It soon recognized him as a curious child in magic. It started talking. Marvin didn't understand a single vibration yet he listened. After several minutes he realized this was the magic of earth, metal, and fire, the magic of the forge.

It sang a beautiful melody to the beat of the hammer in the forge, one he had never heard before, with words he couldn't understand. The rhythms reminded him of the tales the Dwarves had told of Feldspar the Great. He didn't understand much of what the ax was saying, but he was happy to listen.

They took a break at the next station. The princess and queen left the coach and spent some time together in a small break room. A large metal pipe fitted over the water tank. The honor guard relaxed as soon as the rest of the guards surrounded the carriage. They passed several large mugs of mead up to the guards. They drank and passed them around. They gave one to Marvin, he took a drink, and then he passed it on.

The guard next to him smiled and said, "Young Atlantian, I heard you listening to my battle-ax. She's beautiful don't you think?"

84

Marvin said in return. "She is beautiful. I've never seen anything like her. I'm sorry if I broke any customs by listening to her, please forgive me."

The guard laughed, "Nothing to forgive. You are young in years, and your magic is younger. The curiosity of youth is expected in our culture. Besides, my ax was teasing you to look at her. But then she played shy, and finally accepted you, and like a lady, became talkative."

Marvin smiled and said. "I didn't understand many of the words she spoke, so she sang me a beautiful song. I heard the beating of the forge hammers and the same rhythms I had heard a few days ago at the telling of the sagas of Feldspar the Great. She is a beautiful weapon."

The Dwarf smiled and said, "Ah, she must like you to introduce you to Dwarven magic. We consider it an invitation to listen when one listens to you. Your clothing is flowing with Atlantian magic, and I can see it flow inside you, yet you are wearing unusual material with unusual colors and style. You carry unknown dead metal. It's perhaps not polite, but I am very curious about you."

Marvin thought for a second, "I would like to satisfy your curiosity, but Princess Shandria asked me to remain silent for now. I can say that the Princess and I have been traveling together for what seems like years but is only months, and the last few days among Dwarves has been fascinating and enjoyable."

Marvin continued, "Queen Olivine is amazing. After holding her warm hands, I suspect she may have learned things about me that even I don't know. I can see why she is loved."

The Dwarf smiled and said, "Loved she is. King Feldspar is the strength of the Dwarves, and she is our heart."

Shandria had a good conversation with the queen. They talked about the loss of the Atlantian arch crystal, finding Marvin on Earth, their travels together, and their mutual need to visit Alfamara. Much of the story the queen already knew, some she had guessed.

The queen shared with Shandria what the Dwarves knew about what had happened while she was away "Your father sent out a messenger to each of the realms telling them of the theft. For safety, we put magic wards on the arc, which prevented anyone from using it to gate into our realm. I'm afraid the ward bounced your gate to the north and caused it to unravel. I am thankful you are okay.

"The thief has been amassing an army, Darfarins, ogres, and creatures from different worlds. She has probed the magic wards on the arch several times, and she will undoubtedly continue. We believe she will soon be on the offensive. She may not be able to gate to the arch gates, but all realms have places which connect to other realms and are sympathetic to portals, and she has an arch crystal to help her to create a gate that can be sustained for long enough to march a large army across.

"I apologize we won't be having a big week-long ball to celebrate your arrival. But I'm sure we can throw together something. Having a princess from

Atlantis visit us is a grand occasion. My seamstress would love the challenge of making a gown for such a lovely princess, and I know she will be disappointed if we didn't give you an opportunity to wear it.

"Tell me how your grandfather is doing. We visited Atlantis when he was a child. He took me on a small boat, trying to bless me, but I fell in, and since Dwarves are too heavy to swim, I almost drowned. He rescued me with his magic, and in the process, I learned to talk to water." The Queen laughed, "But not to breathe it." She was happy to hear everyone in the Atlantian court was doing well.

Shandria and the queen talked endlessly, sharing old stories about the various members of the royal court. Shandria knew her grandfather had visited the Dwarven court when he was a prince, but she had never before heard the stories of when the Dwarven royalty had visited Atlantis.

Chapter 19

Crystal Mountain was the most remarkable feat of architecture and engineering Marvin had ever seen. It was far more than the three-dimensional maze of tunnels it initially looked like. It was a beautiful and well-designed three-dimensional city, built into a mountain. There were walkways and roads for steam-powered carriages and horses. Steam-powered elevators, gears, belts, and pulleys were everywhere. Marvin was impressed with the air circulation and purification system. There were magically generated lights, and the stones were glowing with magic. Dwarves had decorated almost every pillar and wall with colorful stone carvings. He was looking forward to exploring it.

The Atlantians had a maintained but unoccupied embassy inside Crystal Mountain. Half a dozen Dwarven servants stood at attention as they entered in. The head servant, Alluvial, introduced himself, along with the permanent embassy staff. Shandria met and shook hands with each of them. Alluvial gave them a tour and then took them to the private quarters. The embassy had a public area, a guest area, and the private quarters. Atlantian embassy personnel occupied a wing of the private quarters. Royal visitors were housed in a second wing.

They entered the private area and were in a large garden room with an artificial sun. Vegetation filled the garden area. Marvin was amazed at the amount of light and water works that the magic maintained.

Shandria thanked and dismissed Alluvial, wanting to explore the royal quarters herself. She said to Marvin, "This is a smaller copy of the palace gardens at home. Join me."

Shandria took off her clothes and jumped into the clear blue pool. Marvin was a lot less self-conscious about nudity than he had been in his backyard pool what seemed like years ago. He stripped naked and joined her in the pool. The pool was a lot larger than the one in his backyard and a lot deeper. It reminded him of the dolphin pool at an amusement park.

He was treading water when she said. "Let's race our bodies to the other side." Shandria started swimming. He had lettered in swimming in high school. Shandria won, but he came in a close second. It was five years since he raced competitively.

Shandria laughed and said, "Not bad, once you learn to weave water you will swim like the Atlantian you are." A wave rose up around her and carried her back to the other side. Then she dove off the wave and into the water. A ten-foot-high peak of water rose up in the center of the pool, and out of the top rose Shandria. She stood at the top for a few seconds, then she slid down as if she was on a water park slide. She rode the wave back to where Marvin was standing on the gently rising floor of the pool near the far edge.

Marvin's first attempt to raise a wave was a disaster; the wave he tried to create exploded and launched water in all directions. Shandria swam away and yelled, "Splash party." Her well-directed, magically aided attacks were making it hard for Marvin to catch a breath.

He spun around before her next wave hit, took a deep breath, and dove into the water. He pushed off the bottom straight towards her. Shandria was laughing and wondering where he was when he grabbed her ankle from below and pulled her underwater. He kicked up and took a breath. The waves in the pool kept rebounding off the sides, and the once smooth water was choppy. Then Marvin felt the threads, and he commanded the waves to reduce in size. The waves got smaller. Shandria surfaced and started laughing. She yelled, "You cheating ogre, you grabbed me from underneath."

Marvin's joking turned to anger and frustration. Something he had been upset about came out. "That's all I am to you an ogre from Earth. I'll never be good enough for you." He turned and swam to the edge of the pool. He mentally knew he needed to stay with Shandria, but emotionally was still fighting with his decision when he could have taken his portal to Earth. He was just an ogre from Earth. He wanted to get out but realized he was naked. In her mind, he was just a naked monster, and he wanted to hide his nakedness.

Shandria thought he was playing and then realized he had taken it personally. He was standing at a shallower spot near the edge of the pool. She swam beside him. He turned his back to her. Then she thought about everything she had said to him. "Oh no! You thought humans from Earth are ogres. Ogres aren't even from Earth. I called you an ogre in jest as part of the game we were playing."

Slowly it sunk into Marvin. He turned towards her.

Shandria said, "Thousands of years ago the Darfarins invaded Elder Earth with their allies the ogres. They are evil, vile creatures. They consume flesh raw, and Darfarins kill and defile magic. The magical races resisted for a while, then we realized we won every battle but the one that mattered, they were consuming the natural magic of Elder Earth, and the ogres were slaughtering the humans.

"The Anastasi came up with a plan to leave Elder Earth. In the process, we used all the natural magic.

The invaders magic consumed magic. The Darfarins had no magic and quickly died. Without support from the Darfarins, the people of Earth were able to defeat the ogres. We gave the magic free race of humans on Earth a magic-free, safe realm, where they could grow and develop their unique culture. The ogres and their allies would never be able to attack them without magic.

"Elder Earth spawned all the great races. We are all related to each other as a lion is to a tiger. Only humans have no magical ability. You have Atlantian magic. You are an Atlantian, raised on Earth. How or why I don't yet know. You are still learning magic, but you are as much an Atlantian to me as my father the king or my brother, the future king of Atlantis.

"I know you love humans and think of yourself as one. But humans were never our enemy. When we left, we made the realm of our birth safe for them and gave it to them as a gift of friendship."

Shandria reached around and gave Marvin a big hug. He returned it and held her tight. She said, "I know you miss your home. I felt you open the portal to Earth a few nights ago, yet you decided to stay with me. You are a true companion and always will be my friend. I will make sure Atlantis accepts you. I know you will soon realize it is your new home and will have many friends. You may not be a royal, but the title I gave you of Sir Marvin is well deserved and makes you a noble in our society, I'm sure the rest of the Atlantian Court will acknowledge you as noble. And I will always be your friend."

She kissed him then released him. Marvin dipped his head, still fighting with his emotions. He backed away. It was a lot to take in.

Shandria asked, "What's wrong?"

Marvin felt better but still refused to accept he was something other than human. He said, "You're a real ogre to have played that joke on me." He splashed her, dove under the water, and pushed off the wall. He saw the threads of magic. He had them lift him up in a wave, and not by his intent, it splashed him out on the side of the pool. He hit the ground, and said, "Ouch!" He lay on his back laughing.

Shandria smiled at hearing him laugh. They played for a while. Then she climbed out of the pool and walked over to an antique, carved dresser by a wall, and pulled out a beautifully decorated gold colored comb from the drawer. She said, "I knew there would be one of these in here." She dove back into the water, hung out under a waterfall at the edge for a minute, then stepped to the side and started combing her hair. She said, "It feels wonderful to comb all the dirt out of my hair."

Marvin was looking for a towel. Then he realized Atlantians might not use them. He lay down on a lounge seat to dry off in the artificial sun that was providing light for this area. The warmth of the artificial sun felt luxurious after all the days of ice and snow.

Shandria finished combing her hair and lay down on a lounge beside him. She said, "The Dwarves built this garden for us after seeing our palace gardens. Everything you see is Dwarven except for the sun and the sky, which is Atlantian magic. Everything in the ceiling reflects the sky above us. The sun is low in the artificial sky. Soon it will be sunset and dinner time.

Pd MICHEL

Shandria told Marvin what the queen had shared with her. Soon she said, "We need to get dressed for dinner time. The servants would think we had the manners of ogres and would be embarrassed if we showed up free. There should be clean clothes that fit you in one of the rooms."

Marvin realized that the Atlantian word for naked and free was the same word. He followed her as she walked away from him.

Shandria opened an ornate door to reveal a hallway. She walked down the hall and opened doors until she found the room she wanted. She entered, opened up the wardrobe, looked at Marvin carefully, and then selected some clothing.

Marvin dressed as she handed him the clothes. He recognized what looked like boxer shorts, but there was no elastic, and it tied at the top. The shirt was a vibrant blue pull over, and the pants were brown and baggy. They had a tie on them that secured them in place.

Shandria said, "You look as good as a prince. Any of the boots in the wardrobe will match that outfit. You may want to try on a few pairs to find one that fits. I'm going to get dressed, and I will see you in a few minutes. He watched her still naked body leave the room. He looked around and lay back on the bed for a few moments. After sleeping on the ground for weeks, the bed would be like sleeping on a cloud.

He closed his eyes and then sat up, realizing he would fall asleep if he lay there too long. He felt a twinge in his abdomen. His cancer was starting to grow back. He could see it in the way the magic moved through his body. He wasn't sure whether he should mention it to Shandria. He didn't think he would get to visit the Alfarins with the arch not working. Besides, tonight was the first time he had heard her laugh in a while. The news of his cancer could wait until morning.

He walked out to the garden and sat down near a stone wall. He put his hand on the stone wall and tried listening to the magic, but it was shy.

Shandria wore a beautiful dress that made Marvin stand up and watch her as she walked by him. She insisted it was only a housedress, but still wore her sword tied to its side. She wore eyeshadow and lipstick that gave a soft pink color to her lips.

Shandria was carrying his camping knife and the belt he had worn it on. She said, "You are Sir Marvin. It's proper for you to wear this all the time." She also handed him the wolf's tooth necklace, which he had taken off at the pool. He smiled and put it over his head.

Dinner that night was spicy meat, cut up vegetables, which he realized were all tuber-based, and roasted potatoes seasoned with a citrus and garlic sauce. It was in one big bowl. There was a second smaller bowl with a green colored sauce. There were green colored crackers, which he dipped into the sauce. A fragrant red wine, which Shandria assured him came from the Atlantian palace gardens, accompanied it.

At the end of the meal, Shandria showed him where to clean up.

90

Then she met him back in the garden. The overhead showed a sliver of the fading twilight and a star-filled sky. They played a game of sticks and stones. The stones were smooth flat stones. The sticks were polished wood. They played the first game to a tie. Then Shandria beat him in the second game.

They had finished off the bottle of spiced wine between them and both starting to yawn. They walked down into the royal area. The magic now dimly lit the hallway. Marvin turned to go into his room, but Shandria said, "No, we sleep together in the royal room. How can we protect each other from different rooms?"

There was a small nightstand on each side of the bed. Shandria put her sword on her nightstand, and he put his knife on his. He watched Shandria strip naked and crawl into bed. He followed her lead and crawled naked into bed beside her. They soon fell asleep.

The room lighting followed the sun and grew brighter in the morning when the sun rose.

Shandria stood up out of bed and stretched. She touched the floor with the palms of her hands and did what looked to Marvin to be five minutes of tai chi and yoga, all naked.

Marvin got out of bed.

She said. "There should be clean undergarments in the other room. I will be with you in a minute to help you select an appropriate outfit in which to meet the king."

He entered the room with the men's clothing. He saw the embassy staff had cleaned and folded his travel clothes. They had cleaned his pack and laid everything out on the bed. He thought about Shandria's necklace and saw the aluminum box. He picked it up and was glad to hear it rattle. He peered inside and saw the necklace was still there. He relaxed and repacked his pack with the box on the bottom, then he changed into a fresh set of undergarments.

Shandria walked through the door wearing just her undergarments. She opened the closet and selected an outfit for him. Once she held up a shirt towards his body. She put it back into the wardrobe and decided on a different one. She said, "Get dressed and then come return to our room. These formal dresses require two people to tie them. I may need your help." She left the room.

He dressed in the outfit Shandria had chosen for him. The pants were comfortable, but there were several ties on the shirt of different lengths. The shirt should show off his muscles. What it showed was a disappointment. There was a vest and a cloak to go with the outfit. It took him a minute to fasten the clasp on the cloak. He strapped back on his knife. Wearing his knife camping was one thing. But it would take him time to get used to wearing it all the time. It always seemed to be in the way when he sat down.

He joined Shandria in the royal bedroom. She had put on a top with half a dozen ties on the back. He tied them from top to bottom.

Shandria slipped on a dress. Marvin had expected a huge Victorian style dress, but there were no underwires to balloon it out, and it lay flat against her.

She strapped on her sword and then walked over to a mirror. She spun in one direction, then spun in the opposite direction. Marvin thought she looked amazing, but she said, "Well it will have to do. I hope the Queen likes it."

He watched her touch up her makeup using a small brush, dipping into a liquid to paint it on her lips.

He thought she rocked the look of a fairytale princess. Then he laughed when he realized they were underground below yards of stone in a Dwarven mine and wondered where the seven Dwarves were.

Shandria asked, "Are you laughing at me?"

He replied, "Yes, I mean no. I mean, anyway, it's a compliment." He tried to explain the joke. He thought she got it, but he couldn't be sure.

They sat down for breakfast in the dining room. A layout of honey-covered pastries was there. There was a blue colored fruit that Shandria cut in half and shared with Marvin. It tasted like a cross between an apple and a pear.

Soon Alluvial entered the dining room. "Princess, your honor guard is here."

"Thank you, Alluvial. Tell the honor guard we will be out soon."

Alluvial bowed and left the room.

Shandria touched up her lipstick, and said, "Let's go meet King Feldspar."

The honor guard consisted of several dozen soldiers dressed in the royal blue color of the Captain's guards.

They split into two groups of soldiers plus the lieutenant. One group walked in front, one group walked in back, and the lieutenant joined the group in front and led the procession.

Shandria and Marvin had to get used to the speed of the Dwarves. They were marching at a slow ceremonial pace. It was less than half the pace Shandria and Marvin had set hiking. It gave Marvin and Shandria time to play tourists. They started pointing out interesting rock carvings, piping, and ductwork to each other. Artists had carved most of the pillars with impressive artwork.

Soon they reached a guard house. The portcullis was open. Two lines of Dwarves, wearing blue king's guard uniforms, and carrying battle-axes lined the way. Then they were on a bridge over a deep pit, which formed a semicircle around the front of an open balcony. The Balcony extended into a courtyard in front of the palace. The Dwarves had built the palace into the side of a cliff, all inside the mountain.

ATLANTIAN MAGIC

As they approached the front of the palace, they started admiring the relief drawings on its front. It reminded them of something. Then almost at the same time, they looked at each other and said, "King Feldspar the Great." The drawings depicted scenes from the epic battles of Feldspar the Great. Only when they were closer did Marvin realized they weren't just painted, the scenes were in full color, and the color came from the stone. The Dwarven artist had used magic to embed different colored minerals into the rock itself to change the color. It was magnificent.

Chapter 20

Marvin wanted to spend more time looking at the relief drawings. He wanted to spend more time looking at everything, but it was time to enter the palace. He was amazed at the palace construction, the carvings and the colors of the rocks used were beautiful.

The guards in the front split in half to let them go by and the four guards behind them marched up and closed the gap behind them. Once inside the palace, a man dressed in royal finery greeted them and escorted them to the king's auxiliary courtroom. It was the smaller, less formal courtroom, where the king would greet them.

The Dwarfs' concept of small was different than his. So was their idea of what less formal meant. The courtroom was the size a basketball arena. Their escort told them all the regulations for meeting with the king. Marvin was amazed at how many there were. It took several minutes to run through the list. The Dwarves had memorized the regulations and quoted them with their regulation number.

Dozens of troops at attention stood inside the room. Beautifully carved and colored columns held up the roof, or maybe they were there just for the beauty of the artistry. Once again, Marvin had to resist gawking like a tourist. Their escort walked to a location about thirty feet from the stairs leading up to the thrones of the king and queen, and they waited.

A trumpet sounded. Everyone knelt down on one knee. Shandria had Marvin kneel down also, but she stood tall. When the king and queen came in, she bowed her head.

After the king sat down the trumpet sounded twice, and everyone rose together. The rustle of people standing up echoed through the hall. A few seconds later, it was so quiet that Marvin could hear his heart beating. The king looked at the queen, and they stood up.

The king said, "Come up here my niece so we may speak with you."

Shandria curtsied and said to Marvin, "Stay here."

Marvin watched as Shandria walked up the stairs. Once at the top she curtsied to the queen. The queen embraced her in a hug. Then she curtsied to the king, who gave her another hug. They talked for ten minutes before Shandria stepped over to the side by the queen. The king said, "Sir Marvin, you may approach the throne."

Their royal escort walked next to Marvin and started talking, "Go straight up the stairs, and then turn towards Princess Shandria. Bow down by touching one knee to the floor and bowing your head, then stand back up. Wait for the princess to take your hand. She will let you know when to meet the queen, then bow to the princess and repeat the formality for the queen and after she dismisses, repeat the bows to the king." The royal escort stopped at the base of the stairs and motioned for Marvin to go up.

Marvin climbed the stairs to the top, turned to the right, and did the formal bow to Shandria. She took his hands, then took a step towards him and gave him a quick embraced which he returned. She said, "Sir Marvin, you have been a faithful companion and protector. You saved my life from narworms, wolves, and dark spells. I have awarded you my Order of the Wolf, and the title of Sir Marvin. It is my privilege to honor you with an invitation to meet with the queen of all Dwarves. Shandria indicated by looking down that it was time for Marvin to bow again. He bowed down, rose up, and repeated the procedure with the queen.

She smiled and took his hands. "The exploits you have accomplished on behalf of my niece are exemplary, even more so since you are young in your training. I name you friend to the court and allow you to meet with the King. She let go of his hands. Marvin said, "Thank You," then he knelt down on one knee, bowed his head, then stood up and walked over to the king and repeated the process.

The king held his hands, then after a few seconds, he closed his eyes. Marvin could feel the strength of his magic and its warmth. He had the strongest hands Marvin had ever held. Then the king opened his eyes and said, "You are full of the doubts of the young, but you have the heart of the mighty. It is my pleasure to honor you with a private meeting."

The King released his hands. Marvin once again repeated the bow. When he stood back up, he heard the trumpet sound three short blasts. At the conclusion, he heard the soldiers shout, "Long Live King Feldspar and Queen Olivine." Then there was a rush of noise as they filed out.

The king said, "Follow me." He walked around behind the throne, and through a doorway hidden by a tapestry, which a member of the court pulled back. Marvin looked towards the queen who indicated that he should follow the king. He did. Shandria and the queen brought up the rear.

The king sat down in a comfortable chair and motioned for everyone to join him. He pointed to a chair next to his for Marvin to sit in. A servant brought four cups of mead. Copying something he had seen in a movie, Marvin raised his glass, and said, "To beloved King Feldspar and his equally beloved wife."

The king said, "Here, here, and everyone drank the toast.

Then the king said, "To our beloved niece and her Atlantian traveling partner from Earth.

His wife said, "Here, here, and they drank another toast."

The King put his mug down and said, "In here we relax all the formalities. So, tell me about Elder Earth."

He told the king about the major countries, with some population statistics, which surprised the king. Soon they started talking about Earth's technology. The king was interested in how internal combustion engines had replaced steam-powered engines for carriages. The idea of stamping out hundreds of identical parts from one master mold interested him also.

Marvin reached into his pocket and pulled out his multi-tool. He showed its functionality to the king than he handed it to the king. The king looked at it and said, "Could you part with it for a few days, I would love to have my craftsmen look at this. The metal is dead, but it would be wonderful if everyone in the army could have a multi-purpose tool like this. If as you say, we put the craftsmanship into making the mold, we could stamp the pieces out quickly. Of course, we would still take considerable time to enchant and harden the metal, but back during the war against the ogres, we enchanted many battle-axes at the same time.

Marvin said, "I would love to let your craftsmen look at it."

The Queen and Shandria were talking about family members and court intrigue and had left once the King and Marvin had started talking about technical things. They were back now. The queen cleared her throat.

The king looked at his wife and said, "I guess it's that time." We have a gift for you.

He stood up, and Marvin stood up with him. He escorted them through the soldier's armory. Thousands of axes and crossbows lined the wall or were packed and stacked into crates.

He proceeded through the armory past the king's guard and the queen's guard. He could tell the king was listening to the magic in the air. Marvin's senses were overloaded. They were strong and deafening. He was having a problem trying to separate the sounds and the colors. There was just too much. All he could tell was the weapons were somehow excited.

The king took Marvin into the protected area of the royal armory. Marvin felt something calling to him. He saw a glowing light in the distance. He almost involuntarily asked, "What's that?"

The king saw the look on his face and felt the magical feeling in the room. King Feldspar smiled and said, "Let's walk over and see my son." The protected area of the royal armory held enchanted weapons. Most were weapons used by the Dwarves, but there were a few swords. As Marvin walked closer to the object, he became more excited. A sword on display longed for him to pull it from its sheath. He took another step towards it and realized where he was. He turned to the king and said, "I hear that sword talking to me. May I touch it?"

The king laughed and said, "Touch it, talk to it, and handle it. It is calling you."

Marvin hurried over to the sword. He took it down from the rack. He slowly pulled it from its scabbard and looked at it. It was beautiful. It felt strange to Marvin, and at the same time familiar. It was like a chance meeting in a bar with a stranger and finding out you had known each other in elementary school and now have the same job at a different company. The sword was talking to him. The sword was happy, and so was Marvin. Marvin couldn't believe how the sword fit perfectly into his hand. He barely felt the weight.

Marvin turned towards the king, and the king said, "I had planned to give you a magic sword so you could better protect my niece, but it looks like a far better sword has given itself to you. This sword is one of the ancient swords of old. King Feldspar the Great and one of the great kings of Atlantis forged and enchanted him. And he has chosen you as his companion. Do you accept the choosing?

Marvin said without hesitation, "Yes, yes. He is so handsome and so happy."

The king laughed. He realized that his job as the king had made him neglect his battle-ax, also one of the ancient weapons. He made a mental note to have his schedule changed so he could once again work out with him on a daily basis.

Marvin undid the knife that was around his waist and strapped on his new sword. He turned to the king, and said, "I guess I have no more use for my old knife. It's from Earth. If it can be of use to you, then it's yours." There were several guards at the entrance to the chamber. And there were several members of his staff outside.

The king yelled to one of the guards. The guard rushed over. The king said, "Give this to one of the ministers outside to give to Sir Geode. Tell him it is from the Earth and is for his research."

The Guard said, "Yes my king." The guard bowed his head. He grabbed the weapon, carried it outside, and handed it to one of the ministers. Then he walked back to his post at the entrance to the armory.

The king told his wife. "I need to talk to Marvin in private for a few minutes. We will join you soon."

They left the armory. The queen and Shandria took a direct path back to their chambers. The King took a more roundabout way. The sword selecting Marvin told the king much he had suspected when he met him. There was much the king wanted to tell Marvin, but he had a promise to keep. He said, "The ancient swords themselves tell you their stories and teach their wisdom. And I don't want to ruin the fun for you. But this sword was the last ancient sword to journey to Earth. It was many centuries ago. Ancient swords have their reasons for choosing who they choose. It will only become apparent over time."

They met up again, and then the king left Shandria and Marvin to talk about his weapon for several minutes, while he spoke to his queen. Then the king wanted to speak to Shandria, and the queen wanted to speak to Marvin.

The queen said, "Sir Marvin, I see the sickness in you and the sickness in Princess Shandria. Your condition is getting worse. Fortunately, Shandria is stable, but her magic is fragile. Shandria has learned to weave magic through paths that are not healthy for her. I have cautioned her to use her magic infrequently. If she uses her magic too much, she will break the paths apart and lose her magic.

"There is a minor conjunction in two moons. It will allow you to generate a portal to Alfamara, the land of the Alfarin. Shandria doesn't have the power to create a portal. You have the power, but not the experience. Fortunately, your sword has been there and can help you. We will give you a writ of friendship with the Alfarin and a request that they help the two of you.

"One last thing, tell me what happened to the cursed necklace. Shandria said you threw it into the river after she forced it back from you the first time. Is that right?"

Marvin looked at her and knew she could be trusted. "It is a half-truth. After I took the necklace from Shandria the second time, I put it in an aluminum box I had. Aluminum is an Earth metal. It proved effective in stopping and destroying the dark magic. I did go to the river and throw it in. That's what I told Shandria.

"What I didn't tell her was that immediately afterward, it occurred to me that maybe the necklace could be useful in either curing Shandria or tracking down the traitor who cursed the necklace. I grabbed the box from the river. I hid it under the rocks by the porch until the magic no longer controlled Shandria. When we were ready to leave the way station, I retrieved it and hid it in my backpack. It is at the embassy."

The Queen said, "You need to give me that necklace in its protective box. We need to make sure neither Shandria nor anyone else stumbles upon it by accident. I will have it evaluated, and the spell inside it destroyed forever."

Marvin was surprised at the forcefulness of the queen. There was an implied "now" in the statement.

Marvin said. "Yes, your highness. Let's do it now."

The Queen laughed, "Your Highness, what a strange honorific. Here you stand a head taller than me and you call me your highness."

Marvin returned the Queen's infectious laughter. "I'm sorry. I'm new to kings, queens, and royalty. All I have is stories from Earth about royalty, and some of them are conflicting. What should I call you? I don't even know your name."

The Queen said, "What should I have you call me? Most people refer to me as the Queen or just Queen. In some places, they call me King Feldspar's queen or Queen of all Dwarves, but few call me by my name. My name is Olivine.

I have always liked my name. You may call me Queen Olivine, or in private, Olivine."

Marvin said, "Thank you, Olivine."

She grabbed his arm as if she had known him all his life. She yelled, "Squire! I need two horses ready to ride at the front door." The squire ran off.

They walked through the palace to the entrance. She said, "It will take several minutes before the squire saddles the horses and brings them from the stables.

They looked at the carvings on the front of the palace. Marvin mentioned how much he admired the craftsmanship. The queen was pleased. He told her about singing the songs of Feldspar the great with the guards of the north gate.

The queen said, "I miss those days when I could enjoy a mug of mead with the troops. It's just not proper now."

Marvin said, "Maybe you should make it proper, at least one day a year. Perhaps have a festival where the queen comes down off the stairs and joins with the people or the soldiers for a saga or two. Surely, a queen so loved as you should be with the people who love you."

Marvin saw Queen Olivine staring at him. He said, "I'm sorry. I guess I don't understand royalty or Dwarven culture."

The queen wasn't staring at Marvin because he said something wrong. She was thinking about what he said. "You understand it rather well. I need to make some minor adjustments so I can convince ten ministers and the king. And like you did with the necklace, tell a half-truth. I won't tell them I'm joining in. I will set precedence, and it will then be proper."

She smiled at Marvin. "You will keep this secret won't you Sir Marvin?"

Marvin returned her smile and said, "I could never violate the trust of so gracious a lady and queen."

They both laughed.

Chapter 21

The horses arrived. Even though Marvin had grown up in Arizona, and his grandmother had lived on a ranch when she was younger, he had never ridden a horse, other than the plastic one kids put a coin into for a two-minute ride. His horse knew it and acted skittishly.

The queen figured it out right away. She said, "Listen to the horse. Touch him. Stroke his mane. Let him know you are a friend. Let him know your smell." The horse settled down.

"Now hold the reins and the saddle. Step up in the stirrup with your left foot and swing your right foot over to the other side."

Marvin noticed his sword. It was speaking to him. It had ridden a horse thousands of times. And through it so had Marvin. Marvin stepped in the stirrup and swung his foot over the top of the horse. He expertly held the reigns. The horse settled down and was his to control.

The queen stepped into the stirrup and mounted her horse. She led the way across the bridge and back to the Atlantian embassy. Marvin expertly dismounted at the front door. He then held the bridle of the Queen's horse as she dismounted.

The queen looked at Marvin. "I thought you had never ridden a horse before."

Marvin replied, "Only a pretend horse, but my new sword has ridden a horse countless times, and I'm learning it's a good teacher."

The eyes of Alluvial grew wide when he saw the queen enter. He knelt and bowed low. The queen had him stand, asked his name, talked to him for a couple of minutes, and then walked inside. Marvin handed the reigns of the horse to a servant before entering the embassy. The servant looked at the reigns as if he had never seen a horse before. Marvin said, "We will need them in a few minutes."

Marvin followed the queen inside the embassy. Soon the rest of the staff lined up, and the queen greeted each of them. She said, "Forgive my rudeness but we are in a hurry, or I'd love to spend some time talking to each of you. But today we shall not bother you for long."

Marvin said to Alluvial, "I'm giving something to the Queen, and I need a small pouch that can carry something this size." Marvin made gestures with his hand to indicate the size. "Can you have one ready for us? Alluvial bowed his head and then hurried away.

The queen took Marvin's arm and allowed him to escort her to the private area.

Olivine said, "It's been over a decade since I have been here. I forgot how beautiful it is."

There was a chair near a table. Marvin said, "Why don't you enjoy the garden. I will go get the box with the necklace and be right back." He bowed and walked to the private quarters.

Marvin rushed into the bedroom and found the box at the bottom of his pack where he put it. He pulled the box out, peeked inside, and verified the necklace was still there.

He brought it out to the queen. The queen was walking through the garden when Marvin returned.

She said, "I love this garden. It's too cold to grow plants outside this time of year, and we grow most of our flowers outside." The servant arrived with a purse that had a shoulder strap. Marvin was impressed that it was a good color match for the queen's dress. The Queen asked to see the box. He handed it to her. She spun the box around and said. "You're right. This box is a strange metal." She opened up the box, peeped inside, and then quickly shut the box.

She had a concerned look on her face and said, "I'm glad you brought this here. The necklace is still enchanted with vile magic. Fortunately, it is inactive. It could have caused a lot of problems if someone found it." She quickly put the box in the purse and put the purse over her shoulders. She continued, "I would love to stay and enjoy the garden, but we have to get back."

Marvin was surprised at how quickly the Queen's voice went from enjoying her time with Marvin to concern and anger when she saw the necklace. Marvin was glad she wasn't angry with him, and quickly shifted back to being happy.

They walked to the front of the embassy and exited out the front door. Marvin took the reins of the horses from the servant and saw the relieved look on his face. He held the bridle of the Queen's horse as she mounted. He then mounted his horse. They rode back to the palace, waving at several people as they passed.

Shandria and the king were outside, waiting for them. Several stewards helped the queen from her horse. But Marvin could see she didn't need the help. It was a formality. She immediately walked over and talked to the king.

Shandria watched Marvin get off the horse. The Atlantian royal clothing he wore reminded her of her older brother. She said, "You sure rock your sword, on that horse."

Marvin laughed. Shandria said, "Did I say it wrong, why are you laughing?"

Marvin said, "You used it correctly. I just didn't expect you to say it, and in Atlantian."

The king and queen walked over to Marvin and Shandria. The King said. "We both enjoyed your visit, but necessities of the crown are waiting. We will see you again soon."

Shandria said "Thank you for sharing the warmth and friendship of the Dwarves with us, and for treating me like your niece. She curtsied."

Marvin said, "Thank you. No gift can match the sword you gave me. I am so honored." Marvin touched his knee to the ground and bowed his head."

Marvin and Shandria rode back to the embassy, handed their reigns to the Dwarven honor guard, and watched them ride away.

Shandria asked Marvin where he had gone with the queen. Marvin realized Shandria would soon find out, but he wanted the necklace disposed of before she did. He didn't trust the magic that had almost killed her. "We briefly visited the embassy, and I gave her a gift. I won't tell you what now, but I will in a couple of days. And this afternoon, I have a sword to listen to."

Shandria was curious about what he wouldn't tell her, but she understood his desire to be with his sword. She said, "Well at least help me get out of this dress first." They walked back to the royal bedroom. He untied her dress then walked back to the garden. He unsheathed his sword and started listening.

Shandria changed into a comfortable house dress and walked out by the garden, looking for Marvin. She watched him do some basic exercises with his sword. He was a beginner and slow, but the sword was thousands of years old and patient. It was not so much teaching his mind as it was teaching his muscles and his reflexes. He would learn far more in a few hours with his sword, then in weeks with any other.

Step forward, thrust, step forward, and thrust.

Step at a 45-degree angle with a parry, then slash.

Shandria continued to watch him practice, after a few minutes Marvin took off his shirt and pants, stripping down to his underpants. She watched him continue fighting against an imaginary opponent. He was training his muscles, training his reflexes

She could tell he was tired, yet he continued. Then he switched the sword to the other hand and practiced on his left side. She knew what he was feeling. His forearm and shoulder muscles must be burning. The deep stances made his leg muscles burn painfully.

Developing both sides for balance was important. It was important enough that for a while Marvin would be spending more time training his weak side, his left side until it caught up with his dominant right hand. Soon Marvin would learn that the motions he was learning applied to unarmed combat also. A thrust with his sword was a jab with his fist or a spear-hand strike. The slash is a knife-hand strike or a hammer fist. But they would be back at the royal palace before he was ready to learn unarmed combat.

She thought about working out next to him, but she knew the intensity of her workout would be intimidating to him for quite a while.

Marvin stopped. He put down his sword, took off his underpants, and jumped into the pool. Shandria thought, why not. She stripped down and jumped in. Her body glided through the water, carried by her momentum towards the bottom of the pool. She arched her body upwards and continued her glide. Her head emerged from the water a few feet from him. They gave each other a quick splash, but neither was in a mood for a water fight.

She said. "The first few weeks of training with a sword are hard. After that it gets brutal."

Marvin let out a quick outburst of surprise. He smiled and said. "You caught me off guard with that one."

Shandria said, "I can help you out with some of the muscle pain."

Marvin quickly and firmly said, "No. Queen Olivine told me your use of magic could damage you."

Shandria said, "It's not that serious."

"That's not what the Queen told me. She said it would seem okay to you, but you are close to breaking your magic. You are using fragile threads to move heavy magic. It won't grow stronger. It will tear. It will break, and you will lose your magic. You have always strived, pushed your limits, and watched them increase. But this isn't a limit. It is a trap imposed by the curse. It will break, not grow stronger. I am your sworn protector. I insist we trust the Queen's judgment on this."

Marvin continued, "Besides, I'm scared."

"You don't have to be afraid; I can take care of myself."

"You proved with the wolf and the tiger you can take care of yourself without magic. But how long can I help? How long can I take care of you?"

Shandria saw the sadness in Marvin's eyes. "What do you mean, what's going on?"

"We both know we have a much better chance at success if my magic increases. But I also need to be physically strong. My magic shows me my cancer is growing. I am trying to gain as much strength as I can. Hopefully the stronger I get, the longer I have before I start to get weaker. But I will get weaker, slowly at first, but then faster towards the end. My cancer will start to eat me from the inside out."

Shandria said. "We can help you with magic."

"I talked with my sword. You can't help me. I spoke to the queen. The Dwarves can't cure me, but they can help me strengthen my body, and the Alfarin might be able to heal both of us. If we want to win, we have to fight smart. I have to gain strength. You have to restrain your magic for an emergency. I have to gain enough confidence in myself to open that portal as near to the Alfarin arch as I can."

Marvin's voice changed, almost begging he said, "Please do this for me. I have a death sentence inside me. You don't. But even if I die, I want to be sure that my life meant something. I need to complete my vow to get you to Alfamara. You know I care for you, and Atlantis needs you healed."

Shandria thought about Marvin dying. He was more afraid for her than for himself. She started to cry. She moved towards Marvin and hugged him. He hugged her back.

After several seconds, Shandria's crying died down. They separated. Marvin didn't know what to say and wanted to avoid awkwardness. He said, "I need to train some more." He ducked down under the water and kicked off the side towards the other end of the pool where his sword was.

Shandria realized her emotional connection to Marvin ran deep. She didn't want him to die, and it wasn't just her promise. She watched a pseudopod of water lift him out of the pool.

Marvin had found a towel and dried himself off. He looked at his clothing, then he looked at his undergarments, and then he picked up his sword. He decided that getting them all sweaty was silly. He commenced another drill. This time he started with the sword in his left hand. It was similar to the move Shandria had used against the wolf.

He squatted down and stepped backward with his right foot behind his other foot. He twisted and stabbed. Shandria watched for a few seconds. She knew the twisted horse stance was an awkward position for a beginner, and it would take a while for Marvin to feel comfortable in the stance. She grabbed the side of the pool and pulled herself out. She picked up her sword. There was another room at the embassy designed for training in combat. Marvin wasn't ready for it yet. She would work out there.

She knew Marvin was right. Shandria needed to save her magic weaving for when they needed it. And she needed to get stronger and faster with her sword. She had taken her sword fighting abilities for granted for too long. Much of her recent training had been using her magic focused through her sword for a power attack. She was good without her magic, able to best even the palace knights, but she could be better. It was time for her to take the next step in learning how to fight and to do it without using magic.

After dinner, Shandria and Marvin enjoyed some spiced wine while looking up at the evening sky. Marvin was staring at the ceiling. Shandria did too. Finally, she said, "The stars are wrong here."

ATLANTIAN MAGIC

Marvin said, "You are right, but they are correct for Alfamara. My father taught me how to navigate from the stars when I was little on camping trips. I was homesick for the stars of Earth back on the ridge. My magic showed them to me, and the portal opened. My sword knew the sky of Alfamara was available to display, and it showed me how. So, I plan to learn the map, or at least enough of it to find it in the sky, and to open a portal."

Chapter 22

Marvin was so stiff and sore that it was painful to get out of bed, but he got up before sunrise anyway. Unlike his exercises the previous day, his sword led him in slow movements and deep stretches. He had adapted the Atlantian clothing-optional style of working out and then swimming in the pool to bath the sweat off at the conclusion of his workout. He cooled down, let the tiredness in his muscles subside, and then climbed out and did another set of slow stretches.

Shandria had gotten up before him. She came into the garden area dripping with sweat. She put her sword and its sheath on a table near the pool and jumped in. Marvin, feeling looser after his stretching routine, jumped in and joined her. They talked for a few minutes, and then Marvin watched Shandria comb her hair. Then they both dried off in the artificial sun. They walked back to their room to dress for breakfast.

Marvin wasn't sure how Shandria was training, but he could see abrasions on her knuckles and bruises on her wrists and her shins. It didn't seem to bother her, so he decided to wait until breakfast to ask her.

Marvin was glad to see potatoes, eggs, and bacon for breakfast. Potatoes, or at least some tuber, were at every meal. Shandria said the Dwarves raised birds for their eggs and meat, but it never occurred to him that they would salt pork and create bacon. The slices were thicker than he expected, but it was bacon. He enjoyed his "taste of home" meal so much he forgot to ask Shandria about her bruises.

A messenger arrived after breakfast with two messages sealed with official court seals. One was for Princess Shandria of Atlantis, and the other was for Sir Marvin, Friend to the Court of King Feldspar.

Queen Olivine had invited Shandria to join her and her daughters to go horseback riding. The Royal Metallurgist invited Marvin for a meeting. Escorts would arrive in about an hour. Shandria told Marvin what he was wearing was all right. But she had to hurry and find something suitable to wear for horseback riding with the queen.

Marvin's escort arrived first. They rode away from the embassy and palace area. After several minutes, they arrived at a stable where they left their horses. The steward took Marvin to an elevator, which took them down several hundred feet. Steam generated by magical heat rotated gears and moved cables to cause the elevator to go up and down.

The steward escorted him past a maze of gears and steam piping. Ventilation pipes ran through the compound blowing cooling air to counter the heat of the steam piping. The ventilation kept the air fresh and cool.

The steward led Marvin to a room that reminded him of a messy Earth office. He saw tables covered with hand-drawn prints and technical drawings, piles of leather-bound books, and scrolls, some rolled up, and others rolled out. Several small metal objects, and geodes, cut open rocks with crystals inside, served as paperweights. Small random pieces of forged and shaped metal pieces were on shelves or fighting for space on the table.

A Dwarf dressed in an outfit right out of a steampunk novel walked over and extended his hand. Marvin looked at his smile, returned it, and shook his hand. His hand was thick, callused, muscular, and strong like the kings.

The man spoke, "Welcome, Sir Marvin. I am Sir Geode, Grand Master of the Forge, and Chief Metallurgist to the court of King Feldspar. Welcome indeed.

"Please don't mind the mess. I never seem to get the time to file anything away."

Marvin replied, "A scientist on Earth did a study and concluded that our most brilliant scientists and engineers had cluttered desks. I am honored to meet so brilliant a person."

Sir Geode laughed, "I would love to visit Earth sometime young Atlantian. I'm sure you have some fascinating tales to tell over a mug of mead. Oh my, we just met, and I don't have any mead to share or even an extra chair. Please forgive my rudeness."

Sir Geode walked over and opened his door. "Please follow me," he said.

Marvin followed Sir Geode down the hall and into the break room. He pointed to a chair by a table where Marvin should sit. Marvin sat and watched Sir Geode grab two mugs from a shelf. He filled them from the barrel of mead. He gave one to Marvin, raised his glass, and said, "To King Feldspar."

Marvin raised his glass, and repeated, "To King Feldspar." He realized that rather than just saying it to be courteous, he meant it.

They started talking about the metal in Marvin's old knife. Marvin was way over his head; all he knew about metals was from a few science shows, a show about how they made samurai swords, and the periodic table he had to memorize in high school chemistry but had mostly forgotten.

Sir Geode was interested in the various trace minerals they added to the metals of the knife. Marvin didn't know anything about them. All he knew was the knife company stamped out the blades from hot steel, and then heat-treated and sharpened by hand. Sir Geode said it was the finest knife not made in a forge he had ever seen. He was surprised they could make such a blade without the magic of the forge. Sir Geode could tell that it had been heat treated to harden it.

Marvin apologized to Sir Geode for his lack of knowledge about metal. He tried to remember a show he had watched on the making of samurai swords. Sir Geode became excited when he mentioned how they applied clay to the sword to provide differential cooling. The clay kept the quenching that made the sword edge hard from over-hardening the back part of the sword making it less prone to breaking.

Sir Geode started telling Marvin more about crystalline structure of metals then he could absorb. It didn't help that he had never heard the English terms before, so his language magic had no way to translate it.

After they had finished their drinks, Sir Geode said, "Come with me. You need to see our forges."

Marvin was amazed at the interior of the Dwarven mine. There were gears, pulleys, and moving belts all powered by steam. It was close to his idea of steampunk. Even with the ventilation, it was warm near the forges.

Steam-powered sleds moved buckets of ore from the mines to the refinery. Large machinery crushed the ore, and then sifted it. Pieces that were too large were crushed and sifted again.

Dwarven workers wearing helmets and goggles filled large metal containers with the crushed ore and then moved the container to a place outside the large metal furnace. The workers poured a layer of crushed ore, then a layer of finely powdered coal into a crucible. They mixed it together using a large wooden pole. They repeated the layering and mixing several times, filling the crucible to the proper level. The crucible waited outside the furnace.

They opened doors on both sides of the furnace. A large metal ram pushed the crucible into the furnace. In the process, it pushed another crucible out the other side. Brightly glowing metal filled the crucible exiting the furnace. Workers used metal tools to slide the crucible away from the furnace and to close the doors.

They pushed the crucible further away from the furnace and poured the drowse, the impurities which floated on top the molten metal, out into another container, along with a continuous flow of water to cool it down. The rapid evaporation of the water and cooling of the dross emitted a loud hissing noise and filled the area with a cloud of steam.

They moved and poured the dross free crucible into a long trench of fire clay, where it cooled and solidified. Dwarves with mauls chopped the glowing hot metal into bars while it was still soft. The process destroyed the clay mold. They used metal tongs to move the hot bars of iron. They took some straight to waiting blacksmiths. They allowed others to cool and stored them for future use. Dwarves cleaned up the clay and then built another mold for the next batch. The clay from the broken mold was reprocessed for use another day.

ATLANTIAN MAGIC

Sir Geode guided him through the full process. The blacksmith worked the metal, hammering and folding it, and then heating it up again. In the process, they removed the remaining impurities from the metal. Then the blacksmith worked the metal to form it into its final shape, many were singing a continuous rhythmic chant.

Marvin could feel the magic from the metalsmith entering into the metal. It accumulated outside, waiting, and then entered with each stroke of the hammer. He watched fascinated, lulled by the sound of the hammer and the melody of the magic. In the process, he could see the magic glow of the blacksmith's hammer, formed over years of working in the hands of the blacksmith.

The rhythm of the hammer fascinated Marvin. Marvin lost track of time. He realized he was humming a tune to the rhythm of the hammer. The finished product was a plow blade, enchanted never to break. It would glide through the soil, would never rust, and would last for many lifetimes.

Several of the blacksmiths had watched Marvin. They were all smiling, remembering the first time they had heard the song of the forge. Somewhere in the process, Sir Geode had gone back to his office. A blacksmith smiled at Marvin and broke him from his trance by saying, "It's time for mead in the break room. Please join us."

Marvin followed him into an open elevator that took them up several floors and shared a mug of mead with the blacksmiths. Sir Geode entered. He may have been in charge, but they were all equal here, and he could see the camaraderie and mutual respect.

Sir Geode told him, "The king said you need to get strong before you leave, and you have the music of the forge in your heart. A horse and escort will be waiting for you a half hour past dawn tomorrow. Join us, if you have the courage and choose the calling of the magic and strength of the forge."

A young Dwarf escorted him up to the stables, then to the embassy.

Marvin noticed it was already sunset. He felt stronger than he had before, and he hadn't even lifted a hammer. Coal dust covered his clothes and face. He may have ruined his Atlantian outfit. He definitely needed to clean up before dinner.

He arrived at the embassy, dismounted, and gave the reigns of his horse to his escort. The embassy greeter looked at him and said, "Dinner is in an hour, sir."

Marvin thanked him, walked into the garden, took off his sword, stripped, and dove into the pool. Shandria came out from her workout and joined him. Either her bruises were worse than yesterday, or they had turned purple. He touched her and felt his magic flowing into her body.

Shandria pulled her hand away and yelled, "What did you do to me?"

"I don't know I was concerned about your bruises and magic flowed into you. I felt it give you strength."

Shandria yelled again, "You never, ever, weave magic into a person without their permission!"

She turned her back on him, pulled herself out of the pool, and, stormed off. She grabbed the comb and her sword and headed off to the royal quarters.

Marvin yelled, "Dammit!" in English. He slapped the water in front of him. A wave, powered by his anger-activated magic, charged to the far end of the pool. It splashed out of the pool, taking enough water with it to noticeably drop the level. The slope of the deck caused the water to flow back into the pool. All he wanted to do was tell Shandria about his day, and his magic had flowed into her on its own.

He left the pool and picked up his sword, thinking he would exercise out his anger. But his sword refused to assist him. He tried doing a drill from the previous evening. There was no life in it. He realized it may have been an accident on his part, but he had violated some Atlantian rule or custom. He needed to apologize. He sheathed his sword and started walking towards the door to the royal rooms.

The door opened just before he arrived. And Shandria walked out at the same time, they both said, "I'm sorry."

They stepped towards each other and hugged. Shandria loosened her hug and said, "I'm sorry I yelled at you, I know you didn't mean anything wrong, and you are still learning to control your magic. Besides, it wasn't a magical weave. It was spillover magic from your time with the Dwarves. And my body was calling to it."

Marvin said, "I'm sorry. I would never have done any magic that affected you without asking, but when it happened, it felt right to let it happen. Now that I know I shouldn't, I will be more careful.

"What is spillover magic?"

Shandria smiled. "Your body absorbed more magical energy than it can hold. The extra energy was leaving your body. Like a glass too full, it was spilling over. And like water from an overflowing glass, it flowed to the lowest spot, which was my body. It was beyond your control, and I shouldn't have been so sensitive."

Shandria hugged him again. Marvin hugged her back. Then he realized they were once again naked and giving each other a full-frontal hug. His hormones started to respond. He released her and said. "I'm starved. I'm going to dress for dinner. He grabbed the door and pulled it open. Shandria walked through first. He stopped and opened the door to the room that held his clothes, put on some underwear, and picked out and put on an outfit.

Shandria told Marvin about the wonderful time she had with the Queen and her daughter, Amethyst. Amethyst was older than Shandria, but because Dwarves lived longer and matured slower, they were at the same maturity level. They rode through tunnels all the way to one of the settlements outside the wall.

Inside each entry-hill was a tunnel. The tunnels continued for several hundred yards from the entrance to a settlement of over a hundred Dwarves. Each community stored their wagons and farm implements underground and raised relatives of the ostrich, chickens, pig, and lope. Closer to the mountain there were small shop owners and craftsmen.

They exited the tunnels through one of the entry mounds. Snow covered the fields they rode by, but food grew during the spring. Amethyst said, "Beautiful wildflowers grow in the spring past the farms."

They returned in through the tunnels and ate lunch at a random diner. The queen used to eat at small restaurants when she was younger and decided she was going to start doing it again.

Marvin told Shandria about his experience with the blacksmith. He was going to work there if she thought it was a good idea.

Shandria thought about it and said, "It's your decision. If it grows your strength as fast as they say, it will be of benefit. It will make our evenings busy. Your magic has been growing incredibly fast, and I realized that I have to teach you more weaves, starting tomorrow night. But tonight, after dinner, I have a surprise.

Marvin was curious as to what the surprise was going to be. Shandria seemed extremely excited.

Chapter 23

Marvin was happy to see Shandria smiling, so he feigned excitement, but he wasn't. Shandria's surprise was she had visited the royal seamstress with the queen and her daughters after lunch. The seamstress was going to make her several new outfits. She was excited because she had arranged a visit from the court tailor for Marvin.

Alluvial announced, "The Queen and her entourage are here."

Marvin hadn't expected the queen. A visit from her was the real excitement.

Shandria rushed to the door herself to greet the Queen, followed by Marvin. She curtsied and greeted her and the Princess. The staff all bowed low. The queen told them to arise and greeted each of them fondly. Her daughter followed her mother's lead. With the queen were several people dressed in court attire, six soldiers of the queen's guard, the court tailor, and his assistants.

Marvin put one knee on the ground and bowed his head to the Queen. She stopped in front of him, smiled, and nodded her head. He stood up. She took his hands, and said, "The King and I are pleased that you will be learning the way of the forge. I can already feel its magic has touched you. I know it will give you strength. All of Crystal Mountain is excited for you. You are the first Atlantian to learn from the forge in many years. I know you will do well."

She introduced him to Princess Amethyst. He started to bow, but the queen held him up. "Since she followed me, and is junior to me, the proper way is to bow your head."

Marvin said, "Let's try this again from the top." He bowed his head, and said, "It is a pleasure to meet you." He raised his head high and smiled.

They looked to be about the same age, but Marvin knew from Shandria that she was far older. Princess Amethyst took his hands and held them for a second. He could feel the beating of the forge magic inside her. Marvin looked surprised. She saw the look on his face and said, "I spent many decades forging iron, and now I'm working as a journeyman silversmith. All members of the royal family get to spend time at the forge."

Marvin said, "All I met were men, and the job is so strenuous that I thought only men worked the mines and the forge. I owe you my apologies."

She said, "Would it surprise you to know that I am a warrior, just like Shandria? That I carry a crossbow into combat and a battle-ax?"

He replied, "I am surprised but in a pleasant way. Shandria is amazing in her abilities, and I have no doubt you are also." He shook his head. "I have a lot to learn about everything."

She smiled and said. "You will learn fast at the forge. But mastery takes a lifetime."

Shandria talked to Alluvial. A member of the staff escorted the guards to a room to relax. Alluvial accompanied Marvin and the tailors to another room for measurement. And Shandria accompanied the queen and her daughter on a tour of the embassy.

One of Alluvial's assistants brought in mugs of Mead for the tailors and Marvin. He had drunk spice wine with Shandria at dinner and would have preferred water, but it was the custom. He was glad the mugs were small. He suspected there was a nuance to the custom he didn't know.

The court tailor stood by and directed the junior tailors as they measured Marvin in places he would never have imagined needed measuring. On his left arm alone, they measured him around the wrist, from his wrist to his knuckles, and around the palm of his hand. They slipped rings on each finger and measured his ring size. They measured the length of his fingers. They measured him from his wrist back to his elbow, then from his elbow to his shoulder. They measured the circumference of his wrist, his lower arm, and his upper arm. At the same time, a second assistant measured his other side. They took what seemed like an endless number of measurements on the rest of his body.

But the weirdest measurements were the ones they took on his head. They measured his head not just with a tape measure, which he would have expected for a hat, but they used a set of large calipers to gauge the distance from the front of his head to the back, and from the left side to the right side. They measured his nose height, width, and length, as well as the distance between his eyes. Finally, the measurements were complete.

The tailor seemed irritated when Marvin told him he was going to start working in the foundry tomorrow at sunrise and needed some appropriate clothes. Maybe working clothes were beneath the tailor.

After the tailors had finished, Alluvial escorted them to the exit. She told Marvin, "Sir, Shandria and Queen Olivine request your presence in the garden."

The Queen, Princess Amethyst, and Shandria were girl talking, drinking out of wine glasses, sitting on lounges, and looking up at the sky. Marvin smiled and noted it was the first time he had ever seen Shandria keep her clothes on near a pool.

Shandria said, "I'm glad you are here. We want to look at a familiar sky."

Marvin wove magic towards the ceiling. He decided to show off, "Which do you prefer?" He changed the sky above them and said, "Crystal Mountain?" He let the stars stay for about fifteen seconds, and then he changed it again and said, "Or Atlantis?" The sky changed.

Princess Amethyst clapped. She turned towards Shandria and said, "I've never seen the stars of Atlantis before, how exciting."

Marvin chose a lounge near the ladies and looked up at the sky. He listened in, and they included him in their group, but it was obviously a woman's party.

He realized he needed to memorize the stars of Atlantis as well as Alfamara. He was glad it was the winter night sky. His favorite constellation was Orion, and he was using it as his focus for his magic. He closed his eyes trying to concentrate, to remember what he was seeing. His sword started talking to him. It hummed a beautiful melody that he knew was from Atlantis.

He heard his name called and opened his eyes. It was time to escort the queen and her daughter to the door.

After their guests had left, Marvin asked Shandria when they were going to select clothes. Shandria replied, "Don't worry. I know you are new to court and Atlantian fashions, so I am meeting with the queen and her daughter to select fabrics, colors, patterns and accessories. I'm sure you will be pleased."

Marvin hoped so. He was a casual dress, off the rack, clothing shopper. He even bought his suit off the rack for his fiancée and parent's funeral, and then wore it for his job interview. He told his grandmother to bury him in the suit when he died of cancer. Whether he lived or died, he doubted he would ever wear that suit again.

Marvin was up early since he needed to meet the escort at sunrise. He slipped out of bed and dressed. There was nothing appropriate for working in the mines, so he chose something plain to wear.

He ate a large breakfast. He was sure he would expend a lot of energy today.

His escort arrived early and presented him with a box. It contained a proper work outfit.

Marvin slipped into the closest room with a door and changed clothing. Part of his clothing included a large leather apron that extended from his neck down to his knees and large leather boots. The bundle contained a magically hardened leather helmet that was the Dwarven equivalent of a hard hat and a set of goggles. Once again, Marvin thought, steampunk.

Marvin followed his escort to his new job.

Chapter 24

No one starts at the top in any job, and iron working was no exception. Marvin moved more iron ore than he ever imagined existed.

He was sore, famished, dehydrated, and drunk at the end of the workday. The Dwarven concept of lunch was a large glass of mead. And they served Mead at every break. He started to wonder if Dwarves ever drank water, or if they could get drunk.

He thought to ask a Dwarf about the mead, but knew the Dwarven answer would be something like, "Why would any sane man drink water when he could drink mead?" or perhaps, "Every Dwarf knows the health benefits of mead." He joined in on the mead breaks they had every few hours to stay hydrated in the heat. If he didn't have his magic protecting him from the heat of the foundry, he would have passed out from heat and dehydration.

At the end of the day, the foreman thanked them as they filed out. He gave everyone a friendly punch on the shoulder or a slap on the back. The back slaps seemed to have no effect on the Dwarves, but they were hard enough to make Marvin's back sore.

He stripped and jumped into the pool. He drank as much water from the pool as his stomach would hold. Unlike his pool at home, magic purified the water, and there was no added chlorine. He relaxed in the pool.

Shandria came out already dressed for dinner. He saw her. He was too exhausted to climb out of the pool, so he crafted a magic weave, which picked him up like a pseudopod from a strange organism, set his feet on the deck, and collapsed back into the pool.

She was excited. She had a good day and had a lot to tell him. He smiled and said, "Let me dry out in the sun for a couple of minutes, then I'll dress and join you." He lay down on the lounge and closed his eyes.

When Marvin woke up the sky above him showed he had slept well into the night. He got up, thinking how he had planned to eat with Shandria. On the table next to him sat a basket of fruit and a covered plate of cooked vegetables, potatoes, and meat. His stomach responded by growling at him. He realized that Shandria must have left him the food since the staff stayed away from the pool area when anyone was there. Dwarves had a Victorian culture when it came to nudity. He was famished and ate his fill. His body was less exhausted, but he was still tired. He was surprised he wasn't sore, and even more surprised he wasn't hungover.

He did his best to be quiet and slipped into bed behind Shandria. After a few minutes, she backed into him, and he put his arm around her. She didn't say anything, and he didn't know if she had woken up or not. He fell asleep.

Shandria woke up later in the night. Marvin's arm was around her. She had wanted to tell Marvin about her busy day. They had selected fabrics and designs for their dresses and Marvin's new clothes. And she had started to work out with Princess Amethyst. They were using blunt wooden weapons and padding, but still, she was sore. Usually, she would have used healing magic, and the bruises and bumps would disappear in a few minutes, but she knew that could hurt her magic more than it helped her body.

She hoped Marvin could help her as he had the previous day in the pool, and she was interested in how he was doing. She could feel his strength growing daily. His arm around her felt stronger and bigger than it had just yesterday. She felt his magic spilling over and strengthening her body. She felt guilty as if she was stealing his magic, but she knew he had no control over it. It was helping her, and he would have not only volunteered but also insisted on helping her. She felt sad and ashamed that her magic wasn't able to heal herself or his cancer. She grabbed hold of the tiger's tooth around her neck and remembered she was more than her magic.

The next day Marvin cut the amount of mead he drank to less than half. He found a place in the foundry where the water wasn't too bad. It was warm, but easily cooled and purified with magic. The other ironworkers joked about their water-boy. But at one break, a coworker confided in him that they all understood his strength as an Atlantian was water, and theirs was earth and fire. He earned a big laugh when he said human slang for drinks containing a high alcohol content was firewater.

The ore containers felt lighter than they did yesterday, and he had more energy at the end of the shift. The chief metallurgist saw him and said, "Tomorrow don't just move the ore, look at the ore."

Marvin was recovered enough that evening to talk to Shandria during dinner. They talked about their day. Shandria mentioned his spill over magic. Marvin smiled and said, "I'm excited that I am helping you, even if it is accidental. I need to pay more attention to it so I can learn to do it as a weave and not just as spillover magic. You will have to teach me how to do a healing weave."

Shandria replied. "In time, but healing magic uses complex weaves. Atlantians have a natural aptitude for the magic of air, water, and sky. Air and water are elemental magic as are the Dwarven magic of earth and fire. So, earth and fire are easy for us to learn. Nature magic or wood magic is the magic of life. Life is complex and so healing weaves tend to be complex. Healing magic takes more time and practice for us than our natural magic. The master level magic that most Alfarins know is impossible for all but a rare Atlantian to weave.

After dinner, Marvin insisted on letting his spill over magic strengthen Shandria. He paid attention to the magical flow. The powerful magic in the foundry was supercharging him. He not only wanted to share it with Shandria, but his magic also wanted to be shared. Or as Shandria would say, magic wanted to help her friend Shandria.

He yawned. He apologized to Shandria for his tiredness and headed off to bed early.

Lifting the heavy containers of ore seemed easier the next day at the foundry. His foreman asked him if he was looking at the ore. Marvin said he was trying to but hadn't seen anything change.

The foreman walked over to a bucket of ore, selected a fist-sized piece, and handed it to Marvin. Then he walked with Marvin further into the mine. They took a rail car to an old elevator. The foreman rode with Marvin down the shaft. It was dark and became darker still. Marvin wove light magic as the elevator descended into the darkness.

The railcar stopped, and the foreman led Marvin through a maze of tunnels. He told Marvin, "Stay here until you see the ore." The foreman released the light weave, and it was suddenly pitch dark. The foreman said, "You will never see it with the lights on."

Marvin heard the foreman's steps get quieter as he walked away.

Marvin couldn't see anything. He closed his eyes for several minutes to get his eyes adapted to the dark. It didn't help. He put his hand in front of his face. He wiggled his fingers but still couldn't see them. It wasn't just dark. There was no light from anywhere. Marvin understood where the phrase "dark as the inside of a coal mine" came from.

Marvin tried looking at the iron ore. It was as just as dark as the rest of the tunnel. Time passed. He sat down with his back to the wall. His mind wandered. His magic showed him the inside of the tunnel, but then Marvin realized, he could see the magic in the air, but the rock of the tunnel was dark. He tried probing the rock in his hand with magical threads, with no result. After what seemed like hours, Marvin found himself nodding off, and his stomach was growling. He realized the foreman had grabbed him just before lunch.

He didn't know how long he sat there. He must have fallen asleep because he found himself waking up. He had a brief moment of panic. "How long was I asleep? What would I do if they left me here? Could I get out?"

Marvin calmed down. If it came to it, Marvin could craft a light weave. But for now, he was determined to stay here in the dark. He shook the iron ore. He talked to the ore. He yelled at the ore. He banged his fist against the ore, and nothing happened. He even tried tasting the ore with his tongue.

He closed his useless eyes and started thinking about the time in the mines, the hard work that made him stronger, the exciting but scary heat and glow of the furnace, and the song of the forge. He started to hum to the rhythm of the forge. Then he saw a flash from the ore, then another. He kept humming the rhythm. Slowly the ore responded. It was generating a dim magical light, which was starting to glow brighter. Then he saw it. The iron ore was composed of several different colors. It was translucent, like looking at the different colored fruit inside a bowl of gelatin.

Around him, he could see the glow of the ores and minerals in the tunnel. He saw veins of several different colors and a few rocky outcroppings. The earth magic was responding to his humming. He stopped humming and realized it wasn't the hum. The song of the forge had introduced him as a friend to the magic. Earth magic was slow and shy but had accepted him. It was now talking to him and showing itself.

He stood up and walked around. He could see the tunnels around him like a three-dimensional cutout. Even the floor was translucent. He could see the multi-colored veins of rocks and minerals running through it. There were many different shades and intensities of color. Marvin realized he would have to learn what each was.

Marvin identified the shaft he had come down and walked back. The elevator was at the top of the shaft, and there was no way for him to have it lowered. After waiting for several minutes, he looked around some more. Several hundred yards away there was another vertical shaft with an elevator. He walked to the second elevator. Then he saw some movement in a distant shaft. He walked there and found several Dwarves mining rock and shoveling ore into a mine car. The workers were surprised to see him without a pick and wearing the wrong helmet. But their foreman wasn't. He handed him a pick and a new helmet.

The foreman said, "I guess I lost the bet. I was sure I would have to get you at the end of the shift."

The foreman yelled, "Break." and all the miners stopped working. He said to Marvin, "I am now your foreman for the next few days, starting right after the break."

One of the Dwarves handed him a mug of mead. His nickname of water boy had stuck with him, and the foreman had a pitcher of water, which Marvin was happy to drink along with his mead. They talked during their break. The Dwarves laughed and kidded him because seeing rock and ore was some of the first magic their children developed.

Marvin had a pseudopod of mead poke out from a pitcher and point back and forth like it was a strange creature looking at them and said, "And liquid magic is one of the first things Atlantians learn." Everyone laughed.

There were no lights in the underground mines because the miners didn't need them. On the way out, they took Marvin through a tunnel to a chamber filled with various crystalline minerals. It was beautiful; the colors were spectacular. Marvin's jaw dropped open.

ATLANTIAN MAGIC

Marvin saw one craftsman working with a small hand tool, carefully exposing a large crystal. It was a place of reverence for the miners because of the beauty. But today they were here to see Marvin's reaction. He realized that few people other than the Dwarves could see this beauty. He felt humbled. He didn't know what to say, so he said, "This is amazingly beautiful. Thank you for showing this to me, my friends."

He didn't even mind the slap on the back from his new foreman. That evening he took a different hard hat home. More dirt covered him than coal dust.

The fastest way to the mine was closer to the embassy, but he had to walk all the way back to where he had stabled his horse. This time when he returned to the embassy, he found Shandria in the pool. He joined her. He had none of the overflow magic from the refinery. But he had activated his earth magic when he saw the ore, and he allowed it to flow into Shandria.

Shandria had asked the staff to serve dinner later so that they could spend some time in the pool. She decided Marvin needed more time soaking to get the dust off. After dinner, Marvin spent time training with his sword and Shandria taught him a new water weave.

Shandria was training with Princess Amethyst, and they had added in several other warriors. Marvin was surprised to find out that even though the regular army was almost all men, the militia was nearly all women. Men took the field in battle, and women protected the home from attack.

Marvin worked in the mine the following two days. He learned how to listen to and see the rock, and to tell differences in layering and stratification. He watched the veins of gold, copper, and silver winding through the mountain, and he saw the stress inside the rock. Too much stress and the rock would crumble. Dwarves dug carefully and strengthened the rock as they dug to prevent a collapse of the tunnel.

He reported to the mine for his third day. They took him to a place that had pillars of sandstone and granite. He learned how to weave earth magic to make the sandstone as hard and compact as granite and to make the granite soft and brittle as sandstone, or to turn it to sand. Builders magic-hardened the stone pillars in the city to make them as strong as any steel construction beam. Then Marvin learned how to weave earth magic to strengthen his body. After that, the foreman's slap on the back became the mark of camaraderie it was supposed to be.

Marvin had the next two days off, and he wanted to spend some time outside. His arrival back at the embassy found Shandria excited. The tailor had a new set of clothing he was bringing over for Marvin to try on. Shandria had already tried on everything but her gown, and she would have a final fitting tomorrow morning. They splashed around in the pool for a few minutes. Then they dressed and waited for the tailor.

The tailor arrived with his assistants. Marvin tried on his first outfit. He was happy with the fit, but the tailor wasn't. The tailor thought it was too tight. Marvin's muscles, aided by magic, had grown at an exponential rate while he had worked in the mines. Dwarven society wore loose clothes on their arms and legs. Marvin was happy with the fit of his clothing, but to the tailor, it was too tight. The tailor refused to let Marvin try on the outfit for the ball. Marvin asked, "What ball?"

Shandria replied, "The King and Queen invited us to attend a royal ball tomorrow evening at the palace."

Marvin went into shock, so did Shandria but on a different subject. Shandria was all worried Marvin's suit wouldn't be ready, but the tailor assured her he would get Marvin's suit read by lunchtime tomorrow. Shandria calmed down, but not Marvin.

He was going to a royal ball. He didn't know the customs, he didn't know the music, and he didn't know any of their dances. Carol had insisted they take a semester-long dance class, which taught his two left feet to dance the two-step, which they jokingly called the two left feet step, but Marvin was sure the Dwarves had never heard of the western waltz or the country two-step.

He told Shandria his fears right after the tailor left. Shandria said, "That's why we have a dance instructor coming over in an hour. Let's eat."

The dance instructor included a complement of six advanced student dancers and a six-piece orchestra. He was shocked that Marvin knew none of the dances and none of the melodies.

Marvin, the instructor, and Shandria became frustrated and tired after three hours of dance lessons. Shandria knew all the standard dances. She thought the dance lessons would be fun. Maybe she would pick up some new variation. But Marvin was starting from scratch. He failed to learn any of the six couple dances, the men only circle dances, or the line dances.

Shandria pleaded with the instructor to come back tomorrow. He huddled with his people. Then he relented. The instructor and his dance group would be over an hour after sunrise. Maybe he could teach Marvin one of the basic dances. They would pass the word that their dances and music were far different from Earth, and they should feel honored that he had worked so hard to learn even one dance for the ball. But Marvin had a different idea.

Chapter 25

Marvin told Shandria he would get to bed late. He had to practice with his sword. Shandria woke up sometime after midnight. She searched and found he wasn't in the royal wing. She threw on a night robe and walked out to the common area. She found him in the ballroom, with his sword, but he wasn't practicing swordsmanship.

Marvin was holding his sword high in his extended left hand. His right hand was on his right hip. He danced in a circle around the sword. Then he spun 180 degrees, now his hand with the sword was on his left hip, and his right hand was up in the air. He rotated around his right hand, then backed away and bowed. Then he walked with both hands on his hips to the next imaginary lady in line before raising up his sword again and taking her imaginary hand.

Shandria watched him until the dance was over. Then she started clapping.

Marvin sheathed his sword. He had closed his eyes as he concentrated on the dance, so he hadn't seen her watching him. He was a little embarrassed. Shandria ran over and gave Marvin a big hug. His invisible partner and silent music were memories from the sword. Just like his sword training, he was learning how to dance. Since the memories included all the muscle movements, he had condensed months of dance lessons into a few hours.

He picked Shandria up around her waist and set her down, something he didn't have the strength to do only a few weeks ago. Then he stepped back, bowed and held out his hand. He started humming a song. Then he started moving, all the while humming. Shandria was impressed. He was having some minor problems with his hand position, but then she wasn't a sword. She had no doubt they would quickly correct it tomorrow morning. He was already getting the feel of her hand and starting to correct it. Once more around the circle and he stopped. They both laughed. Marvin's mouth opened wide in a big yawn. Shandria said, "It's past our bedtime. I can't wait until dance lessons tomorrow." Marvin was asleep as soon as his head hit the pillow.

Marvin was tired when sunrise came. Of all the things he missed from Earth, coffee was at the top of his list this morning. He had dance lessons in the morning, a meeting with the tailor, and then time for a nap before getting ready for the ball.

Pd MICHEL

The dance instructor was shocked. Marvin had gone from a failing, hopeless student to the top of the class overnight. He was dancing an older version of two of the dances, but Marvin quickly shifted from a 'side, cross, side' to a 'side, spin, and step.' One of the men only circle dances was entirely different. Marvin would skip the dance.

Last night the instructor was afraid someone would know he had tried teaching Marvin to dance. But now he wanted to brag about it.

Marvin was wondering if he could take his nap early, but the tailor showed up. The suit for the ball fit well, but Marvin felt ridiculous in it. The suit was an aqua color with shiny sequins. The legs were wide bell bottoms. The collar stuck up like a tail fin of some fish. When he moved to the side, his collar lagged behind and then flowed back towards the middle. He felt like his collar was a fin swaying in the ocean current. All he needed was a black hair wig, sunglasses, and a sign saying "Elvis Live" to complete the outfit.

The tailor was proud of Marvin's new suit, but almost died when he saw Marvin strap on his sword. The old leather sheath did not complete the outfit. He hadn't realized that Marvin had the title of Dwarf-friend, which allowed him to wear his sword in the king's presence, or that his being the princesses' protector demanded him to wear it.

He asked Marvin to remove his sword from the sheath. He measured its dimensions. He hoped he would be able to find something to either cover the sheath or to make a new sheath for the sword. When he realized it was one of the ancient swords, he decided to cover the sheath. If the sword didn't like the sheath, it would complain. He grew frantic when he found out the king had given Marvin the sword. The king could consider it an insult if Marvin didn't wear his sword.

He may have a secure job with the court, but he also had a reputation to keep that both ensured the crown wanted him, and that nobility wanted him also.

Marvin managed to catch a couple of hours of sleep after lunch. Shandria spent all afternoon getting ready. At dinner that evening, she looked stunning. And after another half hour of putting on makeup, which Marvin didn't think she needed, she looked even more so. Her dress was beautiful. The sheath for her sword matched the dress. Shandria was wearing an aqua colored dress. Hers was a greener shade, and his outfit was bluer.

Princess Shandria sat at the royal table with the king, queen, and several members of the court. Sir Marvin sat at a table to the side as her official protector. There were various other guards in their formal military dress. No one wore anything like Marvin, but then most of the dancers were in formal military uniforms. He felt out of place wearing his Elvis suit.

They served mead and spiced wine. The king and queen danced the first dance. Then the princes, princesses, and the officials of the realm danced. Marvin

122

stood up when Shandria did. He held out his arm when she approached. She took it, and he escorted her to the floor.

Marvin almost panicked when he didn't know the song. Shandria helped him recognize the beat. It had the same beat as one he knew, and then he knew which dance to dance. At the conclusion of the dance, he escorted Shandria back to the table, but the king took Shandria's arm. She curtsied and walked to the dance floor with him.

Marvin walked back to his seat and sat down. He saw the queen approach him, stood up, and then bowed low. Queen Olivine said, "It's Dwarven dance custom to allow the queen to take your arm so you can escort her to the dance floor."

Marvin smiled and held out his arm. Queen Olivine took it, and they exchanged smiles. It was a lovely dance. Marvin escorted the Queen to her seat. The queen had a servant place Marvin's chair at the table. Some of the initial formality was now relaxed. Several of the ministers added a lady of the court to their part of the table.

The king and queen had taken on an almost parental interest in Marvin. And they were both happy with his progress. The court metallurgist came over. He presented an ornate wooden box to the king, who handed it to Princess Shandria. She opened it and then quickly shut it and put it down.

The Queen said. "The cursed stones have been destroyed and replaced. It can no longer harm you." Shandria said, "Where? How?"

The queen said, "Sir Marvin pulled it out of the lake. We destroyed the cursed gem and restored the necklace as a gift of friendship to you."

Shandria looked at it again. She realized how much the necklace meant to her. She spontaneously hugged the queen, then the king, and finally Marvin. She asked Marvin to put it on her and turned around for him to fasten it. Her outfit had felt like something was missing. Now it felt complete. She had scars caused by the cursed necklace on her neck, and the new necklace covered them. She grabbed Princess Amethyst and ran to find a mirror.

Marvin thanked the queen and king for their generosity and for the way they explained about the necklace. Queen Olivine said, "She will ask you how and when you retrieved the necklace. I suggest you tell her the full story soon."

"I will." promised Marvin.

After they had returned from looking in the mirror, Princess Shandria took Marvin out onto the dance floor. It was a slow, low volume dance. The first thing out of her mouth was. "How did you recover my necklace?"

He told her the full story. She said, "Thank you. I couldn't ask for a better protector and friend." She hugged and kissed him lightly on his lips.

When the dance was over, Princess Amethyst asked Marvin to dance. They walked onto the dance floor. Dwarven courtesy required they respect a couple's right to only dance with each other. Marvin dancing with Princess Amethyst was the social signal that both Shandria and Marvin would dance with someone else.

Since Shandria and Marvin were the guests of honor, they were hot commodities. Shandria understood the court social power points. Each dance added to or took away social points. Being a princess, she made sure to stay neutral and spread around the points.

But Marvin was oblivious and danced with anyone who asked. He only turned down one dance. He apologized and told the lady he didn't know the dance. She was upset. But Marvin recognized the next dance. He walked over to her and asked her to dance with him.

To ask someone from the court table to dance was a questionable social move. If they said yes, it was a social positive. If they said no, it was a minor social negative. Marvin, asking her to dance, was far more positive than his initially turning her down, so she earned double points. Marvin shook his head when Shandria tried explaining it to him.

Shandria and Marvin danced together for the last two dances. She was in her element, and Marvin was glad to see her smiling. Dancing the last two dances together neutralized any thoughts that they were interested in anyone else. There would be no talking of suitors, even though cross marriage was rare and children were impossible. Shandria was destined to marry an Atlantian Prince, and dancing with Marvin in her mind was the same as dancing with her brother.

After the ball, Marvin and Shandria let their coach wait, while they looked at the front of the building once more. The pictures of Feldspar the Great were not just artistic. They were a masterpiece of Dwarven magic. Marvin could have spent hours looking at the internal construction of the stonework, which his earth magic sight now revealed, but Shandria was tired, and so was he. They rode back to the embassy.

Chapter 26

The following morning, they both slept late. Marvin felt recovered and stronger than ever. Shandria was still sleeping when he left the bed.

Shandria woke up and dressed for breakfast. She found Marvin practicing with his sword. The added strength in his leg muscles allowed him to perform the deeper stances. She watched him. He was performing the water kata of the Atlantian Kings. The water kata simulated a fight and trained muscles and movement. An outsider would consider it a choreographed dance done with a sword, but the moves in combat were lethal.

Shandria took off her clothes and grabbed her sword. When Marvin finished, she joined him and said. "Again." She followed Marvin at his speed. Unlike Marvin, still following his sword's instruction, she had mastered the kata and molded it to reflect her personal style and body type. Water was fluid and likewise was the kata. The basic kata remained the same, but each student made subtle changes on their way to making the kata their own. Today she performed the base kata to mirror Marvin.

After breakfast, Shandria and Marvin packed a lunch and spent the day horseback riding. They traveled through the tunnels. The tunnel complex amazed Marvin. Non-magic vision only saw rock and stone, but the magical eye showed the full beauty. The Dwarves had built the tunnels and woven them with magic for strength and beauty. He was surprised to find out Shandria had never developed her earth magic to where she could see into the rock.

Colorful patterns decorated much of the tunnel, but relief drawings, like the front of the palace, adorned many areas. The reliefs didn't just bulge out. Each drawing was three-dimensional. Most of the drawing was inside the rock and could only be seen using magic.

They stopped in a small farming enclave before leaving the tunnels. The people were excited to meet the Atlantian princess. And they were thrilled when Marvin admired the artistry of their tunnel, particularly as it was invisible if you didn't see the earth magic.

Some of the children were shy of them because of their size. Shandria sat down on the ground and soon she was talking to them about the seas of Atlantis. They thought she was making up the stories. All they had ever seen was a few fish that brave Dwarven entertainers would catch and put on display.

Marvin started asking them about the beauty of a relief drawing in one of the walls. It was a story of planting and harvest. It would have been in a museum on Earth, and they would have missed the real beauty and layering of ore and crystals. The drawing was a 3-D masterpiece extending several yards deep below the surface of the rock and was only visible through magic.

On the wall opposite, was an unfinished work, and Marvin realized it never would be finished. The children used it as a chalkboard, honing their talents and drawing pictures of animals, some real and some imaginary. At least Marvin hoped the scarier animals were imaginary and not real. But after seeing a picture of a narworm, he couldn't be sure of anything.

They convinced Shandria and Marvin to stay for lunch. They all ate out of a series of large bowls. The farmers were far from the palace, yet they had hearts as big as the mountain.

Too soon, it was time to go. Shandria saw how tiny the children were and how much love their parents had for them. She knew that once she returned to Atlantis and was well, the process to choose a prince would begin. A drop of desire for motherhood touched her heart. She hoped she would find a suitor as funny, gentle, and brave as Marvin for her prince.

They said goodbye to their friends and exited the hill. The sunshine was blinding, reflecting off the snow. Their horses shied away from the sudden brightness of the outdoor sun. Marvin and Shandria turned their horses, so their backs were towards the sun to allow their eyes a chance to adjust.

They rode their horses through knee-deep snow to the main road. Only a few inches of snow was on the road, and they found they could coax their horses up to a slow trot. Soon they came to the Northern gate of the city. Shandria showed them a royal seal, which allowed them free transportation through any gate.

They rode north until a gentle hill put them out of sight of the north wall. Shandria dismounted, and so did Marvin. Marvin sunk knee deep into the snow. He would have to enchant his new boots. Shandria said, "Let's see how your water magic is coming along."

Marvin pointed and said, "The river is that way."

Shandria said, "Your magic isn't powerful enough to affect the river from this far away. Did you forget snow surrounds us?"

Marvin hit his forehead with the palm of his hand and laughed. A few weeks ago, everything was snow and ice. He saw a mound of snow and blew it apart to warm up his magic. Then he wove the magic that created a wave of water in the pool, but it didn't work well. Shandria was smiling. She said, "Listen to the snow then try again."

Marvin discovered that snow and ice were sleeping water. Marvin had to tickle the snow awake, then the snow responded. It gathered itself together into a mound

ATLANTIAN MAGIC

He was playing in the snow, making shapes and converting the snow to water, ice, and back again, when something hit him in the back. He turned around, and another snowball hit him. Marvin grabbed a large mound of snow with his magic.

Shandria yelled, "Not fair! I can't use my magic!"

Marvin used his magic to toss the mound high into the air, and it came down as snow. He picked up some snow and compressed it into a snowball while trying to dodge several snowballs Shandria had already made. He threw a snowball. Shandria dodged and threw three back. This wasn't working. She had a pile of snowballs already made and ready to throw.

He made another one and rushed her. She threw one more snowball and then ran away. He pursued. He was sure she wasn't running her fastest. He hadn't enchanted his new boots, and he was sinking knee-deep into the snow with each step. He soon caught up with her. He grabbed her from behind, and amid her laughter he half laid, half threw her into a snow bank. She repaid his gentleness by pulling him down beside her, laughing all the time, then getting up and running back to her mound of snowballs.

He stood up amid a hail of snowballs and chased after her again. This time he picked her up and used a high school wrestling move to get on top of her. They were laughing uncontrollably. Marvin felt like a kid again, rolling in the snow in Flagstaff with his girlfriend. Then he realized that girlfriend was not part of Shandria's reality. He rolled off her and lay in the snow beside her.

She said, "That was so much fun. It was what my sister and I used to do when we visited the snow. Thanks for reminding me of her."

Marvin swallowed his feelings. She was reminding him of spending time in Flagstaff with his fiancee. He stood up, reached down and said, "Truce." She grabbed his hand and said, "Truce." He helped her stand up.

Shandria said, "One last weave before we leave. I want you to clear as much of the snow from the road north of us as you can in one weave."

Marvin sent a blast of energy, which removed the snow for a dozen yards.

Shandria said, "No I want you to use complex weaves and powerful magic. Don't blast the snow in front of you. Talk to the snow. Weave magic to have it pass the message on down the road as far as it can, then concentrate hard and weave the strongest magic you can. Let the snow accept it and use its own energy."

Marvin collected and focused all the magic he could. He asked the snow particles to talk to each other like a signal passing over the internet. Then he released his weave. The snow particles spoke to each other and used the magic around them to augment Marvin's magic. The snow parted, and the road was clear beyond the next rise, which was as far as they could see.

His heart was racing, and he was breathing hard when he finished.

Shandria was clapping. She hugged Marvin. "I knew you could do it. You opened that portal a few weeks back, but this was your first use of controlled master level magic. And it was your own weave, and not one I taught you. I'm so proud of you."

Shandria whistled and their horses, which were digging through the snow with their hoofs and noses looking for vegetation, started walking toward them. They walked and met the horses partway. This time they rode down the king's road towards Crystal Mountain. The guard saw them coming, but once again, he quoted regulation 1128.3. The portcullis was always open during the day.

They practiced with their swords that evening after eating a tasty dinner. It was a good day.

The next two days Marvin spent tending the fire at the refinery. Shoveling the coal was hot, dirty, dangerous work. But Marvin's magic reacted and protected him from the flames. Midway through the second day, Marvin started seeing the magic in the fire, not just the threads, but the weaves the Dwarves were using to control the heat. He could feel the fire, but the fire no longer burned him. The third day, the foreman of the flame had him practice controlling and manipulating the flames. Dwarves could have used magic to heat the furnace, and they did to start up a cold furnace, but the burning of the coal in the furnace ate up the oxides in the ore and was part of the traditional refining process.

Marvin worked for a blacksmith the rest of the week. The blacksmith and Marvin would alternate hammering on the glowing red steel. The Smith would rotate the iron and keep it at the best temperature. The blacksmith's trained eyes could tell how hot the metal was by the glow and by how much his hammer had shaped the iron. Marvin saw the blacksmith's magic keeping the fire at the optimum temperature. But the iron, now no longer ore, was dark to Marvin's magic. Halfway through the day, the blacksmith had him change arms. He wasn't here just to hammer iron. He was here to gain strength in both arms. The pace of hammering slowed down until Marvin grew better at hammering with his left arm.

The following week was more of the same, but Marvin's arms were no longer sore. And the rhythm of the pounding became monotonous. He started daydreaming and humming to the melody of the forge. Then Marvin saw it, first as a flash and then later sustained. He saw the crystalline structure of the metal. It changed colors as the hammer, and the heat forged the metal. And he saw the magic jump like a spark between the blacksmith's hammer to the metal, each time the hammer struck.

His hammer was affecting the shape of the metal, but there was no magical spark. It took him two more days of hammering before the first sparks jumped as his hammer struck the metal. Several more hits later, it repeated, but it was random.

His blacksmith started to sing. The blacksmith around him joined in. Marvin began to hum. He could feel the rhythm of the forge. It was in the cadence of the hammer rising and falling. The blacksmith had felt the first sparks of Marvin's forge magic, the magic of iron, and so had the other blacksmiths. They knew he was close and they wanted to help him over the edge. The forge was alive with magical threads, each of the smiths was sending him help, sending him magical threads.

Then the magic started to spark through his hammer into the metal. But it was their magic, not his. Their magic was now flowing through him. It became easier with each strike of the hammer, more natural, and then he felt the magic join his. His magic had made room for the magic of metal to join his magic family. The magic of metal grew and started to come from him. With each strike, it became stronger and stronger. And the magic of earth and fire learned and grew stronger inside him.

Marvin was lost in the hammering; the rhythm became a soothing new friend. It reminded him of how he would get lost in the rhythm of his footsteps on a long-distance run or the rhythm of his arm strokes on a long-distance swim. The blacksmith finished his plow and started hammering metal straight from the furnace. Soon Marvin saw the impurities that were still in the metal. He saw how the hammer of the smith and his magic were driving them out of the metal, but the metal needed some trace elements. The magic responded to the blacksmith and distributed the trace elements as directed. The blacksmith controlled both the temperature of the metal and the enchanting magic.

Marvin was lost in the process, mesmerized as he helped to finish the new plow. Marvin was shocked back to himself when they poured a tankard of cold water on top of him.

There were half a dozen Dwarves around him. All were laughing, happy for him. Each one slapped him on the back and congratulated him. They escorted him to the break room, where they passed around the mead. Dwarves drinking and singing filled the break room. It was halfway through the afternoon shift, yet no one returned to work. The forge magic had made a new friend. It was worth celebrating.

Forge magic, like all magic of solids, had a natural persistence, and the magic in his system was still there. Marin needed a break for the magic to normalize and find its place in his body. Being Atlantian his balance came from cool fluid magic, and the heat and solidity of forge magic were pulling him off his center. The foreman said he was done for the week, with a prescription to stay cool and practice Atlantian magic.

The head forge master would evaluate him come Monday and see if he was ready to continue. They kept Marvin's mug full during the celebration. And they kept offering him toasts. His foreman escorted him to the stables. Marvin doubted there were any laws against drinking and riding, but he realized he was too drunk to mount his horse safely. He walked the horse home, taking his time to sober up a little.

When he arrived home, Shandria saw how drunk he was. She saw the strange magic inside his body. He apologized and told her the story in a slurred voice. She had him lay down on one of the lounges. He quickly fell asleep.

He woke up several hours later. He felt like every strike of his hammer had hit him in the head. He drank a pitcher of water, relieved his bladder, and fell back to sleep. Later that night he woke up again and joined Shandria in bed.

The next morning, he was hung over, but he still worked out with his sword before jumping into the pool to clean off. Shandria finished her morning workout and joined him. He told her in a much more coherent manner what had happened, including what the forge master had said to him. So, when Shandria said she was going to get her comb, he lifted her onto the deck with a pseudopod of water. She grabbed her comb, jumped back in, and started combing her hair. Marvin played with his water magic until Shandria climbed out to dry off. Then he joined her. They dressed and enjoyed breakfast together. Shandria talked nonstop about her training with the Dwarves.

Marvin's skin felt hot as if he had a high fever, but he didn't feel sick. He stayed at home. He could feel the heat of the forge and the power of the metal magic slowly receding. Water, air and sky, those were the natural magic for Atlantians. So, he let his sword teach him. And he played with his magic and his sword all day long.

Shandria came home and opened the door to the garden. A cloud of fog so thick that she couldn't see the pool from the door hung in the air. She yelled, "Marvin!"

Then she felt a swirl of air. A small whirlwind pulled the mist and collected it over the center of the pool. A small cloud formed from the mist then precipitated out into the pool.

Marvin yelled back. "Hi, Shandria. I must have lost track of time. How was your day?"

"Tiring."

Shandria started to take her clothes off. She saw that Marvin was in the smaller pool above the main pool. The pool waterfall flowed down from the smaller pool. He said, "Join me up here."

Shandria climbed and sat down in the pool. She was expecting cool water. "How did the water get so warm?"

Marvin replied, "I found the weave where water and fire magic can exist together. I heated up the water in the upper pool, making it into a hot tub. We use hot tubs of water on Earth to relax sore muscles. I can cool it down if you like."

Shandria wasn't sure whether she should be upset or not. It was hotter than the south sea on Atlantis. "I guess I will give it a try."

Marvin smiled. "May I weave magic to strengthen your body?"

Shandria reluctantly said, "Yes." She felt the strange magic inside him and realized that even after playing with water magic all day long strange magic still supercharged his body.

The warm water of the upper pool and the magic boost from Marvin relaxed Shandria. She was happy about the progress of Marvin's magic and enjoyed honing her non-magic sword work. And each evening she was his magic instructor. But each day she missed using her magic more and more. And she was starting to resent her dependency on Marvin. He knew far fewer weaves than she did, yet he was weaving magic as complex as she had ever used. And he was learning Dwarven magic few Atlantians knew.

She knew it was wrong; she owed him a debt for stopping the necklace from killing her, twice, but she resented depending on him a little more each day. And she was resenting his growth in earth magic, fire magic, and the strange magic he called metal magic or forge magic. She was angry with herself. Here she was in the perfect place to learn new magic, and she was unable. That evening it all came out at dinner.

Chapter 27

"I am not a cripple! I'm a princess of Atlantis. I don't need your help!"

Marvin stepped back from Shandria's chair. He had gone around behind her after dinner to slide her seat back so she could stand up. He was trying to show respect for her, a custom his grandmother from the south had taught him, and it was also a show of respect in Atlantis.

"You're treating me like I'm some frail old great grandmother and I'm about to break in two. I've killed wolves and bears with a sword, and I rode the waves of the riptide of Sebastial in a shallod. I don't need some peasant from Earth to treat me as if I'm a frail old great-grandmother! Why did I ever go on this stupid journey with you? Leave me alone!"

Shandria stormed off towards their personal quarters.

Marvin was stunned. He felt his anger flare up, and it continued to build. He yelled at her as the door slammed behind her, "You're a self-centered, selfish princess who treats me worst then your horse. You convinced me to go on this quest so you would have someone to order about and to help you get healed. This was never about me being healed; It has always been about you."

She didn't care about him or his feelings for her. She found him vulnerable, took him from his home, and convinced him to follower her on this foolish quest.

He realized the fire magic inside him, strengthened by the magic of metal inside him, and the pounding of the forge magic was reinforcing his anger. He tried controlling his emotions. But the illogic of his anger fought against him. He knew his emotions were too extreme a reply to her outburst. It was the wrong thing to do. But his frustration and anger, fueled by the imbalance of his new magic built up. Marvin started to take deep, slow breaths. It began slowly to cool down the fire within him.

He walked into the garden with the intent of jumping into the pool and saw Shandria coming out from the private quarters. She glared at him.

Marvin saw the look in her eyes as she stormed past him. His anger responded and burst past the damn of control Marvin was trying to erect, and this time he was pushed past his desire to control it. He now felt justified in his anger. Marvin had lost the battle. The out of balance magic inside him was now controlling his reason, "It is the right thing to do!"

ATLANTIAN MAGIC

He became madder and madder. Not just at Shandria but at everything. The last rational thought he had was to take off his clothing and jump into the pool. But when he looked at his clothing, all he saw was an Atlantian costume, the one he wore at her insistence for their evening meal. He thought, "Hell, she didn't even let me choose my own clothes but chose them for me. She likes this outfit, well I don't!" He grabbed his shirt top, and using his forge-hardened muscles, he ripped it in half. He never asked for this crazy adventure.

He wanted to decide his fate, not have her decide for him. He was a free man, and she had convinced him to be a second-class citizen in a world he didn't understand.

Her companion? Damn it, he treated the dog he grew up with better than she treated him. He was just the body she used to stay warm at night. She cared nothing about him, his feelings, or his needs. She would have preferred to kill him when they first met. Well, he wouldn't be a bother to her anymore. He wasn't the property of a spoiled Atlantian princess. He was a free man from Earth!

The anger inside him controlled him, and he didn't have the emotional energy to fight it. The fire of the forge inside him flared. The pieces of his shirt, still hanging from his body, caught fire. He finished ripping them off and threw them on the ground. He stripped out of the rest of his clothing and tossed them into the pile of burning clothes. They were Atlantian clothing. He didn't need them, and he didn't want them. He had his clothing from Earth. He stormed back to the room where his clothing was.

His blue jeans were tight around the leg muscles and the seat, but loose around the waist. His shirt was too small to put on. His arms were too muscular, and so was his back and shoulders. He grabbed the sweatshirt out of his pack. Rather than being baggy, it was tight around his shoulders, but it stretched and covered him. He put on his Earth socks and boots. All he had left that was Atlantian was his sword.

But Shandria hadn't given it to him. The sword itself had called him, and the Dwarven king had given it to him. Dwarves forged it in the fires that now fueled his anger. And he had traded it for his camping knife, so it was his.

He threw on his pack and grabbed his poncho. Alluvial met him at the front. He sharply said, "I need my horse, now."

Alluvial saw the fire of Marvin's anger in his eyes and heard it in his voice. He hurried away.

Alluvial ran and told one of the other servants to get a horse. Marvin stormed out the front door. The fire of the forge was fueling the anger inside him. It was baby magic. Like a crying child, it demanded its way. It was yelling too loud to ignore, and it was winning. Marvin grew angrier at the wait, and his anger was beyond his ability to control.

When the servant handed him the reigns of his horse, he grabbed them, mounted the horse, and galloped off towards the mountain entrance gate. It was always open, and he rode through the gate, and down the road. Several minutes later, he came to the first wall and stopped at the gate.

The Dwarf yelled up at him. "Passage through the gate is closed after sunset without proper authorization per regulation number…"

Marvin didn't bother to listen to the rest. He galloped along the wall until he came to a large snowdrift. The snow picked him and his horse up in a large pseudopod of white and placed them on the wall. A pseudopod met them from the other side of the wall, grabbed them and set them down on the other side. His horse was scared and wanted to run. That's what Marvin wanted also. He encouraged it.

He hung on as it galloped back to the road and headed towards the second wall. He horse was exhausted when he arrived at the wall. Marvin didn't care. He didn't need the horse. It was only slowing him down, so he dismounted.

He grabbed another pile of snow. It lifted him up in another white pseudopod. He wove another pod on the other side of the wall to let him down the other side. Then he stood on the pseudopod, and it started to move. The pseudopod became a small mound, then a wave. He glided over the snow, powered by magic. He headed northwest, riding on the top of a wave of snow. He knew his destination. He had formed a portal there and almost left for home. He could do it again.

Snow was falling. It started to snow harder, and the wind was blowing. Marvin let out his air magic, and the wind started howling.

Marvin was hot. He took his poncho off. Then he took off the sweat-shirt and shoved them into his pack. Rolling hills of snow covered the field in front of him. He rode them up and down like a mad captain of a ship at sea riding the waves. The howling of the wind was blowing in his ears and his face. "It should be at my back," he thought. "The wind is always at the captain's back. And I am the captain of my fate, not some princess."

The winter storm should have cooled him off and allowed him to regain his senses. But he wasn't a candle. He was a hot forge fire. As a bellows caused coals to glow hotter, the wind fueled the heat inside him and his anger. It just made the baby magic inside him cry louder.

He wove magic and controlled its direction. The wind swung around and soon was at his back. He looked up at the stars. He couldn't see them through the clouds. But he could see them with magic. He was the captain of a ship made of snow in a blizzard. His Atlantian magic was trying to exert itself to help Marvin balance himself, but it was overwhelmed.

ATLANTIAN MAGIC

Marvin was half hallucinating in a fantasy. His course was north by northwest. The wind was blowing his ship onwards. He heard and felt the thunder of the storm beating against his bare skin, the rhythmic thunder, like the sound of a hammer hitting metal. The thunder of the hammer inside him matched the crash of waves against the bow of his ship. The crash was harder and louder with each strike. On and on he sailed his boat of snow. He was mad from his anger, mad from his lack of balance, and mad from the new magic inside him that he hadn't learned to control.

Chapter 28

Shandria smelled, before she saw, the pile of burnt clothing after working out most of her anger in the training room. She was frustrated at the course of events in her life and not at Marvin. Seeing him grow stronger and using magic, she could no longer use, made her jealous of him. Marvin had done nothing wrong. She was woman enough to apologize, but she needed time to work out her anger first for the apology to be real. But he wasn't by the pool. She hurried to their private quarters. There was no sign he had been in the royal bedroom. She checked the room where the men's clothing was kept. His backpack was missing, and so was his Earth clothing.

She hurried back to their room to quickly dress. She ran to the common area. Alluvia told her he was wearing his pack and his strange clothes and had galloped away.

Shandria changed into her travel clothing, while Alluvial prepared her horse.

She trotted her horse to the gate at the mouth of the mountain. The guard remembered Marvin riding through the gate. How could anyone miss him? They had closed the main entrance when the snowstorm hit. But a smaller door was open. She dismounted and led her horse through the door. She remounted on the other side. The ferocity of the wind and the snow was almost as bad as on the glacier. Her horse hated it and expressed a desire to go back.

She grabbed the reins tighter and forced the horse's head in the direction she needed to go. A quick kick with her heels against her horse's side let the horse know she was in charge. The horse wasn't happy, yet he trotted to the first wall. Shandria's cloak and her magic prevented the weather from having much effect on her. But her horse felt the wind and the cold.

Shandria saw the guards had shut the gate and the portcullis was down. She closed her eyes, and she saw a patch of wild magic through the wind. She knew it was Marvin. It was miles away and traveling faster than the fastest horse. It would take her hours to get to him even if he stopped.

She could feel the strong magic coming from him, air, water, fire, forge, and then the bright blaze of sky magic. He had opened a portal. Several seconds later, the portal closed. Shandria searched and searched, through the noise caused by his out of control magic, but he was nowhere. The noise died down, and she still couldn't find him. This time he had taken the portal. This time he had left her, no, she had driven him away. He had told her how unstable and susceptible to anger the new magic would make him for a few days and her self-centered jealousy had pushed him over the edge.

She searched for several minutes until her horse started fussing. She allowed the horse to turn around and head back to the mountain. The tears running down her cheeks froze into ice crystals as they dripped off her face.

Chapter 29

Marvin woke up. He smelled burning smoke from a campfire, and a pine forest. His whole body hurt.

"Ya'ah'tee. You rode a wild buffalo."

Marvin looked up. There was a man dressed in a leather outfit. Something in the man's eyes reminded him of a Native American friend from college. "Where am I?"

The man said. "You are at the place where your portal took you."

Marvin asked, "Who are you?"

The man replied, "I won't truly know until my life is over. 'Who are you?' is the question you need to answer."

Marvin replied. "I am Marvin."

The man said, "That is your name. Not who you are."

Marvin asked, "What is your name?"

"You called me Tonto while you were feverish. It will do."

Marvin felt a twinge of guilt for calling the man Tonto rather than finding out his name, but he was feverish at the time, and the man didn't mind. He said, "I remember feeling hot. It must have been the fever."

Tonto said, "You rode too far too fast. You lost balance. You lost control."

Marvin looked around. He was lying on a blanket he thought might be buffalo hide, and he was covered by another one. He was inside a mud-bricked house. There was a closed wooden door on the other side of the room.

Marvin asked, "Why am I here?"

Tonto replied, "Because you don't know who you are.

"Where you were, where you are, and where you go means nothing if you don't know who you are." Tonto placed a bowl of food that looked like stew next to Marvin. "You need to eat and decide who you are."

Tonto left the room.

Marvin didn't know why, but something about the man made him pay attention to every word he spoke. The man left the room and shut the door behind him. It was the same question Marvin had been asking himself, "Who am I?"

Marvin realized how hungry he was. He took a bite of the stew. The meat reminded him of his mother's stew. He took a bite of a vegetable. It reminded him of the spice Shandria had used in the stew she had made at the way station. He bit into a potato. It reminded him of the meal he had eaten at the Dwarven community. Who had he been? Who was he now? And who will he be? I was. I am. I will be. He would never truly know who he was until his life was finished.

Each taste of the stew brought back a memory, many of Earth, some of his travels. He slowly ate it all, enjoying every bite and every memory. He was naked, but his clothing was lying beside him. He slowly dressed, putting on his blue jeans and sweatshirt from Earth. He strapped on his sword from the forges of the Dwarves. Last, he picked up the necklace Shandria, Princess of Atlantis, had made for him from the tooth of a wolf. He looked at it for a few seconds before he put it on and walked to the door.

Chapter 30

Shandria felt like she deserved to freeze outside all night long, but her horse complained, and she allowed it to head back to Crystal Mountain. It traveled quickly back to the embassy, looking forward to its familiar warm stall. Shandria dismounted from the horse and shuffled her feet on the way to the royal quarters.

Shandria knew what the forge master had said. She had seen the out of balance magic inside Marvin and acted like a selfish, spoiled princess. She had driven away her companion, her friend, the man who had saved her life, all because she refused to acknowledge she needed him, and that she cared for him.

Three days later, while brooding, Shandria felt a portal open. The guards had found Marvin's horse and returned it. She had the staff saddle her horse and Marvin's also. She led it behind her as she left the mountain.

It was a cold winter's day, but the sun was shining. The warmth and brightness of the sun felt good on her face. She dismounted after she exited through the first gate. She closed her eyes. Someone was traveling fast in her direction. Someone from Atlantis could have opened a portal, but she knew it was Marvin. It had to be Marvin.

She mounted her horse and trotted towards the next gate. They recognized her and quickly opened the gate for her. Shandria rode several dozen yards from the gate and dismounted. She listened and looked. It was strong Atlantian magic. She couldn't tell if it was Marvin. It felt more mature, more balanced, less like a child's wobbly magic. Maybe it was her brother, but it didn't feel like his. She was both excited that it was Marvin, and afraid to be disappointed if it wasn't. Then she recognized the signature of her magic, the magic she had woven into Marvin's poncho.

Chapter 31

Marvin had a new balance in his body. It was a balance of his emotions, his physical condition, and his magic. There was no longer a constant internal struggle. He had been weaving his magic like a child learning to ride a bicycle without training wheels, wobbling on the verge of falling. It had grown worse as he learned Dwarven magic. He had lost his balance on the bike and fell off. But he now had a new stability, a new harmony between his magic and his body, as he controlled the wave of snow.

Marvin's new maturity and balance allowed him to see and listen even as he was controlling the magic for his wave of snow. He saw Princess Shandria waiting for him long before he could see her with his eyes. He was excited, but his emotions no longer controlled his magic, nor did his magic control his emotions.

He ended his travel weave and slid down the hill of snow ten yards from her. Princess Shandria dropped the reigns of the horses and ran to Marvin. He picked her up for a second as the momentum of her hug almost knocked him over. Marvin held Shandria as she cried in his arms until her crying subsided.

After they both got their apologies out of the way, they mounted their horses and rode them side by side back to Crystal Mountain. Marvin told Shandria how his lopsided magic and his emotions had combined to take control of his actions. He didn't know what he would have done if he was in control. But his out of control anger had taken over. It had somehow opened the portal.

Then he told her about waking up covered in a buffalo hide blanket, and what he had learned.

Shandria said, "The Anastasi, you visited the Anastasi? They rarely talk to anyone. Grandfather stated that they always have their reasons, but we only learn why if they want us to know."

She then asked, "Did you decide who you are?"

He replied, "I won't know until I die, but for now. I am Marvin, born on Earth but with Atlantian magic, companion and protector of Princess Shandria, sworn to make sure she gets to Alfamara, and her friend."

Shandria smiled, "Friend and companion you are. There is no friend of a princess, or I would make it official."

Marvin joked, "Is that Atlantian regulation number 47."

The next day Marvin presented himself to the forge master. The forge master examined him, looked puzzled, then examined him again. "You have matured more than I thought possible. "We were worried when your fire magic took control. For Dwarves, it's minor and over in a few hours, but for Atlantians, it must be much worse. If we had known, we would have introduced you more gradually to the forge. We were afraid we had lost you for good."

Marvin replied, "Thank you for your concern. I think you did lose me for good, but some new friends intercepted me and helped me get back into balance. They took the edge off the recklessness of my youthful magic."

The forge master said, "Follow me." He led Marvin to a gray-haired old Dwarf.

The Dwarf said. "I've been expecting you. I am Sir Hematite, Grand Master of Weapons. Let's drink a mug and then we can get started."

Grand Master Hematite was a grandmaster of weapons forging. It had been decades since he had forged a weapon with anything but Dwarven magic. Atlantians could heat up metal and give it some magic. But only Dwarven forge magic could give it deep magic. Only Dwarven forge magic combined with Atlantian magic could make a weapon of power. And only a pair of grandmasters could create a great weapon. For, if one wasn't a grandmaster, what greatness could he give the sword?

Today Marvin's job was to watch and listen. Tomorrow he would help hammer out the metal. And if Marvin were ready before he left, he would learn about enchanting.

Time at the forge passed quickly. There was another party at the palace. The tailor once again fitted Marvin for an outfit. This one still had the aqua blue color of Atlantis, but at least it didn't have the high collar. It was going against custom, but they seated Marvin at the main table next to Shandria, who sat next to Princess Amethyst and the rest of the royal party.

Marvin worked his last two days forging a dagger, assisted and mentored by Grandmaster Hematite. Hematite wove in Dwarven magic, and Marvin wove in Atlantian magic. The Atlantian weaves were old and intricate, taught to Marvin by his sword. This was a general use dagger and backup weapon. It was always clean, self-repairing and sharpening, almost impossible to break, and able to focus magic. Grand Master Hematite helped him sharpen it, quench it, and finish the blade. Then they put a handle on it to finish it.

Grand Master Hematite was happy and proud of his student. When he came back, and Grand Master Hematite believed he would come back, together they would forge a weapon of power, if for no other reason than to pass on the lore.

Unknown to anyone, Marvin started coughing. He knew it was more than a cold, but it didn't affect him much. He was afraid it might quickly progress, but for now, it was just an annoyance.

Chapter 32

Shandria presented Princess Amethyst with the skin of the tiger she had killed. She had found a tanner and had him finish the process to turn it into a blanket. Princess Amethyst knew how rare and valuable it was, and how much it meant to Shandria. She hugged her with tears in her eyes and promised to visit.

Shandria gave the embassy staff gifts worth a moon's salary each. She then gave Marvin an Atlantian royalty travel outfit. It was the male version of hers.

Marvin had fun weaving magic into his traveling clothes. He copied the magic from Shandria's clothes. He also wove in some protective magic that Grandmaster Hematite had taught him. His cloak had the strength of steel, and it would stop any non-enchanted weapon. With Shandria's permission, he added the weave to her cloak and her travel clothing.

The Dwarven king gave Marvin a scroll sealed with the king's seal for the leader of the Alfarin.

The entourage rode with them to the north gate. They shared a mug of mead in a toast of goodwill and exchanged hugs. Marvin was grateful and sad. The Dwarves had treated him like a member of their family. Everyone was so helpful to him, and he had nothing to give in return.

Shandria and Marvin rode a snow wave to what Marvin was now calling portal ridge.

Marvin concentrated. He searched and found the Alfarin sky map. He looked down on Alfamara and found a large zone on the planet where magic kept his portal from forming. The disabled arch crystal was in the center. He was going to craft a portal on a mountain that would have been a one-month journey to the arch, then he realized there was a large river that flowed by the Alfarin arch. He formed the portal on a ridge a day's walk to the river. Traveling by river would cut their travel time significantly.

Shandria and Marvin held hands and stepped through the portal, leaving the warmth of the Dwarves and the cold snow of winter behind.

Chapter 33

They exited the portal in a clearing on top of a vegetation-covered mountain. It was raining, and the mountain slope was steep and slippery. Marvin magically looked at the sky through the clouds. It was either midmorning or midafternoon.

Marvin knew the direction of the planet's rotation determined map directions. The sun rose in the east and set in the west. He didn't know what direction the planet rotated. The angle of the sun showed it was either midafternoon or midmorning. If it were midmorning, they would have time to get down the mountain. If it were midafternoon, they would need to camp soon. He discussed it with Shandria.

Shandria said, "Let's follow the ridge. It's not the most direct route to the river, but it's in the right direction, and it does slope downhill. There are some flat places in case we have to stop for the night."

They trudged through the wet vegetation along a ridgeline that sloped downward. Bushes, vines, and trees obstructed most of the route. They took turns, Shandria would chop with her sword through the vegetation for several minutes, and then Marvin would.

Marvin felt guilty for using his sword like a machete, but his sword didn't mind and was encouraging Marvin. Rather than the short chopping strokes that he was using, it had him shift to longer smoother strokes where there was enough space.

Then his sword turned it into a training exercise. The trees and bushes were his adversaries. Marvin blocked, stepped to the side, attacked and counter-attacked. Shandria's sword had her do the same thing when she was leading.

It wasn't a straight line, as the trunks of many trees were too thick to chop through, at least in less time than it took to go around them.

The sun was going down, so they found a natural clearing that was almost flat and pitched their tent. All their clothing was wet. Marvin created a temporary weave above the tent, which deflected the rain. It allowed them to shake off the water droplets from their clothing before entering in.

Marvin crafted a light weave in the tent. After the dreary afternoon, it made the tent feel cheery, even if everything was wet. Shandria taught him magic that Marvin could craft into a weave to dry out their clothes and the tent faster. It was a weak, slow, gentle magic by design. It would take several minutes to dry out everything.

Marvin pulled his new boots off. They were soaking wet on the inside. Shandria looked at the magic he had woven into his boots. She laughed. The comfort weave he had crafted was inside out. The outside of his boot was dry while the inside was filled with water.

Marvin unwove the magic and wove it the correct way. Shandria looked at all his clothing and suggested a few improvements. She said, "You did a far better job than I did on my first set of travel clothes. We had to climb a steep hill, and my glove enchantments were on the wrong side. I was slow and klutzy all day. It took me forever to take my gloves off since they insisted on gripping to my hands. The sergeant pointed it out to everyone and teased me for the rest of the trip."

Shandria saw Marvin's earth and metal magic. She was amazed at how it gave their cloaks and clothes the armor abilities of steel, but still allowed for easy movement. Numerous small magical threads interlocked as rings together. The threads looked like interwoven links of chain armor. It formed an impenetrable but flexible barrier. It also became as rigid as plate armor when hit. Shandria wished she had it on her clothing when the wolf bit down. It was more resistant to crushing than the weave that stopped the wolf's teeth from penetrating her clothing and her skin.

Marvin had an auxiliary bag strapped to his main pack where he used to carry his sleeping bag and then the tiger pelt. Food from Crystal Mountain filled it to the top.

Marvin rearranged his backpack, and a pouch fell out. Shandria asked him what was in it. He put it back into his pack and said. "It is my messenger bag. The Anastasi gave it to me and asked me to give private messages to King Feldspar, the Alfarin Queen, and to members of the Atlantian royalty.

Shandria's curiosity was peaked. "What do the messages say?"

Marvin replied. "I don't know, and the messages are sealed. The pouch is a diplomatic pouch from the Anastasi. They asked me to be their messenger. I am only to reveal the existence of the messages to the recipient. But I was told to confide in you if you found out."

Shandria asked him. "Is there a message for me?"

"I don't know. There is a pouch for the Atlantian Court. We will both find out when I present it to them."

Shandria stuck her tongue out at Marvin. He laughed.

They ate dinner and talked about tomorrow's plan. Marvin let the magical threads of the light go free, and it became dark in the tent. Shandria held Marvin tight as they fell asleep. It felt so good to be beside him, to hold him. She had enjoyed time in Crystal mountain, but she had missed traveling with Marvin. She was glad things were back to normal.

Chapter 34

The weather the next morning was worse than the day before. The rain was constant, and the clouds were dark. As much rain was hitting them from the sides as straight down, due to a brisk wind.

The climb today was down a steeper path. In between the occasional rocky outcropping on the hillside, bushes, trees and long matted-down wet grass and vines covered the ground. Marvin led the way, hoping that if Shandria slipped he could stop her. They inched down, grabbing bushes and clumps of grass to slow their descent down.

Marvin didn't want to worry Shandria and had been trying to hide his cough, but he was coughing more frequently. He hoped the exertion was what had brought it on, but knew it was only aggravating the symptoms of his growing cancer.

A clump of grass Marvin was holding onto pulled free. He slipped on the wet, grassy slope and slid down the hill. He tried to stop, but it was steep and slippery. Marvin grabbed a bush, but it ripped out of the ground. He felt his clothing harden from the impacts as he skidded over a sharp rocky outcropping. There were rocks along the slope that would have scraped him and torn his clothing, except the magic weaves on the clothing protected him. His momentum slowed as he crashed through a section of small bushes but sped back up on the other side. He covered his head with his arms and made his body as hard as a rock. He used his arms to protect his face as the trunk of a tree stopped his slide.

Shandria yelled down, "Are you all right?" But Marvin couldn't hear her through the noise of the rain, the wind, and the rushing water from the river below.

Marvin disentangled himself from the tree. Shandria was at least 100-yards away from him, most of it a steep slope. He could barely see her outline through the pouring, blowing rain. It was too dangerous for her to come down and too slippery for him to go back up. The magical weave on his cloak had protected him, but he had also hardened his body with earth magic during the slide, and he knew she couldn't. He stood up and waved his hands.

He saw Shandria, who was mostly an indistinct shadow through the torrential rains, wave back.

ATLANTIAN MAGIC

Then Marvin thought about the rushing water below him. He wove magic and a mound of water fought against the movement of the stream, collected, and rose towards him. It found grip on the water in the grass and the soil. Water's natural desire was to flow downhill; its natural desire was to flatten out. But his magic controlled it. Just as he had done in the pool, he rode it like a wave up the side of the mountain. When he got to where Shandria was, he said with a bow, "Your coach awaits my princess." He extended his hand.

Shandria smiled, took his hand, and climbed onto the water mound. They interlocked arms. She pulled out a piece of a plant from underneath his hood, and they both laughed.

They rode the wave down to where he had stopped, and then on a gentler slope which fell off suddenly into the river below.

The river was a rushing torrent, catching and carrying all the monsoon rains in the area. There was no way forward except on the river, so they traveled down and entered the river, becoming part of the rushing stream.

They rode the current, standing on top a protective hill of water. The water seemed to slow down and widen out, but then they found themselves falling off the edge of a cliff down a ten-story waterfall. Marvin grabbed Shandria. He pulled the water over the top of them, trapping a bubble of air around their heads. Water covered the rest of their bodies. Then he felt the water below him. They hit the water at the base of the falls hard. Their pod of water squeezed out in all directions, and they lost the air bubble, as their momentum carried them deep into the water below. After a few seconds, Marvin's magic pushed them back to the surface and lifted them up on another hill of water.

Marvin realized he had been holding Shandria tight enough to make a back-cracking chiropractor envious. He relaxed his hold. They saw each other's faces, and both began to laugh.

Marvin was tired. He knew he was draining his magic reserves faster than they could regenerate. His ability to continue his magic was near its limit. He looked around him. The waterfall had opened into a larger lake where the banks weren't as steep. He saw a beach, which was relatively flat, and covered with smooth round rocks. He commanded his wave to head in that direction, and then he let them down on the rocks. He immediately sat down and started coughing.

Shandria asked him if he was okay.

He said between coughs, "Yeah, just too much excitement and I need to rest for a couple of minutes." Marvin looked at the hand he used to cover his mouth. He was glad the rain quickly washed away the red he had coughed up.

Shandria looked around. The rain, blown by the wind was falling at an angle. A nearby wall of rock was blocking the rainfall. She pointed out the natural shelter, and they walked towards it. She felt the gravel under her feet shift and crunch as she walked. Her clothing was wet, inside and outside. At least the comfort weave was wicking away the water that had entered through her clothing.

It felt good to be out of the direct rainfall. The magic in their clothing soon dried them off. Marvin saw a large flat rock that was outside the area of the overhang. He couldn't quite pick it up, but he was able to slide it into the shelter area. Shandria watched him as he wove magic to evaporate the moisture on the rock into a mist, which dispersed with the wind. Now they had a place to sit down for a few minutes. It was a good place to take a break and eat.

Marvin made the look he saw on Shandria at the bottom of the waterfall. She showed him his look in return. They laughed and kidded each other. Marvin said, "An E-ticket ride for sure." He saw the puzzled look on Shandria's face. Some things didn't translate well from one language and culture to another.

Marvin explained, "On Earth, we have places where people build rides for amusement. Some rides are mild, and little kids ride them. Others have quick turns and dips, which teenagers enjoy. The fast high-intensity rides are the E-ticket rides."

Shandria said, "That was an 'Eee' ticket ride."

Marvin realized that letters and writing didn't translate well either. He told Shandria, "I don't know how to read or write in Atlantian. Can most people read or is it isolated to a class?"

Shandria replied, "We have several levels of language and corresponding symbols. Everyone knows basic numbers and the common language. There are special symbols we use for mathematics and magic, and scholars and scientists use other symbols."

Marvin thought about it for a second. It wasn't too different on Earth. Everyone knew letters. And everyone knew numbers. There were signs for plus, minus, multiply and divide in math. But there were specialty symbols. Some people didn't know a square root sign. Calculus and higher math had many symbols that were strange to people outside the field. Greek letters were used in many sciences.

Soon lunch was over. Marvin needed to discuss their plans. He said, "All the tributaries and rivers join into one large river which flows by the arch. We can wave travel until we find a good place to stop, but the violence of the rushing water requires a lot of magical energy to keep us stable. I have already used a lot of energy. You said you made a skiff in sea scouts. We can always make a small boat and float, or paddle. What do you think?"

Shandria replied, "I like your suggestion. Let's travel near the bank and look for a good place for us to build one."

They wave traveled for another hour down the rushing river before they found a sandy area to stop. Shandria looked at the trees and said. "Oh no, you don't know any wood magic. And I can't use what little I know. I'm so sorry."

Marvin asked, "How long will it take you to teach me?"

Shandria said, "I don't know."

ATLANTIAN MAGIC

Marvin said, "I can't sustain the wave magic for a full day. My magic reserves are low. We need to stay here for the night. I don't know if it's the magic I used or the exercise, but I'm starved and exhausted."

Marvin grabbed a piece of fruit from his pack and offered one to Shandria. Shandria was only slightly hungry and wanted to wait until dinner to eat.

Marvin ate the fruit then pointed and said, "There is a sheltered stone overhang where we can make a fire. I could warm up the rock with magic, but I am almost out. You can collect some wood, and I will try to catch us a fish. I should have more energy after dinner. You can give me an exercise or two, and we will see how I progress in wood magic. How does that sound?"

"It sounds good to me. We can decide tomorrow what we will do based on how it goes." Shandria started collecting wood for a fire. It was wet, so she dried it out using beginning magic that wouldn't harm her.

Marvin walked down to the lake. He pulled up a ball of water. The water ball trapped several fish. He let water and fish drain away from the ball until he had one medium size fish still on the ball. He brought the water ball over the rocks and let the water wash away. It left the fish flopping in the gravel. Marvin brought the fish to Shandria.

Shandria started a small fire. She told him to listen to a tree, and she would prepare the meal. He had done the same exercise when they reached the tree line but stopped it once they had started traveling with the Dwarves.

This time there was a difference. Marvin knew how to focus, to listen, and to look. He listened to the tree and heard the whistle of the wind through the jungle. He heard the creak of the branches as they bent. Then he heard the magic threads vibrating. He watched carefully; his eyes focused and he saw the threads.

Rock and metal are the magic of solids, the magic of permanence. Water and air were the magic of fluids, the magic of change, of being formless. But wood was the magic of flexibility. It was the ability to hold form, and yet to change, to bend.

He was on the edge of understanding something new about trees and wood. He stilled his emotions and focused again. It was like catching a few notes of a song carried on the wind from far away. The more he stilled his feelings, the more he detached himself, the less he responded to them. He allowed the notes of the wood magic to stir his emotions. He heard more and more, and then he heard the rhythm, a beat.

This wasn't the steady, strong beat of the forge. It was more constant but changing. Like the polyrhythms of gentle rain falling on a collection of objects, each object making its unique sound when the raindrops struck. Marvin thought it fascinating that in the hard driving rain and the movement of the tree branches caused by the wind, he could tell the difference between the sound of the magic and the sound of the rain.

He relaxed his eye muscles and looked at the tree. Just like his first time looking at iron ore, he didn't see the tree with his magical sight. He saw the magic around the tree and the bark with his normal vision.

Marvin remembered the many times he had cooled off in the shade of a tree in the summer or enjoyed the smell of the forest. He was trying to let the tree know he was a friend.

The magic accepted him. His eyes adapted as nature magic welcomed him. He saw into its center. He saw through the layer of bark, each of the many tree rings, and into the heartwood. He saw fluids rising towards the branches. On other paths, fluids carrying nutrients were flowing down towards the roots. It was incredible and in 3-D. And unlike iron ore, it was constantly in motion.

He watched the magical threads bend and move, stretch and contract, as the branches danced in the wind. He followed to the end of the branches and watched the wind blow around the leaves on the branches. The constant movement of the leaves blurred the magic inside.

Then he touched a thread on a small branch. It responded. He bent the limb at an angle. He could see the fibers inside the branch stretching to compensate. The angle of the branch was wrong. He felt sadness in his magic. It wasn't supposed to be that way. Then the sadness left the tree. The flexibility of the magic accepted the change.

Marvin focused on his body. He could see that inside him was wood magic pulsating, beating, flowing. He looked at his arm. It was fascinating. He could see the fluids inside him flowing; his arteries pulsed with every heartbeat. He followed its flow through the muscles of his arm. He clenched and unclenched his fingers. He watched his forearm muscles expand and contract. He observed the firing of the neurons and the contraction of the muscle fibers. He watched the tendons from his forearm, move through sheaths of tissue and cause his fingers to bend.

The many complex layers of tissue that was his skin, the epidermis, the dermis, the layers of subcutaneous fat, oil glands and sweat glands, surprised him. He had no name for other complex structures he could see inside his skin. He saw the network of nerves in his skin and watched them send a signal up his arm when he touched something.

Marvin shifted his focus to his torso. The ravenous glow of the tumor in his abdomen drew his vision. Like a gnarled, deformed octopus, its tendrils spread out along the larger arteries. The veins inside him unnaturally twisted and knotted to supply it with the blood it needed to grow. It was pushing the healthy tissue around it out of the way, and it was starving the healthy tissue to death by stealing its blood supply. The cancerous tissue's noise was deafening, a discordant banging. It was an out of tune instrument playing in the symphony of his body.

ATLANTIAN MAGIC

Marvin pulled back his magical sights. He couldn't watch. He took a deep breath and forced himself to go back to the tree. It was in harmony. He felt, heard, and saw the beautiful melody of the tree.

Then he looked at the branch he had bent. He grabbed the threads and bent it back. It was better, it was straight, but it was different. He could see the tissues where he had bent it. They were different. It reminded him of the discoloration when a cheap plastic toy was bent and then straightened. The toy was never the same. The branch was different. He had changed it, and he could never make it as it was before. It would forever have a scar where he had bent it.

Marvin was starting to understand why healing magic was so complicated. Part of him wanted to look deeper into his body. He knew the organs of his body would each be as fascinating as his skin was, but he didn't want to see what his cancer was doing. As if on cue, he started to cough again. He stopped looking and hearing. He was tired anyway. Once again, he let the constant rain wash away the specks of dark red he had coughed up.

Chapter 35

Shandria finished cooking the fish. A pot of potatoes and carrots from Crystal Mountain was cooking on the fire.

Marvin told her of his experience with wood magic. She was proud of him. He would try again once he rested. There was so much more to wood magic that he needed to discover. He could see why Shandria sometimes called it wood magic, and sometimes called it nature magic.

Shandria noticed his sadness. He told her about his experience with the tree branch. "It left me sad to see the change I caused. It reminds me of the cancer inside me." Marvin's lungs chose that minute to start coughing again.

This time Shandria saw the blood on his hand. He was unable to wash it away in the shelter of the overhang. "How long have you been coughing up blood?" she asked.

"I'm sorry I didn't tell you. I didn't want you to worry. It just started again. I was coughing up blood back on Earth just before we met. And the doctor gave me some medicine which helped."

Marvin paused then said, "I just realized I still have the Earth medicine that was helping me." Marvin dug down into the bottom of his backpack and pulled out the bottle of pills. He read the directions, two pills twice a day. He saw the sticker on the side of the bottle that read, 'Take with food or water.' And another one that read, 'May cause dryness.'

He grabbed a water bottle, swallowed two pills, and drank some water.

Shandria said, "May I see the bottle?

He handed Shandria the bottle. She looked at it and said. "It's the same crazy letters I saw all over your planet. I can't read a thing."

Marvin said, "It will be the same for me when I get to Atlantis. I will have to learn the Atlantian alphabet."

Shandria said, "I will get you the best teachers in Atlantis. Until then I can teach you at night. It will be fun."

Marvin asked, "Is your writing phonetic or pictograms?"

Shandria replied, "What is phonetic and pictogram?"

"For many writing systems on Earth, each symbol represents a sound. It's called phonetic. In other languages, simplified pictures or pictograms represent words."

ATLANTIAN MAGIC

Shandria said, "We use both. We write most of our language as sounds. But we have specialized symbols for numbers and words like king and queen."

Marvin asked, "If you wanted, could you write out the word king rather than use the symbol?"

Shandria replied, "We could, but no educated person would."

Marvin asked, "How many letters do you have?"

"We have thirty-one letters." Shandria sang a song that reminded Marvin of the A B C song.

He laughed, "In my language, we have twenty-six letters." He sang the 'A B C song.' Unlike the English letters, Atlantian letters were actual words. The sound of a letter was the beginning sound of a short common word. It reminded Marvin of the letters he had heard the military use in movies: Alfa, Bravo, Charlie, Delta, Echo... He asked, "How many unique symbols do you have?"

Shandria said, "We have a couple hundred, more if you count specialties like magic, science, math, or other fields. We also have hundreds from antiquity, which few people know except scholars."

They talked about reading while they finished their meal and preparation for the following day. Shandria and Marvin must have sung the Atlantian alphabet song a hundred times before they retired for the night.

The next morning, they traveled by wave again, staying close to the shore. Shandria twice thought she saw the right tree, but then changed her mind. It was either the wrong tree or the wrong spot. Then she found one she liked. It was tall and straight, and the wood was lightweight and strong. Shandria put some magic into her sword and chopped it down with a single slash.

Marvin was impressed. The length of her sword was barely longer than the tree's width.

Shandria used her sword to cut the top off the tree. They both chopped off the limbs. Shandria cut a two-inch-deep slot down the length of the tree. Then it was time for magic. They selected a growth ring of the tree at the bottom of the two-inch slot.

Marvin felt the growth ring all around the tree. He used magic to bend the outer layer of wood away from the cut, peeling it away along the ring. It was like pulling back the label from around a can of soup. An hour later, they had a U-shaped piece of outer wood, with the center wood intact. Marvin picked up one end of the center wood, and Shandria picked up the other. They put the center wood to the side. Marvin pinched the outer wood together at the front and back ends and sealed the end flat. They had a round-bottomed canoe-shaped vessel. He pinched the knotholes together to finish the main structure of the boat.

Shandria was happy with what he had done. But Marvin wasn't finished. Atlantians sat on the bottom, kneeled, or stood in their skiff. That would work for a short ride, but they would be in the canoe all day for at least a week.

Pd MICHEL

He constructed seats from the branches they had cut from the tree and the wood they had removed from the inside so they would have a place to sit, turning it into a real canoe.

He cut a plank from the unneeded central section and formed it into the shape of a paddle. He rounded the wood and flattened the blade. He made a second paddle for Shandria.

The boat was much heavier and thicker than any canoe he had been in before. But it was strong. He dragged the canoe to the water's edge. It was still raining, but not as hard as the previous day. There was no reason to wade out into the water. He had Shandria sit in front, and he sat in the back. He wove a pseudopod of water, which lifted up the canoe and set it down in the lake.

Marvin quickly saw Shandria expertly using her paddle, but then she had grown up on an island. After a few minutes, they were in the center of the current, so they stopped actively paddling. Marvin created a current that augmented the natural current in the river. The current increased their speed, and an occasional stroke of his paddle kept the canoe oriented downstream.

There was some leaking around a knothole. Marvin reinforced all the knotholes and found no other weak spots. The little bit of water that had seeped in was less than the rain was adding to the boat, but Marvin was sure no knotholes would pop out.

The river narrowed, and the current became stronger. Marvin dropped his magic, and they used the paddles to steer. Soon they came to a set of rapids. Marvin yelled over the roar of the rapids, "Just keep it in the middle, and avoid all the rocks."

Marvin laughed. After they got past the noise of the rapids, Shandria asked him what was so funny. He replied, "I don't believe the boy from the desert just told the girl from Atlantis how to paddle a boat." Shandria laughed in return.

The river widened out again and slowed down. Marvin sped up the river current under the canoe. The rest of the day, they let the river current push them, followed by intermittent paddling, and an occasional rapid. The sun was getting low in the west when Shandria pointed out a flat section of sandy beach. Marvin's magic weave lifted up the canoe and beached it on the sand.

He looked through the water and saw fish swimming near the bottom. He brought one up in a pseudopod of water, then a second one. He asked Shandria to select dinner. She selected one that had an odd shaped head. He let the other fish go. Marvin was once again at the limits of his magic reserves, and he was tired. He had used his magic throughout the day and had a slight headache. He started a fire for Shandria and sat back against a rock. He closed his eyes to rest.

Shandria gutted the fish and walked to the edge of the jungle. She found what she was looking for. The herb was tangy, and it would add a citrus taste to the fish. She saw Marvin had fallen asleep and realized how much magic he had used in the last few days. Magical exhaustion was as tiring as physical or mental exhaustion. She smiled at his sleeping body. She looked and was worried about

154

what she saw. The cancer was larger than when she wove healing magic on it back at Earth. It seemed to be in more locations, small dots of angry growth.

She had kept their agreement and had resisted using anything but beginning magic. Using magic was so natural to her that it was hard, like walking and not opening your eyes. She thought about trying to heal him, she could justify it as an emergency, or at least she would be able to soon. But the state of her magic flow was ugly. The healthy, smooth, wide, straight channels were crooked, narrow, and broken. Magical hairs had formed their bridges, and there were blockages in some channels. Use of any powerful magic could break the remaining channels. She wouldn't get a smooth weave, and it may harm him rather than help him. Shandria had never felt so useless and helpless.

Shandria woke Marvin when she finished cooking. Marvin's headache was gone, and some of his magic had restored. After dinner, she sent Marvin right to bed and said she would join him later. She pulled out her dagger and made a gift for Marvin.

That night she spooned in close to him. She could no longer weave magic to slow the disease or to heal him, but she could safely redirect her overflow magic into his body to strengthen his natural resistance. Magic was alive. Her magic would grow all night. The flow would leave her body. She just asked it to spill into Marvin. It was a tiny amount. It would be a few drops, but even a few drops might slow down his cancer. And as long as she held him, as long as she stayed close to him, it would spill on its own while she slept.

Marvin's cough had improved. He was no longer coughing up blood. The medicine from Earth was reducing the inflammation in his lungs.

Shandria let Marvin discover the gift she made him. On his paddle, she had carved the Atlantian Alphabet. Now he could read and learn the letters he had learned to sing.

The rain continued to fall with no end in sight. The monsoons were continuous. They kept the current flowing fast.

But Marvin had enough of the rainfall. When they broke for lunch, he asked Shandria for her tarp. He made the frame of a hut over the top of their canoe by weaving a frame from driftwood, and then tied the tarp to the top, giving them a roof. When they canoed back out, the rain fell on the tarp and not on their heads. The continuous sound of rain hitting the hoods of their cloaks was now the constant sound of rain hitting the tarp above their heads. The magic woven on their clothes kept the rainwater out, but the tarp overhead gave them an illusion of being drier. Marvin would take it.

Mountains on either side rose up, creating cliffs. They were on a river in a deep canyon. Water raced down the canyon. The rain was flowing off the mountainside, and it created a constant flow of water over the edge of the cliffs into the canyon. Rushing streams randomly entered the canyon and churned up the water.

Marvin no longer used his magic to move the boat. They had decided that Marvin being drained of magic left them vulnerable if anything unexpected happened. So, he just occasionally used it to bail water out of the boat. Marvin found the trip suddenly became more relaxing and less strenuous.

The splashing of the rain and the water from off the canyon walls created a cloud of fog and mist so thick they could only see a few yards in front of them. Then the current sped up. The mist cleared just in time for Marvin to see the river disappear over the side of the cliff as the current propelled them over the edge. Marvin's jaw dropped when he saw how far it was to the bottom. They were falling into a white mist of water and air, over half a mile beneath them.

Chapter 36

Marvin's water magic wasn't strong enough to lift them uphill against the water falling down. The force of gravity was too strong. He knew they were going to die unless he could learn to fly. He felt the wind blowing upwards from the white water below. He grabbed the air and made it blow harder. He had it push the canoe away from the falling water where there was more air for his magic to control. He yelled to Shandria, "Hold on!" but he doubted she heard him through the deafening roar of the falls. He could feel the front end of the canoe start to dip. He leaned back to shift his weight towards the back, and the front of the canoe began to rise up. The canoe overcorrected, forcing Marvin to shift his weight forwards by leaning forwards. The tarp above him flapped like a parachute, but Marvin knew it did little to slow down their fall, maybe it was helping to stabilize them.

Terminal velocity for a skydiver was about a hundred miles per hour. There was an indoor skydiving place where wind machines blew upwards and suspended people. A strong updraft would cancel their downward motion. He wove his magic to yell at the air around him to blow upward on the boat.

He concentrated harder and harder. He could feel the deceleration. But would it slow them enough? He was starting to feel hopeful about their chance of survival. Then they entered a dense, impenetrable fog. A white barrage of droplets blinded and disoriented him. He couldn't tell if he was rising, falling, or suspended in midair.

Suddenly his magic stopped working, and the boat dropped. The mist was so thick that there wasn't enough air for Marvin to control. A second later, Marvin felt a sudden jar when the boat hit the churning water. Their weight and momentum submerged the canoe. Marvin lost all sense of direction. He didn't know if they were right side up or upside down.

They popped back to the surface. Somehow, the boat had stayed right side up or at least returned to that direction.

The churning of the water below the falls was worse than any of the rapids. The constant twisting and up and down motion made it impossible for Marvin to get his bearings. The rolling water repeatedly drove the boat back under the water, and the continued heavy mist made every breath an inhalation of water and air. A large spinning current caught the boat and spun it around several times until the main current of water pushed them clear of the churning water and mist. They were in choppy, rushing water, but at least they were in the main current flowing away from the falls.

Marvin kept blinking his eyes, trying to see Shandria, but the constant spray in his face made his reflexes keep his eyelids closed. He could feel she was in the boat in front of him with his magic, but he had an emotional need to see she was there; an emotional need to see she was all right. He reached out and touched her shoulder. The mist cleared as the current pushed the boat farther away from the falls. Marvin could see Shandria through the droplets as a warped fuzzy image between the blinks of his eyes.

Shandria had never been as frightened as when she saw them falling over the edge of the waterfall. She yelled at Marvin to hold on. She knew he didn't hear her since she didn't even hear herself.

She froze, unable to think of any magic she could use. Then she felt Marvin's air magic and the updraft he was causing. She was amazed at the strength and power of his magic. Her weak magic could do nothing to help. She didn't know if she could help even if her magic was normal. She knew there would be an impact, so she held on, bracing for when they hit the water.

She felt the boat tip forward and leaned backward, then it overcorrected, and she leaned forward. The noise and the constant spray of water hitting her face made her completely lose any sense of orientation.

Then they hit. The impact wasn't as bad as she expected. Marvin's magic and the bubbling water below them had slowed them before they hit the more solid water.

She felt her clothing turn stiff and hard, protecting her from the impact when they hit. She was thankful Marvin had woven his metal magic into her clothing. She instinctively held her breath. As she had expected, the wooden boat bobbed back to the surface. The water flow from the falls ejected them from the churning water, away from the falls and the mist. Her first thought was for Marvin. His magic had stopped when they hit the water.

The noise of the waterfall and the sudden loss of Marvin's powerful magic deafened her senses. She was unable to find him and feared the collision with the water had ejected him from the boat. Then she felt Marvin's hand reach out and touch her on the shoulder with a firm but brief squeeze. It wasn't on her shoulder for long; he had to hold on too. Shandria's senses soon cleared and she once again could feel his presence in the boat.

Every minute of travel lessened the ear-splitting noise of the waterfall. Marvin held on tight to the canoe in the fast-moving water below the falls. He had expended more energy coming over the falls than he had in a single magical effort before. Another minute and he would have completely depleted his magic reserves. He pushed the canoe upwards with a magical wave of water and drained the boat with more magic, but the impact had split the wood, and the water came back in through a wide crack. He let the boat settle back into the water.

ATLANTIAN MAGIC

Their makeshift roof was gone, and so was Shandria's tarp. Marvin looked around and found the signature of Shandria's magic on her tarp. They recovered the tarp, still tied to the broken off roof support.

The sound of the falls had diminished, but it was still loud enough they had to yell to talk. Marvin spun the boat around to look at the waterfall. It was the largest waterfall he had ever seen. There were multiple large rainbows in the mist. Marvin saw that the rolling whitewater at its base was several stories high. He marveled at the volume of water falling over the waterfall. He was glad he had blown the canoe away from the base where the falling water hit jagged rocks at its base. He doubted they would have survived.

Part of Marvin wanted to stay and look at the impressive sight of the falls, and part of him wanted to get away from the noise. He allowed the current to carry them away from the falls, away from the deafening roar. Only when the roar of the falls had reduced to a low enough background level that they didn't have to yell to talk did he look for a place and beach the canoe.

He asked Shandria, "Are you okay?"

She replied, "Eee ticket ride."

Marvin laughed and said, "Almost a one-way ticket." Marvin didn't have to explain what a one-way ticket meant. They both started to laugh, more from relief than from the joke.

They exited the canoe and held each other; emotions spanned the full range from fear and excitement to relief. They alternated between crying, laughing, and talking. Marvin sat down on the sand, too exhausted to care where he sat. He felt exhausted, drained of physical, magical, and emotional strength.

He lay back on the sand. The feeling of the sun on his face after several days of constant rainfall felt wonderful. It was only then that he realized it wasn't raining at the lower elevation.

Shandria saw him lying on his back, "Are you injured?"

"Nothing lying on a lounge under the garden sun won't fix," He replied

Shandria agreed. She joined him on the ground and laid her head on his shoulder. "I thought our journey was over. Thanks for saving my life again."

Marvin replied, "Everything happened so fast I didn't have time to think about anything but stopping our fall. I lost contact with the water and couldn't form a bubble or a wave. I felt the rush of the wind and remembered you saying you had jumped off a cliff and used air magic to control your descent. It may have been my magic, but it was your idea. So, thanks for saving my life, again."

They lay there for several minutes, then Shandria heard Marvin's stomach growl. She sat up and said, "Leviathan has awakened. We better get something to eat."

Marvin laughed and replied, "Just five more minutes, mom. Do I have to go to School?"

Shandria smiled. Some jokes were universal. She opened her backpack and started looking for some food.

Marvin sat up, and then he rose to his feet. His clothing had hardened and protected his body from the worst of the impact. He rotated his neck, his shoulders, and then his hips to stretch a little, to reduce the soreness he would feel tomorrow. He looked at the damage caused to their canoe. The canoe had a long wide crack. He wove magic, which brought the wood back together and sealed the crack. He found several smaller structural cracks and repaired them.

They were lucky the boat hadn't splintered apart. The rest of the hull looked good. He removed the remainder of the broken canopy supports. Maybe tomorrow or the next day they would put back up the tarp, but today they would enjoy the sun. He untied Shandria's tarp from the wooden supports. He spread it on top the canoe and used his magic to help it dry quicker before folding it up and giving it back to Shandria.

Shandria handed Marvin a vinepear from the stores the Dwarves had given them. She also ate one. The sweetness of the fruit was what they needed to restore their spirits and energy. She was amazed at how much three minutes of terror had sapped her strength. She handed Marvin a strip of Jerky and grabbed one herself. They had replaced the jerky they had made on the trail with fresh jerky from Crystal Mountain that had a preservation-weave on it. It was good for lunch, and Shandria was sure there would be plenty of fish for dinner.

Marvin thought it curious that when they should have been hanging onto the canoe with both hands, they had both held onto their paddles. They climbed back into the canoe.

Marvin was sore, not only his body but also whatever magical muscles he had were exhausted. He guided the boat towards the center of the lake, where he hoped the current would be strongest, and they lazily paddled downstream. Even with the inside of the canoe mostly dry, the canoe was heavy and rode deep in the water. Their paddling wasn't very efficient, but today it didn't matter. They both needed a few minutes of relative peace after surviving the waterfall, and the rhythm of the paddles stroking through the water was a relaxing relief. Besides, Marvin's magic needed time to recharge. He had thought about just calling it a day, but he wanted the noise of the waterfall to disappear, and he realized he was enjoying the gentle movement of the canoe and the sun. Even the slow, lazy paddling was relaxing and therapeutic.

After their drop down the falls, the river had widened out and slowed down. It was flowing at walking speed rather than racing speed. The landscape became plains with scattered trees on the right side. Trees were denser on the left bank of the river.

Shandria and Marvin occupied their time watching birds and animals on the plains. Shandria pointed out a large heard of animals that looked to Marvin like a buffalo with less hair. Marvin wondered if the climate was milder here. It was definitely much warmer and drier here than above the falls.

After a few minutes, Shandria took off her cloak, her pack, and her shirt, and enjoyed the sunshine on her upper body. Marvin stripped to his waist and joined her.

An hour before sundown they pulled onto the shore near a grove of trees. It would provide some protection from any animals. But it didn't provide any from bugs. Marvin put his shirt back on. The bugs stopped bothering him. Shandria pointed out the weave on his clothing that acted as a bug repellant. He had copied many of the weaves from her clothing and had to admit he didn't know what some of them were. So Shandria told him.

Marvin spent some time examining and learning the weaves, or more precisely the vibrations that Marvin was associating with words on the magic strings.

Shandria prepared the fire, and Marvin caught a large fish. Marvin watched Shandria. She said a few words of thanks to the fish and the creator of the fish before she prepared it for cooking. Marvin often thanked God for his food, but he had never said anything to his food.

He found a branch that was large enough to sit on. He pulled it over by the fire for Shandria and him. Then he did his evening chores of filling up and purifying their water bottles. He sat down next to Shandria when he was done.

Marvin said, "Shandria, I notice you thanked God before you prepared the fish, but you also thanked the fish. I have never thanked my food. We talked about it once, I am wondering if you could tell me more."

Shandria said. "We almost never use God as a name. Some people, such as the Asgardians, and the Olympians call their leaders gods. In their language, god also means a powerful leader. So, we usually use one of his power names like Creator, or we use one of his relationship names like Father.

"We also acknowledge the food he gave us. As a princess, there are times when I have sent an official to tell a servant to give a gift to someone who has gone through hardship or deserving of a special reward. That person is thankful to the servant for the gift that came from the royal court. So, by thanking the royal servant, he is thanking the royal household, and thanking the creator who gave the resources to the court. By thanking the fish or saying words of respect, I am thanking the creator of the fish for giving me nourishment.

"I am also acknowledging the fish as a unique living creation of our Creator, and worthy of respect."

Marvin asked, "By Atlantian customs, should I be thanking the fish when I catch him?"

"I acknowledge a deer that I kill and then hand him to our kitchen staff to prepare. But it's up to you. Just follow your heart.

"You have always thanked me for meals and for cooking our food. So, by thanking me, aren't you thanking the food, thanking me as an individual, and thanking our Creator who made it all?"

Marvin replied, "I never considered how saying thank you worked its way back to God, I mean, our Provider that way."

"Shandria smiled, "I like the name Provider. It is both a power name and a relationship name. I am sure to use it sometime in the future."

Marvin said, "One more thing. You have been doing all the cooking. And tonight, I just sat around and watched. Should I be helping?"

"You are my companion. You are exhausted, and I am rested. I have taken the lead in things I can do to help, and I have given you the lead in things you do best. I never once questioned your decision about how or when to use your magic. I didn't question your decision for us to portal into the rainforest and follow the river. Today, I followed your lead and enjoyed the sunshine and our lazy paddling of the canoe.

"I enjoyed cooking the fish not only for myself but also for you. It's my way of thanking you, my companion, and our Provider, who put us together and is my Eternal Companion.

That night the sky was clear. Marvin peered up at the stars. His magic allowed him to look back onto the land. They were making rapid progress. They had traveled half the distance, but most of that was under the swift current of the rapids. At their current pace, it should take them about a week to get to the capital.

Marvin was glad they would be their soon. The Earth drugs were helping the symptoms, but they weren't slowing the growth of his cancer. He could see the illness inside him when he looked, and it was scary. He was physically much stronger since when he left Earth, but he could feel his cancer sapping his endurance. Marvin guessed that he had a week before his cancer started noticeably to affect him. Soon he would take the last of his pills. The pill bottle had another refill, but he doubted he would find an Earth pharmacy on the banks of a river in Alfamara.

Marvin wasn't sure whether the use of his magic was making him tired or the cancer was, probably a little of both. Tomorrow he would try alternating between magic and paddling. He could paddle all day but it was slower than using magic, and he was anxious to see if the Alfarins could heal them.

Chapter 37

The next morning Marvin and Shandria talked about how to make the canoe lighter. A lighter vessel would ride higher in the water and be easier to paddle and to steer. Marvin removed half the weight of the canoe by peeling off half the thickness of the wood. Marvin knew the canoe was still thicker and heavier than an aluminum canoe, but to make it any thinner he would have to use ribs to reinforce the wood. He was unsure how to do that properly and afraid he would ruin the boat.

That day Marvin alternated using his magic to propel the canoe and paddling. They were going at least three times as fast as paddling alone. His goal was to finish the day with at least half his magic reserve. It was smarter than completely draining his magic during the day, and then being unable to handle an emergency in the evening.

They spent their morning paddling with brief periods of magic propulsion. Once again, they took their shirts off and enjoyed the warmth of the sun. They had learned their lessons about the bugs and put their shirts back on before they pulled into shore for the night.

Marvin once again used magic to catch a large fish for the two of them, and Shandria prepared it. They were sitting down waiting for dinner to finish cooking when a man appeared in their camp. His sudden appearance startled them. He said a sentence in a language they hadn't heard before.

Marvin's language weave translated it as "Aloha," which he knew could mean both hello and goodbye.

Shandria invited him over, but he declined and stood on the edge of the shadows just watching. After a while, he found a log, pulled it closer to the fire, and sat down.

The man was wearing leather pants held up by a tied leather-belt, and was naked from the belt up, except for an ornate vest made up of different pieces and colors of wood held together by fibers or threads. Marvin could see the shirt had different wood magic weaves on it, but he knew it was rude to look too hard. At least it was rude by Dwarven and Atlantian customs.

He had a knife on his belt in a leather sheath, and he was carrying a spear. The spear shaft was straight and smooth. It was a long spear tip made of a green crystal substance. Marvin could see it had magic in it, but he couldn't tell what type. There was a small pack on his back.

When the fish was ready, Shandria offered him a piece. He took it and ate it. They ate their share, cooked some sun roots and carrots from Crystal Mountain, and shared what they had with the man. The man pulled three pieces of fruit from a bag Marvin hadn't noticed before. He gave one to each of them and kept one himself. He said, "Thank you for nourishing me," and took a bite of one.

Shandria said to their guest, "Thank you for the fruit." Then to the fruit, "Thank you for your energy."

Marvin repeated what Shandria said and took a bite. It was an unusual flavor, sweet and tangy. He liked it.

He looked up, but the man had disappeared. He listened and looked. He could detect several living things but not the man, and none were human size. He turned towards Shandria, and said, "Alfarin?"

She replied, "I'm sure he was. I'm glad they are friendly. Their primary magic is wood, nature, healing, and camouflage. There could be an army watching us right now, and we would only know it if they wanted us to know.

Marvin asked, "The Dwarves greeted us like long-lost cousins. What is the status of the Alfarin?"

Shandria replied, "I asked one of our scholars once. He said the Alfarin are cautious when you first encounter them. But they are good friends. They try to live in harmony with nature. In general, the manufactured products of outsiders have little to offer them. Back on Earth, the ogres kept invading their lands and destroying things. So, they have an initial distrust of outsiders.

"Cultures tend to reflect the nature of their magic. Dwarven magic is the permanence of rock and metal. With the Dwarves, we have a permanent treaty of friendship. It will never change.

"We are aligned with the Alfarin to fight against the Darfarins and ogres and to respect each other. But they are more flexible in their nature. They believe change is a natural part of life. Plants grow and die, and in dying, they fertilize the soil for the next plant to grow. So, our treaty is more changeable, adaptable.

Marvin thought for a second, "Atlantian magic is water and air, which is always changing. How do we view our alliances?"

"Water needs walls, or it dissipates and evaporates. You can easily hold a rock in your hand, but water escapes through the fingers. It requires the rigidity of a container. Through the rule of hundreds of kings and thousands of years, our society has developed customs and laws that we maintain to keep us a society. Our treaty of alliance is the container for our interaction with the Alfarin.

"Our treaty with the Dwarves is unnecessary for them but necessary for us. To the Dwarves, we are best friends, people you treat as family. That will never change in their hearts or their minds. You don't need a treaty with family. But the treaty is our container. We need one to keep us true, and to define our relationship with them."

"When Queen Olivine, Princess Amethyst, and I rode through the farming communities, we were honored like we were patriarchs of the family. We sat down, and the Dwarven children crawled on our laps and played with us, just as they would crawl on their grandparent's lap."

"The treaty is for Atlantians to define our boundaries, not for the Dwarves to define theirs."

Then Marvin asked, "Where will I be in Atlantian society?"

Shandria said, "Your case is unique. You could be a merchant, a scholar, or a tradesman. Your sword plus training would make you an officer in the military. Once you learn more about Atlantis, it would be easy for us to make you an assistant ambassador to Iron Mountain. I gave you the title of sir for saving my life. It was confirmed when the sword chose you. The council will approve of it. It makes you a noble and marks you as having favor with the crown. That opens a lot of doors. And of course, you could always become an apprentice smith."

Shandria saw the look in Marvin's eye. It was time to address the subject once again. "I am a princess of Atlantis. I will marry an Atlantian Prince. I have the fluidity to marry the prince of my choice. My parents and royal advisors will help me choose, but I will marry a prince. That is my container by birth and by choice. I will fulfill my obligation to our society."

Marvin asked, "Is there any way to move between containers?"

Shandria said, "Sure, many children born into one trade group find they have aptitude in another trade group. An apprenticeship is found, and the child will flow to the new trade group. It's almost impossible to stop water from finding its level so we let it flow when we can, especially if it is beneficial to the person or society. Lateral movements are a normal part of our society. Water also exists as steam. Steam rises, and water flows down. There are ways for people to move up and down the social structure. But continuity requires birth to govern some positions. My being a princess is a position of birth."

The next morning Shandria and Marvin started out early with a sword kata. Shandria was impressed with how well Marvin was doing the water kata. They had practiced every day at Crystal Mountain, and he had improved. Even before they had left Crystal Mountain, he had switched from the step, move, pause, of a beginner to the more continuous fluid movement of an advanced student.

Shandria liked his progression through each sequence. Marvin's center was deep and balanced. Like water, he smoothly flowed into each new direction. Shandria had taught the kata to some young teenagers to prepare them for the military. After six moons, only a few were starting to get the concepts of fluid balance and movement. In only a few weeks from no training at all, his sword had taught his nerves and muscles the moves to near mastery. They did the kata twice. The second time they reversed it with the sword in their left hand.

Pd MICHEL

Marvin was more out of breath than normal. Shandria didn't say anything knowing it was his cancer. Once he caught his breath, Marvin wove water magic and walked out onto the slowly flowing lake. Shandria watched as Marvin performed the kata again. This time he added the magic. The kata was in three parts, mist, rain, and water. As he started the kata, he pulled water from the lake and formed a mist. It dispersed into a fog so dense she couldn't see him except with her magic eye. She watched him weave the magical threads of the kata. Each movement of the sword or his free hand wove, concentrated, activated, and released the magic.

Then the second part of the kata began. This time Marvin's magic formed a cloud above him from the mist. It grew dark and started to rain. He controlled the rain, swirling it around his body. The falling rain embraced by his magic, becoming his willing servant. Like a swarm of bees, it obeyed the magic commanded by his movements. Every sweep of his sword or his trailing hand included a magical instruction that caused the water to move in a thrust or slash. The water was an extension of his sword or an extension of his free hand. The freehand confused, balanced and protected him. His sword hand parried and attacked.

Marvin released the rain. He was breathing hard. He was supposed to perform the last part as a continuation, but cancer inside him had sapped his endurance. He waited until he caught his breath.

Once more, he wove the magic of the kata. The water responded to his weave. Large choppy waves formed. Then he began to move. The waves flowed and danced, choreographed and directed by his movements, and his weave, much as the raindrops had. The water formed into waves, never losing contact with the surface of the lake.

Marvin moved with the waves. Each step of the kata caused a wave to move him a dozen paces. Each sweep of his sword caused a wave to crash down. Each movement of the free hand rose up a new wave, to defend, to crash down, or to join the motion of his sword. The kata ended with Marvin thanking the water. He then stood up straight with his hand and sword lifted to the sky, thanking the creator of water.

Marvin sheathed his sword and rode a wave almost to the shoreline. Just before he arrived, he sunk into the river to cool off and waded the last few yards into shore. Marvin started to cough, and blood was once again on Marvin's hand. He quickly washed it off.

Shandria rushed out and hugged Marvin at the shoreline. She was so excited for him. He not only did the physical portion of the kata, he performing the magical weaves, unleashing the power of water through the kata. Few people knew the kata; fewer still could exercise it while weaving magic. Shandria could name everyone alive who could execute it, and each was an Atlantian Royal, a noble, or high in the military.

Marvin said, "Tomorrow, my sword wants me to practice the air kata."

ATLANTIAN MAGIC

They started out paddling, letting Marvin's magic and his body return to normal. They paddled most of the day, mainly out of boredom and the need to do something. Occasionally Marvin would grow bored and generate a current to increase their speed. The river varied from several hundred yards across to over a mile. There were sandbars in the areas where the river spread out. On one sandbar, there was a flock of huge flightless birds, which reminded Marvin of ostriches. The birds had sentries surrounding the flock. Some of their guards lined the bank of the river and made a loud barking-honk, warning them to keep their distance. Marvin's curiosity fought with his common sense, as he tried to get as close as he could to observe them without disturbing them too much.

Near another sandbar was a herd of animals the size of hippopotamuses. They had decided they owned this part of the river. Marvin lifted the canoe up out of their reach and had a wave carry them safely past the animals.

The river split apart. Marvin looked at it from a sky magic vantage point and chose the branch with the fastest current. They reached an area where large trees anchored numerous sandy islands in place. The trees on the islands seemed to be favorite roosting places for multicolored birds.

The terrain had been changing. The west side of the river was rolling hills and trees. The opposite side had waist deep grasslands with scattered trees. Many of the trees towards the east had wide, thick trunks. There was a grove, which either was one tree the size of a football field with hundreds of trunks, or it was hundreds of trees with intertwined branches forming one large canopy. Marvin couldn't tell which. When they were passing by, a flock of birds, too numerous to count, took off from the grove, flying over them, and like a cloud passing over them, dimming the sun.

They beached their canoe at midday. Both Marvin and Shandria noticed numerous large animals hiding in the bushes nearby. Bones on the beach indicated the area had seen its share of predators. They quickly ate lunch. Shandria noted large animals were spreading out and encircling them right as they finished eating. They quickly retreated to the canoe.

Marvin saw movement in the grass heading in their direction. He quickly picked up the canoe in a pseudopod of water, lifted it out of reach of the predators, and put it down into the deeper water. A pack of Hyenas ran onto the beach. They stopped at the water's edge and started barking in frustration as their lunch paddled away.

They saw a defensible spot on the west side of the river, near a rocky outcropping and a wooded area, about an hour before they would have normally stopped. They decided to stay there for the night because of the predators they had seen. Shandria spotted a long snake, killed it, stripped its skin, and gutted it while Marvin collected wood and started a fire. It was far more than they could eat. They were discussing how they could preserve the rest of the meat, and seven Alfarins entered the camp.

Shandria said, "Welcome, The Provider gave us a meal large enough to share, and friends to share dinner with."

She offered the snakeskin to the chief, who said, "Thank you." Her magic translated the term also as the chief's Blessing.

Once again, the group was silent. Marvin watched as the chief cleaned and scraped the snakeskin. He seemed pleased with the gift.

Their guests were silent. Shandria said a blessing on the snake and shared it with each of their guests. She also put some potatoes and carrots into a pot and cooked them with some spices. After sharing the snake, which Marvin was surprised to find actually did taste like chicken, their guests gave a red fruit to Shandria. They gave a purple fruit to Marvin. The rest ate a red fruit. Marvin's fruit had a thick skin like a banana. He peeled the purple fruit and ate it. It was bitter, and the fruit smelled odd. Marvin finished the fruit so as not to offend their company.

The chief handed out two green fruits to everyone and said a word of blessing before throwing one of the green fruits into the trees. All the men stood up and threw one of their fruit into the trees. Marvin and Shandria did the same thing. They peeled the other green fruit. It had a thin green skin, which covered a large wrinkled seed inside. Marvin watched each of them use wood magic to crack the hard shell.

Marvin broke both his shell and Shandria's shell. It wasn't fruit. It was a nut that tasted like a macadamia nut but was the size of a walnut.

They ate the nut, and the chief of the Alfarin handed Marvin a fist-sized cup made from the shell of a large seedpod. He said to Marvin, "Drink and feel better." Marvin took a sip and almost gagged. It tasted like a rancid, alcoholic drink. He was encouraged to drink all of it, so he did. As he finished the drink, Marvin could feel powerful nature magic from the beverage spreading throughout his body, along with warmth from the alcohol in the drink. The rancid taste soon left his mouth, and Marvin felt happy and sleepy.

Then, as suddenly as they appeared, the Alfarins disappeared.

Marvin crawled into the tent and fell right to sleep. Marvin's falling asleep early turned into a night of tossing and turning. He left the tent before sunup, ran to the edge of the forest, and threw up. Marvin couldn't keep anything down that morning and had a fever. He developed diarrhea. They decided to stay until Marvin felt better.

Shandria explored the area near them. None of the plants she found was medicinal, but then most of them were unknown to her. She saw the tracks of a large predatory cat, but she couldn't sense the predator anywhere. And the tracks were a couple of days old.

Marvin was tired all day long and spent much of it sleeping. He was still asleep at night. His fever broke late in the afternoon the next day, and he woke up fully alert, thirsty and starving.

ATLANTIAN MAGIC

Almost on cue, Two Alfarins entered the camp carrying a large pile of dead wood. They prepared and started a fire. Then two more walked in, carrying a medium size animal on a spit. More walked in when they had completed cooking the animal, carrying a large basket of prepared vegetables and fruit. Then two dozen Alfarins children walked into camp.

The chief looked at Marvin and handed him another mug like the one he had drunk the previous day. The chief ordered, "Drink."

Marvin wondered if the drink the chief had given him had made him sick. Then he realized that if they had wanted him sick or dead, he would already be dead. Marvin drank it down. It had a pleasant fruity taste. He could once again feel the warmth of nature magic flowing from the liquid into his body. The drink settled his stomach and made his tongue feel numb.

Marvin walked to the lake and caught a large fish to share in a pseudopod of water. It was as long as he was tall. They watched him thank the mighty fish and their Provider. Marvin planned to hand it to Shandria, but several women took the fish from him and prepared it along with the rest of the food. Unlike the previous encounters, where they were silent, everyone was talking and sharing.

The language weave Shandria crafted on Marvin started to take full effect. Marvin's knowledge of the Alfarin language increased quickly with all the conversation around them. It was intriguing to Marvin. The men talked in one dialect, the women spoke in another dialect, and the children spoke in a hybrid of the two. The older children shifted to their adult dialect, but still spoke in the mixed dialect to the younger children as did the adults when they were talking to the children. Men and women talked to each other, each using their unique dialect.

All the men were passing around a large mug that they continuously refilled. It never seemed to run empty. It was different than the drink they gave him earlier, but it was also alcoholic. Marvin suspected it had other drug-like qualities in it. His typical guarded nature when he was with strangers disappeared, and he answered every question they asked as if they were trusted friends.

The drink affected the Alfarins the same way. Marvin asked them about the drink they had given him yesterday. The chief said the purple fruit and the drink they gave him yesterday had strengthened his body and caused it to fight against his sickness. His body now identified his sickness as a disease. His body reacting to his cancer caused the fever and diarrhea. The magic in the drink had accelerated the process. Otherwise, he would be sick for several weeks. The drink they gave him today would help bring his body back into harmony. The worst of it was over, but it would be another couple days before the disease was fully gone, and another week before his body repaired the repairable damage done by the disease.

He asked about Shandria.

The senior woman replied, "Princess Shandria isn't sick. There is no illness inside her, and nothing is physically wrong. Nothing we can do physically will heal her. The dark spell twisted and broke her magic, not her body. Perhaps the grandmasters in the capital can regrow her magic."

The word Marvin's magic translated as "Perhaps" also contained an expectancy that they could.

Shandria was both worried and excited, but tonight she was under the influence of the Alfarin wine. They were soon free dancing and singing around the fire. The Alfarins shared much of their culture through song. Shandria shared an Atlantian song about hunting a giant sea monster that had been destroying ships. It was a song designed for children, and there were parts where everyone made the noise of the Kraken.

Marvin couldn't think of a song that would translate from the music of Earth to the world of Alfarin music. Then he remembered a childhood song. He stumbled with a few words, because of the translation, but when he was done, all the children were practicing the hand movements to "Itsy Bitsy Spider."

The next morning, Marvin woke up. He was laying on the ground. The sun was high in the sky. His arms cradled Shandria. He had no recollection of how or when they had become that way. The last time he had a hangover, it was caused by dwarven mead, but part of that was his sickness.

Last night Shandria had shared with him that she loved him and would formally have him court her if Atlantian custom allowed it. Then, with all their inhibitions down, she had kissed him like he had wanted her to kiss him since her feelings for him had revealed them self to her. He knew, on the one hand, it was an acknowledgment of their mutual desire, but it was also a goodbye kiss to those feelings. An electric shock from her chastity weave had kept it far shorter than either wanted.

Marvin realized that all he could do with his feelings would be to cause pain to Shandria. He would always love her, but never as her boyfriend or husband. He would have to put barriers around his feelings, using the strength of his love for Shandria, to wall off his desires and needs and to help her fulfill her duty to her society.

Chapter 38

Marvin was still sick and weak, as if he had the flu, exactly as the chief had said he would be. His body was still treating his cancer as an illness and fighting against it. The tribe usually camped at this location when they were in the area. They said no large animals would bother them here. Any fruit they found in this grove was good to eat. But it was time for the tribe to move on.

Marvin said to Shandria, "My sword has been teaching me a new kata, and it says I'm ready to do the movements. Marvin started out with the gentle, slow movement of the air kata, which increased in speed. He stopped at a natural break, breathing hard before he continued to the finish. Shandria watched and smiled. She then performed the kata herself. She was out of breath at the end.

Marvin laughed. "If the purpose of the air kata was to get our lungs pumping lots of air, then it worked."

Shandria joined in the laughter. Marvin practiced the kata for an hour each day without the magic.

Three days later, Marvin performed the air kata all the way through. He even completed the acrobatic moves without stumbling.

He felt better than he had in a long time. He looked inside himself, and there was almost no trace of cancer. The fist-sized, spread-out mass in his abdomen was now the size of a pea. The long tendrils were gone. Some holes and scars were left behind by the cancer. Marvin hoped most of that would repair itself over time.

Marvin grabbed ahold of Shandria's hand. He asked her to look at him. She saw the great remission of his cancer and gave him a strong embrace.

Marvin looked sad. Shandria asked. "What's wrong?"

He replied, "Your debt of life to me is now complete. I swore to be your companion and take care of you until your magic has returned, which may only be a few days away when we get to the arch at the Alfamara capital. As I understand Atlantian honor, my obligation to you is then over, and I don't want it to be."

Shandria realized she didn't want it to be either. She said, "We also have obligations as companions and protectors. Let's extend that until we get to Atlantis."

Marvin said, "I agree."

She continued. "What else is wrong? You have done a great service to Atlantis and me in protecting me. I won't just dump you into our society. I will make sure you get a position of value, and that you are allowed to flow to a place where you are happy and productive. Our ancient swords bind us together to protect Atlantis. The arch crystal is missing, and there will be trouble. I know we will be defending Atlantis together."

Marvin said, "I know you need to get your magic back, and Atlantis needs you to get your magic back, and I am committed to that end. After our talk the other night, I now understand and accept your obligations as a princess. I don't like it, but I accept it, and I will help you to be the best princess ever. When you marry a prince, I will drink to your long happy marriage, but I feel guilty because part of me hopes you don't get your magic back, perhaps then maybe we can be together."

Shandria said, "I've thought about that too. But something would be missing to me if I don't get my magic back and return to Atlantis. Part of me would never be happy."

Marvin said, "I know. So just like the Dwarves, I want you to know you will always have my friendship, and that needs no formal contract."

Shandria said, "Me too."

Marvin said, "I was looking at the sky last night. We have a half day of travel until we get to where the river passes near the arch crystal. Then we have to find the Alfarin Queen."

The next morning, Shandria and Marvin ate breakfast and boarded the canoe. They were enjoying the calm of the river and the rhythm of paddling. Then they saw a group of Alfarins lining the shore and waving. Marvin and Shandria waved back. Then the Alfarins disappeared. Increasingly they saw more and more groups of Alfarins. All of them waved as they paddled by.

Marvin was wondering where they should get off when they saw several wooden piers jutting into the water. A group of Alfarins was motioning for them to come over to one of the piers.

Marvin and Shandria paddled to the dock. One Alfarin had a rope in his hand. He frowned. Then he touched the front of the canoe, and the boat changed, a large handle shaped tie down point grew out of the wood. The rope, which he was touching, moved like a snake and tied itself onto the tie-down point. Marvin stepped onto the pier and saw Shandria step onto the pier beside him.

The man with the rope said, "Welcome to the capital. We are happy you are visiting."

Shandria said with a smile, "We are honored and thankful for your warm welcome."

Marvin looked around, and his jaw dropped. The piers that were empty a few seconds before were busy and had dozens of boats tied up. He remembered that Shandria had said. "You couldn't see them if they didn't want to be seen."

Marvin had thought Shandria meant they were good at hiding. Now he wondered how many villages and piers they had canoed past.

Many of the Alfarin were saying and signaling with their arms, "Come with us. The Queen wants to see you."

Excited families escorted Shandria and Marvin. A young girl took Shandria's hand, and another one took her other hand. Marvin couldn't hear what everyone was saying, but he could tell they were excited.

Two young boys took Marvin's hands and escorted him. Marvin's jaw dropped as they walked through the wooded area. The houses of the village were living trees, shaped by Alfarin magic. The Alfarins seemed at ease climbing them. Many Alfarins, including young children, had climbed the trees around them and were watching and waving, some from the higher branches. Marvin could see openings in the large trees, which were houses or rooms. It was an apartment complex made out of living trees.

The children excitedly asked Marvin about his travels, and about the Dwarves. Information in Alfarin society quickly spread, and they already knew everything they had told the chief at the celebration.

Soon they came to a large tree, or was it a grove of trees? Marvin couldn't be sure. At the entrance, there was an elegantly dressed woman. She wore a gown that seemed to flow and change in color with each step. A beautiful necklace made of different colored wood and jewels that Marvin thought might be different colors of amber adorned her neck.

She said, "Princess Shandria of Atlantis, and Sir Marvin, the Atlantian from Earth, I am Queen Juniperia. Welcome. Would you care to join me for a drink?"

"We would be honored your majesty," said Shandria who curtsied.

Marvin knelt down on one knee, bowed his head, and then stood up.

The queen escorted them into her home. The inside was large enough to fit a hundred people. Several different trees growing together made the walls of the room. There was no solid roof, but crisscrossing branches covering the top. There was a subdued light entering in through the branches. Vines with beautiful flowers and colorful fruit covered the wall.

The Queen asked them to sit down. The chairs were all made of ornately carved and decorated wood. Marvin was surprised to see wood magic enchanted into the chairs. Marvin sat down and the seat molded into the shape of his body. It was one of the most comfortable chairs he had ever sat in.

A young girl brought in a large wooden pitcher and three wooden cups. The queen walked over to one of the vines and pulled off a fruit. She pulled a piece of fruit off of three other vines.

Marvin watched her magic squeeze the fruit. The juice ran into the pitcher, which already had a liquid inside. The queen did the same thing with the other fruit. She swirled the pitcher around to mix the juice. She put the squeezed-out fruit on a wooden tray. A different girl picked up the tray and took the fruit away. The queen poured juice into each of their glasses.

They took a drink. The drink was sweet with a tangy taste. It also had an almost hidden taste of grapes.

Shandria was amazed at the beauty and fragrance of the room. There was a sweet smell of citrus, garden, and flowers.

Marvin listened as Shandria, and the queen caught up on royal business, in other words, they discussed their families, the kings, queens, princes, and princesses of Atlantis, their relationships and how they were doing. The queen talked about her children and her grandchildren. Marvin realized she was referring to several generations deep as her grandchildren, yet she seemed to be only a few years older than Shandria.

She turned to Marvin and said, "My condolences on the death of your fiancée and your adopted parents."

Marvin said, "I wasn't adopted."

The queen paused a second then replied, "Your Earth parents must have loved you deeply, and thought of you as their own not to tell you. But blood never lies, and you are full-blooded Atlantian, not a human. The healing medicine required magic that would not have worked on a human."

Marvin had denied it, but he knew it was true. His sword was confirming it.

Marvin looked down for a second then he looked back up and said, "My parents told me all my life I was their child. This adventure with magic is making me question everything I knew. Now I don't even know who I am."

Queen Juniperia replied, "Wisdom tells me the answer needs to be discovered by you. In time, you will learn. Perhaps there is something in the messages."

Marvin had almost forgotten the messages he was carrying. He didn't remember sharing that information with anyone but Shandria and wondered what he had said during the party by the river that he didn't remember. But then realized they could have been watching him from the moment he arrived in their realm, and he wouldn't have known it. He opened his backpack, opened his messenger pouch, and handed the queen the messages from the Anastasi, then he handed her the parchment from Queen Olivine, and then he gave her the scroll from the Dwarven king.

"I hope you will excuse my distraction. I do want to talk to you more, but I am anxious to read these."

She read the letter from Queen Olivine first. She laughed and smiled as she read it. She said, "I do owe them a visit, during their spring I think. I love the flowers in their fields. I will have to write her back a message."

She then opened the letter from the king. She smiled at first, but then her face grew more serious."

"I will have to answer him also. We will do what we can do."

Then she opened the scroll from the Anastasi. She concentrated hard on the message. The paper turned into smoke and disappeared. She said, "Anastasi almost always communicate in questions or riddles. Solving the question gets you to the message, but you learn much on the way."

Queen Juniperia raised her soft voice and said, "Daffodil!"

One of the girls appeared and said, "Yes Grandmother."

"Could you please give Princess Shandria a tour of the gardens?"

"Yes, Grandmother."

Daffodil offered her hand to the princess and escorted her away.

Queen Juniperia said to Marvin, "This conversation is for your ears only. Princess Shandria is severely injured. I can stabilize her magic, and she will live a long life. If I do, she will cease to be a princess. She will have to choose between dedicating her life to the temple or exile from the main island of Atlantis. If she chooses exile, she will need a protector, a husband. We both know she will choose exile with you. But she will never be happy without her full magic. She will both love you and resent her dependence on you."

She paused for a second to let her words to Marvin sink in. Then she said, "Or I can offer her a chance to be restored to full health. You will need to go through the procedure with her. You will share your energy, your strength, your magic, your mind, and your sanity with her. But it may not work. It may kill her, make her insane, or strip her of her magic entirely. If it kills her, it may kill you. If she goes insane, you may go insane. The process will take several moons. The Magic is powerful. It may change you. It will change you.

"Shandria will risk everything to get her magic back. But she will not choose to risk another's life, especially yours. If I told her of the risks to you, she would choose a life of exile and will never be completely happy.

"Only you have a real choice. The risk to you is your choice. You can decide not to tell Shandria of the risks to your health, and we will try to restore Shandria's magic, or you can tell her of the risks to your body, and she will share her life in exile with you. "Take a few minutes and decide. We can delay the decision if you like."

Marvin said, "The Anastasi gave me a question I have had to answer several times. Now I will answer it again. I am a man who will risk all I have to give the woman I love a chance at happiness. Even if it means that happiness is not with me."

The Queen stood up. She smiled. Marvin stood up also. She held out her arm and said, "Would you be kind enough to escort me to the garden?"

Marvin smiled and bowed, "It would be my honor. Your… I don't know the proper way to address you."

The queen smiled. "My name is Juniperia, but you may address me as my children do. You may call me Grandmother."

Marvin returned the smile. He realized she considered all Alfarins as her children. "I am honored to escort you, Grandmother."

She took his arm. Her grip was firm. Marvin was amazed at how strong she was for someone who must be over 100 years old.

The next morning the Alfarins escorted Shandria and Marvin to a grove of trees.

There were a dozen Alfarin. The leader asked them to remove all their clothing. They stripped naked, including their necklaces. They were indifferent to Shandria's princess necklace. It was useless metal. The man spent some time looking at Marvin and Shandria's tooth necklaces. Marvin explained how they had gotten them. The man smiled and nodded his head in understanding.

The Alfarins asked them to sit in wooden tubs of warm water. They scrubbed both of them clean. Marvin's skin felt raw when they finished.

The Alfarins gave them large wooden mugs filled with a concoction that Marvin was sure must be thick fermented pond scum. He tried to ignore the taste as he drank it. There were dozens of large pods attached by vines to a tree. An Alfarin used magic to open two of them. They looked to Marvin like giant-sized coconut shells. Marvin climbed into one and lay down, curled up in a fetal position. Shandria got in another.

Whatever they drank began to work. Marvin felt a strange warmth flow through his body. He didn't have a care in the world. He didn't care when they sealed the shell, or that he couldn't move. He didn't care that it was filling with a thick green fluid. He didn't care that vines inside the pod had penetrated his skin and were growing into his body. He didn't care that the fluid was over his head, or that he felt like he was drowning. He didn't care that he was falling unconscious.

Chapter 39

Marvin woke up. He was floating in a green glowing fluid and didn't see his body. His body must be somewhere, but he didn't know where.

He saw a strange girl crying. She was hurt and needed a friend. Marvin became a child. They ran, laughed, and played together. Then they jumped off a ledge into the garden pool and splashed each other and swam in the pool. There were other people in the dream. But they were like statues or mannequins hiding in shadows.

Soon they were exhausted and crawled into bed together. She held him. He was a giant, stuffed turtle. He held her. She was a stuffed black bear named Smokey.

The next day they played together again. He was Shandria's big sister. They laughed and chased each other around the palace. Then she was Marvin's friend Tom. They ran and played kickball together at the park down the road from his house.

They lived and relived each other's memories together. Sometimes they were themselves. Sometimes they were each other. Other times they were an object in the other person's dream. They played or learned together. And they slowly grew up. Shandria was struggling to learn Earth mathematics, and Marvin was struggling to learn Atlantian math.

Then Marvin was Shandria, learning Atlantian magic, and Shandria was Marvin, learning how to play football and baseball. She was helping his father change a flat tire on their car.

Shandria became Carol the first time Marvin kissed her. They saw a movie in the basement of the student center. A few weeks later, they were in Carol's dorm room. They were kissing and undressing each other. They lay down in bed, but instead of what happened they fell asleep. It was a special, personal moment Marvin wanted to keep private. He was glad that Shandria's nonsexual experience with men in bed took over and they fell asleep, but not really.

Last, they shared the experiences from when they had just met until the present, from the attack of the narworms to pulling into the dock. Then they started back at the beginning, sharing their most vivid memories several times. The memories began to change. Each time they became more bizarre, tangled, and warped.

Marvin was a stuffed turtle, playing football with Shandria, who was Smokey, the Bear. Sometimes Shandria was the ball, and sometimes Marvin was. Shandria was wearing a Santa Clause outfit. She was riding on an elephant and giving out fish and sweet cakes to all the children.

Marvin was an eighty-foot dinosaur, eating cake and ice cream with a narworm. Shandria was a baseball glove. She was catching all the red and blue flowers and turning them into pastries, which became gingerbread children. Marvin was a large, proud stallion, and Shandria was riding on his back. Marvin and Shandria's memories were being replayed and relived, and they were changing each time. Soon they would start to be rewritten, and reality would be lost.

Then a group of Alfarin joined them. They taught wood magic to a bear and a turtle. Then they taught nature and healing magic to Alfarins Marvin and Shandria. They were learning about wood and fiber, plants and grasses, roots and seeds and life.

Then Marvin and Shandria became Atlantian again. They learned how to camouflage their presence, their magic, and their energy. Magic bent light around their physical bodies, creating a chameleon effect. They learned how to move with silence, and with speed. Magic sped up their metabolism and strengthened their bodies. They learned to run faster than a cheetah, for longer distances than a horse could travel in a day.

They learned to change their vision with magic. They could see a mouse move a mile away. Their perception changed. It wasn't just a few displaced grains of sand on the ground. They had fallen off the foot of a gopher whose burrow was fifty feet away.

They hunted with the Alfarin bow, and they learned how to fight with the Alfarin spear. They learned how to grip to a tree with wood magic and walk up the trunk.

They learned the local plant life. And then they repeated everything. But they were themselves during the repeats.

Then Marvin woke up. He was lying on a strange rug, in a strange place. He was back in his body, and not in the green goo. He was back to reality, a reality that had become strange to him. He laughed, cried, and slowly remembered, what was real. Then he remembered the question asked by the Anastasi, "Who are you?" and he remembered who he was.

Shandria was lying on a mat next to him. She was tossing and turning as if she was having a nightmare. He put his hand softly on her shoulder. He sang her the Atlantian alphabet song. It seemed to calm her.

He told her the story of what they had done since the day they had met. He sang a mnemonic she had taught him in the goo, which contained the names her forefathers, traced back two-dozen-generations. Finally, he named her grandparents and parents. He repeated their names. He told her the names of her older brother and sister.

He stopped more to catch his breath than anything else. He also had nothing more to say. He opened his mouth to speak her name, but she sat up and said, "And Princess Shandria of Atlantis, companion of Sir Marvin, the Atlantian of Earth."

Marvin and Shandria embraced each other. They cried in each other's arms, an overwhelming flood of emotions.

When their emotions had calmed down, an Alfarin girl walked in. Marvin recognized her as Daffodil from the queen's palace. She handed a mug to Shandria and a mug to Marvin. "Please drink it all, and spend some time composing yourselves. I will be waiting outside when you are ready."

They finished their drinks, looked, saw their traveling clothing, and dressed. Shandria said, "I didn't understand how much my nudity affected you when we first met."

Marvin replied. "I didn't understand how little my nudity affected you."

They both laughed and finished dressing. Marvin asked Shandria, "May I look at you?"

She replied, "Please do. I'm almost afraid to look at myself."

Marvin looked at her. No dark places where magic wouldn't go remained. The channels of magic were straight, thick, healthy and alive. He looked up at Shandria with an excited smile on his face and said, "It's the most beautiful sight I have ever seen."

Shandria looked down at herself and started to cry tears of joy and relief. Marvin reached out and held her hand. She embraced him and finished her crying.

Arm and arm they walked out together.

Daffodil said, "Please follow me."

She led them back to the Queen's palace.

The queen asked, "How do you feel?"

Shandria said, "I feel wonderful. I feel whole inside again. I can feel the strength of my magic. I can't thank you enough."

The queen smiled and turned towards Marvin. She asked, "How do you feel?"

He replied. "I feel good also. It was the most amazing thing I have ever done. I can't wait to try out the new weaves I learned. Did you teach those to us?"

Queen Juniperia said, "The growing took longer than we had hoped. Your minds were starting to unravel. Each time you relived your past, it was different. Soon you wouldn't know reality from the truth. To stop the cycle, you had to learn something new. One of our grandmasters volunteered to teach you. He taught you our magic through the intermediate level, and it still wasn't enough. Then he showed you our weapons combat. Even though your mind knows the magic, you still have to practice it to teach it to your body and your magic.

"Shandria, I know you are anxious to return to Atlantis, but we have several weeks until the conjunction to Atlantis. We replanted the broken tree of your magic with a new tree. No two trees grow alike. You still need some time to adapt. Our grandmaster physician wants you to stay here so he can evaluate you and help you relearn your magic."

"Also, I have a favor and a challenge to ask of Sir Marvin."

Marvin said, "We owe you our lives. I will be happy to help."

Chapter 40

The next morning, Shandria left with the Alfarin grandmaster of magic and their grandmaster physician to practice magic. He had her start with simple light weaving. She had been able to do it without thought. But weaving magic felt awkward to her. It was simple magic, but she felt like she was weaving complex magic while drunk. Each time she wove the magic it was easier. After half a day of weaving light, the grandmaster had her advanced to another beginning weave. This one felt more as if she was weaving magic while tipsy. It took her a few tries before it felt natural. Each new weave was easier than the last. The initial discouragement she felt evaporated as it became easier. She was a determined and attentive student and relearned quickly. Tomorrow she would try more advanced water magic weaves.

The Alfarins treated her like a member of their tribe. She needed the diverse company. She had spent the last several moons with Marvin alone as her contact inside the green fluid. And he was gone. She felt as if a part of her was gone, and in a real way, it was. But she also needed to reestablish her individuality.

Queen Juniperia had Marvin talk to their arch crystal and teach it the changes the Dwarves had made to their arch. Their crystal was now communicating with Crystal Mountain's arch.

Marvin left through the arch to Crystal Mountain. The queen was quiet about his mission to Shandria and told her he would return in two weeks. She further shared that it was best for both of them if they stayed away from each other for a time so they could regain their independent identity.

Two weeks later, the portal from the arch opened up again. A full delegation of Dwarves led by Queen Olivine and Princess Amethyst arrived through the portal. The two queens met and embraced each other. It had been years since they last saw each other. Queen Olivine and Princess Amethyst were also excited to see Shandria again.

The green fluid had changed Shandria's perception. In some ways, it felt like she had just seen Queen Olivine a few days ago. In other ways, it seemed like a lifetime.

Several dozen Dwarves pulling wooden wagons laden with gifts came through the portal. The winding paths between the trees made cart movement difficult. Countless Alfarins carried the crates and bags to storage areas. Marvin brought up the rear and closed the portal.

Shandria ran to him. She had used her Alfarin speed magic without thinking. Their embrace was instantaneous. Marvin smelled different to Shandria. He needed a good soaking in the river. He was clean, but he smelled like the forge. It wasn't just his smell. He overflowed with earth, fire and forge magic, as he did when he worked the forge. Even if he were covered in dirt and coal dust, she would have embraced him. She missed him so.

Marvin said, while still holding her. "You look beautiful. I've never seen your magic so radiant and powerful."

Shandria said, "My Sir Marvin I missed you so. Every sunset was so lonely while you were gone. And at every sunrise, I awoke, and my heart felt empty."

Marvin smiled knowing it was a quote from an Atlantian poem. He repeated a line from the same poem, "Tonight we shall enjoy each other's warmth and sleep in each other's arms again." Marvin changed the line from "fan each other's fire" to "enjoy each other's warmth."

Marvin said, "The carts are almost unloaded, and one of us needs to open the portal so they can return."

Marvin bowed low. He straightened up, smiled, and said, "Would you do the honors, my Princess?

Shandria smiled and curtsied.

She drew a circle in the air, and the arch opened a portal back to Iron Mountain. The carts moved back through. Then she closed the portal.

Marvin said, "I could be mistaken, but I believe they are waiting for us at a party."

Shandria took his arm and Marvin escorted her to the party. It was a mixture of Dwarven food and Alfarin food. The whole Alfarin city seemed to be there, and it was more people than Shandria imagined could live in the capital. Shandria and Marvin drank and danced. It was a mixture of ritualized dancing and free-dancing.

They left for their tree-hut, stripped naked, and fell asleep in each other's arms. They woke up late the next morning. Shandria looked happy and radiant. She had the best night's sleep since Marvin left. But she could tell something was bugging Marvin. She asked, "What's wrong?"

Marvin replied, "I wanted us to have a happy evening together, so I didn't tell you last night, but this afternoon Queen Olivine and Princess Amethyst need to go back to Crystal Mountain. The drums of war are beating loud. They will ask you to join them and you should for the sake of the Dwarves and that of Atlantis. I must stay here with the Alfarin. We will see each other again before the conjunction and travel to Atlantis together."

ATLANTIAN MAGIC

Shandria grabbed Marvin and held him tight. Marvin held her for a long time. He had been inside her mind, and she had been inside his. Nothing could change that bond, and they didn't need to say anything else.

Shandria opened the portal that afternoon and departed with the Dwarven Queen, her daughter, and the rest of the Dwarves. Several of the Dwarves looked hungover. Shandria thought Dwarves could never get more than a little tipsy. They must have been drinking the strange mix that was the wine of the Alfarins.

Chapter 41

Two weeks later, a week before the conjunction, the portal opened, and Marvin returned. Shandria met him as he descended the trail from the top of Iron Mountain where the arch crystal was. The snow of winter had all but melted away. Soon the wildflowers would be in bloom. This time when they hugged, Shandria smelled trees, woods, and flowers. He was overflowing with Alfarin magic and the magic of air and sky. He had apparently been practicing the sky kata.

He had learned how the Alfarins enchanted their weapons. They were all made of wood. They shaped and hardened tree resin to form the tips of the spears and arrows. They enchanted their bows to make the arrows fly straight and accurate even at long range.

He had drilled with the Alfarin army, or more precisely, operated with their warriors. They traveled in small independent groups and often operated in groups of just two people. Their opponents never knew they were there until it was too late and they were gone. They never operated on one plan, but had several, and were opportunistic and flexible. Marvin practiced their stealth tactics and their stealth magic. The Alfarins used speed and camouflage in their attacks and defense.

Shandria had drilled with Princess Amethyst and the Dwarves, continuing what she had learned before, only now she could use her magic. And in the process, she had picked up some earth magic. She used Marvin's experiences from the green goo to help her to learn earth magic faster.

They talked and strolled down the mountain towards its base, where the entrance was. An honor guard met them with horses. The king requested Marvin's immediate presence.

The king's guard escorted Marvin into the courtroom. They escorted Shandria to another room to share some nut covered sweet cakes with the Queen and Princess Amethyst.

The king exchanged the necessary courtesies with Marvin then escorted him back into the iron room behind the throne.

The queen, Shandria, and Amethyst put some toppings on some small bite size pastries. Then they joined the men.

ATLANTIAN MAGIC

The King and Marvin were conversing about the forge when the women arrived. The men stood up. Marvin bowed to the Queen, who waved away the bow and gave Marvin a motherly hug. "Let me look at you," she said.

Marvin offered his hands. She held them and shut her eyes. She said, "Every time I think you can't get stronger you do.

"So, what was so important you needed privacy to discuss it with us?"

Marvin replied, "Just a king's eyes-only communication from Queen Juniperia. And I have one for the queen."

Marvin opened his pack and pulled out his messenger bag. He presented a sealed scroll to the king. He put his messenger bag back and pulled out an ornately carved, sealed, wooden container, and handed it to the queen along with a scroll.

The queen read the message and laughed, "You men have your secrets, and us women have ours."

Marvin and Shandria enjoyed a private meal with the king and his family.

The next day Marvin and Shandria rode their horses through the North gate. They greeted the guards who wanted to share a tankard of mead with them. Marvin said, "We are on the king's business and need to be prompt. I'll miss the mug as much as you do." The phrase was the equivalent of saying he would miss spending time together.

The north gate looked like the construction site it was. The Dwarven farming community had expanded outside the second wall. They were in danger if the enemy attacked. The Dwarves were constructing a series of guard towers in a zigzag formation, heading all the way to the mountain pass. The zigzag pattern allowed towers to fire at attackers by adjacent towers

The wall extended east to the nearest guard tower. Another tower nearby was being constructed. Hundreds of Dwarves, working together, were building the tower. Earth magic filled the air. Marvin watched Shandria's face as she marveled at the intricate magic the Dwarves were weaving. Rock and soil from the area were magically migrating towards the tower. The tower grew visibly taller as they watched.

Most of the magic weavers were singing a Dwarven song of construction. Much like the song of the forge, it was rhythmic. It kept the weavers synchronized, turning a hundred individual efforts into one.

Marvin turned towards Shandria. "This is the fourth of several hundred towers to complete the outer defense. Most of the builders have never constructed a tower before. Many learned on the first two towers. Tomorrow the teams will split in two; each team will add new workers. Then we will have two teams building towers. A few days later, the teams will split again, and we will have four teams building towers. The process will continue, adding new workers to the experienced workers, and doubling the number of teams every few days. They will complete the towers in only a few weeks, just in time to plant the early crops.

"Two other groups are also working on the towers. One group is rock masons. They are adding the battlements at the top. The other is constructing connecting tunnels between the towers underground. And of course, there are many masters forging iron parts for gates and sundry items.

"Most of the builders are Dwarven farmers. They will start planting their crops right after they complete the towers. Their earth magic ability is amazing. They taught me how to build a smaller section of a wall the last time I was here. It took me half a day to raise a narrow sixty-foot long wall to chest-high. Building the tower is harder. It is master-level earth magic and is past the abilities of all but a few Atlantians, but to the Dwarves, it's as easy as when we create a current of water. They hired and trained Dwarven farmers to do the enchantment.

"I want to show you one last thing." He walked over to a place on the tower, which had Dwarven writing. Marvin told Shandria, "Put your hand on it and tell me what you feel inside."

Shandria put her hand on the inscription and closed her eyes. "I feel strong magic. There is wood magic, earth magic, forge magic, and Atlantian enchantment. It feels like your magic."

Marvin replied, "The wood magic came from the Alfarins. The earth magic and forge magic came from the Dwarves. Inside each tower is a seal that I helped enchant. King Feldspar and I wove the enchantments on a seal provided by Queen Juniperia. It was at the edge of my abilities. It will take me months to understand the magic my sword taught me to weave.

"The warding magic in the seals will grow and seek its own. The magic will join with the towers on either side. It will be able to block and repel dark magic spells. The next phase will be to construct walls between the towers, but that is scheduled to start based on the when the farmers have some time between crops. It will take a while to complete."

Marvin looked at Shandria and had to ask. "Are you impressed?"

Shandria said, "I'm impressed, but shocked. It's illegal for Atlantians to perform enchantments at this level for warfare purposes without approval from a king or a prince acting on his behalf. Depending on the circumstances it can be considered treason."

Marvin said, "I am Alfarin-friend, and I am a Dwarf-friend. I have never been to Atlantis. How am I to know what Atlantians are allowed to do or not do? I'm from a planet that the Atlantians abandoned. I have never sworn an oath to the king of Atlantis, so I don't come under his jurisdiction. I performed a service for a lifetime friend of Atlantis to help them defend their home."

Shandria was mad and got madder when Marvin started to defend his actions. "How can you be so smug? I never thought you could betray Atlantis like this, that you could betray the king like this, that you could betray me like this. Stay away from me!"

Marvin's betrayal had ruined what started out as a perfect day. Shandria ran off angry and jumped on her horse. She sped back to Crystal Mountain. Marvin walked back to the guardhouse. He turned towards one of the guards who was watching Shandria speed away. He asked, "Is that offer for a mug of mead still available?"

An hour later, Marvin left the guardhouse. He must be developing the constitution of a Dwarf. Two large tankards of mead should have had him staggering, and he had drunk three, but they had barely fazed him.

Marvin thought about going to the embassy, but Shandria was furious with him. Besides, she probably locked the door on him. Their whole relationship had been her playing princess in her container and trying to fit him into a container he didn't fit, a round Atlantian container for a square, Earth-raised kid. He had done the best he could do, but the best he would ever be able to do was to become an oval. He would never fit the container she wanted to put him into.

The only container he wanted to fit into was one the shape of the two of them together, and she had told him at least a hundred times that wasn't going to happen. The worst thing about being inside her mind was he knew she loved him, but they would never be more than friends.

Marvin thought, "To hell with her, to hell with Atlantis, and to hell with this whole crazy world out of a Tolkien nightmare." He pointed his horse towards Crystal Mountain and slapped its hindquarters. He knew it would find its way home. He walked a hundred yards to the end of the next guard tower. He waved at the guard, walked around the end, and down the hill to the now flowing river. He wove some magic, stepped on the water, and rode a wave north until after sunset.

Chapter 42

Shandria was angry with Marvin, but she was angrier with herself. She was angry with Atlantis; She was angry with the Alfarin queen, and with the Dwarven king. She doubted Queen Olivine knew what was happening, but she had enough anger to be mad at her also, just in case. She waited for Marvin to show up for dinner. He didn't. She waited for him in the garden, doubling her anger because he didn't show up for dinner, but he didn't show.

Holding anger that long was exhausting and she fell asleep on a lounge in the pool area. She woke up several hours later. She ran and checked all the beds, hoping to find Marvin in one of them. She walked back to the royal bedroom and crawled into bed. She saw the pillow his head was supposed to be on, grabbed it, and threw it against the wall. She tossed and turned in bed for several minutes, her anger fighting with her worry. She climbed out of bed after a while, grabbed his pillow, held it in her arms, lay down in bed, and cried herself to sleep.

Early the next morning, she looked in the mirror at swollen red eyes that had been crying all night. She quickly dressed and apologized to the staff. She wasn't hungry for breakfast. She walked out of the embassy to the exit from Crystal Mountain.

She exited the mountain and found a quiet spot near the entrance. She looked but couldn't find Marvin anywhere. She climbed the stairs to the top of the mountain by the arch crystal. All the guard could say was that no one had come or gone since he started his watch an hour ago. She thought Marvin could have gone back to Alfamara, but she could feel that no one had used the portal in over a day.

But Marvin could weave a portal without an arch crystal. The Alfarins had healed him. He could go back to Earth if he wanted to. Could he have left without her knowing it? Not all portals were noisy. Had he become good enough to balance his magic and create no wasteful noise? And with his Alfarin magic, you couldn't see him if he didn't want to be seen.

Shandria needed to get back to the embassy. The tailor was going to check her formal dress for the ball. She didn't have time to have a new one made, but a quick alteration here and there and the tailor assured her it would look like a new gown.

ATLANTIAN MAGIC

Being fitted for a dress wasn't what she needed. Normally it would be fun. But today she only went through the motions. She would try to cheer up for the ball. She was a princess, and she would act like one. She would tell them Marvin had to go somewhere. She would smile and dance and have fun at the ball. But then she would come back to the embassy, drink too much wine, and cry herself to sleep.

Chapter 43

Marvin headed north until he found a copse of trees. He wove the Alfarin magic that would protect him and hide him during the night, and he lay down. The third mug of mead finally caught up with him, and he fell right asleep.

The next morning, he opened his pack. It was full of trail rations provided by the Alfarin. The honey and citrus cakes were better tasting than most deserts yet were nutritious. But the sweet taste in his mouth didn't reflect the sour taste in his mind or his heart.

He had spent most of his life trying to fit in. Every time he thought he found his niche, life had taken it from him. Marvin had found out why he was different, and with the discovery of his magic, he felt for the first time as if he had a place in the world, and someone to share it.

Okay, He wouldn't share his life with Shandria the way he wanted to, but she would be his friend for life. It would be hard, but he would tough it out and let her go. But now, even that plan was gone. The Atlantians would charge him with treason. All he had tried to do was to learn and to help. He was so upset he didn't know what to do.

He walked out to the road and continued north. He had spent several months in the green goo trying to keep his sanity, followed by two weeks of minimal sleep enchanting for and with the king, then two more weeks training with the Alfarin military by day, and enchanting for the Alfarin queen by night. The herbs they gave him had condensed his needed sleep time to just an hour a night while he was there.

But now he was mentally, emotionally, and magically exhausted. He needed to think. Or in Atlantian terms, he needed to flow, so he flowed. He must have wave traveled farther north than he realized. He was near the stone hut where they had battled Shandria's necklace. The necklace had burned her neck so bad that the skin was wrinkled, scarred, and discolored. The green goo had healed all her scars, a happy side effect. He was thankful she no longer had scars from her cursed necklace. When he looked inside himself, he had no scar tissue or evidence he ever had cancer. Another happy side-effect.

He reached the hut where they had stayed and walked inside. Nothing had changed. Even his sleeping bag was still in the corner. He exited out the back door. The green of spring was replacing the white of winter. Soon flowers would accentuate the landscape with their colors. There were a few traces of snow left, dirty and hiding in the shade.

The river flowed fast with the meltwater of early spring. Marvin decided to walk along the bank. There were bushes along the way. Without thinking about it, he wove Alfarin magic about himself and blended into his surroundings. It allowed him to slip past bushes without being scraped or pricked by thorns. He felt the magic of wood and nature around him, and he blended in. The question the Anastasi asked him came to mind, "Who was he?" Tonight, he would try to find out.

He fell asleep that night next to a mother bear and her two cubs in a den. The mother had broken her ankle. Her children were growing hungry as the last of her milk dried up, and she was growing weak. She had shared her den and her body heat. Marvin had to admit it was a test of his Alfarin magic to blend in so well. Part of him just needed to belong somewhere. It was perhaps childish, but part of him knew she was a substitute for his childhood bear Smokey. And part of him was trying to prove he was Atlantian.

He no longer belonged on Earth. He realized Earth's lack of magic had turned it into a world of black and white with no color. He knew he was Atlantian, but he was still stubbornly holding on to being from Earth. The Dwarves would accept him, but he wasn't a Dwarf. The Alfarins would welcome him, but he wasn't an Alfarin. Atlantis might charge him as a traitor. Could he find a place where he belonged?

Marvin felt sorry for the struggling bear. He wove healing magic as she slept. She would wake tomorrow morning with her ankle healed. An infected open wound on her shoulder she had received in a fight would be cured.

Marvin reached his decision. Tomorrow morning, he would go back to Crystal Mountain. If Shandria rejected him, that was up to Shandria. If Atlantis exiled him, that was up to Atlantis. He owed King Feldspar and Queen Olivine an apology for missing the ball. He owed Shandria enough that if she wanted to yell at him, he would quietly take it. He would be firm in his forgiveness, even if he disagreed with her.

He had promised Shandria he would be her companion until they arrived at Atlantis. He had promised the Anastasi he would deliver their messages to Atlantis. He still didn't know who he was or where he belonged. But he knew who he was until he completed his promises.

The next morning, he left the den just before sunrise. Marvin found a giant boar that was foolish enough to chase him to just in front of the bear's den. The animal charged. Marvin slid to the side and chopped part way through the boar's neck with his sword. The animal squealed, turned around, stumbled, and fell to the ground. Marvin thanked the boar for providing for his friend and her family. The bears woke from the racket and came out of their den to investigate. He saluted the bear and her cubs with his sword, cleaned and sheathed it, and blended into a bush. Once he saw them eating, he walked back to the river.

He jumped on a wave and headed back to Crystal Mountain.

Marvin was traveling fast. He was flowing with the river and adding the speed of his wave to it. Another tower was complete. He had a pseudopod of water deposit him near the tower. The amulet was in place, and the wards were growing in strength.

Marvin talked with the guard for a few minutes. The king had given him a special exemption to the regulations. They allowed him to do almost anything he wanted to when it came to gates, roads, towers, walls, and not paying taxes. Marvin couldn't believe that he almost missed their quoting regulations to him.

Then a second guard came over Marvin hadn't met yet. The guard quoted special order from the king number 1241.08 regarding Dwarf friend Marvin, special assistant to the court of King Feldspar. The Dwarf saluted Marvin. He awkwardly waved back, and then he held out his hand and shook the young private's hand. Marvin slapped him on the shoulder.

He could walk for an hour back to Crystal Mountain, or he could run like an Alfarin and cut the time to a fraction. The Dwarven Sargent gave him a horse and offered an escort. He accepted escort from a young private and rode to Crystal Mountain. Marvin thanked him and gave him the reigns of the horse to take back.

Shandria didn't feel like being social. She spent the morning sulking around the garden. Then she felt Marvin before she saw him, as he entered the private area. She ran to him, hugged, and kissed him. It wasn't just the kiss of a friend; it was deeper and full of passion. Then Marvin's lips and Shandria's lips felt like they had touched a live coal. They quickly withdrew. They were unharmed, but they discovered Shandria's chastity weave was still working.

They both started apologizing. Neither of them cared whether it was for the argument, or for burning each other's lips. Marvin smelled like he had spent the night in a bear's den, so he took off his clothes and jumped into the pool along with Shandria. They tread water while they talked about Marvin's adventure and the ball.

It was lunchtime. Marvin and Shandria dressed in appropriate clothing and sat down to lunch. After lunch, Marvin said, "I need to apologize to King Feldspar for missing the ball."

Shandria said, "Good, I owe an explanation to Queen Olivine. We can go together."

Chapter 44

Shandria put on makeup and a beautiful dress. Then they rode their horses to the palace. The court wasn't in session. They waited while the official greeter told the king they were there. He returned after a few minutes and said. "The king is waiting for both of you in the war room. Would you like an escort and for me to announce your arrival?"

Marvin replied before Shandria could say yes, "No thank you. I know where it is and he knows who we are."

"Very well, Princess, Sir Marvin." He bowed and waited for them to walk away.

Shandria said, "The war room, when have you been there?"

Marvin said, "It's where King Feldspar asked me to help perform the enchantment and showed me the defensive plan. It's the most secretive room they have, containing battle plans for defending the realms, and some other things I think you will find interesting."

There was a long hallway leading to the room. The guards let them pass. The Dwarves decorated the hall much like the drawings of King Feldspar on the outside of the palace. Screens from the mighty battles the Dwarves had fought lined the walls. Marvin stopped at each one. After a while, he asked Shandria a question, "Have you noticed anything unusual about these battles?"

He continued before she could answer. "There is relief picture where almost all the races are fighting against the ogres attacking Earth. Most of the other pictures show Dwarves answering the call to protect other homelands. A dozen times, Dwarves have defended Atlantis from attack. One turned into a sea battle. Dwarves are heavier than water. They are born afraid of open water, yet they responded with aid.

"Dwarves have fought several battles to defend their home, and only two are depicted here. One is when Atlantians and Alfarins helped them protect their home. They are as proud of defending their friends as they are of defending the Dwarven land. Dwarven friendship is as solid as stone. They will never forget how Atlantis and Alfamara once helped them. They are prouder of the battles they fought with friends than the ones they fought alone."

They reached the end of a hallway. A guard opened the door for them.

The king, queen, and several advisors were inside the room.

Before they could say anything, the Queen came forward and said, "Apology accepted. We missed you at the ball, but even more, we missed the happiness of Princess Shandria."

Shandria looked surprised. She thought she had played the part well.

The queen continued. "We already know about the argument at the North gate, so you don't need to explain what happened. Now come give me a hug."

The queen came over before Shandria could respond. Shandria was surprised to find a battle-ax strapped to her back when she hugged her. It was one of the ancient axes.

The queen hugged Marvin. The king hugged Shandria then exchanged forearm handshakes and slaps on the shoulder with Marvin. The king was wearing his battle-ax. It was obvious that the axes and the swords were good friends.

There were several large tables. On the first sat a three-dimensional model of Crystal Mountain and its terrain. The king had already added the completed towers. Small markers showed where the future towers would go. Marvin looked at the numbers on the towers and asked with concern, "Why are we projected to be behind schedule on the towers?"

The king answered. "Every family in the kingdom is excited and wants to help build the towers. We decided to rotate out people to allow others to take their place. This schedule is still well within the earliest that we anticipate an attack. The nearest natural portal point will take two weeks for the enemy army to travel here. This way we will have more Dwarves trained to build defensive towers. They will also have the experience to help build walls after the crops are planted, and to complete it after the harvest. We will be training teams from Iron Mountain and Silver Mountain as soon as they get here."

Marvin looked at the king with respect and said, "You once again show your wisdom King Feldspar."

The king smiled and said, "Shandria. There are three high-value targets for this war: Alfamara, Atlantis, and Crystal Mountain. Alfarin magic can resist and counter dark spells. The enemy detests the Alfarins for that ability. Crystal Mountain has the crystal mines. Atlantians, using the great weapons, can enhance magic, and create the portals. You are the key to the rest of us.

"We are prepared to send both troops and aid to Atlantis and Alfamara. The new towers will give us a greater ability to do that since it will better defend our land and allow us to send more support. The walls we plan to build after the harvest will help even more so.

"We have prepared for dozens of possible battle scenarios. If Atlantis is under attack, we will send troops to defend Atlantis."

After two hours of discussing scenarios and battle plans, refreshments arrived in the form of some spiced pastries. Shandria asked, "What's that wonderful spice?"

ATLANTIAN MAGIC

"I fell in love with the spice when we visited Queen Juniperia," said Queen Olivine. "She wouldn't tell me what her mix of spices is, but she did send me some in the box Marvin brought."

After their refreshments, the king wove some magic, and the table changed. Crystal Mountain and its walls sunk into the table. In its place, the island of Atlantis rose up. Light blue rock representing water surrounded the island.

The King shared his ideas to help defend Atlantis. Atlantis was the name of the realm, the name of the main island, and the name of the capital city. The island was long and roughly the size of Florida without its panhandle. It ran north and south. The city and its harbor occupied the southern part of the island. A string of hills covered the center of the island. Mount Atlantis was north of the city. On the top was the Arch gate.

The basic plan was for the Dwarves to come in from the portal, and to defend the arch and the northern part of the island. They were hoping the Atlantian king would allow Princess Shandria and Sir Marvin to assist them with their magic. Queen Juniperia had agreed to help also.

The king handed Marvin a dozen scrolls inside a cloth bag, which contained combined battle plans for King Vandian of Atlantis, and Shandria's grandfather, King Baracian. King Feldspar had met Baracian years ago. He had followed his maturing as a king and highly regarded the official decisions he had made. He gave Marvin a letter to that effect.

He handed Shandria an amulet, which hung just below her necklace. It had a small crystal that would glow red near anything touched by dark magic, or by anyone who had used dark magic.

Marvin said, "The Alfarins crafted the amulets from beautiful hardwood. And Queen Juniperia and I enchanted them. I know enough Alfarin magic that I can protect myself, and a small group from a spell, but I'm a beginner, and this will provide us automatic protection and alert." There were several dozen like it in a box.

Marvin pulled one out from his shirt that was a little different. He said, "This one also signifies me as a friend to the court of Alfamara. The crystals came from King Feldspar."

The queen walked over to Marvin and asked him to take a knee. She placed a silver and gold medal over his head. It had a single white crystal in the center. "This will tell all you are a friend to the Court of Crystal Mountain. I'm sorry it took so long to get this to you. But Amethyst and I insisted on crafting this medallion ourselves."

She kissed Marvin on both cheeks and had him stand back up. She turned towards Shandria and said, "The kneeling isn't necessary, but he is so much taller than me." Then she started to giggle as if she was much younger. Shandria and Marvin joined her laughter, and everyone smiled.

They ate that evening with the queen, the king, and their family in a private area of the palace reserved for them.

The king and queen saw them off the next morning. King Feldspar couldn't create a portal, but he could open the portal using the portal stone to Alfamara.

Queen Juniperia was waiting at Alfamara. She hugged them both. She whispered something into Shandria's ear which must have been an inside joke, as she smiled in return. They walked down to the docks, where they had prepared a boat of Alfarin design, with many Atlantian features.

They pushed the boat off the dock and drifted out into the river. Marvin told Shandria, "You handle the boat, I will weave the portal."

Marvin focused. He saw the star configuration he had memorized from the sky map at the garden of the embassy. He looked down and saw the Island of Atlantis and the Seven Jewels. Shandria said the current flowed to the north. The arch crystal was gone. But Shandria knew the Atlantian army was weaving and renewing magic that would keep an enemy from coming in uninvited through a portal.

Marvin could see the rippling edge of the magic that would prevent him from going directly to the island of Atlantis. He focused and found a spot south of the anti-portal weave.

Marvin used his magic and opened a portal large enough for their boat, and Shandria used her magic to push the vessel through the portal.

Chapter 45

The transition through the portal caught Marvin by surprise. The portal opened up ten feet above the ocean below. The boat started to drop, but only fell a few feet before an ocean swell hit the bottom of the boat's hull, stopping their plunge and accelerating them upwards. They hit the water with a splash, which sent the salty water over the side and onto the deck of the boat. The portal closed behind them, and Marvin held on tight. The rise and fall of the boat from the constant up and down wave motion made him afraid to let go.

He heard Shandria laugh. She wove some magic, and the sail rose up the mast. She moved the tiller and set a course for true north. The tipping of the boat as it turned made Marvin hold on tighter. Shandria started to happily sing an Atlantian sailing song. She put Marvin's hand on the tiller, told him to keep it steady, and stood up. She stepped out of the cockpit of the boat and walked forward around the port side of the cabin.

Marvin had one hand white-knuckled on the tiller, and the other held tightly onto the edge of the cockpit. Marvin fought against his fear while Shandria walked and laughed on the rising and falling deck.

Shandria's song matched the rhythm of the waves, the occasional flap of the sail in the stiff breeze, and the sound of the boat gliding through the water. Marvin forced himself to relax. There weren't any breaking waves, just the slow up and down swell of the dark blue ocean and some occasional white topped swells in the distance. They were sailing downwind and with the current.

Shandria yelled. "Keep us heading north."

Marvin looked at her like she was crazy. She laughed and said, "I guess you have never been on a boat like this before. "Just keep us sailing straight,"

She adjusted the triangular mainsail. Then she walked forward and unfurled the triangular jib sail. Shandria was in front of the mainsail. All Marvin could see of her was her feet beneath the boom. Marvin shifted his posture so he could better see her. She was the only familiar thing on the boat providing him any comfort.

Shandria came back and lithely stepped down into the cockpit. "It's such a beautiful day," she exclaimed. She opened the door to the small cabin and descended below deck. She came back up a few minutes later, without her clothes, wearing only her necklace and her dagger in its sheath on her calf.

She looked at the boat and adjusted its direction, "That way." she said.

Marvin replied, "It's all ocean. How do I know what way that way is?"

Shandria thought for a second and then said, obviously trying not to laugh, "I forgot. You grew up in a desert. Just keep the tell-tails pointing in the same relative direction to the sails. You won't have to move the tiller much."

Shandria pointed up at the strips of canvas blowing on the side of the sails. "We are headed downwind so it should be easy."

Marvin confirmed the canvas fabric was the tell-tails. Shandria watched him for a couple of minutes. Then she said, "I miss Atlantian water so much." She dove overboard into the ocean.

Marvin, overwhelmed by the boat, its motion, and the vastness of the water around him, felt a spike of adrenalin and a touch of fear when she jumped in and disappeared below the waves. He leaned over the edge of the boat where she dove into the ocean. All he saw was the vastness of the water and the undulating swell of its waves.

Marvin had moved the rudder when he leaned over to see Shandria. The ship shifted suddenly. He regained his composure and pushed the rudder back where it belonged. Then he noticed he was no longer heading in the correct direction. He readjusted his course, all the time looking for Shandria.

All he could see was miles and miles of dark-blue ocean as far as he could see. Swells of water were rhythmically going up and down. Most were higher than the deck of the boat.

Marvin was fighting with the irrational thought that it had been hours and Shandria must have drowned, against the reality that she was Atlantian; this was her swimming pool, and she had gone for a quick dip.

Then he remembered he was Atlantian too. He looked with his magic and quickly found her. She was swimming next to a round shape that was wider but smaller than she was. There were several dozen shapes in the water. He could tell that she was doing fine. He had to readjust the course again. Holding the tiller straight was something he would have to get used to.

He saw Shandria swimming to the surface near the boat. She picked herself up with a pseudopod of water and stepped into the cockpit.

"The ocean feels wonderful. There is a school of sea turtles right underneath us. They don't travel together very often. Maybe they are going to lay their eggs on one of the southern islands." She reached over and took the tiller. "Why don't you get free and take a swim with them? They won't be with us for long."

Marvin looked at her as if she was crazy, "I'm overwhelmed right now, maybe later."

Shandria laughed at the look on his face and said, "Well at least go below and get out of those clothes. You have to get rid of your iron mine tan, so you look like an Atlantian. The sun feels warm and beautiful."

ATLANTIAN MAGIC

Marvin went below deck, unsteady in the constant motion of the boat around him. The cabin wasn't quite tall enough for him to stand up straight, but there was more horizontal room than he thought there would be. The motion of the boat made him undress with one hand. He used the other against the wall or roof of the cabin to steady himself. He finally realized he could lean his back against a wall, or bulkhead as Shandria would call the wall later, and free up both his hands. He reluctantly took off his clothes, replacing his slowly subsiding anxiety with a touch of vulnerability. Just like Shandria, he left his dagger attached to his leg. He carefully exited the cabin, not sure he wanted to leave.

He was holding onto the doorway of the cabin. Shandria saw him and said, "Look!" she was sitting on the starboard side of the boat. "See that splash?"

Marvin carefully inched over to the side. Before he could grab ahold of anything firm, Shandria moved the tiller fast. The boat tipped at a steep angle. And he started going overboard. Shandria helped him over with a push and started laughing.

Reflexively, Marvin took a big gasp of air before he hit the water. He was shocked rather than afraid. He lettered in swimming in high school and did well in the state competition. But he had gone in head over heels, and at first wasn't sure what direction up was.

Unlike the Dwarves of Crystal Mountain, he had always felt comfortable in the water. The motion of the boat and the ocean swells were new and frightening. But the water was an old friend.

He stopped for a second and looked with his magic. It was incredible, frightening, exciting, and beautiful. The water was alive. Algae, diatoms, plankton or something gave off the magical green glow of life all around him. As far as he looked down, there was no bottom. It was somewhat disconcerting but exciting. He could see off in the distance the turtles swimming away, and the boat slowly getting farther away. He wasn't worried. He initially panicked but then realized he could easily catch it using magic.

The up and down motion of the ocean swells felt relaxing. His natural buoyancy drifted him upwards towards the surface. He kicked his feet, sending his body partway out of the water, took a deep breath, and did a feet-first surface dive, letting his momentum and his hands clapping together above his head force him downward. He let the waves carry his body up and down with each pass. It was regular and timed, like the slow breathing pattern of Shandria when she slept.

Then he felt it. It was water magic, but the ocean had its own accent. He felt it welcoming him, and he felt at home, enjoying the heartbeat of the ocean as its swells moved him up and down.

Shandria was getting farther away. Marvin was drifting back up towards the surface again. He kicked himself above the water, took another breath, and did a surface dive.

He wove magic and made a current to ride in. He didn't know if it was how deep the water was or the salt, but his magic seemed to have a greater effect in the ocean. He felt like he was flying through the water like a bird gliding through the air. He caught up to the boat on one breath, popped out of the water on a large pseudopod that lifted him out of the water, over the top of Shandria, and landed him on the deck.

He unwove the magic of the pseudopod, and it came crashing down on Shandria. The sound of her yelling as the water hit her from above, and the fun of the splash fight that only lasted a few seconds until the boat's cockpit drained, almost got her back for pushing him overboard. Of course, he would never let her know that.

Marvin sat down and quickly grabbed ahold of the side of the cockpit, still uncomfortable in the rocking boat. Then he realized he had put water into their boat in the middle of the ocean. So, he asked Shandria about it.

She replied, "Okay desert boy, the part of the boat where we sit is called the cockpit. It is above the waterline and angled backward. It has small holes in the back, so water drains out. The area below, where you changed, is the hold, cabin or sometimes called below decks. I sealed the cabin when you slipped on the deck and fell overboard."

"An assisted slip I might add." He retorted.

She ignored his statement and continued. "Anyway, it prevented the water you put in the boat from draining into the cabin. We need to keep the doors and hatches closed. Occasional, random waves do happen at sea you know. Any water that spilled below drained into the bilge."

Marvin asked, "What's a bilge?"

Shandria looked at him and replied, "You are a desert boy. The bilge is the lowest part of the ship. On this boat, it's the bottom of the V-shaped part of the hull or keel. All ships and boats get some water inside. The water accumulates in the bilge. I checked when I was getting free, and there was no water in the bilge. Bilgewater is magically pumped out. The Alfarins built this vessel well, and it knows it's a boat. Look at the magic on it."

Marvin looked at the threads and listened to them. There were several he recognized, giving the wood strength and self-repair. And a few he didn't. One weave that was new told the boat it was a boat. It combined many magical threads. Boats are watertight and float on top of the water. They are stable and resistant to tipping over. A boat always stays or return to an upright position.

Shandria said, "It amazes me that the Alfarins did so much with wood magic. We would have used water magic. I will remember this weave."

Marvin asked, "How will we sleep and steer the boat?"

Shandria answered, "Tonight you get to stay awake and follow the north star. I will sleep downstairs and relieve you in the morning."

Marvin gave her a dirty look.

ATLANTIAN MAGIC

She laughed and said. "Look at the water. Do you see how it's changing color? The wave motion will soon be changing. We are approaching the southern edge of the Atlantian shelf. We started in the deep ocean. The water is becoming shallower. We will see reefs and an occasional small island.

"Soon we will start to see some seabirds. Many birds swim around the reefs eating fish. Others eat seeds or fruit from trees and insects. They sometimes fly between islands where other fruit may be ripening. The coral reefs contain many species of fish.

"We will anchor the boat in the shallows near an island and sleep on board for the night. We should have fresh ocean fish tonight, and if it is a fertile island and we have time, maybe I can find some herbs to add to our meal. Otherwise, we have enough provisions for a couple moons journey."

Marvin asked, "How long until we get to Atlantis?"

Shandria said, "We have a week to ten days if the navy doesn't intercept us. We can always magic the boat along faster, but desert-boy needs to get rid of that iron mine tan and get more acclimated to the ocean. And this is the first time I have gotten to be free in several moons.

"Our island nation of Atlantis sits on a sunken continental shelf. We moved here from Elder Earth along with seven other large islands, and dozens of smaller ones. We call the large islands the Seven Jewels of Atlantis. Most of the small southern and eastern islands grew over time from coral communities brought from Earth when Atlantis moved here. North west of Atlantis are islands that were part of a volcanic chain, which has slowly been rising.

"The ocean current that had been flowing north is starting to split around the shelf, but the primary flow over the shelf is still north.

"We are right on the edge of the split and will follow the current over the shelf, sailing north with the current. The current will slow down over the shelf. We will average eighty miles a day in a good breeze, and anchor at night. We can sail faster if we used magic, but we currently have no need. And I want to enjoy the ocean with you."

Marvin jumped back into the ocean. He felt like playing in the water. His dread of the boat had mostly gone, but he still felt unsteady on it. The water of the ocean felt comforting. Marvin thought it strange that he was afraid of drowning on the boat but completely at home in the middle of the ocean. After an hour of swimming, diving, and playing, Marvin came back on deck.

Shandria saw the smile on his face. She knew the ocean water of Atlantis had welcomed him home. It was her turn. She yelled, "You're such a whale," which had the same connotation as calling him a water hog and dove overboard into the ocean. Marvin grabbed the tiller of the boat and laughed.

The dark blue of the ocean around them changed as they sailed onto the Atlantian shelf. The water turned a lighter aqua color, and they could see the bottom. Marvin was glad smaller swells had replaced the large deep ocean swells.

They alternated steering the boat and playing in the ocean. The colors and shapes of the coral and fish fascinated Marvin. Shandria had told him not to touch the coral until he learned more about them. Some would leave a painful rash if he scraped against them.

Shandria navigated the boat around the backside of a small island where it was, out of the current. The water level was shallow, and they anchored on the coral reef. She called out orders to Marvin on the tiller as she adjusted the rigging. Tomorrow morning, he would be the deckhand, and she would direct him from the tiller.

Shandria activated a magic weave, which dropped and tied up the sail for the night. She grabbed a trident, a three-pointed fish spear from below deck, and jumped feet first into the water. Marvin watched from above through the clear water. After coming up for air several times, she came up with a fish that was wiggling on her trident.

Shandria handed Marvin the trident, complete with fish. She said, "Hold this while I get what we need from the cabin." She entered the cabin and soon came upstairs with a small wooden cutting board. She laid it on the deck near the front or bow of the ship and told Marvin to clean the fish.

Shandria returned below decks and came back upstairs with a double bottom clay pot. The pot had vent holes between the top and the lower part, which kept the bottom of the clay pot cool enough to place on the deck of the ship. In the top part of the pot, she had laid out several dark rocks. She heated the rocks with magic and cooked the fish on wooden skewers at the top of the pot. She let the rocks cool down after the fish finished cooking. Once everything had cooled down, she carefully cleaned and put it away. Marvin watched her. Tomorrow was his turn to perform many of the chores.

After dinner, they relaxed for a few minutes before going into the cabin to sleep. They slept well that night, cuddled in each other arms, rocked to sleep by the gentle ocean waves of Marvin's new home.

Chapter 46

The next morning Shandria and Marvin wove magic and walked out onto the water and practiced the water kata together. Marvin raised himself up with a mound of water he created and performed the air kata on top the mound. Shandria watched. She was impressed at how fast he had learned it.

Then he surprised her. He let the mound of water below him sink away and stayed floating above the water on a magically generated updraft, Marvin performed the kata again, dipping and diving in the air currents. He rose up a mound of water to meet him again at the conclusion of the kata and had it bring him back to the water surface. Shandria greeted him with loud applause and a hug. "I'm so proud of you. You have worked hard and learned so much."

Marvin smiled and thanked her. "I'm still not confident enough to do the air kata without the water below me. But soon I will try it. I started learning the sky kata on land when we were apart. I'm hoping that tomorrow we can find a large enough beach for me to practice it. It's very unlike the others, and it will be a while before I can try it on water, and then move further up the levels."

Shandria was still working on the second level on the sky kata, and she never made it to the third. Few Atlantians had since it took a lot of practice, a lot of magical focus, and the aptitude. Only a few people, her grandfather one of them, had ever performed it at the highest level. She had never seen anyone progress as fast as Marvin in Magic. At this rate, he would soon be doing the sky kata in the sky.

Shandria let Marvin recover for a few minutes, and then she had him pull on the anchor rope until their boat was above the anchor. She said, "Dive down and free the anchor."

Marvin jumped feet first into the water. He should have dived in. The clear ocean water made the bottom seem closer than it was. He had guessed the depth to be around 20-feet, but it was double that. He kicked back to the surface, took a breath, and then pulled himself down quickly using the anchor line. At the bottom, he pulled the stone anchor out from under a coral ledge it had snagged on and put it on top the ledge.

Marvin was glad he was a good swimmer and wondered how much of that had to do with being Atlantian. Many of his friends complained about pain in their ears when they dove down to the bottom of the deep end of a swimming pool. He never had any sensation, maybe his ears cleared faster. He had always been able to hold his breath longer than anyone he knew. Maybe that was part of it. He looked around at the coral and the fish before kicking off the sandy bottom near the coral. He wove a pseudopod and lifted himself back into the boat, grabbed the anchor line, and pulled the anchor back up on deck. Shandria showed him how to coil the rope so it wouldn't tangle, and where to stow it and the anchor.

Shandria was at the tiller. She told Marvin, "Look at the weaves on the mast. See if you can find the trigger to lower it."

Marvin looked. He replied. "I see three triggers. One trigger is activated. That must be the one to stow the sail."

Shandria yelled back, "Pick one of the others and activate it."

Marvin activated one. The sail rose partway up the mast. Shandria Yelled. "That reefs the sail. Activate the next trigger."

Marvin activated the next trigger. The mainsail rose to the top of the mast. Shandria yelled, "Turning hard to port."

They were facing into the wind and moving slightly backward. It took a while for the boat to turn enough so that the wind caught the sails. As soon as it did, the boat slowly twisted to the left, the port side, and the wind filled the sail. The sheets, or ropes as Marvin wanted to call them, which attached to the sail, stopped its movement. The boat started to move forward. Shandria yelled, "Move the Jib sail to the starboard side of the ship."

The jib was lying down on the port foredeck. The front corner attached to the bow of the boat. Marvin moved it to the starboard side. Shandria yelled, "Tie off the starboard jib sheet." She pointed to where he should tie it, and he did.

"Now activate the jib sail trigger."

Marvin looked at the sail and found the trigger. He activated it. The jib sail moved up a line to the top of the mast. Shandria had Marvin hold the tiller. She walked forward and adjusted the sails where she wanted them. They were still heading downwind. The mainsail was sticking out on the port side. The Jib sail was sticking out on the starboard side. The two triangular shaped sails caught the wind and pushed the boat forward. Shandria spent part of the morning teaching Marvin how to rig the sails and explained tacking into the wind. Once they were farther from the island, she turned the vessel around so he could practice moving the sails and tack into the wind.

That morning Shandria told Marvin her secret for navigating the boat. First, she knew the Atlantian islands and currents. Second, she knew where they were at and could check their position by listening to the magic, and last, she could tell the direction of north using sky magic. It gave her both a magnetic and a magical sense of true north. And of course, she could look down and see their position and the other islands.

Shandria had Marvin swim and explore the ocean around the boat. He was exploring a coral outcropping near the boat and saw a shark. He kept his distance until he saw another one. So much for his bravery. He wove a pseudopod high above the water, caught up to the boat, and got out of the ocean.

He talked to Shandria about his fear of sharks. She said, "Sharks are beautiful and beneficial to the reef community. Only a few species are dangerous, and then only if they are feeding." She further replied, "Even aggressive sharks are no worse than wolves." It didn't instill much confidence in Marvin.

Later that day a pod of bottle-nosed dolphins swam near them. Shandria had Marvin dive in. After a few minutes, she dove in also. Marvin was concerned that no one was in the boat, but Shandria wasn't so they swam with the dolphins. After a half hour, they wove a wave to take them back to the ship. Shandria had woven some magic to keep the tiller pointing the boat towards the north. Strictly speaking, they weren't supposed to leave the boat at the same time, but it was only illegal in the shipping lanes. And Shandria wanted to enjoy swimming with the dolphins and Marvin.

They spent another night anchored by an Island before continuing their journey. Later on, the next day, Shandria had Marvin hold the tiller. She entered the cabin and returned fully clothed. She said to Marvin, "Get dressed, we are about to have some company."

Marvin walked below decks, dressed, and returned.

Shandria said, "Look straight north and tell me what you see."

Marvin looked and saw nothing. Then he concentrated, and he saw something, or rather, he saw the magic. "I see magic moving the water."

"Good, now keep concentrating. As you get more detail tell me what you see."

Each time he looked his focus was getting better. "They are moving fast. It looks like three of them. They are riding on top the surface of the water. I guess they are boats."

Shandria said, "Good, they are Atlantian patrol boats, probably from the Southern or Eastern Jewel fleet. I suspect they saw the portal we opened, and they are on their way to inspect the area. They aren't heading straight towards us. We aren't using magic to move, and this boat is almost all Alfarin magic, which tends to be quiet. They probably don't know we are here yet but will soon. Let's help them out."

Shandria wove magic and above the boat appeared a bright blue circle of light. In the center was a blinking white dot. The light identified them as an Atlantian vessel from Atlantis. They might be too far away to see the colors in the daylight, but they could see the magic. It was purposely noisy. Marvin watched the ships change course and head in their direction. They were closing fast, and soon he could see them clearly. Shandria triggered the magic to drop the sails. She walked out onto the foredeck and tightened the sheets on the boom and the Jib sail.

Marvin told Shandria he was impressed at the size of the naval vessels.

She turned to Marvin and said, "They are powerful, but now it's our time to impress them back." She unwove the beacon, and in its place wove a beacon with a different pattern.

"The pattern identifies me as a member of the royal family from the Island of Atlantis. That should put them on their best behavior."

The Atlantian fleet was following the patrol boats and stopped about four hundred yards away. Shandria told Marvin it put them out of bowshot range. The patrol boat sent out a small vessel, which soon pulled alongside them. An officer on board the boat asked, "Permission to come aboard?"

Shandria replied, "Permission granted Lieutenant."

The Lieutenant boarded the ship.

Shandria said, "I am Princess Shandria of Atlantis. This is my companion, Sir Marvin. I am under his protection, and he is under my protection. We are not in need of assistance. This vessel is of Alfarin manufacture. The Queen was gracious enough to provide it for us since we had to portal into the ocean. We opened a portal south of here from Alfamara. We are the only vessel that came through, and we closed the portal.

"We have a diplomatic dispatch for the eyes only of the Kings of Atlantis. We also have items for the king that qualify as diplomatic items under Atlantian law. So, this vessel qualifies as both a royal vessel and a diplomatic vessel. Do you have any questions about our status?"

The lieutenant dropped to one knee and said, "My Princess. I am satisfied and excited for your return. All of Atlantis will rejoice. I will report it to Admiral Parathian. Is there any way we can assist you?"

Shandria said, "You may rise. You have a good admiral. I have known him all my life and am looking forward to his invitation. Tell him I am heading to Atlantis. I would prefer to flow and enjoy the ocean, but I suspect the court may prefer us to arrive sooner. Signal us, and we will join the fleet or continue on our own. You have permission to leave this vessel."

"Thank you, my princess." The lieutenant did a military about face and left the boat.

Shandria watched him turn his boat around and head back towards the fleet. She turned towards Marvin. "The Admiral is a friend. I expected them to send a vessel south to check on the portal. I didn't expect them to send an admiral and part of his fleet. They must have been on maneuvers. I also hoped to have at least one more day alone on the ocean. Law requires us to declare who we are. Since we have diplomatic status, we have to report that also. They will offer assistance, and it's almost impossible for us not to accept it."

Ten minutes later a green signal started flashing above the patrol boat. Shandria sent up a green signal of her own. She wove water magic to move their boat near the Atlantian vessels. Once they arrived at the ships, they rode north on a wave generated by the Atlantian sailors.

ATLANTIAN MAGIC

When they got close to the flagship, which was considerably larger than the patrol boats, Shandria asked Marvin to grow the wood of the cabin door together. She used her magic to carve a royal seal into the door. Then she placed a warning ward on the door. She said, "No one will open that door without us knowing it. A traitor cursed my necklace. I don't expect anything wrong, but all your messages and the gifts are downstairs, and we can't take chances."

She yelled up to the flagship, "Permission to come aboard?"

The captain of the vessel yelled down, "Permission granted to you and your crew."

Shandria lifted Marvin and herself up on a pseudopod of water.

The captain yelled, "Boatswain's mate! Take care of this vessel and get the Boatwright out here to modify the small boat dock."

The captain said, "If it is your desire, my princess, the admiral is waiting below deck for you and your crew mate."

Shandria said, "Then let's not keep him waiting."

Chapter 47

The Admiral was in the Admiral's Wardroom. He walked over, bowed his head forward, and then straightened up. "Welcome aboard your flagship, my princess." He extended his hand.

Shandria took his hand, then stepped towards him, and gave him a hug. She kissed him on the cheek and said, "I am excited to see you again uncle."

He smiled and replied, "Likewise my child. I am so proud of you. I always knew you had the heart of a warrior." He released his hug and took a step back. "May I look at you?"

Shandria nodded her head.

Her uncle took hold of her hand. He closed his eyes and looked. He opened them again. A tear formed in his eye. He said, "I can't believe how beautiful and powerful you have become. I see you have befriended some other magic also. We heard that you had become separated on a mission and feared the worst, especially when you missed your brother's coronation last moon."

Shandria said, "Handrian is king now? Who is his queen?"

Her Uncle said, "I forgot that you had been away for almost a year, and with the arch crystal gone, regular communication has been spotty. He chose Alandria for his queen."

Shandria smiled and said, "It's a good marriage. She is smart and beautiful, and it's a good diplomatic marriage. I've only met Alandria twice. Both times we met, I admired her intellect. We had a lot of fun together. And Handrian was visibly attracted to her."

The admiral turned around, and said, "Steward, please get us some wine from my stores and three glasses. Then have the cook prepare us some treats worthy of a princess. She has been away from the sea for a long time."

The steward said, "Yes Admiral," and left the room.

The Admiral turned back towards the princess and offered them seats.

A sailor entered into the Admirals wardroom, "Admiral, I have a message from Atlantis." He handed a communication to the Admiral.

The Admiral read it to himself, and said, "Excuse me for a second." He left the room.

He returned a few minutes later and read the message aloud. "The message is from King Baracian. It says, 'Please provide all accommodations requested for

Princess Shandria. If she desires it, please escort her back to Atlantis if it is consistent with your military mission. Tell her we love her and are anxious for her return.'"

Shandria started to cry. She turned towards Marvin and gave him a quick hug. After a few seconds, she composed herself.

The admiral poured the wine, and said, "I had the captain set a course to a point southeast of Atlantis. Tell me about your adventures and the royal with the ancient sword I have never met, and who you chose for your companion."

Shandria took a drink of wine and said, "Thank you, uncle. This is the best wine I have drunk in several moons." Then she said, "It's a long story. Why do you call Sir Marvin a royal?"

The Admiral replied, "You, as a princess, I ask permission to look at, but it's my job and responsibility to know everyone aboard this ship. His magic aura is as powerful as any Atlantian I have ever seen. He has Dwarven and Alfarin magic. He carries an ancient sword of power. His sword won't reveal its name, and my sword won't tell me, but my sword says it has always bonded to a member of the royal family. I know all members, yet here he is.

"I wanted to talk to you first, but since we are on the topic. Sir Marvin, who are you?"

Marvin looked at Shandria. She nodded her head. He said, "The Anastasi gave me the same riddle. The answer is I am still finding out."

The admiral's face changed when he heard the name of the Anastasi. It changed from someone who had just issued a command to someone who was intrigued and awaiting the answer.

Marvin continued, "What I know is that I am full-blooded Atlantian. I don't know who my parents were or how I got to Earth. An Earth family adopted and raised me. I unexpectedly ran into Shandria, her brother, and their party. My magic, which was dormant all my life on Earth, awoke. My baby kick of magic saved Shandria's life. I was ill and would die in a few months. Shandria took me on as her companion and after a long journey together, here we are. She tells stories better than I do, so Shandria, please elaborate."

Shandria loved to tell stories, and Marvin loved the way she told them. Part way through Shandria's tale, the admiral ordered his steward, "Tell the captain I will be dining alone tonight with my guests and prepare us a meal a princess who has missed the sea would enjoy."

Shandria continued her story. They took a pause from the story for some rare delicacies from the sea. Shandria enjoyed them all.

Marvin found to his surprise that he like most of them, although the flavors were new.

Shandria told much of her adventure. She included her sickness but left out the cursed necklace, and their time together in the green goo.

He offered the princess the Admiral quarters for the night. She didn't want to be a bother and insisted on an empty stateroom for the two of them.

Pd MICHEL

They sailed for two days and said goodbye to the admiral when they were a half day's travel from Atlantis. Shandria and Marvin boarded their boat, which now flew a pennant from the top of the mast, courtesy of the Admiral. It identified them as an Atlantian royal vessel. They watched the Admiral's flagship sail away towards the east, then they set sail for the island of Atlantis.

It was a beautiful day, and as soon as they finished rigging the sail, Shandria insisted they sail free. Marvin had never seen Shandria this excited. Every reef, every beach, every buoy, and every vessel had a story behind it. Marvin saw many Atlantians swimming free. Some were on boats, some were on Shallots, and some were traveling by magic over the water. Marvin was a little self-conscious about being naked when he saw the amount of boat traffic. But when he realized most of the non-commercial traffic was free, he relaxed.

They received many onlookers, curious about the strange boat with the royal pennant. Shandria and Marvin waved to them. Several vessels sailed parallel to theirs. Soon it was a mini-flotilla, sailing behind them and giving Shandria a royal escort home. Just before they arrived at the royal harbor, they put back on their clothing, and their escort left. Shandria said, "Only royal and military vessels are allowed in this area of the harbor."

They dropped their sails and wove currents to push them into the royal dock. The guards at the royal dock initially met the strange vessel with suspicion as they pulled into the dock. Then the suspicion turned to excitement as they identified Princess Shandria.

A minister and several attendants were already waiting on the pier. They bowed low and knelt down on one knee. Princess Shandria said, "Arise. I am eager to see the faces I have missed for so long."

They stood up. Shandria jumped off the boat, hugged and kissed a minister she had known all her life on the cheek. Something from the surprised look on his face, she didn't often do. A smile replaced his surprise. She hugged his assistants.

The minister said, "King Vandian requests your presence in the courtroom as soon as you arrive. He called a meeting of all the ministers to welcome you back. The word has gotten out, so I am sure others will attend."

Shandria said, "I can't wait to see everyone. We have two large boxes of gifts I agreed to present to the court on my arrival. I need a cart to carry the boxes. Second, I have a companion carrying an ancient sword. He is sworn to me and will accompany me into the courtroom. Make sure the guards allow him and his sword. We will be waiting for the cart."

The ministers hurried away. A few minutes later, all but one returned, followed by a small cart pulled by a pony. Shandria and Marvin helped them remove the boxes from the boat. Several excited people in military uniforms carried the boxes to the cart.

ATLANTIAN MAGIC

At the end of the pier stood several hundred mounted knights. The captains of the Knights had dismounted, and they were down on one knee with their heads bowed and their sword arms crossed on their chests.

Shandria had them arise. She greeted each with a forearm hug, talked to them, and addressed them by name. They had been her friends and mentors all her life, and she was excited to see them again. The excitement was obviously mutual.

Soldiers led two horses, which were much taller than the ones at Crystal Mountain. The stallions were adorned in beautiful Atlantian-blue capes. Shandria was excited. She knew the names of the horses, and they recognized her. She stroked their manes and then hopped up on one. Marvin introduced himself to the other horse, allowed the animal to smell him, and then he mounted it.

The honor guard escorted Shandria and Marvin to the palace. It was several miles and slightly uphill. Several hundred yards past the end of the pier stood a tall wide wall. It surrounded an enormous and busy courtyard that was several square miles in diameter. Inside the wall, near the wharf, was the commercial district. Farther back were military barracks. At the far end, an inner ring of thick walls surrounded the palace grounds proper. Shandria was excited and talkative the whole way, pointing out every detail to Marvin. They were continuously waving to the well-wishers lining the pathway. The news of her arrival had spread quickly, and a crowd was cheering, waving, and talking excitedly.

Marvin was amazed at the number of people and the size of the city.

They entered the walls around the palace grounds. Shandria raised her sword in the air, and Marvin could hear the sound as the Knights pulled their swords from their scabbards. She pumped her sword into the air three times, then all the knights yelled, "For Atlantis!"

The knights sheathed their swords.

Shandria and Marvin dismounted their horses. A squire grabbed the reigns. She grabbed Marvin's arm, and they walked on a path through some ornate shrubbery to the palace. As they walked, she could hear conversation and speculations about the person who was accompanying her. Shandria wondered why they were speculating what island Marvin was the prince of. It must have been his sword. Her Uncle was convinced he was a royal. They didn't know he was from Earth.

Shandria had instructed Marvin how to act at the court on the boat, and once again reinforced it. The most important rule was never to cross a line on the floor unless called to by a king, or the guards would respond as if you were a threat to the king's life. The line was about twenty feet in front of the stairs.

They entered the palace through doors that must have been twenty feet high. The courtroom was twice the size of a basketball gymnasium. Magical light lit the hall. Columns supporting the cathedral-arch style ceiling ran on both the sides of a wide central aisle. On the left were soldiers. On the right were people dressed in Atlantian high fashion, mixed in with people wearing armor, and guards carrying weapons. It reminded Marvin of the court of King Feldspar.

At the end of the aisle, was a raised platform with seven stairs leading to the top. Marvin found out later the stairs represented the seven jewels of Atlantis. At the top were three thrones. On the nearest throne, on the right, was Shandria's brother. In the center of the stage was her father on his throne. On the left side sat her grandfather on his throne. Smiles and obvious excitement were on everyone's faces.

They followed the minister's direction and stopped behind the line. Marvin stopped one pace behind Shandria and to her right. Marvin knelt down, but Shandria just bowed her head. Her father stood up and said, "Arise my daughter and come to me." He opened his arms wide.

Shandria jumped up, and ran like a small child to her father; she took the stairs three at a time into his arms. They held each other for a long time. Marvin wasn't sure what to do so he stayed kneeling. The rest of the court, which had been standing, started clapping. Marvin looked up. He saw her father hold her at arms-length and shut his eyes, after a few minutes he opened them. He said something to her and then embraced her again. Shandria talked to him for some time as the noise died down.

Then her father released her and looked at Marvin. His hand touched the pommel of his sword, and he sat down.

Shandria looked towards her grandfather, who stood up and outstretched his arms. She ran over to him and gave him a warm embrace. She talked to him for a few minutes. She then looked towards her brother who was standing, and he extended his arms. She hurried over to him, knelt down on one knee, and said something to him, which Marvin couldn't hear. He grabbed her hand. She rose up, and they embraced and kissed.

Marvin heard a minister whisper to the person next to him. "She just swore loyalty to the new king since she missed his coronation." Marvin watched the grandfather's hand travel to the pommel of his sword. After a while, he took it away. Marvin could tell they were ancient swords. He knew the swords talked, and he wondered what they were saying. His sword was talking, but not to him.

Marvin realized that until recently he would have never noticed the movement of the hands to the swords. It must be part of the reflexes his sword had been teaching him. He noticed how aware he was of the position of each of the people near him, especially the guards. He was sure that awareness had been taught him by his sword.

After talking to her brother, Shandria walked down the stairs and stood by Marvin. She almost succeeded in not smiling when she saw Marvin's discomfort at having been on his knees for so long. She motioned to him to stay down. Marvin had been looking at the crystal in his amulet glow. It said someone here was a user of dark spells. Shandria's amulet was glowing also. Marvin focused.

There were two users. One was near the front on the right side. The other was farther back also on the right side.

Shandria's father raised his hand, and two seconds later, the only sound in the courtroom was a person in the back trying hard not to cough.

He said, "Princess Shandria, please have your companion stand and face the court." Marvin looked towards Shandria, and she motioned for Marvin to rise.

Her father said, "Shandria told us you saved her life multiple times. We are in your debt. Please tell this court who you are."

Marvin started talking. "My name is Marvin. The Anastasi gave me the same question to answer, 'who am I.' I am still trying to find the answer myself." Marvin could hear the startled noise when he said Anastasi, which only interrupted the silence for a second.

"What I know so far is I am a full blooded Atlantian who was raised by foster parents on Earth. When Shandria and her brother came to Earth during their quest, their magic ignited mine. My baby's cry of magic killed one of two narworms, the one that was about to kill Princess Shandria. Prince, I mean King Handrian killed the other one.

"I was dying of an incurable disease. Princess Shandria and her brother saw I was Atlantian. She said she owed me a debt. So together, we started a journey, which took us to Crystal Mountain, and to Alfamara, where the Alfarins restored my health. At Crystal Mountain, an ancient sword bonded itself to me. My magic ability has grown strong and is still growing.

"I have sworn myself to protect Princess Shandria. I carry sealed messages from King Feldspar and Queen Juniperia for the court.

"So, who am I? The answer is I will spend the rest of my life finding out, but I do know I am Atlantian by blood and magic. I am a friend to the court of Alfamara, and to the court of Crystal Mountain. Today I am a messenger to the court of Atlantis, and I am a sworn protector of Princess Shandria." Marvin stopped for a second, and then added, "Honored king."

Marvin saw the two elder king's hands move toward their swords. Shandria had shifted her traveling cloak open to reveal hers. Her father commanded. "We know part of the reason you traveled on your journey was to heal Shandria. Please tell the court what caused Shandria's illness."

Marvin looked at Shandria, who nodded her head. Marvin said, "A dark magic curse placed on Shandria's necklace poisoned her. And there are two dark spell users in this courtroom." Marvin saw the dark magic user near the front of the courtroom raise his staff. Marvin started moving towards him. But he was too slow. He saw the weave of a magical blast of dark magic begin to form. It was pointed at Shandria's brother.

Chapter 48

Marvin's reflexes, learned from his sword training and his Alfarin speed magic took over. Everything slowed down as the speed magic sped up his body. The Alfarin protection magic from his amulet activated. He took three steps and dove in front of the dark spell. The amulet flared white as the dark magic hit the amulet's effective radius. The magic spell knocked Marvin back onto the steps of the throne. The metal magic in his clothing hardened and protected him as his back slammed into the stairs. He rebounded to his feet and pulled his sword. The Darfarin was readying another spell.

Shandria had reacted also. Sped up by Alfarin magic, she pulled her sword, slipped through the crowd, who were too stunned to move, and stabbed the spell caster through the chest. Marvin saw the second spell user unleash a bolt of dark magic at several guards. The guards fell to the ground and started convulsing. The spell caster was preparing to unleash a second spell.

Marvin sped towards him, but the spellcaster was towards the back of the court and was too far away for Marvin to stop before he cast his evil spell. Marvin extended his hand, and a flash of blinding blue lightning came from it. It burned a hole in the spell caster's chest, putting an end to the spell. It also knocked several nearby onlookers over. Marvin had practiced the magic as part of the sky kata but had never attempted the magic by itself until now. For a brief second, the air felt charged with electricity. He sped to the back of the courtroom and surveyed the area. He could detect no other dark magic users, only the ozone smell from the energy of his lightning.

His amulet was now glowing dimly; the after-effects of the dark magic still affected it. Marvin sheathed his sword and knelt down on his knees. He put his hand on the first guard on the floor. The dark magic was still active inside. He pulled the dark magic from the man's chest. A dark smoky snake of magic came out and dissolved. He quickly moved to the other three victims and did the same.

The threat was over before many of the guards had time to respond and to recover from the blinding flash of Marvin's lightning. Marvin stood up and saw the two senior kings had descended the stairs and had their blades drawn. Both blades were shining with a blinding light that Marvin guessed was a strong magical ward. Dozens of guards were running to surround the Kings. Others were guarding the doors, and a group holding spears were pointing them towards Marvin and heading his way.

Marvin knelt down, and held his empty hands high in the air, "I yield! I surrender!" He repeatedly yelled.

One of the guards swung the butt end of a spear at the side of Marvin's head.

Marvin's raised arms deflected the blow. He had hardened his body with Earth magic, but the force of the spear sent him sprawling onto the floor. He heard Shandria yelling at the guards. "Stand down! Stand down!" followed by her father and grandfather yelling also.

Shandria ran over and yelled at the guard. "He just saved the king's life and probably yours. Stand Down!" A loud horn blast sounded three times. The guards stepped back but kept their spears pointed at Marvin.

Slowly the guards pointed their spears back towards the ceiling. They watched Marvin intently as they withdrew to their previous positions. The confusion in the courtroom died down as everyone returned to their former spots. Marvin looked up and said to Shandria. "I guess I crossed the line without permission. Can I stand up?"

Shandria's serious face showed the start of a smile then quickly returned to serious. She took Marvin's hand and had him stand up next to her. She said, "Thank you for saving my brother." and kissed him on the cheek.

The Kings returned to their throne and yelled for silence. A loud noise filled the courtroom as the guards with spears banged them on the floor. The courtroom quickly quieted down.

Shandria's father talked to his father and his son. He said, "Princess Shandria, escort Marvin to the throne." Marvin looked at Shandria. She said, "Walk by my side."

They walked up the stairs. Shandria's father held out his hand. Marvin reached for a traditional shake, but the King grabbed him by the more camaraderie forearm shake and reinforce it with his other hand in a hug. Marvin followed suit. The king then kissed Marvin on either side of his face. He turned towards the court and said. "For repeatedly saving the life of the princess and the king, we hereby award the title 'Friend and Protector of the Court of Atlantis' to Sir Marvin and reaffirm the title of Sir Marvin."

Marvin said, "I am honored, king. Forgive me I don't know the titles and customs yet."

The king smiled and replied, "Shandria told us. But don't worry; Atlantians are always forgiving of their friends."

Marvin smiled back. There was something about the king, which Marvin liked and knew he could trust.

The King directed him towards Shandria's grandfather, who shook his arm and pulled him close. "Thanks for protecting my granddaughter, grandson, and this court." He said. The king held onto Marvin's arm and looked closely at his face, then smiled and released him.

Then he directed him towards Shandria's brother. His brother shook Marvin's hand, but Marvin felt like he was doing it as a formality. Her brother said nothing to him and released the handshake.

Her father motioned over Marvin. He said, "Just smile and face the audience. It's part of the honor."

Marvin stood, uncomfortable with all the attention, and looked at the audience, trying to smile. Several notes from a trumpet sounded, and clapping filled the courtroom. After several long seconds, the king raised his hand. The clapping stopped. He spoke, "Today we held court to welcome my daughter back. Thank you for the warm welcome you have given her. But we received more than we expected. The court now has a new friend, and we have found and eliminated two evil traitors." Marvin noted the guards had already removed the bodies from the courtroom. They took the injured people to the infirmary.

"I declare today's session of court closed."

Another set of trumpets sounded. The high minister yelled, "Long live Atlantis! Long live our kings and queens!"

Her father said. "We shall have a private meeting in the blue room to receive our messages and gifts and to share some spiced wine." A minister rushed away to make preparations. A second minister immediately appeared to take the place of the first, in case the king gave any new orders.

A guard pulled back a large ornate curtain hanging down from near the ceiling. There was an open doorway, which the kings walked through from oldest to youngest. A minister instructed Marvin to follow at the end.

They called the room behind the throne the blue room. The large heavy door at the entrance could be closed and barred shut if it was needed. Light magic lit the room at a more comfortable level than the bright lights in the courtroom. Beautiful tapestries, alternating with ornate weapons covered the walls. There was a large table in the middle.

Marvin watched men take off the breastplates of the kings and put them on a rack reserved for them. He heard Shandria's grandfather, King Baracian say, "Thank you, squire." He bent forward and poured wine out of a metal pitcher into each of four large mugs. A servant replaced the pitcher. There was a second tray like the first with four decorative wine glasses rather than mugs.

King Vandian walked over to the second pitcher and filled the glasses with a light red colored wine. Servants replaced the empty pitcher with a full one. He left a chair open than stood up behind the next chair. King Handrian, Shandria's brother, walked over last. He distributed the mugs to each of the kings, and one to a chair across the table from them. Then he did the same with the glasses, placing them on the table in front of the skipped chairs.

A servant came over and asked to take Marvin's traveling cloak and his backpack. Marvin handed him his cloak, and said, "I have messages for the Kings

I need to deliver in my backpack." The servant replied, "The pack won't leave this room and will be guarded, sir."

Marvin allowed the servants to take his pack. A minister instructed Marvin to stand behind a chair, and he did.

Marvin heard the voices of women talking excitedly outside one of the doors. They quieted down and entered.

First Shandria's Grandmother, Queen Elantria entered. King Baracian pulled out her seat and allowed her to sit down before pushing it in. Marvin could see the queen was watching him intently. Queen Elantria saw him look at her and smiled back. He smiled and diverted his eyes. Marvin felt uncomfortable. In some cultures, staring in the eye was normal. In others, it was rude. He had read that in some places staring at a king in the eyes was a challenge and punishable by death. He had much to ask Shandria.

King Vandian offered the chair for his wife Queen Isaria, and so did King Handrian for his bride, Queen Alandria.

Princess Shandria came out last. Marvin pulled out her chair and pushed it back in as she sat down.

The Kings, still standing, grabbed their mugs and raised them. They looked at Marvin and nodded. Marvin grabbed his mug and raised it. King Baracian said, "To the most beautiful women in the realm."

All the men took a drink. Then they sat down next to the ladies. Marvin included.

The ladies grabbed their glasses, and the elder queen raised her glass and said, "To the brave men who love us and protect us." The ladies all took drinks.

Marvin was uncomfortable, afraid he was going to do something wrong and wondering what was next. Shandria's grandmother said, "I'm glad the formalities are over. She stood up, looked at Marvin and said, "Come over here and let me hug you. She came around the table as Marvin stood up. She embraced Marvin with a stronger hug than he expected from a grandmother. But then she looked too young to be a grandmother. He returned the hug. She said, "Let me look at you."

Marvin held out his hands, she grabbed them and closed her eyes. After several minutes, she opened her eyes and gave Marvin another hug. She kissed him and said, "Thanks for protecting my granddaughter and my grandson."

Shandria's mother did the same, so did her sister-in-law. The queens wore elegant dresses, but also had ancient swords strapped to their sides. King Handrian had an enchanted sword, but it wasn't one of the great ancient swords.

The ladies sat back down. The elder queen said, "We award few people Protector of the Court, and they all know about it and prepare for several days. We don't even have a medallion ready for you, and you did fine." She smiled, and Marvin did in return. Marvin felt way underdressed in his traveling clothes, but Shandria was in hers and seemed right at home."

King Baracian said, "Now that the formalities are over, we drop the titles. At this table, we are all friends of Atlantis, and we treat each other as equals. Marvin, tell us how you blocked the dark magic. And we are all eager to see the messages you have brought us."

The servant with Marvin's backpack handed it to him. Marvin opened it up and then pulled out a packet. Marvin pulled out the Alfarin medallion around his neck. This is my friend of Alfamara medallion. It has been enchanted to protect me from, and glows to warn me of dark spells."

Shandria pulled a similar medallion from out of her shirt. Marvin opened the pouch. "Inside are three dozen medallions, enchanted like the one which protected Shandria and me in the courtroom.

"As demonstrated by my collision with the stairs, it protected me against the perverting forces of the dark magic, but not some of its physical effects. I don't know how long its protection will last under continuous attack. Queen Juniperia suggested you wear them at all times and use them to find dark magic in the area."

King Baracian took one of the amulets and studied it. He said to Marvin, "This has Alfarin and Atlantian enchantment in it, and it shows you are one of its enchanters."

Marvin said. "I learned and performed several enchantments, enchanting both in Alfamara and at the Dwarven forges of Crystal Mountain. The knowledge of my sword taught me and assisted me in the weaves.

"I was separated from Shandria at the time. She did not find out about the enchantments until they were complete. She informed me of Atlantian law when she found out and kicked me out of her life for several days afterward.

"Everything I did was to help Atlantis, and its allies, who I owed a debt to for saving Shandria's life and my own. I had never stepped foot or swam in the oceans of Atlantis at that time. I will follow the Atlantian law where I know it and will endeavor to learn it. But I believe I did what was right by the alliances and treaty of friendship."

The Kings huddled together. After a few minutes, King Baracian said, "Atlantian laws apply to Atlantians wherever they are, but your background at the time and your reasons allow forgiveness. Please tell us what you did enchant."

"Along with Queen Juniperia, I also enchanted protective wards they are placing inside new guard towers the Dwarves are building. Eventually, they will have a third outer wall around Crystal Mountain. King Feldspar said the increased protection of his kingdom will allow him to send more aid to Atlantis if needed. At the Dwarven forges, I helped make a couple plow blades and enchanted one dagger.

"Here is the dagger. Marvin reached into the sheath on his lower leg and pulled out his dagger. He laid it sideways on the table where Baracian could reach it. The king reached over and picked it up. He looked at it and said, "It is well crafted and enchanted. It has a good balance. You should be proud of it." He returned it.

Marvin replied, "Thank you. The Atlantian enchantment is mine, and some of the forge work, but the weapons master did most of the finishing work. I still have a lot to learn."

King Baracian handed amulets out to the kings and queens and placed one around his neck. "I wish we had enough for every member of the court, nay every soldier and sailor also if not every Atlantian."

Marvin replied, "So do I king, but the time was short, and we did what we could."

King Baracian said, "What else do you have for us?"

Marvin pulled out the letters from King Feldspar and Queen Juniperia. Then he pulled out the package of scrolls from the Dwarven king. "These are proposed mutual battle plans for Dwarves to help defend Atlantis."

King Baracian opened one of the scrolls. "My Dwarven is rusty, but it looks like he plans to bring as many as two legions of Dwarves in through the arch gate with a few hours' notice and several more soon after. Unfortunately, we don't have an arch crystal."

Marvin reached into his backpack and pulled out his aluminum box from Earth. He said, "The last thing King Feldspar and I enchanted was this." He opened up the box. Inside was an arch crystal. The crystal shined bright at his touch.

Chapter 49

He put the box where the king could look into it. Then after a few seconds, he closed it down.

"King Feldspar warned me I shouldn't let this out of the container. The energy makes it a beacon and target for the enemy. The crystal is ready but needs final enchantment. The arches at Alfamara and Crystal Mountain are set to talk with him."

Marvin continued, "I don't understand all the magic, but to protect everyone if the enemy stole the crystal, the key is tied to my magic. I modified the arches at Crystal Mountain, and Alfamara, and plan, with your permission, of course, to set up the arch at the earliest time that is convenient to the court. It will function just like the old one, but its magic will be younger. Its aura will spread out. In a few days, it will be strong enough to prevent almost anyone from opening a portal into Atlantis and the area around it."

King Baracian looked at the other kings. They nodded to him. He turned towards one of the military men. "Have horses and a mounted escort ready by the end of the hour. Marvin, Shandria, and Handrian will accompany us." He turned towards King Vandian, "Sorry, Vandian, we need to leave a king behind and today is your duty day."

Queen Alandria said. "I would like to go also. It will only take me a few minutes to be ready to join you."

The king knew of her military abilities and said. "You are welcome also my daughter."

Marvin said, "One last thing before you go, Shandria said I shouldn't mention it in open court, but I have messages from the Anastasi if there is time." He pulled out his messenger bag and said. "I was told to hand these only to the person addressed."

He reached in and pulled out a rolled up and tied piece of parchment. On the outside, it said, "King Baracian."

He handed King Baracian the scroll, one to King Vandian, and one to their queens. Then he noticed there were two other scrolls. He said, "This one says King Handrian, and this one is for Queen Alandria." Marvin handed them their scrolls.

King Baracian opened his scroll. He looked at it for a while, and then it disappeared. The same thing happened with all the other scrolls.

King Handrian said after his scroll disappeared. "Is this a joke? It's just a simple stupid question."

His grandfather said. "It's said the Anastasi always communicate in questions. Telling us the answer only gives us the information, searching for the answer causes us to understand the answer. The search changes us and gives us wisdom and knowledge. Mine is personal and direct, yet discovering the answer will take time and much searching.

Marvin said, "My simple question was, 'Who am I?' Searching for the answer has already positively affected my life several times. Without it, I wouldn't be here, and you might be dead."

Marvin said, "That's all I have. We have two large boxes of gifts from Crystal Mountain and Alfamara for the court. I don't know what is in them, but I don't believe they are critical or of military importance." The two kings put back on their armor. About the time they had finished, Alandria came back, dressed in a chest plate and helmet. She carried a shield, and of course, her sword.

They walked out and mounted their horses.

There were a hundred knights. Half were in front, and half were behind the small party. Behind the royal party were several officials of the court.

King Handrian was on the left, King Baracian was in the middle, and Sir Marvin was on the right.

Queen Alandria and Shandria brought up the rear. Through the noise of the horses, Marvin could hear Alandria and Shandria talking, but he couldn't make out what they were saying. They were talking like old friends.

King Baracian asked Marvin about King Feldspar and his wife. He told them they were doing well, and the stories she had heard about their visit with Baracian when he was young. Then Baracian asked him about Queen Juniperia. He related his time with her.

They started talking about his progress with the Atlantian sword katas. Marvin was excited. King Baracian was one of the few acknowledged masters of the katas.

While they were talking, Shandria's brother was stewing. He felt like everyone was ignoring him. His sister and his wife were talking and ignoring him. His grandfather was more interested in the peasant from Earth they had given an award to and a title. He started brooding, "Why don't I have an ancient sword? Everyone else has one but me. I am a king of Atlantis. I should have a sword. Even the peasant from Earth has an ancient sword.

"Getting a message from the Anastasi is supposed to be a life-changing event, but all I received was a stupid question, 'What is love?' What type of an idiot question is that? I expected something that would help us with the war and help us recover the crystal. What a stupid, useless question. Even a child knows what love is.

"I know love can mean different things. I love my family. I love Atlantis. I love my wife. I've loved all my concubines. I even found good marriages for two of them before I was married. I found better marriages for my concubines than they ever would have gotten by themselves, and they were happy and excited about their new lives when they left.

"I only have one concubine left. My wife should have understood how I feel when I found marriages for two of them. She doesn't understand love. She doesn't love me the way she needs to. Many noblemen have concubines. In some cases, their wives have given them to their husband as gifts. Many ladies have presented concubines to their future husband as gifts.

"Sometimes I need someone more understanding to love at night. Everyone does. I have a loving heart. It's big enough for two women. It's big enough for even more. I should have kept my other concubines.

"It's all Alandria's fault. She doesn't know what love is. She acts as if we are still in Sea Scouts together. She is so immature. Why can't she act like an adult? Why can't she act like a proper queen?

"It was a good political marriage. But I wish I had seen how little Alandria had matured. I would have still married her, but I would have kept my other concubines, or helped them find good husbands, and helped other women advance in their social standing by making them my concubine. Now by Atlantian tradition, I need to be married for at least a year before I can find another.

"Look at the way my sister is with that peasant with a sword. She is more in love with him then my wife is with me. And she knows she can't marry him. She's throwing her emotions away. I'm sure it's only puppy love from her time with him. It will wear off, and we can find her a marriage that's good for Atlantis and her." He continued his brooding for most of the trip.

King Baracian mentioned they should have grabbed a bite before they left. Marvin undid a strap on his pack and rotated it to the front. He opened it up, took out an Alfarin travel biscuit, and handed it to the king. King Baracian gave Marvin the thumbs up sign. Marvin gave him another and pointed to King Handrian. He saw the king pass it across to him.

Marvin pulled his horse farther to the right and slowed down. Shandria and Alandria pulled their horse towards the left and Marvin fitted in beside Shandria. He handed her a travel biscuit. She passed it over to Alandria and ate the next one Marvin gave her. Then Marvin ate one. They were small but filling and tasted of honey and fruit. He rotated his pack onto his back.

Shandria asked Marvin, "How was your talk with Grandfather?"

Marvin replied. "I can see why you love him so, and why Atlantis does too. He's a great man. I feel like a kid with a giant. We talked about the katas. I think I am carrying something from the water kata into the air kata, and then into the sky kata. I need to go back to scratch on air and get it out. Once I clean up air, the sky kata should fall into place."

Marvin watched the way Shandria was looking at her brother and grandfather. "I know you want to talk to your family. Why don't you pull ahead? Queen Alandria can keep me company." Shandria sped up. She eased her horse between her brother and her grandfather and started talking to both of them.

Alandria seemed a little shy at first, then Marvin said, "King Baracian mentioned he has been working with you on the sky kata. I am just learning it." Alandria and Marvin started talking about the katas.

After a while, he asked her about her shield. Marvin could feel the strong enchantment. It was one of the ancient shields, as were her breastplate and helmet. She said, "Certain sets are comfortable with each other and often select individuals together. I have one such set. How are you adapting after being raised on Earth?"

He said, "I now understand why I never felt like I fit in on Earth. I mean, I was an Atlantian without magic, who thought he was a human and grew up in a desert. Even though I didn't fit in, I adapted."

Alandria said, "You are Atlantian, and like water, you flowed and adapted."

Marvin continued, "Shandria's customs were strange to me, but during our adventure, we were in a limited situation outside the Atlantian culture, I learned, and I adapted.

"The Dwarves are warm and treat you like family, as long as you don't mind drinking lots of mead, and so rock hard in their culture that it's easy to figure out. They were very understanding of my being young in magic.

"The Alfarins felt us out then accepted us. Their culture is different from anything on Earth, yet it was easy to figure out and adapt.

"Travelling with Shandria we had a few survival rules; they made sense. She is free-spirited and a lot of fun to be with outside of Atlantis. Now that we are in Atlantis, there are so many rules. Maybe I just haven't figured them out yet, but they seem so arbitrary. Quick bow with the head, low bow, high bow, one knee down, two knees down. A guard hit me with the butt of a spear for crossing a line to save the king's life, and then fifteen seconds later I'm being hugged and kissed. I'm afraid I will do or say something wrong and break a rule or a cultural taboo. So, the hard thing right now is figuring out the culture that should have been my birthright.

"How different is it between your island and the court of Atlantis?"

Alandria replied, "The bows are the same. But you're right. Some people turn small differences into major infractions. I seemed to have a lot more freedom before I joined the Atlantian Court. The Court of Atlantis is restrictive in many ways, but the rules have a purpose. Being a queen is exciting. It gives me a lot structure and responsibility, but also a lot of resources and freedom to help Atlantis. You haven't lived long enough in the culture to have adapted, but I'm sure you will quickly."

Marvin said, "Shandria explained to me that water has no structure. Without walls, it flows away and dissipates. Some walls are necessary and expected, like the wall around a family, but many aren't. Walls can be triangles, squares, circles, or crazy shapes at random places, and there is no way of knowing without bumping into one, and then I've violated another rule."

Alandria was having some minor difficulties adapting. She felt better after talking with Marvin. He was starting from scratch and had much more to learn about Atlantian island's unique customs then her.

Shandria slowed her horse down and slid backward between Marvin and Alandria. Alandria rode forward and took a position between the two kings. Shandria was still excited about being home. Marvin didn't mention to her his feeling about being so out of place. He would just go with the flow.

Soon the path became steeper, and the horses slowed down, but the steep portion was short. Then it flattened out to where the arch was.

The arch was a large circle inside an upside-down U, which supported it. Part of the circle extended below ground, leaving a flat area to walk through. There was a broken section at the top of the arch where the crystal needed to go. A large part was broken off, and its rubble lay on the ground. They must have used force to remove it thought Marvin. It needed to be repaired before the crystal could be put into the arch.

Marvin was going to ask for a ladder to get to the top. But he needed to balance on something stronger than a ladder. He needed a platform to the top of the arch he could stand on and repair it.

He closed his eyes and looked around. He could see no one in the area had the signature of recent wood magic use, or any non-Atlantian magic except for Shandria and himself. Sufficient wood and stone were in the area to make the required platform, and to repair the arch.

He told the two kings what he needed. There were stonemasons in town and some woodworkers who used wood magic in their job. But it would take several hours to get them to the area. There were construction workers in the area who could build the platform in a couple of hours. Marvin himself thought he could cut the stone himself before the masons arrived unless they were Dwarves, and then their magic would be superior to his. He mentioned it to King Baracian.

King Baracian said, "There is a small contingency of Dwarves at the Dwarven Embassy, which is dug into the mountain not too far from here. They stayed behind when the portals closed."

Marvin received permission from the king, and told the carpenters what he needed, and that he needed it fast.

Shandria knew where the embassy was. The Kings realized this could take a couple of hours to build the platform, several more hours, maybe all night to repair the stone, and then a couple of hours to enchant the new arch crystal before Marvin could activate it.

They decided to wait it out in a tent, at least until they saw how long it would take. Shandria knew the fastest way to the Dwarven Embassy. Marvin talked to the Kings. They allowed Shandria and Marvin to ride to the embassy, along with a dozen-soldier escort. On his way out, Marvin yelled, "Get mead to serve to the Dwarves."

Marvin and Shandria arrived at the embassy in half an hour. The outside of the embassy was stonework similar to the royal palace. There were a couple of relief drawings on the outside of the embassy. There were others inside.

The ambassador received them and offered them refreshments. Marvin pulled out his Friend to the Court of King Feldspar amulet, and all signs of diplomacy disappeared. He was family. Marvin told the ambassador what he needed. He was pleased to discover they had two grandmaster stone artists, masons who maintained and enhanced the artwork in the embassy. They were excited to use their talents in service to King Feldspar and their friends, the Atlantians. After a small mug of mead to toast their friendship, they grabbed some tools and rode back to the arch area. The ambassador accompanied them to the arch.

The carpenters had just completed the wooden platform. The platform was sturdy enough, but the Dwarves had obvious fear in their eyes. To Dwarves being that far above solid ground on a wobbly wooden platform was suicidal. Marvin touched the platform and wove the wood to strengthen it at its connection points. He also added additional lumber to make it look sturdier. Then he put railings around the outside of the platform.

While Marvin was working on the platform, the Dwarves found some stone in the area, which matched the stone used for the arch. They used magic to cut off a chunk and repaired parts of the arch that was on the ground. Marvin had four strong soldiers carry the restored stonework to the top of the platform. Then he had four more join them on top the platform. He had the soldiers jump up and down to show how sturdy it was before they came down. After his exhibition, the Dwarves felt more comfortable about being on the platform. Still, they cautiously climbed to the top and only did it for King Feldspar and their friends.

Chapter 50

Marvin climbed to the top of the platform. The Dwarves took their time and tested their weight with every step. They only relaxed after they had touched the stone of the arch itself and tied themselves to the arch with ropes that were long enough for them to move around. The two masons picked up the broken stone piece and fused it into place with their magic. Marvin watched, enjoying watching their level of skill and their speed. They used some of the extra rock to fill in pieces of the arch that were missing. Marvin thought the Dwarves had completed their work in a few minutes, but then they spent a half-hour working to move trace elements and aligning crystals of the replacement stone to correspond exactly with the grain and magic flow of the existing arch.

Marvin realized he could never have done this without their help. He thanked them and descended with them. He was glad to find that the mead had arrived. Marvin apologized to the Dwarves. He wouldn't be able to join them yet since he had promised King Feldspar he would activate the portal as quickly as he could and the royal court was waiting.

He asked the royal court if they wanted to join him as he activated the crystal. They had grown bored waiting and now were enthusiastic. They climbed to the top of the platform. Marvin recommended they put a hand on the stone of the arch. The stone carried the magic, and the arch crystal would activate the stone. Marvin removed the crystal from his box and placed it into the receiving hole at the top of the arch. He made the rock grow around the edges of the crystal to hold it in place.

He put one hand on the crystal, and the other on a smaller crystal on the amulet from Iron Mountain. Marvin closed his eyes and started the most complex magic he had ever performed.

The Dwarven arch and the Alfarin arch had already existed. He only had to tell the arch crystals their new friends, in effect their new arch addresses.

But now he was weaving the final parts of the arch magic itself. The magic mesmerized Marvin. He was in total communion and concentration with the crystal and talking to the arch and the stone. Each weave intertwined new threads, new complexity. Each thread vibrated with its unique frequency, duration, and pattern. His threads were speaking the words, the vibrations of magic. He was weaving more threads into it, weaving magical words, paragraphs, and chapters.

The enchantment in the crystal had come from the arch stone at Crystal Mountain. The dwarves had crafted the matrix inside the new crystal, and he had enchanted the crystal by copying the base magic from the Crystal Magic arch stone. He had copied the magic needed to startup the crystal into his crystal pendant. This part couldn't be copied. It had to be rewoven in pieces, in sections, and each section needed to be activated in order.

Marvin depleted he wove and activated each section. He didn't realize it would be this tiring. It took far more energy than when he had activated the other arches. But then they were already activated. The new crystal needed energy, and he was low. The arch magic had a natural rhythm, and Marvin added energy to it. It was like pushing a heavy swing at the right spot, at the right time. Each push raised it an inch higher each time. The magic grew in strength with every push. Marvin's magic called to the royals touching the arch. First Shandria, then the rest caught the rhythm and added in their energy.

Then Marvin felt a beat, a slow beat as the crystal and arch became alive. It was the first faint heartbeat of the arch, the heartbeat of a newborn child. It was time. He gave the crystal the last of his energy. He was holding it in reserve. He told the arch his new name and his new family of crystals, which he had stored in the crystal in the amulet of the Dwarves. He would only respond to his new family and reject all other crystals as outsiders. The arch slowly grew stronger and stronger, tapping into the magic of earth and sky until Marvin no longer had to feed it. The magic was growing on its own.

Marvin was physically, emotionally, and magically exhausted. He stopped weaving and released his hold on the arch. Then he said. "We need to get off the platform and move it out of the way."

Everyone climbed down the platform. Marin went last and stumbled at the bottom of the platform. Shandria and her grandfather caught and steadied him. Marvin said, "Thank you, I underestimated the energy needed to activate the arch."

As soon as everyone was clear of the platform, he put his hand on the platform and the threads of wood no longer bonded together. The platform came crashing down. He yelled to those around, "Clear the wood away from the arch."

Then he stopped and once again steadied himself. King Baracian looked at Marvin. He saw how exhausted and depleted of magic he was. He yelled to the troops, "Remove the wood now!" The soldiers scrambled at the command of the king. They hurried to grab and drag pieces of wood away from the arc.

Marvin called over the rest of the royal party. He said, "Stay away from the center of the arch. You may safely touch the outside of the arch. Watch and feel as the arch magic grows and comes to life."

Marvin moved away so they could see it better. Everyone watched. The crystal at the top was slowly growing brighter and brighter. It was drawing energy from the ground below it and the sky above. The energy, the personality of the crystal slowly spread out from the crystal and around the arch circle, one inch, two inches, a half foot, two feet, and continued to spread. Slowly the magical energy spread around the arch. Marvin stepped back and yelled at the lieutenant in charge of the troops. "Make sure everyone stays at least twenty paces away from the front or back of the arch. Watch the magic and enjoy the show." He heard the Lieutenant give the order to his troops to stay back.

Marvin watched the arch coming to life like a child being born. As the ring of energy completed at the bottom, the arch started vibrating and singing, putting out its own unique musical rhythm. The music grew louder. Then a glow started as a thin ring of light formed on the inside edge of the ring of the arch. The ring of light thickened, growing slowly inward. The empty hole in the center of the circle became smaller and smaller as the ring of light traveling inward until a thin membrane of light filled the whole circle.

Then like the membrane of a drum, the membrane of light started to vibrate. It was vibrating with the song of the arch, the beat of its heart. It vibrated stronger and stronger. Then for a brief second, the light disappeared. Like a sudden pause in a symphony, it was deafening in its sudden absence. And then it exploded. Light spread out to the horizon. Anyone watching could see the star pattern of Crystal Mountain and Alfamara briefly flash in the center of the arch, as the Atlantian Arch found the other arches.

Everyone was silent. Then someone started to clap. The sound of clapping and cheering filled the air. The Arch of Atlantis was working again. Marvin walked away from the celebration and slunk down, exhausted, inside the tent. One of the Dwarves handed Marvin a mug of mead. Marvin muttered in Dwarven, "Thank you, my friend," and took a healthy swallow. He put his mug back on the table. It had to be the worst mead he had ever tasted.

Soon King Baracian entered the tent. Marvin started to stand up, but the king put his hand on his shoulder to keep him seated. Marvin saw tears in the king's eyes. The King said, "Most astounding feat of magic I have ever seen and I have lived many years. Atlantis thanks you for restoring our arch. It has long been a symbol of our city and nation. We missed it so much."

Marvin felt the King sharing his magical energy. He thanked the king for the magic and his gracious words. Marvin felt Shandria's hand on his other shoulder. Marvin realized that tears were streaming down his face. He had never felt such strong emotions, except when his family had died, yet this was different. The birth of the arch was draining emotions that had been bottled up. It was a cleansing, emotional release. He had gone to the edge emotionally, and he didn't have any emotional strength left to hold it in. And it was all coming out. He knew later he would dwell on this moment, trying to figure it out, but now he was too exhausted.

ATLANTIAN MAGIC

Then the king thanked the Dwarves and the ambassador, who insisted the royal party share a glass of mead. They made room at the table.

Marvin wiped away his tears and thanked Shandria and her family for helping provide the energy the arch needed, their help cut at least an hour off the growth time of the magic. Marvin's physical strength was returning. His magic reservoir was refilling. But he was mentally and emotionally exhausted. He needed a good night's rest or at least a few hours of quiet to recharge.

King Baracian wanted to know the details of the arch. Marvin said. "He is ready to open a portal to Crystal Mountain or Alfamara. His protective magic is spreading out and should have its normal range in a couple of days, but the arch is young and needs to learn and grow before he has the power or maturity of the old arch."

The Dwarven ambassador wanted to re-establish transit home as soon as he could. After drinking what passed as mead in Atlantis, Marvin could understand why.

King Baracian yelled, "Commander of the watch!" Several seconds later, an officer ran into the tent and saluted. The king continued, "By order of the court of Atlantis, travel out through the gate for Dwarven Embassy personnel is immediately restored and unrestricted."

The king asked, "Commander, when can we be open for routine business?"

He replied, "Tomorrow morning if we work through the night."

He turned back to the Dwarven ambassador who was all excited, and asked, "When do you plan on going back?"

The Dwarven ambassador replied, "Tomorrow, midday."

The king said, "No one goes through without court approval until our friend, the ambassador of the Dwarves, does. Then we can re-establish normal operation."

The commander replied, "Yes my king." He left and started to give orders to his troops.

Marvin watched a scribe of the court write down the order.

The king said, "Excellent. Ambassador, this is troubled times. I will reestablish the traditional wartime royal protection for your embassy and yourself. It may take a few days for full implementation. Until then, I will have members of my personal guard protect you and your embassy."

He continued, "I know it's not the usual procedure, but do you mind if I send an ambassadorial group through to King Feldspar when you go? I believe he is awaiting my communication."

The Dwarven ambassador said, "Of course, anything for the King of Atlantis and our King Feldspar."

King Baracian raised his mug and said. "To friends."

As soon as everyone at the table raised theirs, He took a drink.

After the toast, King Baracian bent closer to the ambassador and said, "I apologize for the poor quality of the mead. It was acquired quickly and not through normal channels. While different in body and aroma from Dwarven mead, we do have some Atlantian mead of the highest quality. He gave a light slap on the ambassador's back and said, and I look forward to sharing some with you."

The ambassador smiled and said, "I will return with a cask of our best."

King Baracian said, "Excellent. I will match it with one of the finest from Atlantis, and we can contrast, compare and enjoy a friendly disagreement on which realm makes the best mead."

They both smiled. The king drank the last of his mug, stood up, and left the tent. He gave out several orders.

Half their military escort stayed behind as an escort for the Dwarves.

They mounted their horses and rode down the hill towards Atlantis. Marvin was next to King Baracian. King Handrian was riding between his wife and his sister.

King Baracian said, "It was tough swallowing the last of that mead."

Marvin said, "I agree. Even the mead in the Dwarven barracks and mines is of better quality. I heard the ladies talking about washing their mouth out with spiced wine when we get back to the palace."

The king laughed, "Good idea. How did you end up in the Dwarven mines? Only the destitute and criminals work our mines."

Marvin said. "It's a long story, but Dwarves are people of the Earth and the underground. Even the palace is deep inside a mountain. Mining is a highly respected profession and part of the training to work the forge. King Feldspar said the forge was calling me and would strengthen me. So, I agreed to let the Dwarves train me. It was physically the hardest thing I had ever done, but I learned more magic and gained more strength than I could have in ten times as long elsewhere.

"Lifting rock, heating forges, hammering metal, listening to stone and ore, and of course enchanting grew me fast. Once earth magic had strengthened me enough, I sat alone in the dark for hours in the heart of an iron mine trying to hear and see the stones, as Dwarves do. Now I see not just the outside of stone. I see the patterns and minerals within. It's beautiful to my eyes, like the beauty of a coral reef.

"Both Queen Juniperia and King Feldspar lamented how few Atlantians they get to train in the combined magic. I'm still new to wood and nature magic, yet I could have erected the platform by myself in half the time it took the carpenters, and I still had to make it sturdier for the Dwarves to go up it.

"I saw the Dwarven handiwork in the palace. It is beautiful, not just what we see on the outside, but what I see on the inside. Hopefully, I will get a chance to look at it and study it."

The king asked, "I am amazed at how strong you have become for so little time with magic."

Marvin replied, "Shandria and I talked about that. She feels that since my magic was unable to be born on Earth, and had been essential to our survival, it has grown exponentially fast. But I still am a beginner in knowledge."

King Baracian said, "Tonight you will be a royal guest of the court and will be until we determine your status. I know you have mixed feelings about being from Earth or being an Atlantian. I am hoping someday you will choose your blood and magic over your upbringing. But that is unfair of me to ask until you have lived among us for a while."

Marvin replied, "Thank you. I know that I will never be at home on Earth and that I am an Atlantian, yet part of me has no idea what that is. I know it will take me some time to learn the social customs and laws. I still need to learn to read Atlantian. Shandria taught me the basic alphabet, but I am like a young child sounding out each letter. I even read Dwarven better."

The king said, "You are far too valuable to me and the crown not to assign a scholar to teach you. I know you need to spend time here to learn our customs, but if you would like to work for the court of Atlantis, I would like you to be part of a delegation back to Crystal Mountain. You and Shandria are in favor with both courts. So, I am sending both of you. You will counsel King Handrian, who will lead the delegation."

Marvin replied, "It will be an honor to serve the court of Atlantis. Just one question since I know King Feldspar will ask me, am I allowed to perform any enchantments?"

King Baracian laughed, "I will get an agreement with the other Kings tonight, and the delegation will be renewing our alliance under our treaty of friendship. Once that is complete, it is legal for you to help him. You are under King Handrian's strict command. What, where, when, and anything else you do or say needs approval from him. Shandria will assist you in that regard."

King Baracian turned his head around and yelled, "Shandria, please join us."

Shandria excused herself from her conversation and trotted her horse forward, so she was between the king and Marvin.

The king said, "I know the two of you are close. You know our marriage customs, our courtship customs, and our protector customs. You know you are not allowed to share your warmth at the palace.

"Tomorrow I am sending the two of you under King Handrian to Crystal Mountain. Shandria, it is your right to designate Marvin as your protector and companion while away from the palace, which will allow you to share your warmth while on the king's business to Crystal Mountain."

Shandria said without hesitation. "I designate Sir Marvin as my protector and companion."

The king said, "Shandria, I am of split decision to send you because of your close relationship with Sir Marvin. But I trust you and your love for Atlantis. I trust Marvin, and his ability to protect you and his desire to follow our customs and laws. Marvin needs your guidance in our customs.

"Marvin, if you were a citizen we would find you a suitable concubine familiar with our laws and customs to teach you. But we will worry about that when you return."

The king slowed down his horse and fell back to talk to Alandria and Handrian.

Marvin thought he knew but asked Shandria, "What is a concubine?"

Shandria said, "A concubine in our society is a formal female companion for a man of status. For a single man, she performs all the functions of a wife. For a married man, it varies with his relationship with his wife, but she still serves the husband.

"A concubine joins a man's household for a year or two. After that, the concubine or the man may choose to end the relationship or to keep it going. It is up to the man and the concubine to find her a good marriage. Finding her a good marriage is good for the man's status. Sometimes the concubine will choose to be a concubine to another man. Concubines who served the royal families are highly sought as wives of nobles since they confer status to the husband and knowledge of the royal court. Most women consider men who have had a concubine as experienced, desirable husbands.

"My grandfather and father had concubines in their youth. Handrian has had three. He has one now from a noble family that fell on hard times. She is sure to find a good marriage to a noble. I expect the prince I marry will have had one or more concubines.

"Once you chose to stay at Atlantis, I will help you find a suitable concubine to take care of your needs and later a good wife if you allow me to."

"Marvin thought for a second and said. "What if a concubine becomes pregnant?"

Shandria said, "Their womb is magically barren while she is a concubine."

"Can a man marry his concubine?"

"It's done, but not often. It takes a while for the man's status to rise again."

Shandria continued, "You were about to be married. Did you have a concubine? Who took care of your needs?"

Marvin thought about it for a second. "We don't have concubines on Earth. My fiancée and I lived together and took care of each other's needs."

Shandria replied, "So, on Earth, you marry your concubine?"

Marvin thought about it and said, "There are no formal concubines on Earth, but sometimes in our society, a man and women mutually decide to share their bed before they marry."

Chapter 51

Mid-morning the next day, they mounted their horses and rode up the hill towards the arch accompanied by dozens of guards. Marvin had a chance to talk to King Handrian. He apologized for his inexperience in Atlantian Court protocol but assured him of his friendship with the royal family of Crystal Mountain. He then asked Handrian what his duties were, or if he could tell him anything about his experience with the Dwarves. The king was formal with Marvin and didn't seem to want to talk.

People watched them along the route. Several were waving. The king waved back, as did Marvin and the rest of the party. Marvin heard some people call out the names of the royal family. He also heard his name called out. His opening the arch had spread through the city, and probably much of the realm.

The original arch took several kings and princes, and the energy from a dozen people to open. And the people were crediting Marvin with opening it alone. It wasn't a fair comparison. The magic that had coursed through the arch for centuries had seasoned it. The magical channels were open and waiting. Marvin couldn't image spending a week weaving the magic to open the first arch.

When they arrived at the arch, there were dozens of horse-drawn carts waiting to go through.

Marvin said to the king, "It might be good if you open the portal since it's the first time. A king of Atlantis should be the first person through."

The king was reluctant since Marvin had suggested it, but he realized Marvin was right.

The king closed his eyes, found the trigger for Crystal Mountain, and made a circle with his arms. A circle of light appeared on the inside of the portal, and then Crystal Mountain was visible through the opening.

The king rode through with Alandria, followed by Shandria and Marvin. The Dwarven ambassador was right behind them. The rest of the party followed.

A dozen members of the royal guard followed, and several horse-drawn wagons came up the rear. The portal closed after everyone rode through.

Marvin shifted to Dwarven and talked to the ambassador. The ambassador was surprised that more than a messenger was coming through, especially a king of Atlantis. They hadn't follow established ambassadorial protocols for Head of

State visits. He needed at least three moons to properly plan and to coordinate the visit. It was most unusual and violated a dozen different procedures.

Marvin explained that with a war on the horizon they were under emergency military protocols. And that he and Shandria had already delivered war plans to Atlantis from King Feldspar. Then Marvin said in a voice in a manner that the ambassador knew he was joking, "Besides, you know how fluid and spontaneous Atlantians can be. And after what was served at the gate opening I personally can't wait for a mug of real Dwarven Mead."

The ambassador smiled and calmed down. He hadn't realized that King Feldspar had activated emergency war protocols. Normally he would get a diplomatic message, but with the arch down, he realized communication had been out.

A mounted guard from Crystal Mountain met them on the way down to the entry gate from the arch. The ambassador greeted the soldiers. He announced the arrival of King Handrian of Atlantis and Princess Alandria.

The Lieutenant of the soldiers dispatched a messenger to the court per regulations 1732.61. Per regulation 807.16, he had his men form an honor guard and lead the way down the mountain.

The Dwarven king's guard took over from the army soldiers per regulation 1315.2b. The Dwarven guard led them through the streets of the city.

King Handrian heard the crowd say the name of Princess Shandria and Sir Marvin. Then he heard someone say the ambassador's name. It took a while but the word spread that a king and queen of Atlantis had arrived, but no one knew their names. He heard Marvin call down from his horse, "King Handrian and Queen Alandria" several times to questions. The words traveled faster than the horses walked. Handrian heard his name said several times, but Princess Shandria and Sir Marvin were on everyone's lips.

Handrian wished his grandfather and father hadn't insisted he take Marvin. He was the first King to enter Crystal Mountain since his grandfather, and his grandfather was a prince at the time. The last king visited several hundred years ago, yet the name he heard more than anyone else's was Sir Marvin.

Sir Marvin hadn't even acknowledged himself as an Atlantian yet, and he was getting all the credit. Handrian had tried to recover the crystal but had lost the trail of the thief. His father was so upset at losing Shandria that he didn't even talk to Handrian about not recovering the crystal, but he knew his father was disappointed in him. All he wanted to do was make his father proud, yet ever since he had found his sister dead, he had been the bearer of bad news.

And Marvin was getting all the credit for doing what Handrian hadn't. Marvin from Earth had brought back Shandria and restored the arch. He was now the talk of two realms, three counting Alfamara.

His wife Alandria was quickly bonding with his sister. He always thought of his baby sister as immature, but she always followed court protocol. Hopefully, she would be a good influence on Alandria.

ATLANTIAN MAGIC

When Alandria said yes to marriage, Handrian was glad their time together in the scouts with her allowed them to skip the introductory phase, and to get married quicker. He hoped it would boost Atlantian morale, but it didn't work as well as he planned. The loss of the arch and his sister missing had more of an impact on the hearts of the people than his marriage and kingship had.

Handrian stilled his thoughts. He was a king. He was above this, and the Dwarven crowd at least now knew his name. He was sure they would soon forget Marvin's name. And his name would grow. He would make his father proud. Atlantians would see his love for them.

Handrian was impressed when they rode across the bridge to the palace. The trench looked deep and straight down.

The guards took their horses. Marvin saw the king looking at the relief drawings on the side of the palace. He said, "It tells of the exploits of the King Feldspar the Great."

Members of the court led the King and his party into the court of King Feldspar. When they passed through the final door, the sound of a trumpet greeted them. Soldiers, dignitaries, and finely dressed members of the court filled the courtroom, leaving the center hallway open. They started to clap and cheer as the king and queen entered. After a minute, the trumpets sounded again, and the clapping ended.

King Feldspar rose and said, "Welcome King Handrian and welcome to your new bride Queen Alandria of Atlantis. We only now found out about your marriage and coronation. And of course, we welcome Princess Shandria and Sir Marvin as friends of this court."

The crowd started to cheer. After a half a minute, the king raised his hand. The courtroom quieted down. He said, "King Handrian and Queen Alandria, please join us on the stage as equals and friends."

Queen Olivine, who was standing back in the shadows, stepped forward to join her husband. Princess Amethyst joined her a few seconds later.

They exchanged formal introductions. Then King Feldspar called Marvin and Shandria up. Shandria bowed her head, and Marvin bowed and touched his knee to the ground. He greeted them with a hug. The Queen followed, and so did Princess Amethyst. The king announced, "Court dismissed."

Trumpets blew, and they waited as the courtroom cleared. They then headed back to the Iron Room.

King Feldspar poured everyone a mug of mead, and they toasted to their continuing friendship. Marvin was glad to be drinking Dwarven Mead again, rather than what they drank at the arch. King Handrian handed a rolled up and tied document to King Feldspar. King Feldspar opened it, read it, and said, "Done! Our friendship and Alliance is once again reaffirmed." He stood up, reached across the table, and shook hands with King Handrian. Then he raised his mug and said, "To the eternal friendship of Atlantis and Crystal Mountain."

They raised their mugs and yelled, "Here. Here." then drank a toast.

After the toast, King Handrian handed King Feldspar another scroll.

King Feldspar looked at it for half a minute and scratched his beard. He said, "Well it looks like we are into negotiations."

King Feldspar turned towards Marvin, "Have you had a chance to look at the new towers?"

Marvin replied, "No, I haven't. I saw several from the mountain as we came in through the portal. I hope I will get a chance to at least tour the progress before we leave."

The king said to Marvin, "King Handrian and I have court business. I can think of no better person than you to give a tour to the ladies."

He looked at King Handrian, who gave an affirmative nod.

Then King Feldspar said, "Perhaps King Handrian will allow you to show the ladies how to strengthen the towers with magic."

King Handrian smiled and said, "Of course. Marvin explained to the Atlantian Council how essential the towers are to the defense of our friends the Dwarves."

King Feldspar stood up and said, "To the ladies of the court." He took a drink, as did everyone else.

It was an indication for Marvin and the ladies to leave. Marvin heard both kings give orders for their ministers to attend them as he closed the door behind him.

Queen Olivine and Princess Amethyst needed to change into their travel clothes, and Shandria and Alandria needed to freshen up back at the embassy. The queen and her daughter would join them at the embassy soon.

Of course, soon meant something different to the ladies than it did to Marvin. He was anxious to see how the towers were proceeding, and each minute waiting seemed like hours.

Yet Shandria and Alandria were ready in less time than it seemed to Marvin. Queen Olivine and her daughter arrived soon after. The young ladies, Shandria, Alandria, and Amethyst, formed a subgroup. And Marvin paired with Queen Olivine, his Dwarven aunt.

Soon they arrived at a tower. Marvin was proud of the excellent work the Dwarves had done. He became all excited telling how the king's twenty-year plan had become a twenty-day plan because of the possible war, and how King Feldspar, Queen Juniperia, and himself had enchanted amulets that were spreading their protective power into the towers. They would build walls after the harvest to join the towers together, and the magic would flow through the walls.

Marvin had the ladies put their hands on the tower to feel and see the energy flow. The ladies enjoyed feeling and seeing the magic slowly grow and enchant the tower. Marvin thought it was interesting that the Dwarves and the Atlantians saw different flows. The Dwarves sensed the earth magic flow. The Atlantians sensed the general energy flow and the other magic to a lesser effect.

ATLANTIAN MAGIC

Marvin was the only one who sensed all the magic of the Dwarves, Alfarins, and his Atlantian magic at a high level. A few more weeks of learning earth magic and he was sure Shandria would be able to see the flows inside the rock also.

Marvin focused and said. "I'm going to try and add more energy to the tower, to speed up the growth and spread of the enchantment. Marvin wove his magic. He slowly energized the wall segment they were touching. It was rock, so it was slow, but the strength of the tower segment grew noticeably. Every extra encouragement he gave to the tower would speed the growth of the protective magic.

Marvin concentrated and followed the magic flow. The tower magic interconnected to towers on either side, creating a thick band between towers that resisted dark magic. Walls would someday connect the towers and be strengthened and add to the defense.

They continued the tour. But the ladies soon became less interested in the towers than in riding their horses and talking. Queen Olivine continued the tour, explaining the mounds and the farming complex. Soon it was time to ride back to the palace.

Queen Olivine had the palace staff 'throw together' dinner for everyone. The Kings had just finished their agreement. They both looked pleased. King Handrian looked drunk. Marvin thought, "Welcome to Dwarven culture."

The thrown together meal was a banquet. Marvin didn't realize how hungry he was and based on how much they ate; he wasn't the only one.

He filled in the details about the tour. Then King Feldspar said. "King Handrian and I agreed that it would be in the interest of both kingdoms if you would do some enchanting at the forge while you are here. Of course, the decision is yours."

Marvin smiled. He knew refusing the request of a king wasn't a smart a choice. But it was a win-win, and King Feldspar knew Marvin had enchanting in his blood. Marvin said, "It is an honor to serve one court, and to serve two at the same time is ten times the honor. I am eager to serve."

King Feldspar said, "That rocks!" a phrase he had picked up from his daughter who had picked it up from Shandria who had learned it from Marvin. It meant the same thing but for different reasons. The king said, "First thing tomorrow we will expect you at the forge."

After dinner, they rode back to the embassy and cleaned up. Handrian and Alandria got the royal room where Shandria and Marvin had slept before. They chose the room two doors down the hallway, across from the room that held the clothes Marvin had worn.

Marvin checked the bedroom where the male clothing hung on the previous trip. He found his forge gear was clean and laid out on the bed. The staff was efficient as always. Shandria and Marvin took their clothes off, walked out to the pool, and jumped in. The water felt good and was relaxing. Alandria soon joined them.

Pd MICHEL

King Handrian was lying on a lounge, having had too much to drink. He was upset at how negotiations had gone. He had been negotiating deals in the court since he was a teenage prince. But King Feldspar was a master. They settled the easy treaty points quickly. But then the decisions became serious. Near the end of the negotiation, King Feldspar had everything he wanted, and King Handrian had very little. King Handrian was starting to worry.

Then King Feldspar treated the rest of the negotiations as minor issues. He agreed to them all, except for the iron to make five thousand swords. He changed it to five thousand Dwarven-forged swords. Iron to make swords for privates turned into swords a prince would be proud to own.

The only concession King Feldspar asked for was to allow Marvin to work the forges for a few days if he agreed to it.

Handrian was a king of Atlantis, and only the friendship of King Feldspar had given him an excellent assistance agreement. In the process, he had been all but drunk under the table. He knew better than that. He finally understood where the saying you can't outdrink a Dwarf came from. Mead was like water to a Dwarf.

Handrian was upset, what was so valuable about the Earthman Marvin that having him for a week was more valuable to King Feldspar then spending time with a King of Atlantis? He brooded until he fell asleep.

After playtime at the pool ended, Alandria gently kissed her husband on the cheek. He had fallen asleep by the pool. Her kiss woke him up. She invited him to bed.

Marvin and Shandria headed off to bed. They snuggled closer than normal, knowing this was probably the last trip they would ever get to sleep together.

Chapter 52

Marvin ate a big breakfast and left for the forges. Waterboy received many back slaps and was directed to a forge where King Feldspar was working the metal. The hammer he had used when he made his dagger was waiting for him. It was his friend, and he eagerly picked it up. Forge hammers weren't separately enchanted, but with all the magic running through them they became enchanted and picked up their own personality. It always reflected its owner.

The king slowed down his rhythm so Marvin could keep up with him. The rest of the forges slowed down also. The rhythm "TAP... TAP ... TAP ..." of the king's hammer combined with Marvin alternating hits become the double-time rhythm "TAP.tap. TAP.tap. TAP.tap." Marvin watched the force of each of the king's blows. They were several times as hard as Marvin could hit the metal. The rest of the forges synchronized with them. The song of the forge filled their hearts and minds. It was directing the rhythm.

Then Marvin saw the king's magical weave. Dwarven magic filled the air, knocking at the door of the metal with the pound of the king's hammer. The king nodded, and Marvin started a weave taught him by his sword. It was almost the same weave as the one in his dagger. He could see his magic was in harmony with the song of the forge. The magic he wove was near the limits of his ability and took all his concentration. Soon he was lost in the enchantment, the rhythm of the hammer, and the song of the forge.

The Dwarven magic and the Atlantian magic touched each other slowly, shyly at first, and then in a slow dance, intertwined. Together they knocked on the door of the metal with each tap of the hammer, and over time, the hot metal opened up and accepted the weave. Marvin could see the combined weave reproducing, splitting and spreading out to all the forges. It was like the first flower of spring opening up and spreading its petals. It was beautiful to Marvin's heart. Marvin had tears in his eyes from the beauty.

They enchanted three daggers before the break, but with the fires hot, there was no stopping today. A cart came around and gave a tankard of mead to the King and one to Marvin. They also left their water boy a pitcher of cool water. Marvin drank half the water after the mead. They finished another dagger, and Marvin finished his water. They kept filling up his water. He drank some between each new piece of metal. They became faster with each dagger and enchanted five more daggers between break and lunch. They passed on the hot, enchanted daggers to another weaponsmith for final shaping, sharpening, polishing, and finishing. Then a third artisan would build and attach the handle. Marvin would have loved to have worked the daggers to completion, but this was mass production Dwarf style. And his job was the enchanter.

Lunchtime was a quick mug of mead. The forges were hot, and the magic was flowing. After lunch, Marvin drank water for the rest of the day. The king bid him goodbye. He had royal duties.

Marvin moved from the king's forge to the one right next to it with his old mentor Grand Master Hematite. They were enchanting a sword. Marvin's old forge master increased the speed again. It was once again at the limits of Marvin's ability to hammer with precision. Marvin kept up, and there was a noticeable increase in the strength of his hammer strikes. "TAP.Tap. TAP.Tap. TAP.Tap." Soon they were once again enchanting.

The rhythm of the forge helped him keep up the pace. He felt his body and magic responding to the challenge. The Dwarven magic of earth and metal, fire and forge flowed through his body, making him tougher and stronger. The Atlantian magic of water, air, and sky flowed through his body, making him more flexible and giving him more energy. Alfarin magic of wood and nature flowed through his body, making him more resilient and faster. He realized the magic that allowed him to blend into his surroundings was making him able to blend into the forge rhythm easier.

They were hammering at twice the pace they had when he started in the morning, and Marvin knew he was hitting harder. The rhythm of the forge was the pounding of the slowest hammer. He was the slow man, and they had waited for him to learn and catch up.

That evening he rode back to the embassy and jumped into the pool to clean off. After his swim, he quickly dried himself with magic. He walked back to their room and found Shandria had laid Atlantian clothes out for him. He dressed and joined them for dinner. Not unexpectedly, Marvin ate twice what everyone else did.

King Handrian spent the morning meeting with his ministers and his scholars. They were sending communications back and forth through the portal to Atlantis. He spent his afternoon in the war room with King Feldspar, who was fresh from the forge. They discussed combined military tactics over mead.

Shandria, Alandria, and Amethyst had spent the morning chatting and getting the gowns they had brought with them ready for the royal ball, which King Feldspar had called to celebrate their visit. That afternoon they fought with dulled wooden swords, battle-axes, and spears. Shandria wore padded armor that had Dwarven metal magic woven into it. Alandria wore her ancient armor. Amethyst wore her armor and hardened her skin with earth magic. The other ladies were impressed when Shandria showed them her Alfarin speed magic. She was five times as fast as her normal combat speed and could move faster for brief bursts.

Shandria agreed not to use speed magic during their sparring sessions.

Afterward, they decided to exchange magic lesson. Princess Amethyst was excited to teach them earth magic. Shandria and Alandria taught Princess Amethyst water magic. Because of the Dwarven nature of stone and metal, learning anything but the basic in another type of magic was very hard. It was slow going, but finally near the end of the week, Amethyst started to see water magic. They taught her a weave that would allow her to gently move or stir liquid. Amethyst was more excited with her simple water weave then Shandria was when she wove her first lightning bolt.

Shandria tried to teach speed magic after the session to Alandria. They realized Alandria needed to know more nature magic first, so they worked on that. It took all week, but Princess Amethyst learned a beginning healing weave that was only slightly more complex than just asking nature magic to heal. Once again, she was excited as a child in a room full of sweet cakes.

Princess Amethyst gave the ladies a tour of where she was working as a journeyman silversmith. In another fifty or a hundred years she was hoping to apprentice as a goldsmith.

Shandria was excited that Alandria and her were becoming such good friends and they planned to continue working out together once they returned to Atlantis.

After dinner, Marvin practiced his katas with Shandria and Alandria. Both of them joined in as Marvin performed his improving sky kata. He was working to make his kata smoother and more precise.

They jumped into the pool afterward. Shandria held Marvin's hand in the pool after the kata. She had Alandria hold his other hand. They enjoyed his spill over magic from the forge, which they could feel was strengthening their bodies. Handrian was busy, but he did join them in the pool with his wife and sister's insistence, but he soon left. He said he had more historical court decisions to discuss with his ministers.

The next few days continued the same. Only Marvin was finished making daggers. He alternated making battle-axes and swords. Marvin enchanted with the king in the morning, and with different weapons masters in the afternoon. Marvin found out later that everyone wanted to enchant with the "water boy" so he was getting the most senior masters. Marvin liked how each master's techniques were the same but had subtle differences.

The tailors once again measured Marvin for an outfit. They didn't have time to make him a new outfit, so they were going to modify his Elvis outfit. He was glad they thought his idea to go to a smaller folded down collar was a good idea. He was no longer an Elvis impersonator, but a character from Saturday Night Fever in his bell-bottomed leisure suit, although the sequins were a little over the top.

The ladies said they liked his fashion statement. But Marvin knew so little about Atlantian fashion, and fashion in general, that he was wondering if Alandria and Shandria were pulling a prank on him. Even so, he was glad the fishtail shaped collar was gone.

They had fun at the ball. Marvin danced with two queens, two princesses, and two more Dwarven princesses who had come from Silver Mountain with their husbands on royal business to attend the ball.

Once again, Marvin danced almost every dance. He kept hydrated by making sure the dance ended near the head table where he could grab a quick drink of water or spiced wine. Shandria pointed out Amethyst at a table with some of her friends showing them how she could stir their drinks with her magic.

Afterward, they took a carriage back to the embassy. They laughed and had a good time all the way back. Even King Handrian was in a good mood.

They stripped down and jumped into the pool. Handrian joined them for a few minutes then left. He unrolled a scroll and started drinking out of a large tankard.

The ladies started playing in the pool, showing Marvin various water magic tricks. Some Marvin copied right away, but others had the ladies laughing at the results of his unsuccessful tries before he correctly wove the magic. Marvin laughed too. It was all in good fun, and he was learning a lot.

Handrian was watching them out of the corner of his eye. He started to brood again. He watched Marvin and Shandria laugh together. He was upset that Marvin and his sister were still sharing the same bed. This wasn't a tent. There were plenty of bedrooms.

Shandria didn't need protecting except from her protector. His sister needed to let go of their relationship. She was a princess of Atlantis. She needed to hold to a higher standard. She would only get hurt. She was his sister. He loved her and needed to protect her.

And Alandria didn't understand how much he loved Atlantis and how much he loved her. She didn't understand he had his duties to perform as a king and didn't have time to play like a child. She had her duties as his wife and queen. He needed a queen as strong as his mother or grandmother to be the king he wanted to be; the king he needed to be to make his father proud. She had a long way to go. She should be studying past rulings of the court, not playing. Didn't she realize he was showing his love by making her take her job as queen more serious?

Shandria, Marvin, and Alandria ended up in the top pool, which Marvin had turned into a hot tub. They were passing a bottle around and sipping spiced wine. Alandria was telling them how she had created an ice water ball and thrown it at Handrian in Sea Scouts so he would notice her. Handrian had already noticed her, but it broke the ice. She giggled when she said 'broken the ice' with her ice water ball. Afterward, the two of them became partners in crime and pulled some mild pranks on other Sea Scouts.

She was tired of her husband ignoring her. At least he wasn't ignoring her in bed since his concubine wasn't around. She grew frustrated, walked over to him, and asked him to join them in the hot tub. He said, "No, I'm too tired."

She hit him with an ice water ball. She giggled and started to run away. King Handrian blew up and started yelling. Alandria was shocked. She couldn't believe this was the fun-loving boy from Sea Scouts she thought she had married. The ice water ball should have turned into a splash fight and tickle session in the pool. Then her frustration came out. They yelled back and forth. After a while, King Handrian grabbed her by the upper arm, made a fist with his other hand and brought it back as if to punch her.

Alandria stopped talking and stood there with a look of total disbelief on her face. Handrian saw the look on her face. He looked away from her at his mead-powered fist hanging in the air. He looked back at her, and he saw the tears start coming from her eyes. He looked at his hand again, dropped his fist, and with his own look of disbelief at his behavior, let go of her and walked away. Shandria ran over and hugged her, alternating between comforting looks at Alandria and angry looks at Handrian, who had turned his back to everyone.

Marvin watched, wishing he knew what to do, but realized Shandria knew far better what Alandria needed than he did. The two ladies headed back towards the bedroom area. Overhead was the midnight sky. Marvin saw King Handrian brooding in a dark corner with a tankard of dark Dwarven mead. Marvin exited the hot tub and walked by himself to his room, quickly grabbing his sword and clothing along the way. He walked a wide path around Handrian when he saw the king's face was full of anger and frustration.

He heard Shandria with Alandria talking and crying in Shandria and Marvin's room. It was late, so Marvin decided to sleep in the spare bedroom. Soon the events of the week caught up with him, and he fell asleep. An hour later, he woke up when he heard a commotion in the hallway. Someone was opening doors and slamming them shut. His door opened, and a stumbling drunken King Handrian stepped in. He yelled, "Where is my wife? I'm the king; tell me where my wife is."

Marvin said, "I last saw her with Shandria, my king."

He yelled back, "That's right! I'm your king. Now stay away from my sister, you damn peasant from Earth." He threw the empty tankard, which Marvin suspected he had refilled at least once. It bounced harmlessly off the wall above Marvin. Handrian slammed the door.

Marvin lay in bed and listened. He heard Alandria arguing with Handrian in the hallway. The last thing he heard was Alandria yelling. "I will always share my warmth with my husband, but I won't spread my legs for a drunk." Then the door of the royal bedroom slammed shut, and it was quiet.

Marvin lay there. His door opened, and Shandria crawled into bed. She spooned in from behind, with her arm hugging him. He gently held her hand, pulled it up to his lips, and kissed it before letting it go. Shandria kissed his shoulder. Both wished Shandria's chastity weave would let them do more, and that their society would allow them to be together.

Frazzled nerves, combined with Handrian's hangover, put a quiet and somber mood on everyone the next morning. Just before breakfast, King Handrian approached Marvin. Marvin bowed his head. The King started, "About last night…"

Marvin quickly knelt down on one knee with his head bowed and said, "Please forgive me, my king. I was tired from the forge, and I must have drunk too much at the ball celebrating your great treaty. After watching you dance beautifully with your queen, I don't remember anything."

The king halted for a second, then said. "You are forgiven. The night went well." Then he walked away.

King Handrian wasn't the person Marvin expected from Shandria's stories. Marvin wasn't sure whether he should start to hate Handrian, or only to feel sorry for Alandria. But internally Marvin was praying it was just a season in his life, and he would recover.

It was a later breakfast than normal. And it was quiet around the table. Even Shandria and Alandria were mostly silent. They left the embassy midmorning and rode towards the arch. Marvin and Shandria rode their horses behind the king and his wife. Marvin watched them smile and wave as they rode up the mountain towards the arch. The couple traveled together, yet their hearts were realms apart.

Chapter 53

Marvin followed Handrian and Alandria into the portal for Atlantis. He blinked and found himself lying on a blanket he thought might be buffalo and covered by another one. He was inside a mud-bricked house. There was a closed wooden door on the side of the room.

He smelled burning smoke, a campfire, and a pine forest.

This time there was no bowl of food. Marvin saw his clothes and backpack. He stood up and put them on. He opened the door and walked out. The man who said Marvin should call him Tonto was there…

Marvin blinked again and arrived through the portal to Atlantis. He was sitting on his horse. Next to him was Shandria. In front of him were her brother and his wife. He felt disorientated. What a vivid dream. Did the portal cause it? He was sure he had been gone for several months, yet here he was. Marvin reached inside his shirt and pulled out a strange medallion on a chain. If it was a dream then why am I wearing this, and why can I read the inscription? He put the medallion back into his shirt. He looked down at his right hand. He snapped and spread his fingers. He saw the blue glow of lightning jumping between his forefinger and thumb. He ended the weave. Now there was no doubt. He had been away for several months.

It took him a few minutes to remember what he had been doing before he left Crystal Mountain those many months ago. Or was it just a second ago? Somehow, both were true. For now, the last few months didn't happen. He had heard the Anastasi were masters of wisdom and sky. Earth physicist talked about sky, or space, as space-time. He must have lived for a few months and been sent back. Or maybe he traveled backward in time, and then he returned to today. Marvin wondered if he would ever find out.

His last thought when he left had been about Handrian, and they weren't good. At least his time away had moderated his emotions towards the man. His wife could take care of herself. Even after spending several months intertwined with Shandria's mind in the green goo, he still didn't understand the beautiful, fragile, and yet powerful uniqueness that was a woman's emotions. But he knew Shandria would take care of Alandria.

Marvin saw people were waving at him. He waved back. He needed to pay attention. After last night, his companions wouldn't think his being a little detached was strange.

They arrived at the palace. Court officials, after much bowing, escorted them into the blue room.

The ministers took their packs and cloaks. They celebrated with spiced wine and toasted their successful journey.

Baracian turned towards Handrian and said, "King Feldspar gave us a great assistance agreement. When I was young, I tried negotiating with him. I ended up owing him half our kingdom, then he gave it all back. I learned more about friendship, and how to negotiate in that meeting than I ever had before. We sent you because you are good, but also because I trusted King Feldspar would help turn you into the great king that is your potential. I am very proud of you." He raised his cup, and everyone toasted to Handrian. "You can brief us in the war room about the rest of your discussions when we finish here."

Then he turned to Marvin, "Tell us about your experience. I heard you did some enchanting."

Marvin said, "Yes k... I mean Baracian." He motioned to have his backpack given to him. He pulled out seven bundles. Each had a name written on them in Atlantian and Dwarvish. He handed one to each of the queens, and the kings, and one to Shandria.

He looked at their eyes as they looked at the daggers he made. He said. "King Feldspar and I worked the metal and enchanted these. Weaponsmiths did all the final sharpening and finishing work after us. We made eight daggers. King Feldspar thought enough of their quality that he gave one to his daughter. He said they are some of the best daggers made in centuries. They are gifts from King Feldspar and me."

King Baracian said, "The quality, the balance, and the magic inside is beautiful. I would ask you what the weaves are, but I would rather discover it myself."

Marvin replied, "I helped forge and enchant several dozen swords, but the magic spread out into the forge area and enchanted others. Dwarves seldom use swords. They will be part of the Dwarven sword shipment. I also enchanted several battle-axes. The magic spread out also, and enchanted others."

Marvin closed his pack and handed it back to the minister.

Queen Alandria and Shandria gave their accounts of their time with the queen, the Dwarven princess, and the ball.

Marvin expected them to send him to Alfamara, but Queen Isaria and King Vandian already visited and arrived back yesterday. Queen Juniperia agreed to do what she could but wanted to be flexible.

King Vandian asked Shandria what she thought about the Alfarins. She replied, "I owe Queen Juniperia for restoring my magic, and probably my life. It is hard for me to be objective, but we can trust her when she says she will send help."

He asked Marvin what he thought. Marvin said, "Shandria taught me that our magic affects how we think. The Dwarves are masters of the magic of solids. Like solids, they haven't wavered from our treaty of eternal friendship one inch in thousands of years.

Alfarins are masters of wood and nature. Trees bend and are flexible, but their roots hold firm. No two trees grow alike. We can trust that the queen has planted a strong tree. Her assistance will be flexible yet firm. Flexibility is the strength of wood magic, so she is offering us her strength."

The three kings conversed for a few minutes, then Baracian said, "Marvin, your commission with this court is fulfilled. You have three choices. First, you may declare yourself an Atlantian. You are a friend of this court, and that choice will always be open to you when you are ready. Second, you can stay in our society and learn from it, and then decide, or third, you can leave Atlantis and explore. You are always welcome back. The choice is up to you."

Marvin said, "I prefer choice two, I still have a lot to learn about Atlantian laws and customs and where I fit into Atlantian society. I will remain loyal to this court and will gladly serve again if the court desires."

King Baracian looked and verified with the other kings and said, "We offer you living arrangements on a small estate not too far from the palace. The estate is the property of the crown, and it will remain so. It's in what we call the seaside narrows. The estate is on the ocean. A resident family lives on and takes care of it for the crown. They will help you adapt to Atlantian life. It is close to the University. The Crown will pay the university to tutor you in any subject you desire and already has a fund with the university.

"We give you two horses for your stable, and twelve new sets of Atlantian clothes. A court tailor will be by tomorrow to measure you.

"We give you a reward in Atlantian currency for services to the crown. King Feldspar gave you a rather generous reward for services to him. Queen Juniperia gifts you the boat you received from her. The crown will maintain and store it at its present docking location. Certification is required to operate it in Atlantian water. Perhaps that is one of your first lessons.

"The crown extends to you a small weekly stipend, which should be sufficient to cover your ordinary living expenses. These are awarded to you for your service to the crown.

"We also offer you a commission as a scholar to the crown. It comes with an additional stipend and fits your title of Sir Marvin and Protector of the Court. You will perform duties as the crown sees fit. You will get occasional visits on matters to do with your expertise, at your estate. The court may invite you at its leisure and expects you to attend to our needs. It comes with access to the library of the court. It should give you time to study, and the resident scholars will assist you. A court official will periodically visit you. She will help you with your transition.

"Do you accept the gifts of this court?"

Marvin said, "The court is very generous. I accept both the gifts and the commission."

King Baracian said, "Since you carry an ancient sword, and have protected members of the royal family before, there may be additional opportunities to serve the crown. May we call upon you in an emergency?"

Marvin replied. "I will never hesitate to protect or come to the aid of a member of this court, whether in an emergency or under less extreme circumstances. And I am honored to serve."

King Baracian smiled and said, "There is no doubt in the mind of this court that what you have said is true."

"Princess Shandria, will you select two good riding ponies from the royal stable, and have them saddled and equipped for Sir Marvin. You may escort Marvin to his new residence at the narrows and spend the day with him. A squad of royal guards will accompany you there and back."

Queen Elantria said, "Before you go, stand up Sir Marvin." She walked forward. Please lower your head." She placed a medal around his neck. "This is the medal certifying you as a friend and protector to the court. You may want to wear it when you visit, at least until the guards get to know you. It will allow you access to the palace grounds and library.

King Baracian sad "You are dismissed."

Marvin bowed and left the room. Shandria followed him out and then escorted him to the royal stables. She selected two horses and had them saddled. She had them saddle one of hers. She ordered and signed a writ of transference for the two horses and accessories from the quartermaster.

The royal guard accompanied them as they rode out of the stable. It was half an hour on horseback, but then they were in no hurry. Shandria had the guards wait outside the estate. She knocked on the door. A family of four, a husband, his wife, and their two children met them at the door. An assistant from the court was there. After some discussions with Marvin, she said she would be back tomorrow midmorning with the court tailor and would escort Marvin to the university and give him a tour of the city.

The property had a name, Sea Fan Narrows. The property was on a curved section of the Narrows. Rather than a narrow strip, it had a slight fan shape and had a larger than average ocean access.

Marven took the tour of the estate. It was the biggest small estate he had ever seen. It included stables and a swimming pool that was double the size of the one he had back in Phoenix. The property sloped down from the road to a sandy beach where it met the water. The beach was large enough for Marvin to work on his katas. The estate was fully furnished. There was a stand of grape

ATLANTIAN MAGIC

vines and an herb garden. Marvin wondered if he would get to learn how to make wine or if the grapes were for eating.

Princess Shandria explored every nook, cranny, and drawer of the estate with him. Marvin was both overwhelmed and saddened. Soon Shandria had to leave. The loss saddened Marvin. But he could tell it affected Shandria far more. From his perspective, they hadn't shared a bed for several months. From her perspective, this was the start of many nights they would be apart.

Marvin spent time with the White family. He heard the general house rules, but they were up to him to establish new rules as he saw fit. Marvin eliminated some of the main house separation rules. He wanted to be part of the family. He asked them what their established family meal times were. Marvin was happy with breakfast a half hour after sunrise, a midday meal, and dinner at sunset. He wanted to eat together with the family and learn Atlantian customs.

The next day the crown delivered Marvin the clothes he had acquired from Crystal Mountain, and the court tailor visited. Marvin toured the University and the city. Then Mr. White gave him a tour of the neighborhood. Marvin sat down and talked to Mrs. White after she cleaned up dinner. The property had gone through a dozen owners since they had started working here. They weren't at liberty to give names, but there had been both quiet and wild people.

He found out there were several levels of female companions, everything from a common prostitute to a courtesan, and various forms of live-in permanency. Mrs. Write told him he had a high social standing since he restored the Atlantian arch and was in favor with the crown. Gossip traveled quickly, and many families had already contacted her about meeting him, including a rather well to do young widow with high social standing. The widow had stayed chaste since her husband died. Marvin found part of him was contemplating the offer, at least for her friendship, but realized his heart was still set on Shandria, and even though Shandria had offered to help him find someone, it felt like cheating to him.

A week later, the court called him in as an advisor. He rode his horse to the palace. King Vandian asked him a few questions about Queen Juniperia and their military, then dismissed him. He decided to use the palace library to study. He was tired with the "See the fish swim" books his tutor from the university was having him read. He realized he already knew how to read. He just needed to improve his reading speed with the Atlantian alphabet. Another instructor was teaching him the symbols used to read magic. To improve his reading speed, he was toughing it out with harder works of a historical nature and studying magic.

He was glad that most of the language was phonetic. His language weave didn't help with sounding out the word, but it did help him understand once he read the word. He knew his reading would get more automatic over time. He kept bugging the scholars about certain symbols, most of which turned out to be names or locations. They found him a scroll, which had a list of two hundred common symbols. He was using it so often they made him a copy.

He started using the library every day. A few weeks later, Shandria came in. She was glad to see him. Her brother had suggested she be restricted from seeing him until she was over him. The rest of the Kings only restricted her from visiting him at his estate, unless she had a formal reason or invitation.

She saw him using the list of symbols to decipher names. She said, "Most of the newer symbols you can read if you know how. She wrote her name down, then her symbol. She showed him the sideways 'SH' letter, the 'N' letter and the 'DR' letter. All female names ended in "IA," which looked like an open bracket. The stylized letters were different. It was like reading cursive. Then she had him pick out the letters on the rest of the family. All the male names ended in the "N" letter, which looked like a closed bracket.

They took a walk around the palace grounds, and Shandria shared with him the court gossip.

Marvin was glad they didn't bump into her brother. He had no doubt that word of their encounter would make its way back to him anyway. There were few secrets in the gossip of the court.

Her brother wanted Shandria to start courting right away. She said she would do her duty. But the other kings and their queens said marriage is more than a duty. They wanted her to wait a season before courting for her emotions to get back in balance. That was part of the reason that they had given Marvin an estate off the palace grounds.

Shandria shared the gossip and some information of a less formal nature. The Dwarves had delivered the first thousand swords. Shandria said they vibrated with his enchantment. They were some of the best swords in the armory. Shandria was sure they were better than the sword her brother was using, but he was stubborn. Marvin was sure it was because of his feelings about him.

Alandria and Shandria were working out together. Her brother would have preferred she was reading an old musty scroll but couldn't deny that her military training was essential also. Alandria had quickly learned enough nature magic that she was starting to learn Alfarin speed magic.

Her brother was giving Alandria the cold shoulder and spending most nights with his concubine. Alandria wanted the fluidity of their friendship back and not the ice-hard man he had become. She was always ready to receive him in her bed and share her heat, but he only came in about once a week. At least when he did, he treated her well.

Shandria asked Marvin if he was sharing his heat with anyone. He told her he wasn't. Shandria said, "I haven't inquired for you, but I have kept my ears open, and there are several good prospects. Atlantians will think it strange and start spreading rumors if a man of your stature doesn't find a companion soon. You know I will help you."

Marvin said, "I also need a season away."

Shandria thought a second and said, "I know, I will tell people you are honoring your Earth custom of mourning for the death of your fiancée and your family, and that you pushed the mourning period to the side to be my protector but now feel the need to honor it. There is truth in it. It will allow me to speak with you more often since I can't abandon a friend in mourning. It will also add to both your social standing and desirability when your season is over. Then when we find you a suitable companion, I will present her to you. That will confirm us as just friends."

Marvin and Shandria arranged to talk the following week again. It would be infrequent enough that it would be hard for anyone to question it. But other events got in the way of their meeting.

Chapter 54

Marvin didn't know how Shandria had spread the story of his mourning so quickly, but the following afternoon Mrs. Write heard and confirmed the story about the tragedy of his fiancée and family.

Marvin often walked to the palace rather than ride his horse. The weather was beautiful, and the walk felt great. He enjoyed people watching on his way. Many people that were avoiding him or just not paying attention to him suddenly became friendly. One or two handed him a flower and walked away. Maybe the guards were getting used to him. But even they were friendlier. He asked Mrs. Write.

She said, "Someone of your status is expected to ride a horse to work. Now, not riding a horse makes sense to us. We know you are taking long walks to help with your loneliness and grief, and we all support you."

Marvin found out different flowers in Atlantian society meant different things. One day Marvin received a red waluia flower from a woman down the street. The waluia flower was a beautiful flower, common in Atlantian gardens. He showed it to Mrs. White.

She said, "The nerve of that slut! She knows you are in mourning and she invites you over to share your heat. She only wants notoriety at the cost of your reputation. She even propositioned my husband once."

Suddenly Mrs. White's tone changed. She said, "I'm sorry. I will be discrete about this. If you want to visit her, then I will help you send an affirmation."

Marvin asked, "What's her reputation? Is she any good at satisfying a man in bed?"

Marvin saw the shocked look on Mrs. Write's face. He started to laugh. "I'm just joking. When I'm ready, she won't be a slut. And I value your input like you're my sister." She realized Marvin was only teasing and she giggled.

He asked, "Is it the flower or the color?"

She said, "It's both. The waluia Is a message flower. The red waluia is for love or romance between a husband and his wife or concubine. It's used to ask a lady for marriage, or for a clandestine meeting."

"What about the white waluia people have been giving me?"

"They are given to show good wishes or emotional support. They can also signify a romantic relationship is over, but the man still cares. A man gives a white waluia to a concubine saying it's time to end the relationship, that he cares about her status, and he will help her find a good husband."

He received a similar message from another woman in the neighborhood, only it was a blue Waluia. Mrs. White said, "She is a lovely woman of noble birth. Her parents died when she was young, and she has never married. The blue says that when you are ready for a female friend, she would like to meet you. There is the implication of a possible relationship in the future that will go through proper channels."

Marvin asked, "What should I do?"

"We can either arrange for you formally to meet her. We can turn her down. Or we can thank her for her invitation, but that you aren't ready yet. I would recommend the last one. She is a proper lady, and it keeps your prospects open."

Marvin chose the last option. He was trying to be realistic. He wasn't ready yet, but when Shandria's waiting period was over, he would move on for Shandria's sake and his.

The next day, Mr. White showed Marvin a crack in the foundation that a professional would need to repair. Marvin sat down on the floor and looked at the ground. They had built the house on sandy soil. The sand had compacted and subsided. He took a deep look at the entire estate. The estate was concrete, brick, wood for the interior, and ceramic for the roof.

He spent the rest of the day using earth magic to shift sand from the beach to under his estate and to harden the footing and foundation. Next, he used wood and stone magic to repair and strengthen the exterior walls, and critical walls inside the house. Almost as an afterthought, he added magical wards to protect his home. It was fun to use his magic for something useful rather than just practice it.

Marvin saw Mrs. White working in the herb garden. He showed her a few earth and nature weaves that would help her. He was surprised that few Atlantians studied their secondary magic. They considered it more of a hobby when they did. He found Mr. White grooming the horses. Marvin had Mr. White show him how to brush his horse.

A few days later, Marvin was reading in his office. A loud knocking on the door made him run downstairs. A messenger bellowed, "Message from the King, message from the court of Atlantis."

The Court Messenger said, "The court has an emergency need for your services. King Baracian told me to tell you, 'Code Black.'"

Code Black meant war. Marvin said. "I will be ready in five minutes." He ran upstairs and changed into his travel outfit. He grabbed all his medallions and amulets and put them on under his shirt with his wolf's tooth.

He grabbed an envelope from his nightstand and ran downstairs. He handed the envelope to Mr. and Mrs. White and said, "Once I am gone, please read and heed this." He hugged them both. The kids were gone, so he told Mrs. White to give them a hug.

Marvin activated the wards on his house and left with the King's guard escort.

Mrs. White and her husband read the note in the envelope. "Dear Mr. and Mrs. White."

"Since I gave you this message, it means I have been called away to serve the court under emergency orders. Most likely, none of that will involve you, and it will be something that is easily resolved, so there is no reason to worry. I have strengthened this house with advanced level magic. This is the strongest building in the narrows. I have crafted strong wards and activated them. It will withstand all but a sustained magic attack. I will sleep well knowing I have done what I can to give you added protection.

I want you to know how blessed I am by your treating me as part of your family."

"Full instructions about the wards are on the next page."

It was signed, Sir Marvin.

Chapter 55

A small unit of the king's guard was waiting for Marvin with a saddled horse. They rode as fast to the palace as they could safely travel through the crowded streets. Marvin hurried through the palace into the war room. It was busy and looked like a military operation had been going on for a while.

King Baracian greeted him. Marvin bowed his head and touched his knee to the ground in respect. The King said, "Something is going on with the portal. It's causing interference. We've lost communication with the other islands and our ships. Can you help?"

Marvin thought for a second. Then he replied, "I may have to go to the arch, but I might be able to find out what I need to from the roof. Can I get an escort?"

Princess Shandria spoke up. "I grew up here and can get you there faster than anyone else."

Marvin excused himself by saying, "My King." and followed Shandria. She headed up some stairs, then down a long corridor that opened into a tower. There was a circular staircase on the inside. They hurried up the stairs. The stairs ended in a floor with eight large open arches. Marvin followed Shandria on a series of decorative stone steps that stuck out of the side of the tower, creating a ladder to reach the top of the tower. There was a second ledge around the tower above the arches. Then more steps ascended the remaining distance to the roof. Marvin looked around. It was the tallest tower in the palace. They named it the sky tower for obvious reasons. Marvin sat down and closed his eyes.

Marvin looked through his magic at the portal. The arch itself wasn't causing the interference. The protective magic Marvin had placed on it was. The portal arch was a large source of magical energy. Powerful dark magic was attacking the protective magic. The battle between magic was causing widespread interference. It was like a solar flare hitting the ionosphere of Earth and causing radio interference. The attack was coming from the northwest, from beyond the portal's magic protection zone. Something was there. Marvin held out his hand towards Shandria. He said, "Join me." and placed her hand on his temple. Shandria saw what Marvin saw. She saw some of the strongest magic she had ever seen. It was ugly, and it was dark.

Marvin released her hand. He said, "Let's get back to the king."

Marvin wove some magic, grabbed the sky, and jumped off the roof. His sky magic held him up as he slowly descended to the ground.

Shandria hadn't realized he had progressed so much in his sky magic. She did the same and followed him down into the courtyard.

Marvin reported to the war room what he had seen. They looked at the sea chart. There was a series of volcanic islands to the northwest. Marvin pointed to the islands and said. "It's these islands here. They are using the stolen arch crystal to create a portal into Atlantis here."

Marvin continued, "The volcanic activity makes the island a sympathetic portal area, and the earth magic from the volcanos is powerful. It is outside the protected area of the magic I placed on the arch crystal. The protective magic we put on the arch crystal is under dark magic attack. And the magical attack is causing the disruption of communication. If we assist the arch, it might reduce the magic's disturbance. Have we sent any ships into this area recently?"

An Admiral said, "We have a monthly patrol of the area. I will check our fleet status."

Marvin asked, "Do we have any communication at all?"

The Admiral said, "We can communicate with the fleet in the harbor, and for several dozen miles farther out."

Marvin asked. "Can we set up a line of picket ships to relay the communication back and forth?"

The Admiral replied. "Good Idea. How do we assist the portal magic?"

Marvin replied, "Any Atlantian can harmonize with the arch crystal, not to enhance it as much as to smooth the rhythm and reduce the interference. It will take several soldiers. Rotate them frequently since it will drain their magic."

Marvin asked. "Have we had any interference before today?"

The Admiral said. "We've had some minor interference for the last week."

Marvin paused for a second and then asked, "Admiral, how many ships can you get through a portal in a week?"

The admiral stopped for a second since the question was unexpected. He replied, "Several fleets."

King Handrian said, "Wait we have no evidence of a fleet."

Marvin said, "Not yet, but let's look at what we do have:"

Marvin counted on his fingers. "Point one: They are attacking our communication structure with powerful dark magic. It prevents our scouts from sending critical information to us and gives them the tactical advantage of surprise. Why now, if not because the attack or staging for the attack is underway. Only the stolen crystal in an arch pulling energy from the sky and earth has the power to resist the magic of our new arch and to create this strong interference.

"Point two: We know we are at war with an enemy that infiltrated to near the top level of the court and tried to kill Shandria.

"Point three: They can't use the portal to move their troops inside the magic of our arch so they must be using ships to transport them.

"Point four: For a week we have had interference consistent with a portal being operated right on our defensive perimeter.

A general asked, "What is their objective?"

Marvin said, "King Feldspar said, they would have three objectives: Atlantis, Iron Mountain, and Alfamara. They are after Atlantis to keep us from generating portals and moving allied forces between worlds. Divide and conquer."

The Admiral said, "Our largest fleet is in the Southern Islands. We need to get in contact with them immediately to protect Atlantis. Our second most powerful fleet is on Eastern Island."

Marvin said, "King Baracian, I may be able to make a point to point portal to Eastern Island."

King Baracian said, "That's impossible without dropping the Arch defenses."

Marvin said, "You are correct if we push against it. But we can flow with it. The portal magic is waves of magic flowing away from the portal. It reflects off the ocean. If I time it right, I should be able to open a portal at the ocean's edge that will push me to the next piece of land between the waves. I need to be on a direct path between the island and the portal at the water's edge. I won't be able to use it to portal back against the flow so I will be unable to come back through a portal. It may only work for me. The portal magic won't reject me because I created it."

King Baracian asked. "Is there a risk?"

Marvin said, "There is always a risk. I've been playing catch up with the theory of magic. I've spent the last few weeks learning more about the enchantments I have cast. I find portal magic fascinating, and much of that time I have been studying how portal magic works. I believe the theory of what I have said is sound.

"My portal may fail to form, and I will be wiser than I was before. My portal may collapse when I am part way across. I will get wet, but I can swim and use water magic. There is a small percent chance I will get bounced out of the area protected by the portal and end up at the edge of the protected zone. There is also a slight risk of death so I wouldn't try this except in an emergency. It's up to you to determine if this qualifies as an emergency."

The three kings looked at each other. There were some head nods. King Baracian said, "Admiral, let's discuss tactics. Princes Shandria, it will be a late night. Take Sir Marvin to get something to eat. Have the kitchen staff send us all some food. Along with juice, water, and tea, no wine."

Shandria said, "Yes my king."

She walked with Marvin and asked, "How are you feeling?"

He replied, "I'm just doing my best and hoping the future isn't as bad as the one I'm imagining. How are you doing?"

"I'm scared. The war room is worried. You're worried. And that makes me worried. I'm wondering what the council isn't telling us."

Marvin asked, "What do you mean?"

"They don't know you as I do, so how can they trust you? Nonetheless, Grandfather treats you with more respect than he ever treated anyone who hasn't earned his respect over several years. And the rest are following his lead. Do you realize they are about to commit our fleets on your recommendation?"

Marvin stopped for a second, then asked, "When was the last time our civilization has been to war?"

Shandria said, "We had a minor insurrection where we never committed our troops two hundred years ago. Our last big war was six hundred years ago."

Marvin replied, "So Atlantian generals have no experience at war. Generals with no experience at war trained them, and so on back for six centuries.

"Earth has over two hundred countries. She has been at wars off and on since the beginning of recorded history. A truce here, a peace treaty there, then another conflict starts up. Some wars involved millions of soldiers. I grew up in that culture, I saw movies about war, played games about war, and read books on war. I heard and talked to people who had been in a war. My adopted father and his father fought in wars on different continents. I once read that war tests each generation and each generation of generals. Earth generals learned from each war and passed the knowledge on.

"Do you know why your brother is angry with me? It's because I have an ancient sword and he doesn't. How old were you when you first beat him in a fight, a month after your sword chose you? He's several years older than you are. He has his male strength, and almost since the day you were able to lift your sword, you beat him in every sparring match.

"I have had mine for only a few moons, and it has trained my muscles and nerves to fight for several hours every day. It taught me katas that only sword owners have ever learned. I know all the moves you used to kill the wolf and feel confident I could do the same. Half the time I spend with my sword I am learning military tactics. Do you wonder why? It's because our swords are training us for war.

"I grew up in a culture where we learn military lessons without knowing that we are. My sword is grabbing my knowledge of war from Earth, infusing it with its own, and talking to the generals, who are learning from their swords, and we are all agreeing with the voice of deceased generals and kings, who know we are at war.

"Atlantis is a peaceful country. So why is our army so large? It's because the wisdom of the swords has kept us training our soldiers."

Shandria said, "You are right. I heard what you said to the generals, and I know it's true. One day I was playing with dolls and the next I was playing with swords. At first, I was using a smaller wooden sword. But my arm strength grew quickly, and in a few moons, I was using my sword.

I used to sleep with a stuffed turtle my grandmother made for me, and my sword. I never stopped loving my turtle or my dolls; I just started loving my sword."

Marvin smiled, knowing from the green goo that she was still sleeping with her stuffed turtle.

They reached the kitchen area. Marvin asked the cook what they could quickly prepare. The staff replied, eggs, toasted bread, and fruit, or they could wait a half hour for the evening meal of fish, which they just started cooking.

Shandria ordered the quick dinner, knowing how much Marvin liked eating eggs and bread. Then she told them to triple the size of the evening meal and to send it without wine to the war room as a priority.

Shandria and Marvin found a private place outside the kitchen on a balcony to eat. She said, "I noticed when you talked about Atlantis, you used words like us and we and ours. When you spoke about the Earth, it was they and theirs. It sounds to me that you have accepted Atlantis as your home."

Marvin thought about it and said, "You are right. I have accepted that I am an Atlantian."

Shandria hugged Marvin and said, "I'm excited for you. I know you belong here."

Shandria and Marvin walked back to the war room. They had a pile of documents for Marvin, who put them in his pack. Marvin said to King Baracian, "Before I go I have one request. If I die, I want to die as an Atlantian. To do that, I need to live as an Atlantian, even if only for a few minutes. If it pleases the court, I would like to swear my Allegiance to the crown of Atlantis.

King Baracian said, "Your Allegiance is accepted. You are now a citizen of Atlantis."

Marvin said, "Is that it? I expected a ceremony with half a dozen different bows or something."

King Baracian laughed and said, "We have no precedent since every Atlantian is an Atlantian. Unless you want nine ministers to spend the next five years coming up with one, this will have to be it."

King Baracian continued, "By order of this court, I hereby appoint you a commission in the King's Scout Corps as a general. You will uphold your commission and report directly to this court until the time this court sees fit to dismiss you."

Marvin stood there not sure what to say. King Baracian said, "The proper response is to bow onto one knee and say Yes, my king."

Marvin went down on one knee and said, "Yes my king."

He stood up and asked, "What is the Scout Corps?"

Everyone laughed.

The king replied in jest, "You don't know how to march, so you can't be in the army. You don't know how to sail, so we can't put you in the navy. And you will never be comfortable in a regular uniform. You know more about several realms than you do about Atlantis. So, we recommissioned the King's Scouting Corps. You report directly to the court of Atlantis, and you carry our authority and trust at the highest level. So, we give you the title of general to convey our highest level of authority and trust.

King Baracian handed a small box to Shandria and said. "Since Marvin gave you back your necklace, I think it appropriate you give him this."

Shandria opened up the box. Inside was a general's necklace. It was similar to the one Shandria was wearing, although smaller in size and different in coloration.

Shandria fastened the necklace and gave him a quick kiss.

King Baracian said, "It's time for you to implement your portal. In the top of the papers is your commission and instructions for Admiral Parathian."

He handled Shandria a map and said. "Take General Marvin to this location. A royal guard will accompany you. May the warrior of warriors prosper your mission."

Marvin said, "And Atlantis, my king." He left with Shandria.

Shandria was excited for Marvin. Being a general gave him the top rank and position in society below a prince or princess. They rode their horses down the east road, which soon turned north. Then he rode out onto the beach, handed their reigns to one of her guards, and walked a few more yards. Dramatically, Shandria marked a line in the sand that pointed east from the arch to the main naval harbor of South Atlantis.

Marvin gave Shandria a hug. He stopped for a second and looked into her eyes. They showed a tinge of fear but also resolve. He stepped back and focused his senses on the arch crystal. He soon found it. It would take him several minutes to get the rhythm of the magic. He asked, "Where will you be in this battle."

She replied. "I don't have my official orders, but I'm sure I will be with the knights, defending the palace and Mount Atlantis if they get through our naval forces."

Marvin wanted to say many things to Shandria, but what came out of his mouth was, "We may have to reschedule our secret meeting in the library until the following week."

Shandria smiled, but it was a forced smile.

Shandria's insisted that Marvin take a skiff. He agreed it would be useful in the unlikely event of a water landing. He picked up the small boat and put it on his shoulders. A few seconds later he said, "I'm getting the feel of the arch's rhythm, and I need to concentrate."

Marvin turned and faced the water. He walked out into the surf, which today was gentle. He felt the rhythm of the waves lapping at his feet. He felt the rhythm of the magic in the waves. The sun was low on the horizon behind him. He felt the beat of the arch magic, its steady beat. The Arch magic knew him and accepted him. He watched both rhythms, waiting for them to synchronize.

He wove his magic but didn't activate it. He made a circle with his hand; his other hand was holding the skiff on his shoulder. He saw a point where the rhythms matched, where the ebb of the water matched the ebb of the arch magic. He activated his portal and immediately jumped through.

Marvin found himself dumped out onto a sandy beach. The boat flew off of his shoulder. He did a shoulder roll, stood up, brushed himself off and looked about. The structures to the north must be the port. He ran at Alfarin speed and soon arrived at the outskirts. It wasn't the naval port, but a small coastal village. A fisherman was preparing his nets.

Marvin slowed down and stopped. "Excuse me, but, where am I?"

The fisherman looked up from his nets. He looked at Marvin strangely and said, "You're on the beach. Where did you think you were?"

Marvin said, "I need to get to the naval station."

The fisherman pointed up the beach and said, "That way, an hour's walk."

Marvin thought about running but decided water travel would be faster and less draining. He said to the fisherman, "Thank you." He walked into the surf and collected the next incoming wave. He rode out to sea and turned up the coast.

The fisherman watched him go and thought, "Poor guy didn't even know where he was. He must have pulled an early drunk. And he's in a hurry, I wonder if he's running back home to his wife or running away from her?"

Then he thought, "The moon tonight will attract the fish to the surface. If I don't get out fishing, I'll be the one running away from my wife." He collected his nets, second checked the rigging on his boat, and disconnected the rope from the dock. He wove some magic and sailed his fishing boat out to his favorite night time spot.

Chapter 56

Marvin rode his wave to the naval dock. He had a pseudopod of water deposit him on the pier. A bored guard responded and challenged him. He said, "I'm General Marvin of the royal scouts. The court of Atlantis has sent me with a message for the Admiral."

The guard said, "You aren't dressed like a general. How do I know you aren't just a bum?"

Marvin pushed his cloak to the side and showed his necklace. The man's eyes widened as he saw the necklace. The man said, "You still aren't dressed like a general, but that necklace will get you to the duty officer. I'll let him decide."

The pier guard turned Marvin over to another guard. The guard escorted him to the end of the pier, and onto a slotted wooden walkway to a building. There was a young corporal in the room. The chief said, "We found this guy on the pier. He claims he's a general and has orders for the admiral from Atlantis. I figured I'd let the lieutenant decide."

Marvin heard her say back to the guard. "It's a full moon. He's just another lunatic. Tell him the duty officer is busy."

Marvin heard the encounter and pushed his way around the guard and stepped into the hut. "I am General Marvin and have been sent by the king with urgent orders. I will see your duty officer now!"

The girl looked at his necklace, looked at him and said, "Marvin? Oh my God, oh my God! You're Sir Marvin. You enchanted our arch. Right this way sir, right this way. She burst through a closed door behind her, where a man sat with his feet up on the desk. "It's Sir Marvin. It's Sir Marvin," she yelled.

The man took his feet off the desk and said, "What the hell." Then he saw the necklace on Marvin. His jaw dropped.

Marvin said, "I am Sir Marvin, newly appointed by the court of Atlantis as General Marvin. The court of Atlantis has sent me with urgent orders for Admiral Parathian."

The man stood at attention and said, "Admiral Parathian and the fleet left for sea several hours ago, sir."

Marvin said, "I need to get to him now."

The duty officer jumped to his feet and said, "Let's go see the commander."

ATLANTIAN MAGIC

After several similar encounters up the chain of command, they told Marvin where the Admiral was. He was heading west and should be cutting south around the end of the island. The communication had started to improve. They contacted the Admiral. He was reversing his course, and he would meet them partway.

Marvin found himself on a small boat with four sailors and their chief. It was a fast rescue boat. The fastest boat in the fleet they bragged. The boat left the dock and started out to sea. Marvin said, "I thought you said this boat was fast?"

The chief replied. "Regulations prevent me from going faster than this until I am out of the harbor, and I can't go to maximum speed without authorization from command.

Marvin said. "My commission and authority are from the court of Atlantis. I order you to top speed."

The chief smiled and said, "I've been waiting for ten years to get that order."

The chief yelled, "Alright you land lovers, ahead flank."

The chief excitedly turned to Marin and said, "Now you will see what we can really do!"

Marvin watched as the crew ran around the deck, unfurling sails, and tying off sheets on cleats. Then he saw one of the sailors weaving air magic. A stiff breeze started to blow and filled the sails. The wind steadily picked up speed, as did the boat. At first, the vessel slowly accelerated. Then suddenly it leaped up from the water and started to accelerate faster. Soon it reached its top speed.

Marvin was impressed at the boat's speed. He looked over the side. The boat's hull was in the air above the water. Poles sticking out of the bottom of the boat and into the water were lifting it up. This wasn't a sailboat; it was sail powered hydrofoil. The sailors took turns maintaining the magic. Marvin was impressed. It was the fastest he had ever gone on a boat in his life. It was several times faster than he could travel using his water magic.

Then the chief yelled, "We need top speed, Ahead Emergency!"

Marvin felt the speed of the boat increase noticeably.

Marvin talked to the chief, who was standing up and steering the boat. He was obviously enjoying himself. It was rare the Navy let them air out their sails and go to flank speed, and Ahead Emergency was never used. It was draining on the crew for any length of time, but it allowed them to show with pride what they could do.

Marvin was impressed with the air weave. It was pulling the wind from in front of the sail, spinning it around, and pushing on the rear of the sail. The vacuum in front of the sail and the wind behind it explained the speed of the boat.

What Marvin figured would be a two-hour journey was closer to twenty minutes.

When the fleet was within sight, the chief ordered, "Ahead standard." The sailor changed the air magic weave. The velocity of the boat slowed down. Then he commanded, "Secure Wind!"

The sailor canceled the air weave. The airspeed died off. The boat slowed down and dropped down into the water. The chief yelled, "Lower and secure the sails."

The sailors lowered and tied off the sails. Marvin was surprised that they didn't use magic to drop the sails like on their Alfarin boat. He suddenly remembered he was supposed to take his sailing test for his permit in two days. Another thing put on hold.

The chief wove water magic to move the boat closer to the admiral's boat. Marvin said, "I can get there from here." He shook the crew's hands and stepped over the side. He traveled on a pseudopod of water to the side of the admiral's ship and yelled, "General Marvin with instructions from the court of Atlantis requesting permission to come aboard."

The captain replied, "Permission granted." He greeted the captain and then the Admiral. He followed them back to the Admiral's wardroom and handed the Admiral the documents. The admiral read his commission and orders from the court and said to Marvin and the captain, "Follow me." They followed him to the chartroom. He said, "Captain, deploy picket ships per this order, and set a course for ten miles south of Atlantis, Ahead Standard. Tell me a quarter-hour before we arrive, and I will assign new orders."

Chapter 57

Sir Marvin's words had convinced everyone but King Handrian. He agreed they needed to send out scouts, but not a whole fleet. The council overruled him. If there was a threat, they wanted him to have the resources to neutralize it. Handrian was in charge of the Atlantian Island fleet. One thing everyone agreed on was their hope it was just a training exercise. Handrian obeyed the orders of the council.

The fleet was ready to go, and Handrian ordered them out to sea. He left Atlantis at about the same time Marvin opened his portal to East Island. Handrian sailed west around the island of Atlantis and then turned towards the northwest. He ordered a spread-out picket formation for the fleet to provide maximum coverage of the ocean.

After several hours of sailing, they lost contact with the forward picket ship. Handrian ordered the fleet to close formation. Another ship reported seeing strange ships and abruptly became silent. King Handrian had all communications relayed to Atlantis. More picket ships reported sightings of foreign vessels before they went quiet. They lost communication with several others.

King Handrian plotted where he had lost his ships. It looked like there was an advancing line of attack. He needed to know what was going on. His watchmen were unable to penetrate past the line using their magical sight. He tried and couldn't either. It was like there was no magic coming from the area to see and talk to. He relayed all his observations back to Atlantis.

Suddenly static stopped any more communication. A few minutes later, all the magical weaves that pushed the ship failed. The water around them no longer responded to magic, and neither did the air.

King Handrian saw the enemy ships. He had never seen their configuration before. They were using dark magic to stop the weaves the Atlantians used to move their ship. He called to the captain of his ship, "Raise all sails. Commence firing."

The captain repeated, "Raise all sails! Commence firing!" The ballista bolt, which should have turned to blue and hit their target as magical energy, were leaving the ballista, flying a few dozen yards, and then crashing into the water.

The deck hands scrambled to get the sails raised up and tied off to give them some speed and maneuverability.

Handrian saw streaks of dark magic spells shooting and hitting the boats on either side. The ones coming towards his ship never reached him. They dissipated several dozen yards from him. He noticed the amulet Marvin had enchanted was glowing brightly. He stood by the forward ballista, sure it was inside the amulet's range and yelled, "Maximum height." The archers raised it up. He yelled, "Fire." The bolt shot forward. It turned into a magical blue bolt than burst into fire as it left the area of the protective weave. The flaming bolt followed a standard arch of gravity and crashed into the water. His amulet was protecting him and the ballista as long as it was within its range.

The archers prepared another bolt. He had them adjust the height and yelled, "Fire. This one hit the deck of an enemy ship. It shattered on impact with the ship and sent burning embers all over the deck. The ship's rigging and sails caught fire.

He needed to regroup his fleet. He yelled, "Sound the retreat." A large horn started blowing the retreat. Handrian tried sending up the flashing retreat symbol, but his weave failed before it rose high enough in the air to activate. Handrian yelled, "Send signal rockets to sound the retreat." The captain echoed his orders.

Handrian had enough natural wind to turn his ship, and the sails were starting to fill. He heard the Captain yell at the helmsman, "Hard to starboard." The helmsman turned the wheel, and the boat slowly turned to the right. Men were running around and adjusting the sails.

Handrian yelled to the ballista station, "Target the ship forward of the port side." He yelled, "Fire when ready!" The bolt caught fire and narrowly missed the enemy ship.

Handrian pulled the pendant from inside his shirt. It had grown uncomfortably warm and was starting to burn his chest. It was glowing brightly. More dark magic was targeting his ship. He yelled, "Fire once more. He had success; the bolt caught fire and smashed into another ship.

The pendant, now sitting on top his shirt had reached its limit. It burst into flames. He quickly pulled it off and dropped it onto the deck. He felt the magic of the pendant fail. A dark magic spell hit him. He felt the spell suck the magic from his body. He couldn't stop or control it.

He yelled again, "Retreat!"

His flagship was turning, but its speed was slow, and its size made it turn slowly. A seaman raised the retreat flag up to the top of the mast. Signal rockets launched off the stern of the ship and exploded in red fireworks. It was a signal to all other ships to retreat. Handrian knew all the ships in the fleet would be signaling ships farther out. The ships that had communication would be repeating the order. He saw the retreat signal rise up above ships outside he dark magic area.

Handrian saw a ship coming towards them off their port side. It had dozens of oars sticking out of holes in its side. There was a ram on the front of the enemy ship. It was on a collision course, and they didn't have enough speed to avoid it. He yelled to the ballista crews on the port side to target the ship; several bolts narrowly missed. Only one hit but without magic, it did minimal damage. He yelled, "Brace for impact."

He expected an impact as the ram turned to splinters when it hit the hull of his ship. But the dark spells had caused the enchanted hull's magic to go dormant. The ram smashed through the hull. The wooden deck in the area buckled upward, splintered and shattered. It sent lethal debris flying in all directions. The collision knocked Handrian off his feet. Handrian pulled a piece of splintered wood from his left forearm. He was bleeding, but it wasn't too bad. He didn't have time to worry about it and had no magic to heal it.

From the front of the attacking ship, he saw something he had only seen in paintings. Dozens of ogres were boarding the ship. He heard the captain yell at the same time as him, "All hands repel boarders!" All King Handrian could think to do involved magic, and he had no magic. He not only lacked magic, but the magical lines inside him were sucked dry. He felt crushed, depressed, and wounded.

He fought off the depression caused by his lack of magic and pulled his sword from its sheath. It wasn't an ancient sword, but it was an enchanted sword of the highest quality, and the Darfarin magic couldn't affect it.

The ogres looked barely humanoid. They were large, at least a yard taller than Handrian. Their upper body looked like a cross between a human and a disfigured furless bear. They dressed in poorly-tanned animal fur, which made them look even more like a beast. They carried clubs for weapons. Handrian grabbed one of the wooden shields from the side of the front of the forecastle. It was painted proudly as a decoration, but it was functional, and he needed to use it.

The ogres had no desire to kill the Atlantians. They wanted them unconscious or disabled, so they could strip them of their weapons and keep them alive. To them, Atlantians were food, and they liked their food fresh.

Handrian ducked under the swing of an ogre's club and stepped behind the ogre as the club glanced off his shield and passed over him. He slashed the monster in the front of the leg on his way by, severing the ogre's muscles and tendons. He kept moving forward as the first ogre collapsed.

A thrust from his sword angled upward at 45 degrees cut deeply through the back and through many major organs of the next ogre. The ogre, who had just cornered a sailor, let out a loud howl. The monster tried to turn around, but the pain of the wound caused him to slip and stumble. Handrian saw the frightened sailor dive over the side. He ran to the next ogre.

Handrian gave up trying to survive this fight. The ogres were bigger, stronger, and could run faster over long distance than he could. But he could change directions quicker, and on board this ship, rolling in the ocean, his balance was better. Maybe he could survive long enough to make a difference. He saw another sailor dive over the side and agreed with the sailor's decision.

He yelled, "Abandon ship!" knowing his sailors were better off in the ocean.

He slashed once more into the leg of a third ogre. He preferred a clean kill. But he didn't have the time or the luxury. A serious injury to an ogre was a death sentence for the ogre. The more he injured, the fewer would be around to attack Atlantis. He was no longer fighting for his reputation or himself, no one would see him. He was fighting for his crew and Atlantis. He would kill ogres until he died, the ship completely sunk, or he was sure all the sailors had abandoned the vessel. Then maybe he would escape over the side. Until then he would injure the enemy and give his crew time to escape. He jumped away as a large club came down where he was. There was no opportunity to attack that ogre, so he ducked under some rigging and slipped away around one of the ship's masts.

The rocking of the waves made the now sinking boat shift. An off-balanced ogre came stumbling down the deck. Handrian dropped low and slashed through the ogre's ankle. His sword sliced through the bone.

Then he felt a force hit him and pick him up. He saw glowing red eyes from under a hooded cowl. The Darfarin was holding a staff that was glowing at the end. Handrian started convulsing as energy from the staff assaulted his body. It's the last thing Handrian remembered.

The Darfarin slammed him onto the deck and knocked him unconscious. The impact knocked the sword from his hand. It slid overboard off the slanted deck, followed by Handrian's unconscious body.

Chapter 58

Marvin heard the end part of the battle from the Admiral's flagship. Atlantians used tuned crystals to transmit magical energy, which carries information between ships. Atlantis had lost a quarter of its fleet including Handrian's flagship. King Handrian was on the flagship and presumed missing or dead. The surviving fleet was in retreat.

They pieced together what had happened. A barrage of dark magic spells had neutralized the magic on the hulls of the ships and weapons. It sucked the magic from the crew. Ogres had boarded the ships, and everyone aboard was presumed killed. That was the reports. Then the Admiral filled Marvin in on the ogres eating habits.

Marvin felt sick to his stomach. If only he had known more. If only he had realized how vulnerable their fleet was to dark magic. Marvin was learning about Atlantian flower customs when he could have been weaving wards to protect the ships from dark magic. He sat down hard on a nearby bench and held his head in his hands. He knew how much Shandria loved her brother and felt sick for her.

After about a minute, the Admiral touched Marvin's shoulder and said. "If the ogres captured them they are still alive. King Baracian wrote you sometimes think differently from someone raised on Atlantis, and it gives you new insight. His letter said I should trust your counsel. He doesn't talk like that of many people."

Marvin said, "I need time to think." He walked to a corner of the cabin. He sat down and pulled the hood of his cloak over his head. Marvin remembered a toy his friend next door owned. It was a giant slingshot designed to launch water balloons. They took it to a nearby park to try it out. He was amazed at how far it could shoot. It was a small park, and they launched a balloon that flew over the park fence and hit a neighbor's car. The car alarm started honking the horn. They all ran away scared, thinking they were in big trouble. The water balloon had left the park where they made it, but it still maintained its ability to hit the car. It gave Marvin an idea.

He pulled off his hood. The Admiral, the ship captain, and several members of his staff were talking.

Marvin said, "I have an idea. Our magic can't penetrate their spell but the effects of our magic can. We are people of the ocean, and we have it surrounding us. We can create currents and keep them from advancing. We can make a large destructive wave, and have it crashing into them."

The Admiral said, "We could impede their movement by affecting the wind and the waves, but the distance required for us to stay away from their magic and to do that would quickly drain us. We don't have the magical energy to create waves large enough to affect a fleet. We could maybe take out a couple of ships, but not their entire fleet. Even our two swords couldn't generate that much power."

Marvin asked, "If we had dozens of magical weapons spread throughout the fleet and collecting the magical energy, could we create one large destructive wave?" The Admiral scratched his chin and said, "Maybe."

Marvin said, "I can get the swords. Please follow me."

He led them out of the cabin and onto the deck where there was a large flat area in front of the aftcastle of the ship. He took off his Dwarven medallion. He placed it on the wall and grew the wood to hold it secure. "King Feldspar, his weapons smiths, and I enchanted many magic swords.

"This medallion is tuned to the gate at Crystal Mountain. It allows me to portal there even past the Arch's anti-portal weave. It will also enable me to portal back to the ship with the swords.

"I will need a couple of hours to get the swords. During that time, try to keep this area of the ship free, as a portal may open up."

Marvin activated the portal and jumped through.

He was glad it was morning at Crystal Mountain, and the guards were alert. A quick request from the guards and he had a horse. He gave the horse full reign down the mountain. Dwarven horses weren't fast, they weren't large, but the Dwarves bred them to climb on mountains, and they were strong.

At the base of Crystal Mountain, he entered through the doors. He rode fast to the king's palace. He identified himself, and they allowed him access. The King was in a private meeting and was not to be disturbed. He told the guard at the door to let the King know Atlantis is at war and Sir Marvin of Atlantis needed to see him. The guard left, and a few seconds later King Feldspar opened the door himself. He immediately said, "Is it time yet?"

Marvin said, "Soon King, now the battle is at sea. We need the magic swords."

The King said, "They aren't all finished."

Marvin said, "Do you have a hundred? I need to portal them to a ship as fast as we can."

The King called over some ministers. They ran out to perform his orders. He said to Marvin, "The swords will be waiting at the arch in an hour. That should give you time to fill me in on the details. The King started hurrying towards the war room.

ATLANTIAN MAGIC

When they arrived at the war room, the King offered Marvin a mug of water. It was the first time he ever offered Marvin water as a choice of drinks. Marvin thanked him and told him about the defeat of the Atlantian fleet and the capture or death of King Handrian.

The king offered his sincere condolences and best wishes for the safety of King Handrian. Hearing the news was the only time Marvin had ever seen the king angry.

Queen Olivine and Princess Amethyst had stepped into the war room to hear about King Handrian. Marvin would never forget the Queen's sweet motherly hug. Her daughter was as warm as her mother was. They all asked about Shandria and Alandria.

Marvin said, "Shandria is awaiting her assignment but expects to be in charge of the knights defending the palace and the Mount Atlantis arch. I didn't have time to talk to Alandria."

Marvin summarized the present situation for the ladies. He also filled them in on their counterattack plan and their entire naval battle plan. He told the king about the Darfarin arch.

A messenger arrived saying the cart with the swords was on its way up the mountain. Marvin said a quick goodbye, left the palace, and rode his horse up the mountain. The swords were in sheaths and bundled together into one large package. The package was heavy, but not too heavy for him to carry. He felt the weight of the swords as he lifted them onto his shoulder. The swords were all abuzz. They were happy to see their maker. They didn't have the intelligence and will of his ancient sword. Their happiness was more a statement of how their magic was resonating with his.

He quieted them down so he could concentrate. He looked through the ring of the stone arch that formed the portal. He felt and synchronized with the Dwarven arch crystal. Through the arch crystal, he saw the small crystal in his pendant. He activated the portal and stepped through.

Chapter 59

The enemy was attacking Atlantis. They landed on the beaches between the Imperial docks and the narrows and spread out as they landed. The Darfarin came ashore and protected the ogres from the magic of the Atlantians.

News of the attacking fleet had spread, and many Atlantians ran to be inside the protective walls of the capital. But the enemy cut off the people of the narrows from getting to the walls of the city. Many Atlantians ran to their homes. Their doors were no match for the clubs of the ogres. The Darfarins drained their magic, and the Atlantians were helpless against the monsters.

Mr. White stood in his front yard, encouraging his neighbors to join him. The protective ward Marvin had put on his estate had only a few days to grow. But Marvin had put a lot of energy into it, and it was strong for its age. It had spread and formed a barrier against the dark magic that was wider than his property line. A stand of civilians, most of them with military training, sent their families into Marvin's estate and stood their ground. They found out their magic would work inside the ward from the estate but not outside, where the dark magic was consuming the threads.

The crown had given many of the residents their estate for military service. It included Retired Admiral Persimmian. The admiral sized up the military situation. The whole community knew him as admiral, and they were glad to follow his orders.

From the neighbors, he formed a militia force of fifty people with military training, and another handful with strong combat magic abilities. The rest he sent to stay inside Marvin's home. His ancient sword lashed out at ogres stupid enough to come inside the magical ward, sending lightning and bolts of energy. He was using his magic reserves quickly. Several veterans put their hand on his shoulder. Their magic flowed into him, recharging his magic at a greater rate than he was using it. Several Darfarin, were foolish enough to come inside of arrow range. He commanded the soldiers with bows to fire at them. The arrows found their mark. The Darfarins didn't expect resistance and weren't warded against the arrows. There was a temporary respite. And the magic attack ended.

The admiral took the offensive while it was available to him. He had a grandmaster of water magic pull a wave of water from the ocean. It carried an exposed group of ogres in a river of water out to sea. In the process, it swept a dozen Atlantians captives out to sea, freeing them. Atlantians could swim, ogres couldn't.

The enemy fell back. The militia needed the respite. Their magic needed time to recharge. Even the protective barrier from the estate had shrunk under the assault. But magic was resilient. The estate wards had learned from the attack. The house drew its magic from the Earth, the sea, and the sky. It recharged fast and spread wider and stronger than before.

Ogres weren't high on the Mensa curve, but they weren't stupid. They tried storming the estate from the ocean side. But it was the obvious tactic. And if anything, it was closer to water. Another wave of water left the ocean and washed them out to sea.

The preferred weapon of the ogre was the club. They liked to stun, disable or knock out their prey and capture them, but they also were good at throwing heavy objects. The ogres threw bricks broken from neighbor's property, and a large rock, injuring several of the militia before they crafted a protective weave. Fortunately, none of the injuries were severe. They evacuated the injured inside.

The Admiral and his forces were weary and their magic needed time to recharge. His archers were almost out of arrows. Rather than try to face the ogres with soldiers who had never trained as a unit while low on magic, they fell back into the estate, hoping Sir Marvin's wards were as powerful as his opening of the arch crystal.

While inside, the other citizens shared their magic with the militia. They were preparing to fight again if needed.

The ogres crashed against the walls of the house, but the wood of the house was hard as a rock, and the brickwork was as hard as steel. The ogres attacked the door. It bulged inward but then bulged out stronger than before. Magic was alive and had muscle, and like an athlete after lifting a weight, it recovered and was stronger. Being young, it had a quick recovery rate. After an hour of pounding on a house filled with scared families, surrounded by their militia of soldiers holding weapons, the assault was over. The ogres had easier pickings elsewhere.

The Darfarin were frustrated at the power of the estate. In their mind, it was a blasphemy against their magic. This was a mission to drain magic for the assault, and they had expended more than they had gained from this one battle that should have been minor. Their fight led them in the other direction. The estate could wait. It was time to assault the palace.

Chapter 60

King Handrian woke up and coughed up some water. A sailor from one of the ships was towing him. He finished coughing. He could swim, but he had no magic. And they were miles away from anywhere they could get to by swimming. Wreckage from the destroyed Atlantian fleet surrounded them. He started treading water on his own.

The sailor blew a bubble of air into his shirt and held his collar tight. Every Sea Scout learned the survival technique. The bobble of air would keep him afloat and allow him to rest from his swimming for a minute or two before it leaked out. The sailor looked exhausted. Handrian had no idea how long he had dragged him through the water while he was unconscious. The attack had started a couple hours after sundown, and the full moon was midway on its journey across the sky. The sailor could have drowned, expending all his strength to save his king.

He had done his duty, and he was willing to sacrifice to save his king who loved him, rather than ensure his own survival. Handrian saw a piece of wood floating not too far away. He swam to it, grabbed it, and swam it back to the exhausted sailor. The sailor reached over the plank. Handrian put himself on the opposite side of the wood, reached over, grabbed the sailor by his wet shirt, and pulled him partway onto the wooden plank where he could rest. Handrian said, "Relax. You saved my life and let me recover. I will hold you on this plank while you rest and recover."

The sailor replied, "Any sailor would do the same for another sailor."

Handrian was shocked. He looked at his uniform. Wet and submerged in the moonlight, he looked like another sailor. This man hadn't just followed his duty and rescued the king. He had risked his life for a stranger he didn't even know. Many showed their love for Atlantis by swearing their lives to him as a king. It made sense, and in return, a king shows his love by protecting his subjects, but a sailor risking his life for a stranger?

He looked back at the man. He was exhausted. His arms were crossed, and his head was lying heavily on his crossed arms. He had fallen asleep or at least closed his eyes and was resting.

The man of action side of Handrian knew that sleep was necessary. They all needed sleep. It had been a long night. The gentle current would carry them north along the island of Atlantis. By tomorrow, maybe their magic would recharge. The sailor would need his sleep.

He saw another group of people floating on a broken plank. He whistled them over. They saw him and swam the plank in his direction. Their odds of survival were better in a group. They could form a raft from enough wreckage or a skiff if their magic came back. The plank was towing some rigging with it, which would help them strap the wood together until then.

No one could tell rank in the dim light. The sailors would obey Handrian if they knew he was the king, but they didn't need duty tonight. They needed to recover.

The sailor opposite him woke up, smiled, and yawned. The sailor said, "When we get out of this, let's swirl a glass of cheap wine at The Broken Pier together, mate."

The Broken Pier was a sleazy dive bar east of the naval wharf. The drinks were cheap, as were the prostitutes. No royal or noble would ever go there. But without thinking Handrian said, knowing he meant it, "Only If I pick the wine and buy the first round."

He turned to the other two men and said. "You're also included."

The first sailor reached his hand over and said, "Seaman first class Fletching, call me Fletch. Handrian reached his hand over to shake hands, but before he could introduce himself, the other two men introduce themselves. They had all been on his flagship, and he didn't know any of them.

He finished shaking hands and said. "I am King Handrian of Atlantis."

Fletch laughed, and said, "And I'm the queen of the Emerald Isle. I'd like to give the king a piece of my mind. We got caught with our bloomers down."

No one had talked to Handrian like this since Sea Scouts, except his sisters and a few close nobles. He was shocked but agreed with the statement and decided to follow it. He said, "We got caught with our bloomers down, and the mister had a sword." There were some chuckles. He heard a few coarse jokes about the crown, which he thought was funny. Then one of them asked, "So what's your real, name?"

Handrian undid the collar of his shirt and pulled out the gold and gemstone necklace that signified he was the king of Atlantis. There was dead silence. Fletch said, "Forgive me, my king."

The other two sailors echoed his words.

Handrian decided they needed a laugh, and so did he, at their expense.

"I refuse to forgive you" he paused for effect, "because the truth never needs to be forgiven. I've given medals to men who were less honest. And I still owe you the first round of drinks."

Fletch still worried said, "We don't want to get you in trouble with the misses."

Handrian laughed and said, "Oh I don't need any help getting in trouble with the misses. I have quite the ability to get myself in trouble without any help."

The sailors started to lighten up and smile.

Handrian asked, "So what was that joke you told about the high minister again, "I have to use that one against him."

Fletch was single. One of the men, a man nicknamed Bonzo, was married and had a son. The other man, who was nicknamed Kippy, was single also, but hoping to get married soon.

Soon Handrian was collecting all the gossip about the rest of the royal family. He had to agree with most of it. But even when he didn't, he laughed anyway. They made jokes about many of the ladies in the court, but even in the jokes, they showed high respect for the Royal Family. Handrian was pleased that Atlantis thought highly of them.

Then they heard the creak of a boat in the distance and the sound of oars rowing.

"Get low" whispered Handrian, "Don't let them see you." But the Darfarins were searching with magic, not with their eyes. Handrian felt a spell hit. He was frozen, unable to move. An ogre grabbed his arm and lifted him from the water. The monster tore off Handrian's clothes and his king's necklace. Then he threw him into the hold with several dozen naked people. Someone grabbed him and dragged him away from the opening. He found out later it was so the next person thrown into the hold didn't land on him.

The spell slowly wore off. It was several minutes before Handrian was able to move on his own, but it took at least on an hour before the majority of the numbness and tingling disappeared.

Handrian was surprised. Somehow, they had missed the dagger Marvin had given him. He could see it but no one else could. It was camouflage magic enchanted into the dagger or the sheath. He was sure it was a special touch of Marvin's. The Darfarin magic couldn't drain permanent magic, and Alfarin magic was resistant to its effects. One dagger wouldn't do much against an army, but it was a magical dagger, and it would do more if he waited for the right opportunity to use it.

Fletch waved him over. They had found a spot in the back of the hold. Handrian joined them. Fletch said, "We decided to call you Handy. It will keep your name quiet. You may survive a bit longer that way."

Handrian looked around. He estimated there were eighty-people in the cargo hold. No one but the three sailors knew who he was.

Then two of the Darfarin came down to the hold, their red eyes were glowing and so were the gems on the top of their staffs. One held up Handrian's necklace and said in broken Atlantian, "Whoze diz?"

Everyone was silent. Then a magic blast leaped from the staff. It hit everyone in the hold. King Handrian felt paralyzed; his muscles seized up, and intense pain ran through his nerves. When the blast stopped, the hold was full of moaning and crying.

They heard again, "Whoze diz?"

ATLANTIAN MAGIC

Two seconds later the Darfarin sent another blast of dark magic through the hold of the ship. When this one ended, the Darfarin sent a third blast. Everyone was crying. The smell of urine filled the air. Even Handrian had lost control of his bowels. His people were suffering because of him. He had no options. He had a dagger. Maybe he could take out one Darfarin before they tortured and killed him.

The Darfarin asked, "Whoze diz? Handrian staggered, trying to stand up. Fletch and his group grabbed Handrian and pulled him down. He heard someone towards the front of the boat yelled, "It's mine." Another person shouted, "It's mine." Several others said the same thing. The Darfarin turned to the ogres that were with him and said something in a guttural language. The ogres walked further into the hold and seized the closest person.

Handrian watched in horror as two of the ogres tore the arm off of the man. Then they fought among themselves as they pulled apart the arm at the elbow and started eating their share. Handrian heard the cracking of bones between their teeth. Other ogres came down into the front of the hold. Handrian tried to go forward, but his friends held him down and kept him from going forward. The frightened cries and screams of the prisoners filled the hold. Handrian was glad for the cries of the prisoners. It was loud enough that it almost drowned out the cries of the victim, but unfortunately, he would never forget the sight.

The people in the hold became a single mass, panicking and pushing against him in an attempt to get deeper into the hold and farther away from the ogres. There was no way Handrian could get past them. Held by his friends and the panicked mob, he watched unable to move as the ogres fought over, dismembered, ripped apart, and ate the man. The ogres waited until the end to eat the torso and head.

Handrian remembered the stories that older children used to scare younger children. He remembered a story he told Shandria when they were younger to frighten her and realized it was true. "Ogres eat a person from the outside in, so they can hear their meals scream."

Chapter 61

Shandria screamed at the ballista crew, "Fire!" The iron ore bolt burst into flames and penetrated into the inside of the narworm before exploding. It was the last of the narworms.

The Darfarin army had overrun the wharf. They were attacking the walls of the inner city. Shandria had spent the last few weeks strengthening the wards that protected the palace from dark magic. Then she had woven wards on the city walls. It was the Alfarin magic, which she had learned in the green goo, and copied from her amulet. And it was holding. But the wards on the outer walls were too young. They should have broken down under the relentless onslaught. But they hadn't. They had become stronger.

Everything in nature is alive. It grows to its natural limits. Being nature magic, the wards she made were growing and getting stronger, but it should have taken longer to get this strong.

Shandria remembered the wards in the palace and on the walls around the palace were ancient and robust. They were giving strength to and protecting the baby wards on the city walls.

After the defeat of the dark magic users in the throne room, Shandria explored the palace. The wards that had protected the palace grounds were still there. Why hadn't the wards protected them in the palace? Shandria looked deeper at the wards, and she was shocked. Somehow, a spy had found a way to weave a magic thread into the wards. It was like the trigger she used to secure the sail on the Alfarin boat, and it was set to sleep, and couldn't be turned on. It allowed the dark magic users to infiltrate the palace.

The thread was so intertwined it was impossible for her to remove without compromising the ward. But two could play that game. She wove a parallel thread of her own to neutralize the thread. She then tickled the ward back awake. The now awake ward was upset. It destroyed the thread that was holding it asleep. There was a battle as the ward tried freeing the other wards in the palace. Shandria went to another ward and neutralized the thread, and the second ward came awake.

Shandria listened to the ward, and it asked her to go to the next ward. She accepted the request. She exited the palace by a balcony and climbed up the outside wall. She neutralized the thread in the next ward, and another ward was awake. Then the wards took over.

The three wards working together had enough combined strength and new knowledge, that they neutralized the thread on their own, and brought the ward awake. Shandria felt them moving from one ward to another throughout the palace. Shandria lost count of the dozens of wards in the palace as she watched the battle. Soon the wards were all awake. They then moved to the walls surrounding the palace and freed those wards.

The palace wards asked Shandria to go back into the palace. She climbed off the roof and into a window of the bakery. Three workers in the palace kitchen were convulsing on the floor. The palace wards were pulling tendrils of dark magic from them. Shandria looked at one. Her amulet glowed and added its magic to the attack. Shandria soon removed the dark magic out of the women.

After a few minutes, one of the women awoke. She was crying that it was only an awful dream. For weeks, she had been having nightmares that she had been mixing small amounts of herbs into the spiced wine of the royalty. She ran over to a loose brick that was at the back of the bakery and pulled it out of the wall. Inside was a glass container that was half-full of some crushed and dried herb. She started crying when she realized it wasn't a dream.

Shandria called for the guards and told them to get the court physician. The guard asked which one. Shandria commanded, "All of them, NOW!"

The guards ran out the door. The physicians arrived and identified the herb. The poison was harmless in small amounts, but the body was slow to eliminate it. It built up over time and poisoned the body. By the time it showed symptoms, the damage to the liver was impossible to reverse, and the person would die. It was too late to heal the body. The antidote was a common herb but was bitter and infrequently used in food.

The physicians quickly came up with a capsule that contained the antidote herb. All the royalty took their bitter pill, twice a day for a week. They had the entire palace staff take the herb also. Shandria knew everyone on the staff occasional took a sip out of the spiced wine. The palace staff used a phrase, "cleaning the goblets," for cleaning up after a party, since drinking the remaining wine was considered one of the benefits of the job.

The palace stood in a large private area, surrounded by protective walls. The palace wards were magically strengthened and warded against dark magic. Outside the private palace grounds was another set of defensive walls that protected the inner city. They were miles across, and large enough that they circled the barracks, the merchant court, and the homes of many people. Shandria, aided by the magic of her knights and by dozens of army casters used copy magic to copy her wards against dark magic on each section of the city walls, the walls they were defending now.

The wards were designed to help each other out, and the palace wards found the new wards she had made. They were upset that they had failed to do their duty to protect the palace. So, they had taught and strengthened the new wards. The new wards began this battle much stronger than they would have grown without the help of the palace wards. And the palace wards were strengthening them now. The dark spells weren't just fighting against the wards on the walls, they were fighting against all the wards, aided by the mature, strong palace wards. They would hold.

The Darfarin were bombarding the palace with dark magic. The dark spells hit an invisible barrier that surrounded the palace grounds. Their attack was so intense that the air at the edge of the magical barrier glowed.

Several large, covered, battering rams had been unloaded from the ogre ships. The rams were housed inside of mobile wooden and metal framed carts, which protected the ogres within from arrow fire. One ram was causing some damage to an area of the wall. It must have some magical enchantment on it.

Shandria realized her wards had stopped any magical protection the Darfarins could have supplied to the ram. She wove some magic on one of the ballistae bolts. The ballista crew fired the bolt at the ram. The arrow caught fire and smashed through the ram cover. The ram caught fire. A dozen ogres ran from the fire. Arrow fire and magic from the battlements killed them.

They dropped a huge boulder from the wall onto another of the rams and broke the main beam. It was useless and the ogres running away never made it back to their lines.

Soldiers poured a barrel of oil off the battlements in front of a third ram. It flowed downhill towards the wharf and under the ram. They set the oil ablaze with magic. The ogres fled from the fire. The useless ram burned a few yards from the wall. There were dozens of rams and the soldiers manning the walls torched them with oil or attacked them with ballista bolts.

A dozen siege towers started moving towards the walls. The outside was highly resistant to their magic bolts and arrows. But flaming oil underneath the ramps killed the ogres who were pushing the ramps on the bottom. The flames caught the insides of the towers on fire. Soon ogres were running out the back of the towers. They were easy targets, and few made it back to their lines.

Many civilians had taken refuge in the courtyard. They were sitting, or laying down in groups, keeping lanes free for soldiers and equipment. A large stone flew over the wall and came crashing into the merchant's court. The rocks landing in the courtyard caused the civilians to panic. They started fleeing away from the outer walls and back towards the palace walls.

They needed to stop the rocks. Shandria saw an opening in the enemy's defense. The palace wards had caused the enemy to withdraw back to the area past the ward's magic shell. The trebuchets were just outside the protective magic of the walls. It was time for a limited counter attack. Shandria yelled, "Chief of the guard, take over." She crafted a weave and jumped down from the forty-foot wall. Her sky magic slowed her descent. She ran to her armored horse and leaped into its saddle. A squire handed her the shield and helmet she wore when she was mounted. She put them on. Her horse's armor extended out around her legs and protected them. Around her were two hundred knights of the royal guard. She enhanced her voice with an air weave so the knights could hear her above the noise of battle. Shandria yelled orders to them.

They responded and formed four columns behind her. Each knight carried enchanted weapons and had intricate protective weaves placed on their armor and horse armor. Shandria's shield and helmet were magically enchanted. Along with the breastplate she wore, she was as protected as her knights were.

Shandria looked up and yelled, "Open a path." The chief of the watch, on the battlement, yelled at his men. They directed their fire to the area in front of the gate. Shandria had the chief of the gate guards ready the gate. She wove the password to a trigger on the gate. It swung open, and the portcullis rose. Several knights were wearing protective amulets Marvin had enchanted, and all had some protection from amulets Shandria had made. Shandria had crafted a weave based on her amulet that was easy for the court enchanters to copy. It added resistance to dark magic to the heavily warded knights.

She didn't have to yell. Her knights followed her lead as Shandria charged straight out the gate, planning to take her knights, cut a hole in the ranks of the ogres, destroy the trebuchets, and then to retreat. The plan executed as expected. Shandria and her knights with their magically enhanced armor battered through the line of ogres like a hot knife through butter. They were soon at the trebuchets.

The magic of the palace fought for Atlantis. The princess of Atlantis, who had freed them, needed their help. The amulet that had helped free them needed help. As Shandria left, it saw her reach the edge of its protective zone. It narrowed the protective field from the sides of the palace grounds and extended itself over her knights, over the trebuchets, and the ogres.

Shandria saw the Darfarin magic no longer protected the trebuchets. She cast a weave through her sword, which torched them with a chain of fire that jumped from one to the next. Then she saw a tactical advantage they needed to exploit. They were past the ogres and near the line where the Darfarin were casting their spells.

She called to her knights, "Attack the Darfarin!" Her knight spread out and started to kill the Darfarin. Both swords and horses fought against the enemy.

The Darfarins diverted their energy from attacking the city walls to attacking the knights.

The attacks of the Darfarins would have overwhelmed the knight's amulets, but with fewer attacks against the city wards, they were able to extend their protective zone farther and soon covered the knights and the Darfarins. The city wall wards didn't draw its power from the amulets or push power through them; it used them as markers and stretched itself, like a tree bending over in the wind, to provide shade and protection from their attack.

Shandria's father recognized the tactical advantage of the extended shield. He jumped down from his place on the wall, and he led his guard of knights to join Shandria in the battle. Shandria's men fought the Darfarin, and King Vandian fought the ogres between his daughter and the wall, ensuring a retreat path for his daughter and her knights.

Queen Isaria grabbed her knights and swarmed into the battle against the ogres. Then King Baracian committed the troops. One legion swarmed through the gate Shandria had opened. Two other gates opened and two other legions ran out of the gates and attacked the ogres. It was no time to hold back the reserves. He ordered the remaining legions to join the attack.

The Darfarin stopped attacking the palace grounds. That allowed the wards to bend more and cover much of the wharf district. The Darfarin lost their dark magic casting ability, and their normal combat magic was weak.

Shandria and her knights fought to the point of exhaustion and past it. It was a complete rout of the Darfarin. Even the ogres fled the battle, trying to get back to their ships. Shandria would have none of that. She caused a large, sudden wave to rise in the center of a ship. It lifted up the center of the ship, and the weight of the ship bending over her wave, broke the back of the ship, splitting it in two. Protected by her core of knights, she was free to destroy all the invading vessels, but her magic was almost exhausted.

The eight knights that were her personal protectors had no one to attack. They raised their swords in the air. She felt them infusing her with their magical energy, replacing the energy she had used faster than the magic in her body could regenerate. Shandria paused when she saw naked Atlantians swimming out of the destroyed ships. Her anger flared. She renewed her attack, cracking more ship's hulls.

Her mother saw the Atlantians fleeing from the ships and ordered her knight to create a protected corridor for them to get to the city walls. She lifted some of them up with her water magic and placed them inside the safety corridor.

Queen Isaria saw the exhaustion of her daughter. She ordered the captain of her knights to take over three of her four lines of knights. She grabbed one line as her knights and rode out onto the pier with her daughter. Queen Isaria had her guards transfer magical energy into her daughter, and then together they cracked the back of the remaining invading ships.

A group of Darfarin ran east. They were outside the palace wards. Together they were preparing a spell. Queen Isaria pointed her sword at them. A loud crack and blinding flash of lightning came from her sword, killing all the Darfarin. She yelled to her guards, and they followed as she rode to the east.

She was upset at the loss of her son and the attack on her people. She was determined that no Darfarin or ogre would survive this counterattack. Queen Isaria killed a few more she found trying to hide. They showed no mercy, and so she showed no mercy in return. She used her magic to track down several more running away towards the east. When she was confident she had killed all of them, she rode back with her personal protectors towards the wharf.

King Vandian took his knights west through the city and towards the narrows, killing every Ogre they found. He encountered Darfarins twice. Now that they knew what to look for, their dark magic showed up like a beacon. A quick blast of magical energy killed them.

Soon all the enemy in the city were killed. Shandria and her mother organized volunteer workforces. Clothing, armor, and trash from the wrecked, invading ships filled the bay. Her immediate need was to get clothing to the naked, magic drained survivors, and to throw the dead bodies of the ogres out to sea, where they could feed the sharks and scavengers, and not cause an epidemic.

They requested volunteers to help clean the harbor area and to collect the clothing. Shandria knew the people loved Atlantis, but the crowd of exhausted Atlantians from all trades and levels of society working together to help clear the harbor overwhelmed her. She was always proud to serve the people of Atlantis but was never as proud as she was today.

Shandria and her mother had fought all night and were exhausted, but they had subjects to take care of. The ogres and Darfarin had brutalized and stripped their victims of their magic. The ladies put threads of magic into each person and shared words of comfort. The magic would grow. Their people would heal.

They were happy to find the spell the Darfarin had used to drain the magic had not harmed their magic channels. The palace and army healers were busy with treating the physically wounded. Shandria and her mother called on the remaining refugees with any healing knowledge to help. Most of the court officials were assisting.

Shandria taught the magical weaves to put magical threads back into the Atlantians, and the knowledge quickly spread. Soon many were helping restore their neighbors. Shandria's grandmother, Queen Elantria, joined them and started helping. They had most of the palace staff and over a hundred volunteers helping to restore the Atlantians the Darfarins had stripped of their magic.

Without their magic, their bodies were having trouble resisting the elements. They were cold and wet. They wove magic to warm the bricks of the courtyard to keep the naked victims warm and to dry them off. But the naked survivors didn't stay naked for long. The other Atlantians took off jackets and cloaks and wrapped the survivors. Clothing recovered from the water covered others. Field blankets from the supplies of the troops were distributed, and soon everyone had something to keep them warm and covered as their magic slowly restored itself.

Queen Alandria was doing her best not to be upset. Her husband had ordered her to guard the nursery. How demeaning. She was new to the palace and had only started training with the Island troops, but she had trained with the troops of her island all her life and the differences were small. She was as powerful as any general in the army was. If nowhere else, the battlements needed her ancient sword.

She knew that by the time any attacker fought their way to the nursery the battle was lost and so were the children. But she did her job, reassuring the palace children, and the children of much of the nobility, whose first instinct was to protect their children by taking them to the palace.

All the time she was worried about her husband. His fleet had been lost. He was probably dead or worst, living meat for the ogres. She loved him. She had since their first water fight in Sea Scouts. She believed they would get over their marital problems. She had to. She knew his flagship had gone down. She would be devastated if she found out that he had died. She wanted to and needed to take out her anger and worry against the ogres and the Darfarin, and yet she was stuck babysitting the children.

Finally, someone thought of her. The main part of the battle was over, and the war council requested her help to take care of the displaced refugees. At least it was more in keeping with her duties as a queen.

Chapter 62

Marvin's magic touched each of his swords. They knew him, and he knew them. They looked so beautiful. Each was now finished, sharpened, and shined by Dwarven craftsmen. The handles were beautifully and functionally finished. He only had to spend a few seconds with them, and they were happy.

They distributed the swords among the ships of the fleet. The fleet had moved closer to the Darfarin anti-magic field. They were in a position that paralleled the movement of the enemy fleet. Marvin's wave would have a greater effect when hitting the Darfarin fleet from the side.

Their enemy was close to the main island of Atlantis. The water became shallower as it approached the shore. The shallower water would enhance the wave's destructive power as it moved toward the island.

Marvin jumped off the ship into the water. He concentrated on his sword. Each magic sword in the fleet gave him energy. He sent back a weave to the swords. They were now in sync with him and sending out a request to the water around them to provide water magic energy. And the water magic responded to its friends, the Atlantians.

He formed a wave twenty, then forty, then eighty feet high. Much like Marvin's weave that cleared the snow from the road, his request for magical help was being spread both east and west of his location from thread to thread. The energy from Marvin and the rest of the fleet was a loud bullhorn, commanding the waves to rise. Most of the energy powering the wave was coming from the magical energy in the water itself. Only afterward did Marvin learn he was weaving grandmaster level magic. But he had help. Admiral Parathian, through the link of their ancient swords, was steadying edges of Marvin's weave and keeping it tight, preventing it from unraveling. Marvin had the power of a grandmaster of water magic, but not yet the experience and control.

The magical command spread out. Soon the wave was over a hundred feet high and several miles long. It needed to be. Marvin expected it to spread out as it traveled.

It was time. Marvin commanded it to travel. Energy from the swords continued to amplify Marvin's weaves. Marvin expected the wave to lose energy as it traveled, but the opposite happened, it gained more energy from the water it passed through. Sailors on the ships willingly gave their energy to Marvin through the person on their ship holding the sword. Everyone from the Admiral to the cook on the flagship was helping. Atlantis was their home. The Atlantian Island fleet was their rivals in war games but their brothers in arms. And the sailors wanted to avenge and rescue their brothers.

The wave gained momentum and strength. It was strong. It was tall. It was moving fast. And it was close to the anti-magic shell. Marvin released the wave and commanded the magic to stay out of the anti-magic zone. He was glad to receive the last bit of energy from the fleet to restore what he had used and to ready him for his last task.

He slid down the backside of the wave and waited at the edge of the anti-magic shell. He knew the admiral would order his ships into the area to pick up survivors. The sailors held hostage on the ships could swim, but they would be without magic; they needed rescue.

Marvin saw the dark magic barrier fail. The wave devastated the Darfarin fleet as it crashed over the enemy ships, rolling them over and over and breaking them apart. Seeing the destruction made Marvin pump his fist and in English yell "Yes!" but that wasn't what he was searching for. He rode his own wave towards the destruction. He calmed himself, looked, and listened. Then he found the magical signature he was looking for. He adjusted his wave's direction and traveled as fast as he could.

Chapter 63

Handrian sat in the back corner of the hold. His friends made sure he wouldn't be a snack for a hungry ogre.

He sat on the floor with his knees curled up and his head in his hands. "What is love?" It kept haunting him. He realized it was far more than he thought it was. He now knew it was more than position or duty. He was used to people doing his bidding and equated it as love, and sometimes it was. He had thought love was something you deserved because of your position, and some love was. He was a king, so everyone loved him, and he loved them. He now realized some loved him, but many just served him. Love was not just duty or a positional requirement.

He showed his love by helping them stay in their containers, and by being in control. Atlantis needed both, but was his control love? That was his intent.

Fletch had saved his life, even though he was at the point of exhaustion and could have drowned. Two others so far had stood up and been brutally devoured to protect the other people in the cargo hold. None knew they were protecting their king.

His grandfather had told him that a King has to sacrifice to be a symbol for the people. And he had sacrificed his freedom to be that symbol, to be an Atlantian they could look up to. He did it because he loved them, or did he just love his position? Did he actually love the people of Atlantis?

Then it finally clicked. Love wasn't something you received. It was something you gave. His love wasn't shown in their duty and respect for him. It was shown in his duty and respect for them, not just for their position in society, but also for whom they truly were. They may be inside a particular trade group, or level in society, a container as Marvin called it, but each person was different, an individual. They were more than their container, and worthy of respect and love just because they were Atlantian, and because they were individuals made by the Creator.

They were stifled if he allowed them only to exist inside a container. He did love Atlantis, and his people, but his way of expressing it was harsh and needed to be changed. He needed to be more forgiving and more fluid. He needed to be more Atlantian and let people flow.

Handrian realized he had been harshest on himself. He had formed his own unyielding container and, in the process, sacrificed much of whom he was. He was more than his station in life. His self-imposed container was making him mad and unyielding. He had taken out his frustration on Alandria. He had denied a large part of himself. And worst yet, he had denied it to his wife. Then he realized Alandria wasn't at fault in the marriage. He was.

She was giving all she had. Not just as a woman but as his queen, as his wife, and as his boyhood friend. She was far more than the container he was forcing her into.

He owed her the love and respect to become the queen she could be, the way she naturally flowed, and not his way. He owed her the love and respect to help define their marriage. He owed her the part of him, which was the Sea Scout she loved. And to be honest, he loved and married the Sea Scout he was now stifling and hurting by his actions. He started to cry, praying he would somehow survive this and get to change the current in his life and flow back together with Alandria.

Then the wave Marvin had created hit the ship and rolled it end over end. The ship broke apart. It filled with water and sunk quickly. Handrian saw his fellow captors swimming away from the wreckage towards the surface. He started swimming and looked back. Some rigging had tangled Fletch. It started pulling him down with the ship. Handrian swam back and followed the wreckage as it sunk. The knife Marvin had made for him quickly cut through the rigging, freeing Fletch. Handrian saw him swim towards the surface. Gonzo was caught in the rigging. Handrian swam over and cut him loose, and several other sailors.

Suddenly the turbulent water shifted the rigging. The rigging now blocked Handrian's way out. Handrian had no magic and not enough time to cut through the ropes. He tried conserving his energy, hoping the turbulence would move the rigging away so he could escape. But there was no escape. His lungs were on fire, and his vision started to blur. His last thoughts were of laughing and chasing Alandria after she had hit him with an ice water ball in Sea Scouts; then he lost consciousness.

Chapter 64

Marvin was where he needed to be. He took several deep breaths, hyperventilated, and dove into the water. He relaxed to conserve the air in his lungs, weaving magic, so the water pushed him to where he wanted to go. The water was murky and dangerous. Twice he had to avoid floating debris. He needed to be careful. He could see tomorrow's headlines, "Sir Marvin promoted to general and killed by driftwood."

Marvin was after Handrian. There was no way he could find him, he didn't even know Handrian's magical signature, but he could locate the dagger he had enchanted. He had enchanted cloaking magic into the grip of Handrian's dagger, but it wasn't cloaked from his dagger's magic. It had the same vibration, and it found its brother.

He found the back half of a ship unsteadily resting on the bottom, moving about in the shifting currents. Loose rigging and debris covered it. Inside was Handrian's dagger, and hopefully Handrian. He would never be able to cut past the lines before he ran out of breath. He entrained the vessel in a magic generated current and brought it to the surface with him. If Handrian was on the ship, he needed air. Marvin floated the wreck out of the water. He inhaled deeply several times as he watched the ocean drain through the many holes of the wreckage.

He looked around. The wave had driven them closer to shore than to the fleet. He wove water magic to move the ship and him to the beach. He recognized the magical energy from his estate. It was close, and if anywhere was safe on this part of the mainland it would be there. Marvin knew it would take several minutes to get to his estate. There was no magical signature coming from the vessel other than Handrian's dagger. He prayed Handrian still had his dagger or at least was near it, and that he had found an air pocket in the ship.

Marvin roughly landed the vessel on the beach near the edge of his pool, more interested in speed than in smoothness. He pulled out his sword and started to cut rigging. A few slashes and Marvin had made a large enough hole to climb through. He wove a quick light weave and climbed through the hole.

Several tangled together bodies lie near an opening. They had been pushed there when the water had drained out of the ship. One of the bodies was Shandria's brother Handrian. Marvin pulled the other people off the king and pulled him free. He tilted back Handrian head, pinched his nose, and gave him a couple of mouth-to-mouth breaths.

He felt Handrian's neck. Marvin wasn't sure if he felt a pulse or it was just hopeful thinking. It was the slowest heartbeat he had ever felt. He gave him another quick puff of air. He looked deep into Handrian. Blood was moving through his veins at a slow pace. Marvin saw Handrian's magic was empty. He added a few magical threads.

Marvin made sure the other bodies were breathing, which remarkably they were. He saw blood was moving slowly through their bodies and blew into the mouths of the other five people several times. He went back to check on Handrian and saw he was breathing faster, and his heart rate was slowly increasing. There was nothing more Marvin could think to do. Handrian's body would have to recover on its own.

Marvin checked on the other sailors. They were showing signs of improvement. He added magical threads to each of their bodies. He could do nothing more for them than pray and wait.

He looked at Handrian's heart rate. He counted five seconds between heartbeats. Twelve beats per minute. He hoped the slowing down was an Atlantian adaptation to drowning. Marvin watched for a couple of minutes and saw Handrian's heart rate double. He was recovering. It must be Atlantian physiology. Hopefully, it had protected his brain from damage.

Marvin took off his cloak and respectfully laid it over Handrian's naked body, not so much for Handrian as a person, after the way he was treating Alandria, but because he was a king of Atlantis and Shandria's brother. He then exited the ship to make sure they were safe.

He felt the power of the wards in his house glowing brightly. He knew from the increased power level that they had been attacked and had grown. The wave he had unleashed on the enemy had slammed into the land. It had reached all the way to the house, based on the wetness and debris in his backyard. He saw the body of a dead ogre on the bottom of his pool.

This was the first ogre he had ever seen. He took a close look at it and wished he hadn't. He had avoided lumps floating under the surface of the ocean that were the same size. He grabbed all the water out of the swimming pool and threw it far out to sea. The pool was empty, but the magical weave on a pipe was already pumping the water from the ocean, purifying it, and filling the pool. He would have to put a no swimming sign up on the beach for a while. He hoped it would be the last ogre he would ever see, but he knew that was unlikely.

He walked back towards the ship and cut away more rigging to make the opening wider. He heard coughing and entered through the enlarged hole. A couple of people were starting to sit up. He was thankful they were okay. Then he heard coughing from King Handrian. King Hadrian sat up. Marvin went down on one knee and said, "My king."

ATLANTIAN MAGIC

King Handrian saw Marvin's cloak covering him and smiled through his pounding headache. He looked into the corner and saw Gonzo recovering. King Handrian sat up and said to Marvin. "I take it you saved my life again general. I owe you my thanks."

Marvin reached down to help King Handrian up. He was convinced Atlantian physiology gave some protection from drowning.

Handrian grabbed his hand, and Marvin pulled him to his feet. Handrian was a little dizzy and breathing twice as fast as normal, but otherwise okay. He embraced Marvin. Marvin was speechless and hugged him back. Handrian said, "I have been a fool towards you, please accept my apology."

Marvin stopped for a second and said, "Always my king. But you are no fool. The difference between a wise man and a fool is the wise man realizes he did a foolish thing and changes his ways."

King Handrian laughed, slapped Marvin on the shoulder, and put on Marvin's cloak. He walked over to the sailors, embraced Gonzo, and one by one the rest of the sailors. He turned towards Marvin and asked, "Marvin, where are we and how did we get here?"

Marvin gave him a quick synopsis of the wave and the rescue and then said, "We are at the estate I am living at. Please follow me." They all left the remains of the boat and followed him.

Marvin had a password he had placed on the door. In English, he said, "Speak friend and enter." The bar on the inside of the back door lifted up, and the door opened.

Several surprised men with weapons greeted him. Marvin asked, "Is that any way to greet the owner of the house?" He stepped to the side as King Handrian entered. Handrian was battered and bruised, his magic was weak, and he felt like he was recovering from a bad hangover. But they all recognized him. Marvin reinforced his presence by saying, "Welcome King Handrian." And falling to one knee and bowing.

Everyone in the house bowed and went down on a knee. Handrian thanked them and had them quickly stand up. Marvin escorted the King and the sailors upstairs to his room and found them each some clothing.

Handrian saw how nice the room was decorated, except for a strangely shaped boat paddle that had the Atlantian alphabet scratched into it. He wondered why Marvin displayed it on the wall.

Marvin was initially glad when the king selected another cloak and gave him back his. He had woven powerful protection weaves into it, but then he realized the king needed protection more than he did. He said, "King Handrian, I know it's not fashion conscious, but my travel cloak has some strong protection woven into it. It would ease my worries if you wore it until we get you safely back to the palace and your body completely restores your magic."

Handrian thanked Marvin and put back on Marvin's travel cloak. Handrian looked at the cloak. There were many familiar weaves such as comfort, waterproof, and resistance to tearing. There were others of earth and wood, which would take him some time to figure out. One earth magic weave was strange and powerful. He wasn't even sure it was earth magic. He asked, "Marvin, what is that complex earth magic weave?"

Marvin replied, "Its metal magic. On a violent impact, the cloak becomes as hard as steel. It's what protected me from injury when the dark spell threw me against the stairs. It does have its limits, but it's good for one big impact and its recovery time is reasonably fast."

Handrian was impressed. He had never heard of metal magic, which must have been a subclass of earth magic or forge magic. More and more he realized he had misjudged this Atlantian because of his place of upbringing and his prejudice, no his jealousy, and ego.

Mrs. White ran to give Marvin a hug, so did her two children, followed by Mr. White. Marvin crouched down and told the children he was proud of their bravery. Marvin said to Mrs. White, while still hugging the children, "Please get the king and these sailors some food if there is any left, something quick and filling."

Mrs. White ran downstairs. The king came out of Marvin's bedroom and saw some of the people starting to bow low. He said, "Please stand up. Today we are comrades in arms defending Atlantis. I have no idea what you went through, but I can tell you battled with strength and courage. Tonight, you have banded together to protect each other and shared with each other the best and truest spirit of Atlantis. I am proud of each of you, humbled, and inspired by your actions."

Handrian went down on one knee and bowed his head. Then he stood up and walked downstairs and shook everyone's hands. Many he hugged. Handrian saw retired Admiral Persimmian give him a hug. The strength and the duration of the king's hug surprised the Admiral.

The King said, "General Marvin and I have to get back to the palace."

The Admiral said, "I know you do, and so do I. I retired less than a year ago. I know the fleet better than any man, and I know the court could use my sword."

King Handrian looked at one of his old mentors and said, "Do you agree to reinstatement to active duty for as long as the crown needs your service?"

The Admiral knelt down on one knee and said, "Yes my king."

King Handrian said, "Arise, I reinstate you as an Admiral in the Atlantian Navy. We can use your advice in the war room. After that, it is up to the council." He turned towards Marvin and said, "Let's go."

Marvin said, "Yes my king." He then turned and said, "Sorry Mrs. White. We have to run. I'm glad you and our estate took care of our neighborhood. Please continue to take care of them until it is safe for them to go home."

ATLANTIAN MAGIC

Marvin said, "Follow me, my king. I know you need to let your magic recover. So, let me transport us by water. It will be faster than walking or riding, and I can fill you in on your great victory."

Handrian stopped walking towards the ocean and said, "What great victory? I lost half the Atlantian fleet."

Marvin stopped and replied, "And in the sacrifice, you gave us the knowledge the enemy was about to attack. You gained us the knowledge we needed to destroy their fleet and to evacuate and save the city. No victory was ever achieved without loss, and ours was a great victory. We are wise to their tactics now, and we will use them against our enemy. Mourn your losses but be assured they brought us the knowledge we needed to save Atlantis."

Marvin pulled a pseudopod of water from the ocean. He lifted up himself, the King, and the Admiral. He took them out to sea. They rode his wave up the coast. During their travel, Marvin pulled some travel biscuits from his pack and gave them to the admiral and king. He then ate one himself. Then he told them what they had done to destroy the enemy fleet. The admiral shared the story of the defensive stand at the estate.

Marvin knew the capital had been under attack, but he could tell the dark magic was no longer attacking the capital. Atlantis had won.

Marvin looked at some of the damage on the shoreline. It was mostly just debris swept ashore by his wave. It was superficial damage. The estates were farther back from the water's edge and constructed to survive the occasional tropical storm. The wave had freed many Atlantians from their captors, like a tsunami grabbing everyone and washing them out to sea. Their ogre captives had drowned, and the civilians had swum back to shore.

Soon they arrived at the docks. They saw people cleaning up the harbor. News quickly spread that King Handrian was alive and headed back to the palace. Everyone was excited to see him alive. His mother was the first of the royals to see him. She ran to him and held him tight. Then she saw how depleted he was and sent him off to bed as only a mother can. She had previously sent his wife there, who was helping with the refugees but was on the verge of tears.

King Handrian stopped at the palace garden on his way upstairs. He picked some waluia flowers from the palace garden.

A messenger informed Alandria that her husband was safe and would be upstairs soon. She quickly changed out of her usual night clothes and put on the gossamer gown she had worn under her wedding robes. She covered it with her best night robe. She was nervous and excited. She knew her husband had gone through a lot. Whatever he needed tonight, to talk, to cry, to hold her, or to share her body and heat, she would take care of his needs. She loved him, and she would always take care of him.

She heard a commotion outside her room. Then there was silence. She opened her door and peeked out. She saw Handrian two-doors down at his concubine's room, and he saw a red flower in his hand. Alandria closed the door, sat down on a padded trunk at the foot of the bed, and started crying.

A minute later, her door opened, and her husband walked in. She had always tried to be a loving and dutiful wife, but all the hurt she had endured had built up, and she continued to cry.

Handrian put the flowers down on the bench next to his wife and fell to his knees. He started to cry, "I'm sorry. I'm so sorry I hurt you. Please forgive me. I'm such a stupid, foolish ogre, and you deserve better. Please give me a second chance. I just gave a white waluia to my concubine."

Handrian knelt at her feet, held onto her legs, and cried on her thighs. She saw through her tears the red waluia flower and a blue one. One was for love, and the other was for friendship. She realized that he had only visited his concubine to dismiss her. He was offering her, no begging her for forgiveness.

Alandria held his head gently on her lap, she was still crying, but different emotions fueled it. She had never seen a man cry as her husband was crying. He was emotionally broken. She knew how much he needed her, and that he had just realized it himself. She slowly stroked his hair. She bent over and kissed him on the back of the head.

She said, "When your ship was lost I was afraid you were dead, or worst. But I prayed and prayed, and I knew you would come back from the sea. You had to flow back to me."

Handrian recovered a little and said, "I have been such a terrible husband and a terrible friend. I married you because I loved you and we were friends, and I threw it away. Once I realized what a fool I had been, all I did was pray for one more chance. Please forgive me and give me one more chance. Help me to flow together with you and to be a better friend and husband. I promise to stop being an ogre, and to treat you with the respect and love you deserve."

It took some hugging followed by some kissing, and the stroking of his hair, but after a while, they were in bed together. It was the first time in a long time Alandria felt the fire of his love when they shared their heat.

They lie naked in each other's arms. Handrian said. "The Anastasi's question to me was: 'What is love?' I thought it was a useless joke. I equated love with doing a duty, with obligation. I thought love was due me because I was a king and you were my queen. But when the Darfarins stripped me of my kingship and magic, I saw the sacrifice of sailors who thought I was just another sailor. It made me realize I had the meaning of love all wrong.

"I was waiting to be eaten alive by the ogres, and my heart broke open. Inside I found a beautiful flower that I was crushing, and it was you, and next to it was the crushed love I have for you. I plan to spend the rest of my life loving and helping that beautiful flower grow. I realize now that I can't take care of a flower by crushing it, or by crushing myself. I am such a stupid fool."

Alandria held Handrian, with his arm around her, and her head on his shoulder. She had never given up on their love. Even when he asked her to marry him, he had never talked to her like this. She lay there for several minutes, enjoying their back from the sea relationship. She knew their relationship was now flowing down a better stream. She was thinking about how much she felt his true honest love tonight when she heard his stomach growl. She had been too upset to eat, and she realized she was also starving. She said, "I will have the guard get us some food."

Handrian thought for a second and said, "Wait, I have a better idea. I have something to show you. We use to do it as kids."

The private part of the palace formed a rectangle around an inner court and garden. The outside walls were decorated, but defensive in nature. The inside walls were ornate and decorative. They overlooked the palace gardens and pool. He climbed outward from the balcony and down onto a ledge. Alandria followed him, wondering what he was planning. They traversed along the side of the building and arrived at a window.

He signaled with his hand to be quiet. He saw a cook enter the pantry and then leave. They snuck into the pantry through the window and burned their fingers on some sweet muffins that were cooling near the window. Shandria was having trouble not laughing. She felt like they were pulling a prank in Sea Scouts again.

Handrian put several of the muffins in an empty sack that was in the pantry. He grabbed a large mug from a shelf and filled it with spiced wine from an open cask. They climbed back out the window, climbed up a story, and over to a ledge that was big enough to sit on. They shared the wine, ate the pastries, laughed, and looked at the stars above and the garden and pool below. They saw the sunrise of a new day reflecting off the ripples in the pool water.

Alandria had regained her friend and now had the husband she knew she had married. She would keep him to his promise, and make sure he didn't flow away from her again.

King Vandian looked out his window on his way to bed. He saw two people on a ledge below and realized it was Handrian and Alandria, naked and laughing. He called over his wife and motioned her to be quiet. She came over and saw where he was looking. They had discussed Handrian's ill-treatment of Alandria. But what they saw told them something onboard the ogre ship had changed him for the better.

Atlantian Royals hold the marriage ceremony at midmorning. Then the bride and groom go to their room together for their first joining. Lying in bed after their wedding, Vandian and Isaria grew hungry but didn't want to be part of the wedding party just yet. They had waited a long time to be alone together, and they weren't ready to end it. They snuck out and robbed the pantry. They ate, laughed, and enjoyed each other's heat once more before they dressed and joined the reception later that afternoon.

Pd MICHEL

King Vandian asked, "Are you hungry?"

His wife replied, "I don't want to disturb them."

He replied. "I know another route to the kitchen." She smiled but insisted on throwing on a robe first. There were guests in the palace, and they weren't kids anymore.

Chapter 65

The public areas of the palace were crazy with activity. The palace kitchen was cooking nonstop for all the guests who had enough connection to the court to take refuge in the palace. The Common Court Room, the largest room in the palace, was now a refugee center for the families of court workers, and for those with a high enough position in society to have court influence. Not a single guest room in the palace was vacant. The military kitchens in the barracks were working 24 hours a day to take care of the soldiers and all the refugees in the merchant's court. The soldiers were doubling up in the barracks, and many refugees were bedding down on blankets in the vacated barracks. It was daytime, but everyone was exhausted.

Shandria and Marvin spent most of the day with the war council reporting on their activities and hearing reports. They were finally released around dinner time. She took Marvin to the palace kitchen, where rank did have its privilege. The kitchen workers hurried together a meal for two.

Marvin grabbed their dinner and Shandria grabbed a small bottle of spiced wine. She led him out into the garden area by the pool. Only the royal family had access, so it was away from all the noise and insanity of the rest of the palace. They ate and talked about everything but what they had spoken to the council about.

After they had finished eating, Marvin and Shandria took a quick swim in the garden pool to clean off. Then Shandria collected her clothes and her sword and told Marvin, "Follow me. He found himself entering Shandria's room from the balcony. He said, "I don't think I'm allowed to be here."

She replied, "Grandfather said we needed to be flexible and make allowances since the palace is so crowded."

She opened her door to the hallway and stuck her head out. The guard was surprised to see she was already in her room but figured that with all the uproar he had received a bad turnover when he started his watch.

She said. "I'm going to bed, and I don't want to be disturbed under any circumstances."

She closed the door as the guard said, "Yes my Princess."

She turned to Marvin and said, "If you prefer, I could order a court minister who snores and has questionable hygiene to share his bed with you." She crawled into bed. Marvin followed her. She released the light weave. Their exhaustion caught up with them, and they fell asleep immediately.

Marvin hadn't realized how tired he had been until waking up the next morning. He used magic to clean his clothes, then dressed and jumped down from Shandria's balcony. He did some morning stretches and a slow routine that his sword led him in. Then he proceeded to the war room. Shandria did her morning preparation and joined him there a few minutes later. Unlike Marvin, she exited her room into the hallway.

Many people in the war room had been up most of the night. Even the ones just arriving could use a few more hours of sleep.

Then Shandria came in and asked what breakfast plans were. No one replied so she had a squire order a hearty meal for eighty people and some juice and tea for the war room as a priority. There were forty people in the war room at the time, but soon others came in. Everyone must have been hungry. Almost every person that entered the war room asked about breakfast.

King Baracian and his wife came and heard breakfast was on the way. Baracian said, "And when it arrives, order eighty more." Everyone was hungry. Shandria was surprised at how much everyone ate. With court officials, messengers, and officers coming and going the food didn't go to waste.

There were reports of landings up north. King Baracian had sent the first and the second legion to guard the arch before he went to bed. Third and Fourth Legion had been ordered to guard the area west of Mount Atlantis.

The Southern fleet was sending a string of small, fast ships up the west side of Atlantis. They were in constant communication and looking for any indication of dark magic. Now that they were familiar with the area where no magic came from, it was easy to detect. The main fleet was close behind, ready to fall back or advance as needed.

Admiral Persimmian boarded a hydrofoil, along with fifty enchanted swords. King Baracian had assigned him back to the Southern fleet. It was his old command, and he was the right person to lead it now. His new title was Senior Admiral. The current Southern Fleet Admiral kept his fleet but would return on the hydrofoil and was temporarily reassigned to the war room as a strategic naval advisor.

Shandria and Marvin were almost shocked to see the change in Handrian and Alandria. They were acting like newlyweds, holding hands, looking each other in the eye, and sharing private jokes.

The elite guard units would be mustering and ready to depart in an hour. Shandria would accompany them. King Baracian ordered Marvin, and Handrian to go with them to the arch area.

Handrian said, "I want Alandria with us. I may be a fool, but I'm less a fool than when I insisted on her guarding the nursery." King Baracian smiled and quickly agreed.

ATLANTIAN MAGIC

Handrian grabbed Marvin and said, "I need to get a replacement sword from the armory. The sea claimed mine. You know more about magic swords than anyone I know so I would like you to come with me."

Marvin said, "Let's go." He couldn't believe that Handrian had changed so much. He had asked him to come like a friend, and not ordered him. Marvin could tell that Handrian was no longer fighting against him. He could feel the bond of friendship and camaraderie that Handrian was offering. Marvin was quick to grab and return it. He was pleased with the change.

Handrian realized that Marvin had never been to the protected royal armory where Shandria's sword chose her so many years before. Handrian had been there many times hoping to be befriended by an ancient sword, but he had resigned himself to the fact it wasn't to be. He knew Marvin would enjoy seeing the weapons and armor. Afterward, they would look at the other enchanted weapons and select a sword to replace his.

Marvin entered the armory and fell in love. The craftsmanship and the magic in the room sang with him, both as an enchanter and with his sword. It was a family reunion for his sword. His sword had fought alongside these weapons in hundreds of battles and been displayed alongside them for millennia until left at Crystal Mountain. There were several dozen ancient or powerful weapons and an equal number of enchanted pieces of armor in the restricted armory.

Marvin allowed his sword to greet each of them and enjoyed the love they had for each other. Then he saw it, mounted on the wall, and it was calling to him. His sword encouraged him to go over. Marvin had felt that call once before, the day he received his sword. The armor and weapons around him were vibrating, singing a magical song that was a mixture of forge, combat, and camaraderie. But the breastplate on the wall was calling like a lover, like a friend, and Marvin had no desire to resist. He grabbed the breastplate and hugged it to his chest for several seconds like a long-lost friend. Then he made the relationship complete by putting on the armor.

He was glad the straps fastened themselves by magic, as he would have fumbled for far too long trying to figure out how they worked. Marvin stood back from the wall, and he started to dance. It was a dance of sword and breastplate, two friends, no, two best friends, reunited after centuries apart. Marvin enjoyed how the armor caressed his chest and back. The armor adapted to his body, and every curve of the breastplate matched the curves of his chest, with just enough space for his muscles to move.

Marvin and his armor started dancing, moving, and swinging his sword, slash, parry, riposte, attack, retreat, sidestep, spin, and block. They were all familiar drills he had done with his sword, but now his sword was complete with the armor, and his balance was slightly different.

Marvin was enjoying his new friend. Then he realized he had lost track of time. He didn't know how long he had been practicing, no dancing with his sword and breastplate, and he had promised King Handrian to help him find a sword, and they were under orders to protect the arch. Marvin sheathed his sword and turned around. He saw the king hadn't noticed how long he had taken.

Handrian saw Marvin enjoying his time with the breastplate. He was glad the armor had rewarded Marvin this way. But then his eye saw the glint of light on a set of armor he had looked at hundreds of times. The breastplate was so beautiful. It shone like a diamond in the sun, beckoning him to come over.

He picked it up and held it to his chest, holding it tight. Then he turned it around and placed it on his chest. The latches closed by themselves. He laughed and leaped into the air. He was reunited with a dear old friend he never knew, and they started celebrating.

And there was more. A helmet called to both Handrian and the breastplate. He pulled it from its display and held it, no him, with both hands, one on either side of the helmet. He looked at the face of the helmet. He was beautiful and glowed with a magical light Handrian had never seen before. He put him on. The helmet was as anxious as he was and conformed to his head. He spun around, tilting and twisting his head, getting used to the weight and feel of his new friend.

A glowing shield caught his eye. He didn't hesitate. He grabbed hold of him and hugged him against his breastplate. Without thinking his hand slid through the straps. He spun around, feeling the weight, and saw a sword. The sword was calling Handrian and talking to the armor. He grabbed the sword and started to dance with his new family. Handrian had held the finest crafted swords, magical and non-magical, and yet his hand fit the sword so well it felt like part of his hand.

Marvin saw Handrian thrusting and slashing. It was his dance, and Marvin smiled at his new friend and watched. Marvin had sheathed his sword and realized his arms were crossed over his chest. His fingers tracing each design on his breastplate.

King Baracian sent Shandria to find Marvin and her brother, whom they expected to return to the war room. She saw her brother practicing with his new sword and armor. Her sword was singing, and she started crying tears of joy for her brother. She walked around him towards the back of the armory where she saw Marvin was, watching every move of Handrian's dance.

Her brother was an excellent swordsman by anyone's criteria. He could match abilities with any of the elite guards. But by ancient sword standards, he was a novice. She saw his balance, speed, and precision improve with each swing of his sword, and with each step of his foot. The armor and sword were millennia old, and they were teaching him, directly teaching his muscles, nerves, and reflexes. Unlike Marvin who was learning from scratch. His brother only needed minute corrections.

She saw Marvin watching her brother and walked over to join him. Her eye caught a glint of his new breastplate. She smiled and hurried over. But something caught her eye on the wall behind him. It called to her. She diverted around Marvin.

A breastplate was shining and singing. Shandria's sword sang back. She pulled it off the wall, and without hesitation put it on. Its straps secured it to her body. She had known for a long time that her sword and this breastplate were a matched set. She sometimes visited the armory so her sword could say hello to its old friend. So, when it called her, it came as no surprise. She crossed her arms and held the breastplate. She spun around, feeling her weight. She was a little child safe in her mother's arms.

Then her armor called out to Marvin's breastplate. They had been old friends and had fought side by side together for centuries. A married couple often owned the set. Shandria kissed Marvin, and in some ways, it was the armor kissing its spouse.

Alandria came in and found her husband practicing with his sword and his new armor.

Handrian saw Alandria, sheathed his sword, walked over, picked up his wife, and spun her around as they kissed each other. They were wearing a married pair of armor and could feel the excitement of the couple. It was the excitement of being together again, and of the upcoming battle.

Handrian realized he had grown as a person. He had learned what love was. He had turned his queen into his wife and friend. No, he had accepted her love and friendship and committed himself to being her friend and husband. The sword and armor had been waiting for years; now it was time; he was ready. They could now accept Handrian.

The four of them walked back to the war room, but before they arrived, the kings and queens could feel the change. Their ancient swords were celebrating. So, when Handrian arrived, they were excited and couldn't wait to hug him. They knew he had felt like an outsider.

Then they saw Shandria's and Marvin's breastplates. They were happy for them but also curious. The swords and armor all had personalities. All were particular about their owner. Some had established close bonds with other ancient weapons and armor.

King Baracian watched the four of them leaving the war room. He already knew about Shandria's armor and sword. Just like her, he had been waiting for the two friends to join. He knew who the last owner of Shandria's armor had been and who last wore Marvin's breastplate.

Marvin's sword had refused to reveal its name and the other swords and armor had respected it. But King Baracian had already figured out which sword Marvin held, and his new armor confirmed it. He was sure he knew who Marvin's parents were. But his proof wasn't solid enough to present before the council. He knew time would reveal all, and that he would wait to see how it happened.

Handrian was completely against giving Marvin the rank of general. So was King Vandian at first. When he saw how strongly King Baracian argued for it, King Vandian changed his vote. He trusted his father's wisdom and magical insight. Every time Baracian had argued so strongly without voicing equally strong reasons, he had reasons that his wisdom only allowed him to reveal later. He suspected his father knew more about Marvin than he could tell. After Marvin destroyed the Darfarin fleet, all three kings were swimming in the same pool with Marvin being a general.

King Vandian called one of the scribes and ordered him to research the history of Marvin and Shandria's swords and armor. He was growing more and more curious about Marvin, and about what his father knew or suspected and wouldn't reveal.

Chapter 66

When they arrived at the arch, a command tent had been set up. The arch was still under attack by dark magic. And the assault on the arch intensified. The arch was too immature to handle the stress placed on him. The arch's protective shell started to shrink. He was no longer able to sustain the magic weave that stopped people from using a portal to go anywhere on the main island of the planet.

Marvin could see the Atlantian arch crystal was struggling to keep its weave from collapsing. Marvin told him to release the weave. The arch released the weave and felt bad.

Marvin touched him and comforted him, and told him, he was proud. He was young and had done far more than anyone could have hoped. It was time for the arch to rest, recover, learn, and grow. Marvin asked the arch to grow and collect more energy from the earth and sky. Then he gave him a different weave to learn and explore, and said, "This is the one that will soon matter."

The arch felt comforted and studied the magical weave. He was excited; his daddy had given him the same weave as the amulet he wore everywhere. It must be an important weave. His father really was proud of him.

The interference caused by the fight between the arch and the dark magic was gone. Marvin wove his sky magic and looked down on Atlantis. They had been protecting the city of Atlantis and fighting their naval battle against the Darfarin, but that was only part of the Darfarin's plan.

The Darfarin army had invaded the northern portion of the island. They had forces attacking the four northern cities. The cities' walls were well fortified and protected by strong magic. Marvin examined the wards closer. He saw the protective magic wards of the cities were strong and healthy. The more the Darfarins attacked, the more the city wards learned. The level of attack wasn't strong enough to weaken the wards, quite the opposite. The protective wards were learning and growing stronger with every attack. The city wards were thousands of years old, and they were strong. They would hold.

Darfarin's had landed on the west side of the Island. There were no natural harbors and only a few small towns. Most of it was farmland. Inland grew the jungle and a string of mountains and ridges.

Marvin talked to Handrian. Handrian said, "The northern cities aren't their primary objective. If they were, they would be concentrating their forces, attacking them, and taking them one by one. Each city has two legions of troops and several hundred Calvary. The Darfarin are using minimal forces to tie up over half the forces of our island in their cities."

Handrian asked, "General Marvin. You are the general of the Scout Corps. We need to see what we will be facing. What is your recommendation?"

Marvin thought for a second then replied, "My recommendation is to send in a couple dozen Alfarin troops as scouts, but we don't have any. Shandria and I are the only Atlantians with knowledge of the Alfarin magic of concealment, and I'm the only one who has had field training with the Alfarins in its use. Shandria is in charge of the knights. So, I need to scout."

Handrian said, "Take care and don't get too close. I need you back here."

Marvin replied, "Yes, my king." He bowed his head and walked away.

Marvin was still getting used to the change in Handrian. Rather than saying Atlantis needed him, Handrian had said, "I need you."

He looked again at the terrain with his sky magic. There was a hill inside enemy lines, covered by Atlantian jungle. There was a cliff down from the hill where the enemy traveled. There was no indication the enemy was on the hill. It would give him a good view of the area. Marvin didn't think his portal would generate any stray magic, but there was a depression on top the hill, which would hide any magic noise.

Marvin used the arch to form a quiet portal. There would be minimal stray magic to give away the location. He walked through it with his sword drawn and quickly shut down the portal. He hid behind some buses and crafted his camouflage weave.

He snuck to the north side of the hill. As expected, there was no troop movement. He snuck to the east side. As anticipated, there were no troops. Then he carefully moved to the west side. He could see the advancing army through the trees below, if you would call it an army. Ogres and Darfarin's were herding thousands of large animals toward the south. It reminded Marvin of a childhood book where the circus was coming to town. But this was no circus. There was something strange about the animals and Marvin needed to find out.

Marvin found a place where he could do an unobserved climb off the hill. Rainfall running off the top had carved a natural canyon. It was steep but not a hard climb. The water dug into the rock face creating a small canyon-shaped like three sides of a chimney. It protected him from direct observation. There were many good handholds in the cliff, so he didn't anticipate having trouble getting down or backup without using magic.

Marvin climbed down. He had learned in boy scouts how to climb, but he had always done it when there was a rope tied off on top and someone belaying the rope to take up the extra slack, so if he fell, he wouldn't fall far before the rope caught him. But this was free climbing, no rope. He could have used sky magic to let him down, but he didn't want to generate any magical noise. He would only use it if he fell.

Climbing down was always harder than climbing up. When you are climbing up your eyes are close to the handholds, and you are stepping up to a place you have already seen. When you are climbing down, you are reaching with your foot to a place much farther away, that you have never been to, and may not see well.

The climb down was easier than he expected, but he was a lot stronger now than he was in boy scouts, and he had grip magic woven into his boots. He climbed down to the depression, which the runoff water had dug over time. It had some residual water in it, but it wasn't flowing. The almost dry streambed was overgrown with bushes. The bushes and trees in the area made it easy for him to blend into the jungle.

He looked around with his magic. There didn't appear to be any Darfarin scouts. Even so, he proceeded with stealth and caution.

He observed a herd of elephants with long curved tusks; no, they had hair, they must be mammoths. Ogres with clubs and spiked sticks sat on their backs. There were covered with wounds and scars. Some were recently made and still dripping blood. The wounds on the animals made Marvin angry.

Behind the ogres were Darfarins casting spells to help control the animals. Marvin crept as near as he could to the animals. He admired the beauty of the animal and was upset at how they were mistreated.

He looked inside one with his magic and was shocked. The once beautiful animal was an ugly beast inside. Dark magic lines were running along the nerves of the animal. Shandria had her magic ability drained and damaged, but the mammoth had dark-magic scars throughout its body. The wounds caused by the ogre's spiked clubs were as nothing compared to the internal injuries. The ogres were forcing the herds south towards the arch and using pain to keep the animals in line.

It took a lot of restraint for Marvin to stay hidden and not attack the nearest Darfarin. The damage done by the dark magic on the animals looked permanent. He feared that even the magic of the Alfarin wouldn't be able to heal the spell-twisted animals.

He observed other animals, including a herd of long-tusk hairy boars, but there was no practical way to get nearer to them and look inside.

Marvin saw a herd of horned herbivores. They looked like large buffalo.

He headed south for several minutes to see where the front of the group was. Then he snuck farther west into some bushes. He looked down from the sky and saw the front of the herd. He continued to look around and found a small group of Atlantians not too far away towards the east. A high cliff stopped their progress. There didn't seem to be any Darfarins around them.

Marvin stayed concealed and approached the group. It looked like several families hiding from the Darfarins. Marvin couldn't let them be found and taken.

He unwove his concealment and stepped out from the bushes. They were surprised to see him.

Marvin cast a weave that would hide their magical aura from the Darfarin. He said, "I am General Marvin of the Atlantian Scout Corps. Keep your voices low. I will get you out of this. A large group of the enemy is walking past us. In a couple of minutes, it will be safe for us to leave. Until then we need to stay down. We need to stay quiet. We need to stay hidden." Marvin whispered to them, but his focus was elsewhere. He wanted the Darfarins to move farther away before activating a portal. But if they changed direction and came too close, he would activate it right away.

One man owned a farm near the west coast. The Darfarins came ashore and drained his magic with one of their dark spells. He ran inland and alerted other families. They evacuated towards the eastern cities through the jungle. They stayed off the main road, became lost, and missed the passes through the mountains. Now they were hiding from the enemy. Marvin looked at the man who had lost his magic. After talking to the man, he coaxed a magical thread back into him. It would grow, and he would recover.

After a few minutes, Marvin said, "The big group has moved past us. Follow me. Stay close. Stay quiet. If I wave my hand, sit down, and remain still."

Marvin followed the ridge back to the canyon he had climbed down. They encountered no Darfarins or ogres.

There was no way he could expect the family group to climb up the cliff. It's shielding on three sides by the canyon was the best he could do to hide stray magic for his portal. He wove a portal to the dock and had the family step through. He told the families to tell the guards what had happened and to ask for refugee status until it was safe to go home.

Then Marvin opened a portal to the Atlantian arch and stepped through. He reported to King Handrian what he had seen and been told.

King Handrian had hoped the legends of the Darfarin's were wrong. Their dark spells pervert the animals, making them aggressive and vicious. None of the animal Marvin had described lived on the Atlantian Islands, but they existed in various other realms.

The Darfarin must have brought them here from off world. But there was no way they could have formed a portal directly to the island of Atlantis. King Handrian knew Marvin was right. The Darfarins must have used their arch crystal, constructed an arch, and sailed in a fleet of ships to transport them to the island of Atlantis.

Handrian wrote a message down. He sent messengers through the portals to Alfamara and Iron Mountain. He gave another message to Marvin to take to the capital.

Marvin spent a few minutes registering another address into the arch. He temporarily opened the portal and threw an amulet through the portal. Hopefully, they would receive help from the realm.

ATLANTIAN MAGIC

The magic barrier around the palace prevented Marvin from weaving a portal into the palace itself, so he mounted a horse and took the arch to the dock area. He rode as fast as he could through the crowd to the palace, left his horse with a steward outside the gates, and hurried into the palace and to the war room.

Marvin gave the message from Handrian to the war council and told his detailed observation of the enemy forces. King Baracian talked to his generals, and then gave orders to the final legions he had kept in reserve on the palace grounds to join the forces on the west side of Mount Atlantis.

They emptied the armory of long, metal-tipped spears designed for mounted or charging riders. The bottom end of the spears had butt spikes, which stuck into the ground, holding them firm to impale charging animals. It would be their front line, but there would be few impaled animals. The spearmen would cast magic that would stop most animals before they reached the spears.

King Baracian decided to transfer command of the army to headquarters at the arch. He kissed his wife, Queen Elantria, goodbye. She was now in charge of the palace war room and the fleet. He accompanied Marvin out to the wharf with a bag full of maps. Marvin had the arch generate a portal from the wharf to the west slope. The two legions marched through the arch and joined the western forces.

Marvin then wove a portal to the arch and traveled to Mount Atlantis with King Baracian. They discussed the situation with King Vandian and King Handrian, before taking a portal to the western front. King Baracian greeted his generals. They would be controlling their legions, but he was going to be in charge of directing the battle. He discussed tactics with his generals.

The enemy was heading south towards Mount Atlantis on the west side of the island, avoiding the hilly territory towards the center of the island. King Baracian talked to Marvin. Shandria and Marvin both knew enough Alfarin magic to enchant zones that resisted the dark magic. It would take a couple of hours for the two of them to weave the magic, and another one or two for the magic to grow strong enough to be effective. They were given the go ahead.

Marvin wove a portal to get Shandria, and then he transported himself about two miles north of the army's position. The Army's close-in scouts were a half mile out from the army's position, northwest of Mount Atlantis. The Darfarin Army was five miles out. Marvin set up his wards in a staggered zigzag pattern, on large trees two miles out and 100 yards apart. The wards would interfere with the Darfarin's magic, slowing down the Darfarin advance. Shandria set up her wards closer in, a few hundred yards from the army's position, in a much denser pattern. Hers were also staggered and were designed to protect the infantry.

Two hours later, they had constructed over a hundred wards. Marvin and Shandria's magic was near depletion. Marvin used most of his remaining magic to portal back to the army. Shandria asked volunteers to help them recharge. The positive response was overwhelming.

They insisted on receiving only a few percent from each person. The soldier donating the magic would recharge to full in a couple of minutes. The volunteers supercharged Marvin and Shandria. They were both at over twice their normal magic potential. The magic would spill over if they didn't use it, much as Marvin's forge magic had spilled over to Shandria, what seemed like a long time ago. The two wove portals and reinforced some of the wards near the army, strengthening them with more magical energy.

The Atlantian forward scouts started their retreat after sunset. The ogres preferred to fight in the dark, and the Atlantians preferred daylight. An hour later, the herd of animals hit the first trip line of magic, where Marvin had woven the wards. Many animals became difficult to control. Others acted the same as always. Marvin's wards were merely a distraction to slow down and disrupt the Darfarin. It might buy them an extra hour or two, longer for Shandria's wards to grow and adapt, and longer for their allies to join them.

Marvin talked to the arch. The arch had been growing and learning. Marvin had it contact the palace and learn from the mature wards there. Then he had the arch teach the wards Shandria had set up to protect the soldiers.

Marvin had Shandria set up the second set of wards because she had fought against the magic when she had attacked the Darfarins in front of the palace. The ward on her amulet had grown and learned. When she wove her wards on the trees, they began stronger and more experienced than Marvin's wards.

The arch was a large source of magical energy. It had been actively growing, and it was significantly stronger than it had been only an hour ago. Marvin had the arch feed Shandria's wards magical energy.

Shandria's wards had to hold since they protected the army. The arch was supercharging her wards, teaching and accelerating their strength and maturation.

Defensive wards against magic acted like a glass wall. Different colored glass blocked different colors of light and lets others through. Initially, the color is faint, almost transparent, but as it grows and learns, the color becomes darker, and it blocks more magic. New wards are thin and fragile; they break easily. Mature wards are thicker, stronger, and as hard to break as steel armor. Shandria's wards were growing thicker, stronger, and less transparent with every passing minute.

The arch was growing and learning from the wards at the palace. It was powerful enough to spread out now, but Marvin wanted to hold it in reserve. If the Darfarins diverted around the wards and made a direct assault on Mount Atlantis, the ward on the arch would be ready. It would catch them by surprise. In a day, it would be robust enough to protect most of the Island of Atlantis. Marvin would love to have it wait and spread out all at once. It would catch the Darfarins by surprise and take away their dark magic from the Island. But he knew the Darfarins would attack tonight. And he would have to use it then.

Soon the Darfarin army had destroyed and passed through Marvin's wards, but the wards had served their purpose and delayed the Darfarins. They also had passed on information about their attack to the other wards, which had learned.

The Darfarin army reached Shandria's wards. They attacked them and tested their strength. The wards weakened a bit with each attack, but then grew back stronger. The Darfarin magic would attack, and the ward magic would adjust. Marvin knew a strong attack against the wards would destroy them. But they were probing rather than directly assaulting them. Each time they tested the wards, the wards grew stronger. The wards were slowing down the enemy's advance, working their way around the wards. It was what he had hoped. The arch registered every probe and resistance. It was learning from the encounter, and as it learned, it was instructing all the other wards.

Chapter 67

The standard Atlantian Legion was roughly 4000 soldiers, composed of 40 septia of 90 men. The septia was named after the septia, an ancient gold ring used for currency. It would pay ninety soldier's wages for a day. The remaining soldiers were field officers and logistical support staff. Each soldier wore a helmet, breastplate, shield, and a sword. In each septia, the first 30 men carried long spears as their primary weapon. The next 30 men carried Atlantian bows. The last 30 soldiers were the most senior soldiers, called the third line or just the third and they carried only their swords and shields. They filled in the gap when anyone else fell in combat, but primarily used magic for combat. Each septia was a self-contained fighting unit. But they were fighting as part of their legion, and the septias lined up side by side in their standard formation.

Each septia formation was five men wide and eighteen men deep, six rows of spearmen, six rows of archers, and six rows of the third. Combined to form the legion they were a solid line of 200 men across. There was a small gap between the spearmen and the archers, and another gap between the archers and the third.

It was starting to rain. The third had combined their magic to control the weather. Their magic condensed the natural high humidity in the ocean air, creating clouds and rain. Atlantian magic was water, wind, and sky. The water and the energy in the air added to the magic ability of the troops. It took a lot of energy to start the rain, but after that, it was easy to maintain. So much so that the magic reserves of the third would recharge to near normal in less than an hour. The energy in the air and rain increased the rate the soldier's magic recharged and reduced the energy to weave a spell.

The Darfarins started their attack by sending a herd of buffalo through the wards near the troops. Buffaloes were perhaps not a good pick for an assault through the woods. The Darfarins could no longer cast any dark spells on the animals since they were inside the arch warded area. But buffalo were herd animals, they would stay together, and the dark spell scars inside them made them violent, aggressive, and took away their self-preservation instincts. Thousands of buffalos burst through the woods into the clearing in front of the Atlantian legions.

ATLANTIAN MAGIC

The front row of the Atlantians lowered their spears. The spearmen shot powerful beams of energy at the animals heading towards them. The archer's magic enhanced arrows shot straight and true towards the buffalo. The third line shot magic enhanced ice lances and arrows of ice at the beasts. The arrows and the ice lances penetrated deep and released their energy. One shot one kill.

The back row of the third line wove a combination of loud, confusing sounds and bright flashing lights, which disoriented, dispersed, and slowed down much of the herd. But several-hundred buffalo made it through the magical assault. They crashed into the spears set up by the front line of troops. The spears mortally impaled them, but their momentum crashed them into the line of soldiers. Some soldiers were injured. A few died from the impact.

Marvin wanted to help, but his sword cautioned him to stay in reserve. The buffaloes were a probe to deplete their magic reserves, and they were successful. Marvin saw the magic reserve of the Atlantian legions had decreased.

Marvin mentioned it to King Baracian. The king said, "It's like the game of Soldiers and Knights, attack with the soldiers to weaken the enemy, and save the knights for later." Marvin was glad that Atlantians played a game similar to chess so he could understand the analogy. The animals were the pawns.

King Baracian had command of six legions. His legions were set up in a defensive hexagon pattern, three in the front, and three in the back, with the command and control structure in the center. One legion formed a straight line across on the enemy side. Then a legion on either flank angled backward to form the front half of the hexagon. A mirror of the front three legions completed the hexagon in back.

He had the three front legions exchange places with the back three. They would regroup and recover their strength during the next attack. The back three legions were from the eastern isle. Several other islands had sent legions also. The legions from the other islands were defending Mount Atlantis. King Handrian and his father, King Vandian, would be in charge of them. More would come as soon as the princes determined that their islands were not at risk of attack.

The second assault was much like the first, but it was a herd of wild boars. The boars were large, weighing several hundred pounds each. The boars weighed half as much as the buffalo, so their initial charge into the line of spearmen caused fewer spearmen injuries. But the boars were more aggressive by nature, and the dark magic made them even more so. The boars spun around, regrouped, and attacked again.

A large group attacked towards the left-front corner, which a previous herd had just weakened. Marvin used his Alfarin speed to sprint to the area. He wove a blast of lightning through his sword, killing the front boars, and shocking boars farther back. Many dispersed. The remaining boars hit the line of defenders. The spearmen would have stopped them if the animals spread out evenly, but they attacked at the same spot. Some broke through. Marvin sidestepped from in front of a charging boar and stabbed it in the side. He jumped back to the right, dropped low, and chopped through the knee of another boar.

Marvin's left hand came up, froze and exploded the head of a third boar. He advanced into the breach, sidestep, chop, slash, leap to the side, dodge, use magic, and repeat. Behind him, several of the third stepped up and closed the gap.

Marvin raced forward and soon found himself on the front line. The spearmen had all dropped their first spears, which had impaled boars, and were using their second spears or their swords. Many of the boars were still in their death throes. He heard the septians, the leaders of the septia, yelling orders to the formation to close ranks. The bowmen had changed to swords when the boars broke through ranks but now had gone back to their bows.

Marvin entered the gap between the two legions at the left corner. The boars were running around, forming into a herd, and then stampeding back into the line. Another group of boars formed. They swung around and charged towards him, and the weakened line behind him. Marvin wove magic and jumped. The sky magic he wove broke the bond between him and the earth. He was fifty feet in the air and rising.

He extended his sword and took control of the ionization in the air caused by the rain. His weave formed the ions together and created a large bolt of lightning. The lightning was far stronger than he could have generated himself. It struck the herd of boars, spread out on the ground, and killed the newly formed herd and many other boars in the vicinity. Others fell down from the electric shock. The flash and crash of the lightning temporarily deafened and blinded Marvin. His weave was ending, and his magic expenditure was high. He was of earth, and the earth regained control of his body. He landed hard, but without injury.

Marvin examined the dead boars and found the Darfarin had warped them with their dark spells, which explained some of their lack of fear and their aggressiveness. He was glad to see that the death of the boars killed the dark magic inside. He retreated behind the Atlantian lines.

The orchestrated attack by the boars ended, but they were still in the area. They reformed their herds and attacked, but the herds were small. The front line easily dispatched them.

King Baracian saw Marvin and placed his hand on his shoulder. Marvin felt some of his magical strength return. The king called over some of his advisers. He said, five percent. Each gave Marvin some magic. Marvin was close to 100 percent. He knew the rest would recharge quickly

Marvin asked the king what the overall strategy was. King Baracian said, "Ultimately they will have to assault the arch. We have brought the battle to the lowlands with our legions on the west side.

"If they tried to assault the mountain with us here, we would pivot and attack them from their flank. Our reserve legions would move in through a portal to protect the arch. If we weren't here, they would flood up the western side of the mountain, attacking the arch from the west and the north. Many of our vineyards, much of our fruit, and many Atlantians live near the western slope. The majority of the farmers have evacuated. But it is necessary for us to protect our fields and property. And this way, we determine the site of the battle, not the enemy."

King Baracian stopped talking. Marvin watched King Baracian's eyes glaze over. Marvin felt a type of sky magic he had never felt before coming from the king. The king said, "You and I are part of the power pieces on the game board. The enemy is strong, and they will fight hard to the end. Near the end, we will fight together at each other's side, to the limit of our wits, magic, and strength. How we will fare is closed to me."

Marvin watched the King's eyes turn back to normal. The king smiled when he saw the look on Marvin's face. He said, "On rare occasions, sky magic can pierce not only space like the portal, but it can pierce into the future. The future is much like a game of Soldiers and Knights. Each move leads to dozens more, but only a few key moves make sense. Each move allows one or more counter moves. Even a master can see only a couple moves into the future, and many of our choices obscure the future until we make them. Even looking into the future can change the future, because the knowledge will cause us to change what we do now, so the future compensates by hiding itself."

Marvin asked, "How much about me has the future revealed to you?"

The king smiled and replied, "Right idea wrong question. The real question is, 'What can I tell you about your future?' The answer is that I have told you all I can, or at least all I should. Knowing things changes what we will do. It restricts our choices, taking away free choice, and affects the future. There are things the future allowed me to know, and others I have guessed at, but which needs to be veiled from you for a time. If we survive this war, there are things that time will reveal to both of us. If we don't, then it won't matter. Until then we need to fight with strength and wisdom for our friends, family, companions, and for those whose lives we have vowed to serve and protect."

The king slapped Marvin on the back and left to talk to one of his generals. It reminded Marvin of the slaps of camaraderie and acceptance he received from the smiths at the Dwarven Forge.

Marvin yelled, "For Atlantis!"

He heard many of the troops around him echo his words.

Chapter 68

Marvin felt the Atlantian arch open up a portal. He asked the arch where it came from, then told King Baracian the portal was from Alfamara. As soon as the portal closed, the king opened a portal to the arch and traveled through with Marvin to greet the Alfarins.

Queen Juniperia had arrived with several hundred of her warriors. She greeted King Baracian and then hugged Marvin. Marvin talked to Queen Juniperia in Alfarin and then knelt down. Queen Juniperia placed her hand on his head. Images since the beginning of the battle flooded Marvin's brain, and into the brain of the queen. Marvin was glad he had knelt down. It took him several seconds to come back to his normal senses and to regain his balance after he had given her the battle information.

The queen was holding hands with the man next to her. He had also received Marvin's report. He said a few tactical commands to the Alfarin troops and they disappeared into the trees and bushes north of Mount Atlantis. The queen introduced the man next to her as the General of Alfamara. The title she used for general implied he was the bonded husband of the queen. Marvin was surprised he had never met him before. It was obvious looking back, but he never realized the queen was married, or in Alfarin terms, had a lifelong bond.

She turned towards King Baracian and said. "Our warriors will do what they can."

King Baracian ordered a command tent to be set up for the general. He turned back towards Queen Juniperia and said, "We thank you for your assistance. Let me, my generals, or any of my officers know if you have any needs and we will do our best to help you."

She thanked the King and asked Marvin, "May I instruct your arch crystal?"

Marvin saw King Baracian nod his head. Marvin smiled at the queen and held out his arm for her to take. They closed their eyes and joined each other in a conversation with the arch.

Marvin was impressed at the level of magic the queen was communicating to the protection ward. The ward Marvin wove was like a first-year band student playing a recorder. His ward had matured to the level of a horn in the band. It had grown as much as it could from Marvin's level of Alfarin magic. However, Queen Juniperia was a grandmaster. She wove in the instructions, and the ward soon became like a complete symphony of instruments. Marvin pulled his sword from its sheath and raised it into the air. Many around him raised theirs also.

He felt the magical energy from the swords flowing into his sword from the volunteers who had raised their swords. The magical energy helped power the Queen's weave. The ward grew in strength and power. After a few minutes, the energy flow stopped and then reversed. Everyone received their energy back. The arch didn't need the energy. It just needed the information carried by the energy.

Marvin sheathed his sword. He still held hands with the queen. They ended their conversation with the arch.

She looked at Marvin and smiled. "I am proud of how well you have learned and are using the magic we taught you." She hugged Marvin, reached up and pulled his head down. She kissed him on the forehead and said. "Visit when you can."

He replied, "Yes grandmother."

The queen said in Atlantian for all to hear. "Duties call. I must return to my home." Marvin opened a portal for her back to Alfamara. The queen walked through the portal back to her home.

Marvin noticed that the Alfarin warriors had brought dozens of heavy wooden crates of supplies. King Baracian said, "Marvin, I have to get back to my legions. Make sure our guests are at home. Return west when you think it is prudent."

Marvin replied, "Yes my king."

King Baracian opened up a portal through the arch and returned to his legions.

The Alfarin general asked the Atlantian quartermaster to store the Alfarin provisions in the back of his tent. The Atlantian quartermasters couldn't read the marks on the boxes and were troubled that they couldn't sort them. The Alfarin general laughed and said, "Even if I translated them you wouldn't be able to sort them. Just stack them in my tent."

Marvin, Shandria, Handrian, and Alandria met with the General of Alfamara, along with Queen Isaria, and King Vandian. The general was confident his warriors would be a help against the Darfarins. The longer the battle continued, the more efficient the Alfarins became. They were not defensive warriors, they were masters at infiltration and information gathering. Their hit and run tactics were hard to stop, especially once they had entered the field of battle. Their magic quickly learned of any defensive measure the enemy created and helped them to avoid it or to turn it against the enemy. Soon, the general would know much of the Darfarin troop placement, type, strength, movement, and battle plans.

The Alfarin general walked to the command tent and met with the Atlantians. They discussed the battle plan, and contingencies based on what the enemy did. The general suggested a different placement of the archers. The enemy would be coming from the north, slightly to the west. Their main force would assault the troops at that point. Moving the archers out of that direct path, more to the east, would allow them to be out from the main thrust, and enable them to do more damage against the flank of the enemy.

One of the Atlantian generals disagreed with him. The General of Alfamara replied that he had similar discussions with other Atlantian kings and generals during other wars for the last few thousand years. Marvin knew the Alfarins had a long lifespan, but only now did Marvin realized the general had commanded the forces of the Alfarins since before the time of ancient Rome. That meant that Queen Juniperia was several Millennia older than Marvin had guessed. The Atlantian general yielded to the Alfarin general and doubled up the archers on the east side.

Then the portal opened again. It was from Crystal Mountain.

King Feldspar arrived with a dozen of his honor guard. Behind him were several crates of swords. Marvin's magic leaped as the magical swords greeted him. A thousand Dwarven axmen came through next. King Feldspar yelled. "It is always good to fight alongside our friends!" His troops raised their battle-axes and started shouting. Soon the armies of the Atlantians were shouting too.

The portal closed down. Shandria exited the command tent followed by Alandria and Handrian.

King Feldspar saw the new armor on Marvin. The king walked over and gave Marvin a forearm-shake and a hug with his other arm. He said to Marvin. "Finally, my son, you have reunited the armor and the sword. I know they missed each other so." Marvin saw a tear in the king's eye.

The King saw Shandria in her new armor. He gave her a full hug and kissed her cheek. He said, "Another pair reunited."

Marvin wasn't sure whether he was talking about Shandria and her armor, or their two sets of armor.

He greeted Handrian with a forearm shake and said, "I knew you were destined for that armor. I'm glad you found your heart."

Then he gave Alandria a hug and said, "I'm glad you listened to your heart." He kissed her on the cheek.

Alandria was surprised at the kiss, but then she smiled and said in Dwarven, "Thank you, my father." It was an honorific used for a respected elder or beloved parent. Alandria had no doubt that their armor had told King Feldspar all he needed to know about the healing of their relationship.

King Feldspar spoke to Queen Isaria, and King Vandian. Then he greeted the Alfarin general. They had battled alongside each other many times in the distant past. Their tactics were as different as could be, and they had learned to complement each other well.

Marvin was enjoying the excitement of the swords as they greeted their enchanter. The experience overwhelmed him. The axes carried by the Dwarves were also singing. He had enchanted some of them, and they were greeting him also.

King Feldspar broke Marvin's communion with the weapons. Marvin asked him, "How did we enchant so many swords and axes?"

King Feldspar smiled and said, "Several long days, a hundred weapons masters, three hundred forge masters, several hundred apprentices, countless barrels of mead, and one gifted Atlantian to enchant them. You knew your magic was branching to the other forges. You left, but the metal was kept hot, and the magic was nurtured, hammered, fired and crafted before the metal was quenched. I know you have many questions about the process. I look forward to our talking or better yet showing you and teaching you. But for now, I need you to open a portal to King Baracian for my men and me."

Then King Feldspar called Shandria over. "Princess Shandria, Princess Amethyst is waiting to bring her troops over after I have joined with King Baracian. I'm sure she would love you to escort her across."

Shandria smiled and dipped her head in respect.

Marvin looked at the field where King Baracian was and verified there were no active battles. He opened the portal for the Dwarves and King Feldspar to King Baracian.

The Dwarves brought three thousand swords with them through the arch, minus the hundred they had given to Marvin for the sea battle. King Vandian distributed a thousand swords among the troops on top of the mountain. He sent a thousand with King Feldspar to the western front. He sent the remaining swords back under guard to the palace along with a message to store them in the protected armory. King Feldspar said they were finishing the final thousand swords and they should be ready soon.

King Feldspar had left his honor guard to escort Shandria back through the portal. Shandria opened the portal again and left for Crystal Mountain. Soon she returned with Princess Amethyst and a legion of ax-wielding Dwarven women with crossbows slung across their backs. Countless horse-drawn carts filled with provisions followed them through the arch.

Princess Amethyst hugged Marvin and congratulated him on completing his set with his new armor. It was the first time Marvin had seen her wearing full Dwarven battle armor and carrying her ancient battle-ax. He smiled and teased, "I thought Dwarven women protected the home."

She smiled and replied, "Are we not protecting the home of our friends? Besides, we can't let the men have all the fun."

Marvin laughed, and she laughed with him. Marvin and Shandria escorted her to the command tent where she hugged Handrian and Alandria, then she commented on their married pair of armor. She was excited for the two of them.

The Atlantian army quartermaster and his assistants tried to figure out where to put the Dwarven carts. They were happy when they found out most of them were provisions for the refugees, and that much of the rest could be stored on the palace grounds and moved into the field if needed to support the Dwarven army. Queen Isaria opened a portal to the wharves, and escorted the provisions to the palace, along with an Atlantian quartermaster and two Dwarven quartermasters.

They assigned and reordered their armies. It looked like the plan King Feldspar had shared with Marvin in his war room.

Two Alfarins appeared in the command tent. They conversed with the General of Alfamara. Marvin followed their discussion and learned a few Alfarin tactical terms he had never heard before.

The general said in Atlantian, "The enemy is on the move. Many of their scouts are now dead. The Enemy suspects we have joined the defense. They were planning to move more of the troops attacking the cities southward, to harass and deplete the Atlantian resolve and magic, then attack with their elite troops. Now that we are here, they feel forced to rush their attack. So, they will attack soon, but many of their troops will remain up north, so their attack will be weakened."

He turned to Marvin and said in Alfarin. "Carry what you heard to King Baracian. My warriors know you and feel comfortable with you and will report their intelligence to you."

Marvin replied in Alfarin. "Yes, general."

He turned to the rest of the command tent and said. "I am leaving to carry the scouting report to King Baracian. Battle well!"

Everyone in the tent replied, "Battle well!"

Marvin saw the General of Alfamara leave the tent and head down the mountain. He had a minor concealment weave on him. Marvin knew that no one else saw him. Marvin was sure he wanted Marvin to see him go. If he wanted to stay hidden, he would have used a stronger weave. The general was not a man to sit in a tent while his troops were in the field. Marvin was sure he was teaching him leadership by doing.

Chapter 69

Marvin walked through the portal and arrived at the western front. He gave the scouting report to King Baracian and King Feldspar. "There are herds of large double horned animals heading our way. Behind them are mastodons, followed by ogres and the Darfarins and their magic.

"They will start the assault on Mount Atlantis at the same time. But it will take two more hours for the battle on Mount Atlantis to happen due to the uphill climb. They are using different animals, giant lizards and wolves, followed by ogres and more magic."

King Feldspar and King Baracian tried helping Marvin's translation magic along by naming animals that fit his descriptions. The horned animals were a species of two horned antelopes. King Baracian said, "Their herds are nonaggressive unless their young are in danger, then they defend their herd with three-foot-long horns. But the Darfarins have perverted their protective instinct into offensive aggression ."

No one had any idea what the giant lizards were.

Marvin heard many of the outer lines of wards cry as the Darfarin assault broken through. It was time to activate the arch ward to spread and cover the western legions. It would take a few minutes for the magic to spread to the western wards. Marvin could feel the arch's power growing with each passing second. Marvin listened to the heartbeat of the arch. Each beat provided more energy to the wards around them. Shandria's wards were near their maximum strength when the concentrated Darfarin magic hit them.

The wards were strong and initially held against the attack, but then the first one failed. The second one had learned from the first one, and it lasted longer, but not by much. Too much energy would overwhelm a small ward. Handrian's necklace exploding on the ship had shown that in graphic detail.

But Marvin was playing a chess game. The Darfarins didn't have unlimited magic either. They would stop depleting their magic if it had no effect. He heard the cries of a couple of wards as they failed. As soon as the next couple broke, he had the Arch slowly spread its ward forward like thick syrup spreading from a spill. The slower it spread, the thicker and stronger it would be. Three more wards failed before the arch magic spread and protected them.

Pd MICHEL

The Darfarins stopped attacking the wards once they discovered they could no longer break them. Marvin doubted any dark spell could penetrate Queen Juniperia's wards. There was no reason to keep the arch magic hidden any longer.

He asked the arch to expand and cover the whole island, keeping the leading edge at full power. The arch crystal drew its energy from both the sky and the earth. The crystal was growing in maturity and power. It spread its roots deeper into the earth, following the magic paths already established from the original arch. It was dozens of times stronger than when it had failed just a few hours ago. Even a sustained attack from the Darfarins could not break through the arch's ward.

They maintained the same hexagon shaped formation as before, but behind the spearmen, they placed the Dwarven axmen. They positioned themselves so that King Feldspar took a prominent place in the center of the front line.

After the initial attack, the spearman would fall to the rear, and the Dwarven axmen would advance. The axmen operated in groups of four, with two men in the front, and two in the rear. The four soldiers, if isolated, would form into a square with one man at each corner. But, as long as they were in a column formation, the front axmen would alternate with the rear axmen, keeping each of them from getting exhausted.

Spears were thrusting weapons, but battle-axes were slashing weapons. The Dwarves needed the extra room to swing their axes. To increase the distance further between weapons, every other row of battle-axes would step backward, creating a zigzag pattern of axes. After a battle, the second row would advance, and the first row would retreat and regroup if needed.

Marvin took up position near the corner of the left flank. Baracian took up position near the corner of the right flank.

The herd of antelope charged through the forest, horns down. Once again, the Atlantians met them with weaves of flashing lights and loud distracting sounds. Some of the antelope stopped or ran to the sides, but most charged straight towards the soldiers. The blue streaks of arrows once again found their marks, killing the antelope. The dead Antelope's heads dropped down when they died. Their antlers dug into the ground, and the running animals tumbled over onto their backs.

Blue light beams from the spears cut into the herd. Most of the antelope that made it by the energy beams were impaled by the spearmen. But some made it past the line of spears.

Marvin saw one run past the spearmen. King Feldspar jumped in front of it. Marvin was sure the sharp horns of the beast would impale the king.

But King Feldspar had a different agenda. Marvin saw him grab ahold of both horns, one with each hand and lean forward. There was no way any physical force was going to break the grip of a grandmaster of the Dwarven Forge. He held on, and the animal pushed him back. He dug his feet in and slowed the charging animal to a stop. Then he spread his arms apart. The antler in his right

320

hand gave way and broke off the side of the antelope's head. He dropped the horn, put his hand near the animal's head and wove Dwarven fire to kill the antelope.

Marvin stood speechless at the strength of the king. He heard him yell in Dwarven, "Axmen to the front." Then he yelled in Atlantian, "Spearmen regroup!" King Baracian repeated the order. Each legion had men with signal horns. They blew their horns, sounding the commanded pattern. Without missing a step, King Feldspar ran past the retreating spearmen and took up position for the next charge. A few of the spearmen took longer to fall back, helping injured soldiers back to safety.

Dwarven axmen met the next charge of antelope, swinging their axes. Their timing was flawless and their axes enchanted. Single slashes of the axes killed most of the beasts. Repeated swings took out the ones who were still alive. Marvin was impressed at the quick movements of the axmen. They struck quick and quickly repositioned themselves for the next animal.

A few of the Dwarves didn't fare as well as their king had, but their magical armor and the metal weaves on their clothing protected all but a few of them from injury. The second man in each square helped the front man; some of the Dwarves were wrestling four-hundred-pound antelopes off their bodies.

King Feldspar yelled, "Axmen regroup!" The axmen fell back to their protective position behind the spearmen, taking their wounded friends with them.

For the next hour the attacks continued, they were small, random, and disorganized. The Atlantians recovered most of their spears. Some were broken. Marvin used wood magic to repair a few of the spears. A few of the spearmen caught on and finished the work on the rest. It may be wood magic, but it was a basic weave. Marvin wondered why the spearmen didn't already know it.

Every legion has a scribe. Marvin turned to one to record that he wanted the generals to look into teaching the spearman enough wood magic to repair their spears.

The scouts reported mastodons were approaching. Some had ogres riding on their shoulders.

King Baracian ordered the legions into compacted line formation. The lines narrowed. They now had nine men across. King Feldspar had his men form a line in front of the legions. He yelled a Dwarven word, which translated as a battle trench.

Marvin watched depressions form in front of the line of Dwarves. The Dwarven magic dug a long eight-foot-wide, eight-foot-deep trench. King Feldspar yelled, "Camouflage cover."

A thin shell of dirt, the consistency of brittle sandstone, formed a cover over the trench. He had his men split, and form trenches that wrapped around the sides of the formation. Then he had his men do the same in the back. The battle trenches encircled the legions thirty yards out from their formation.

The Dwarves regrouped to the back of the front legions. The tactics had changed. They didn't want to disperse the Mastodons as much as they wanted them to charge straight ahead into the pits. It was a good thing too. Most of the Atlantian soldiers were down to less than a half of their magic reserves. It would take hours to recharge. The Dwarves had used little of their magic. It would soon restore itself. But waiting for magic to recharge during combat wasn't a Dwarven trait.

King Feldspar started humming. The rest of the Dwarves followed him. Soon they were singing. It was a song of battle. Marvin was enjoying the song and picked up the rhythm. It was the rhythm of the forge. Marvin started to hum. With each beat of the music, he could feel the magic of the forge. It was the magic of building, forming, shaping, and of making. Marvin felt his magic level top off and overflow. The Dwarves were soon topped off, and magic was overflowing to the Atlantian troops around them.

Few Atlantians had ever heard the song of the forge. Marvin realized even now, few of the Atlantians around him heard more than the Dwarven singing, but he saw a few joining in. Their rhythm was in tune with the magic. The rhythm of the forge mesmerized them in its simplicity and completeness. He watched their magic levels spike. Their spillover magic recharged the people around them, adding other ten percent to their reserves.

Then it finally dawned on Marvin. The rhythm of the forge was not just a Dwarven chant for timing; it was a prayer to the Forge Master himself. And the magical increase was his response to the prayer. Marvin looked up and said thank you.

Marvin looked at King Baracian. He saw that the king's energy level had spiked also. They exchanged a smile as the Mastodons came stomping through the trees.

Chapter 70

King Baracian gave a command, and the battle horns sounded. The third wove some flashing lights and noises above the mastodons. The flashes made them angry, and the herd charged. The ogres on the lead animals whipped them with their spiked clubs and added to their furry

Marvin remembered reading elephants could sprint for over 25 miles an hour. Looking at a charging Mammoth running towards him, he was sure it was faster. It sure looked faster. But twenty-five miles an hour is fast enough to total a car. He watched the lead mammoth's front legs disappear as his stride broke through the thin shell of dirt that covered the top of the trench. He heard a sickening crunch. The leg bones snapped as the mammoth's leg dropped into and then hit the far side of the trench, propelled by tons of momentum. Hundreds of mammoths broke their legs and met their fate in that initial charge. Even if the mammoths hadn't been injured, their enormous weight made it impossible for them to climb their front legs out of the pit.

The remaining mammoths came at them from other sides of the formation. Marvin saw one mammoth try stepping between the bodies of two others. It stepped on the top of the hidden trench and become its next victim.

The sound of crippled and dying mammoths would haunt Marvin for many years, even though he realized the tactics had saved the lives of hundreds of Atlantians and Dwarves. With each battle, Marvin realized more and more he wasn't in Phoenix anymore.

He pushed his feelings to the side as a wave of ogres attacked. They ran as fast as the Mammoths. The Atlantian magic flared up again. Lances of energy sped forth from the tips of spears. Marvin listened to the sound of the war horns. The horns blew in a regular cadence. There were three different frequencies. Each frequency corresponded to each of the front legions.

Marvin watched the spearmen. In the compact formation, they were six men deep. The horn would blow, and the front line would shoot a lance of energy then kneel down. The second line would fire on the sound of the second horn then they would kneel down. Then the third line would fire and kneel. It would continue until the last line fired. A double blast from the horns and the spearmen would stand up again ready to repeat the cycle.

The bodies of ogres piled up behind the struggling mammoths in the trenches. Few made it past the animals. The trumpeters slowed their horn-blowing cadence to once every few seconds. A sustained blast of the horns made all the spearmen kneel. Any ogres or mammoths would be alone or in small groups. Bowmen killed the last few ogres.

There was a temporary pause in the battle. More horns sounded. The three legions in front retreated to the rear, and the legions in the rear took up positions in the front. Marvin was going to leave the formation with the intent of putting the dying Mammoths out of their misery when more ogres appeared. Behind the ogres were magic wielding Darfarins. It was a full-on charge.

The Darfarin's dark magic spells turned to smoke and dissipated. The arch's magical ward protected the soldiers. Once again, the war horns sounded. The first rank of spearmen lanced out with their energy lances. The Darfarin wove magic, and the Atlantian magic had no effect.

Darfarins were masters of the dark spells, but they also used other magic. Marvin yelled, "Use arrows." Marvin's order caused confusion. Then King Baracian yelled out a military order.

The war horns sounded, and the spearmen knelt down and set their spears. He yelled out another order. The horns blew a sequence of several long and short blasts. Then they blew a blast, and the first rank of bowmen shot their arrows. The arrows turned to blue energy. When they hit the Darfarin anti-magic ward, they turned back into arrows and burst into flames. They struck their targets and exploded.

Marvin looked at the Darfarin magical wards. They were of a frequency he couldn't affect with his magic. He was like an alto trying to sing base. The Darfarin's were changing their wards to adapt to the Atlantian magic. Several more volleys of arrows fired through the wards and found their marks. Then a volley flew through the wards but didn't burst into flame. The next volley of arrows turned into dust. Marvin heard King Baracian yell an order.

The horns sounded. The first volley was inaccurate. The second one was better. The Darfarin magic had no effect on the non-enchanted arrows. But it was no longer one shot one kill. Marvin figured far fewer than half were reaching their mark and a smaller percentage than that were fatal or serious wounds. Marvin ran back to King Baracian. They would soon run out of arrows. They needed to conserve their arrows for closer shots.

The king commanded, "Bowmen Cease Fire." The trumpets sounded a series of long and short blasts.

The long and short blasts reminded Marvin of Morse code. He knew he would have to learn the codes and the formations. He had so much to learn.

King Baracian gave some orders to the generals and called a conference of Marvin and King Feldspar.

They watched the ogres walk forward to the trenches where the mammoths were struggling. The Darfarins were hiding behind them. The arrows without magic were ineffective against the thick hide of the ogres. The ogres were more afraid of the Darfarins behind them than they were of the sting from the non-magic arrows.

Marvin talked to King Feldspar and King Baracian. The Dwarves raised their magical axes. King Feldspar raised his. Marvin could see magic flow into King Feldspar's ax. His ax started to glow red hot, then white hot. Marvin saw King Feldspar nodding his head towards him. Marvin once again jumped into the sky and left the bonds of earth behind. He raised his sword. He looked to his side and saw King Baracian did the same thing on the opposite flank of the hexagon formation.

The fire magic of the Dwarves, hot enough to melt metal, flowed into Marvin and King Baracian's swords. Marvin and King Baracian projected it into the forest where the Darfarins were with a sweeping motion. The forest burst into flames. Then they projected the fire into the trenches with the dead and dying animals. The Darfarins and ogres found themselves caught between the fire in the trenches and the fire in the woods. Marvin and Baracian released the last of their energy into the center of the group. They stopped the flow of energy to their swords and descended back behind the line. The Dwarves shot the remaining fire of their axes into the ogres and Darfarins who had somehow survived between the two conflagrations. It was a grisly barbeque. The dead animals from the previous attacks were on fire.

A wind controlled by the third kept the thick smoke of the burning bodies away from the legions.

The fire was so hot the general ordered his front legions to fall back. King Feldspar and his Dwarves stood in front of the legions. They had nothing to fear from fire. They looked at the Atlantians hunched down behind their shields. At least most of them were. Many had learned enough fire magic that they could resist. King Feldspar laughed. Then he had his men weave magic to deflect the heat away from the legions. The rain falling from the sky cooled down the Atlantian army. But the fire was too hot, and the rain evaporated before it hit the ground. Marvin walked over to the scribe and said, "Have the generals discuss teaching the soldiers fire protection weaves."

The excursion into the sky would have drained Marvin's magic except the Dwarven magic had supercharged him. It became easier each time he left the bonds of earth. He was finding his balance quicker and not spending as much energy to maintain it. The sky was starting to think of him as a friend, and the earth was less jealous of letting him go. It knew Marvin would return soon.

Half a dozen Alfarins appeared near him. If he had been paying attention, he might have seen them enter, but no one else would have. They hurried straight towards him. He talked to them and walked back towards King Feldspar and King Baracian. The fire had killed almost all the Darfarins in the area. There was still a few running away, as well as ogres and different animals, but they were no direct threat. The assault on Mount Atlantis had begun. And they needed the help. Marvin asked the Alfarins if they could help with the wounded.

They were happy to help. But the Alfarin concept of help was different than anyone except Marvin expected. It would be easy for them to heal the cuts scrapes, bruises, and broken bones. They ignored them and healed the deeper life-threatening punctures and lacerations. Then they taught the senior soldiers the weaves to heal the less severe injuries.

Alfarins traveled in small groups. Accidents occasionally happened. They viewed an accident as an opportunity to teach someone a new healing weave. Alfarins had no problem letting someone, or even themselves be injured for days so someone new could practice a new healing weave. Someday the knowledge would save their life or the life of someone they loved, so it was worth the pain and discomfort so someone would learn how to heal and could save a life.

Marvin opened a portal to Mount Atlantis.

Chapter 71

Marvin took one look at the battle. Hundreds of Atlantian soldiers lie on the ground, either injured or dead. The lizards no Atlantian had a name for Marvin did, velociraptor. They stood as tall as an Atlantian, although much longer counting the tail, and they were fast. Unlike the herding animals they faced on the west slope, they were predators. The Darfarins had set their natural aggression to high and removed their self-preservation instinct.

The velociraptors had breached the Atlantian line. Marvin saw Alandria jump into the breach. Handrian did too, leaving the control of the battle to his father and mother.

Shandria was using her knights to attack and disrupt the velociraptors. But they were a tough adversary even for the knights.

Marvin ran to an area where raptors were attacking. He wove magic with his fingers spread, and a fan of branching lightning leaped from his fingers and killed a group of raptors. It saved the lives of several dozen troops by giving them time to reform. He stepped in and disemboweled another one. Step, slash, stab, dodge, and cut, then he ran to the next area and did it again with another pack of raptors. Marvin saw raptors had one major weakness in their attack. They fixated on a target. So, as they assaulted a group of Dwarves, Marvin ramped up his speed magic and attacked their flank until they dispersed.

Marvin's muscles were fatigued, and he was breathing hard. He hurried back behind the lines to catch his breath. It gave him a minute to watch Handrian and Alandria. They were amazing. They were holding off a large pack of charging raptors. They fought side by side, then back to back, then side by side again. Forward, stab, sidestep slash, spin left, shield bash, stab above the shield, stab below the shield. They were moving fast. Marvin caught his breath and watched them dance, for a dance it was. It was lethal but beautiful. Their swords and armor were fighting as one. And Marvin could see that Alandria was using the speed magic Shandria had taught her, and it was covering both of them.

Marvin saw how exhausted Handrian and Alandria were becoming. Muscle fatigue was slowing them down. Nothing in a battle is a marathon. It's a series of sprints separated by periods of recovery. Every dodge and attack were at full power and strength. Otherwise, it could be the last. They needed time to recover.

Then another large pack of raptors came at them. Marvin had taken the edge off his fatigue. He jumped over the line and engaged the raptors from the side at his maximum sustainable speed. There were too many, yet his sword said to wait and not use a magical attack. Then he saw Shandria ride out and crash into a group of raptors with her knights. The knights withdrew, and she leaped off her horse. Her horse retreated and reformed with the knights. She ran to the other side of the line of raptors from Marvin. And their swords found each other.

Their swords and armor were a bonded pair, just like Handrian and Alandria's armor. The swords combined Marvin and Sharia's abilities and gave them a strategy. They attacked the raptors that were attacking their friends from opposite flanks.

Marvin felt his magic resonate with Shandria's magic, and they kicked up their Alfarin speed magic to its maximum safe level and waded into the raptors.

The two of them pinched the pack together and cut them off from their attempt to get to their friends. Slash, sidestep, jump left slash, spin, back together, strike forward strike to the side. The raptor pack now fixated on Marvin and Shandria as their target. Alandria and Handrian stood by, breathing hard and giving their bodies time to recover.

The Alfarin speed magic was strengthening Marvin and Shandria's bodies. Their hearts were beating as fast as a hummingbird; their lungs were inhaling and exhaling a hundred times a minute. And yet their muscles were demanding more oxygen and nutrients than their speeded-up bodies could provide. They had reached physical limits the magic couldn't augment and overcome. And they were operating past them. Alandria and Handrian jumped back into the fight. Shandria and Marvin took a step back to recover.

Marvin and Shandria needed time to allow the Alfarin magic to speed recover their bodies. They watched Alandria and Handrian fight. Then the raptors dispersed and gave them a temporary respite. They returned to the lines, which their attack had given time to reform.

Marvin positioned himself in back on the left flank. Raptor blood covered Marvin. He flicked his sword, and the sword cleaned itself. The rain was washing away the blood from the rest of his clothing. He raised his sword and felt the energy flow from somewhere and topped off his magic reserves.

Marvin closed his eyes. He had seen all he needed to see with his eyes open. Their physical bodies needed time to recover. The troops were exhausted. But his magic was full and ready.

The velociraptors were reforming and about to attack again. And they were together in a large group. Now was the time. Marvin raised his sword into the sky and jumped, releasing earth's hold on him, and grabbing hold of the sky.

The rain had ionized the air. Marvin formed the energetic ions into a bolt of lightning and unleashed its fury into the center of the raptors. The energy of the lighting came from the air. It took far less magical energy for Marvin to collect the ions and form lightning bolts than it did to generate the bolts from his own magic. He repeatedly organized and directed the resulting lightning. Fingers of the bolts hit and spread out on the ground, killing large areas of the enemy.

The sky magic was starting to consider Marvin as a friend. It was easier for Marvin to perform magic. Marvin drifted higher and higher. Or was the sky pulling him? He needed to be in the sky to use the lightning of the sky, but he was using his magic fast and was concentrated on his weaves. He suddenly realized he had used up all his magical energy collecting the ions and producing the lightning bolts, and he was two hundred feet above Mount Atlantis. He no longer had the magical energy to hold onto the sky, and the earth was calling him back. He started to fall.

Then he felt his magic increase, but it wasn't through his ancient sword. The magic flowed from the dagger strapped to his leg.

Princess Amethyst had lost her link to him when he left the Earth. She found him again through her dagger's link to his dagger and when she saw him fall she focused the remainder of her energy to him. It wasn't enough to weave sky magic, but it was sufficient to weave an updraft to slow his descent and to blow him towards the top of a tree. He fell through branches that broke and slowed his descent.

Marvin hit the ground and would smell like a forest for a week, but other than a few scrapes and bruises, his armor and his cloak had protected him from the fall. His armor was quick to point out that it had done the protecting. Marvin wasn't one hundred percent convinced, but he was still learning his armor's abilities. He was coming to realize that his breastplate's protective qualities didn't stop just because the metal did. He was thankful for his armor and let him know. He was exposed and in the open. He ran as fast as he could without the assistance of speed magic and made it safely behind the Atlantian lines.

Marvin was now emotionally, physically, and magically exhausted. He walked back to the tents looking for some nourishment. He saw the Dwarven mead tent. The Dwarves saw how drained he was and several of them gave him strength. Someone handed him a full mug. He raised it in the air and said, "To King Feldspar, the Atlantian Court, the Alfarins, and the eternal friendship of Atlantians and Dwarves." He quickly downed the small mug of mead. He found a pitcher of water and drank most of it before exiting the tent.

King Baracian was directing the reforming of the army. He stopped when he saw Marvin walking over from the Dwarven mead tent. The king pulled a leaf from Marvin's hair and joked. "It's a good thing you have the metabolism of a Dwarf or I would have to put you on report for drinking during a battle."

Baracian laughed and continued. "I know your Dwarven fire magic will convert that mead straight to magical energy and give you the sugars your body needs. You are removed from any restrictions."

Then in a lower voice and with a smile, he said, "How I envy that metabolism right now. You expended a lot of physical as well as magical energy. Your body needs food. Take five, get some grub, and find me."

Marvin headed for the Atlantian mess tent but changed his direction when he saw the General of Alfamara wave at him from his tent. The general invited him in and said, "I know the king gave you five minutes to eat something and speed magic burns a lot of energy." He pulled out a sack and handed it to Marvin. He said, "Some Alfarin war cakes."

Marvin asked, "Why are you so familiar yet we never met?"

The general replied. "I joined you and Shandria in the healing pods, or the green goo, as you call it, and taught you your Alfarin magic. In exchange, I absorbed much about you, Earth, the princess, and Atlantis. I am proud to call you my student, but you still have much to learn to reach your potential in our magic.

"You have been pushing your speed magic to faster speeds and moves that are more energetic than we did in the short period we had to train you. Your body's energy expenditure is exponential as you go up in speed and you need to restore that energy as quickly as possible, or your body will start to consume your muscle, shut down, and you will fall unconscious. Eat one of these and have Princess Amethyst and each member of the Atlantian Court eat one. Then make sure everyone grabs a large meal as soon as they can. Your five minutes are almost up." The general stood up and offered his hand to Marvin. He said, "You can call me Grandfather."

Marvin smiled, shook hands, which turned into a hug, and exited his tent.

He ate one of the cakes and felt an almost immediate boost in his energy level. The fatigue in his muscles disappeared. He saw Princess Amethyst. It looked like she had given him the last of her magical energy to save his life. He gave her one and saw her energy level quickly rise. Marvin thanked her for saving his life. She smiled and replied, "You killed the velociraptors that were going to eat my soldiers and me alive. So, I guess we are even."

Marvin smiled, bowed low, and said, "Always a pleasure to serve princess."

He found and fed the rest of the royal party. They were all low on magic and ate the cakes Marvin gave them. The bag held just enough cakes for the party. Marvin jokingly wondered if the Alfarins made their cakes out of senzu beans.

King Vandian looked tired, but Marvin could see him recovering as he ate the war cake. He had been running back and forth across the lines yelling orders and reinforcing areas with his magic.

Marvin could hear the Dwarves singing one of their battle songs. The large wolves he had mentioned had an Atlantian name. They were dire wolves, bigger, faster, stronger, aggressive, and without a doubt warped to be more aggressive than normal by Darfarin dark spells. They knew the Darfarins were sending their best team of spellcasters and ogres to take the mountain.

Marvin wondered why the mountain had no fortification. Then he realized why. Atlantis was a peaceful society. No one had attacked the arch area since it left Earth, and that was right after they built it. He called over the nearest scribe and said, "Have the generals discuss fortifying the arch area."

For now, maybe they could have the Dwarves dig some trenches or foxholes near the top of the mountain. It would provide some defense, and it might give them a tactical advantage against the dire wolves. Marvin mentioned it. King Feldspar loved the security of rock and earth. He thought it was an excellent idea, He would have preferred a maze of walls and battlements, but they didn't have the time, and magical energy was at a premium. But any Dwarven child could dig holes all day long. He set his men to weave the magic to form trenches.

It was well past midnight. Marvin had eaten a large meal, and a half-hour later was starving and eating another meal. Shandria, Alandria, and Handrian's bodies were in a similar condition. Legion support personnel had delivered battle rations. They were high calorie and nutritious. It was just what they needed.

Marvin looked at the magic level of the troops. The Atlantian troops were exhausted. Almost everyone was low on magical energy. Even Princess Amethyst's Dwarves were below fifty percent after drinking mead and singing their battle songs.

The Dwarves under King Feldspar were doing better, but not by much. King Baracian brought over the strongest Atlantian legions with him. He felt it was important to protect the west side and to let the other legions recover their magic. Fortunately, several fresh legions had arrived from the other islands. King Baracian, King Vandian, and the generals were running ragged organizing the new legions into defensive positions.

Shandria found Marvin resting alone in a foxhole with his hood pulled over his head. Shandria was alert and wide-awake just like Marvin. Whether it was a side effect or a designed effect of the Alfarin war cakes she didn't know. She hopped into the foxhole and handed him a banana. She had found a sack of sweet cakes from somewhere and shared them. "You look like you either need to be alone, or you need company." she said, "Let me know which."

Marvin replied, "I'm not sure what I need and doubt it's available on a battlefield. But whether I'm quiet with you, or conversing with you, I know I'm better off with your company."

Shandria smiled and sat down next to Marvin. She took off her helmet and shifted her body, so her head was lying on his arm. They both munched on their fruit and then started eating the sweet cakes.

Shandria said, "We're not at the palace, so I guess it is okay for me to be with my sworn companion and protector."

Marvin replied, "A wide-awake companion, who is constantly searching the area for enemy movement, and being reported to by random Alfarin scouts.

Then if I hear anything new, I rush out of this hole and tell all the kings and commanders the information. Until then we let the troops rest.

"The Darfarins pulled out to regroup. I thought they had us. This is a temporary respite."

Shandria said, "I'm glad for the break. The longer they are away, the more magic we will have. Do you realize the Alfarins are reporting to you, and it's not just because you are the general of the Atlantian Scouts? They are comfortable with you. Half the time they report to you they don't even bother to uncloak, and they speak to you in Alfarin? You are the only Atlantian who even knows they are here. Well, I sometimes do."

Marvin said, "I hadn't thought about it, but you are right. The General of Alfamara told me they would. I recognize some of them from my time training with them."

Shandria said, "We expected the Darfarins to follow up with continuous attacks, yet we have had two hours of quiet. Enough time to dig in, for some of our troops to get some rest, and for our magic reserves to rise about twenty percent. You ended that last battle with precision lightning gathered from the sky. How did you grow so fast in your magic?"

Marvin replied, "Perhaps in a dream, I was taught by a god."

Shandria was surprised at Marvin's response. It was totally unlike him. It might be his Earth humor, the stress, or too much time with her grandfather, who had a way of leaving you thinking after he talked.

Shandria asked, "How are you getting along with the family?"

Marvin replied, "King Baracian is one of the wisest men I have ever known. He treats me like I'm a member of the royal family, just don't touch his granddaughter."

Marvin smiled, and Shandria laughed.

Marvin continued. "At Crystal Mountain, I was afraid Handrian would treat me to his dagger in my chest. But after the naval battle, Handrian changed so much. Now I'm looking forward to the four of us having a water fight in the palace gardens or the ocean by the estate."

Shandria said, "Handrian does owe us a water fight. He was never that way when we were children. He was a lot of fun. He started to change when our sister died. His heart became harder and harder. Everything became so serious to him. But he came back from the ocean, and now he is my brother and friend again."

Marvin knew that the Atlantian phrase "came back from the ocean" was the Earth equivalent of "coming back from the grave."

Marvin had faced a lot of death in the last few hours. He would have to talk to Shandria or Mrs. Write about it if he survived. He was never a religious person, but after seeing how closely Atlantian beliefs fit in with his personal beliefs from the Earth and seeing so much death, he wanted to learn more. It seemed like it was more than coincidence that the beliefs across realms were so similar. He added it to the long list of important things he needed to learn.

Marvin continued. "I haven't spent much time with your father. I think we are both still feeling each other out. But I do like him. I have been watching him command the troops, and he is a good and respected leader."

Shandria said, "It's the skip a generation thing. We tend to have a different relationship with our grandparents than with our parents. Grandfather said that like waves going up and down, viewpoints of the generations tend to do the same."

They stopped talking and sat together for half an hour. Then Marvin said. "They are coming." They both stood up. Shandria hurried back to take charge of her knights. Marvin disappeared in a weave of speed magic to inform the kings and generals of the impending attack.

Chapter 72

The battle started with a few velociraptors herded by the Darfarin. Marvin closed his eyes and looked. The Darfarin had found a way to make a small bubble around them where the arch wards didn't take away their dark magic. Marvin was sure it cost them a lot of magic to fight against the arch's ward, so they wouldn't be able to maintain the bubble for long. The Darfarins stole and perverted the energy from their victims and stored it in their staffs. He was sure that the Darfarin staffs stored it as dark magic energy. He ran between the trenches spreading the intelligence.

The Darfarin stayed outside of bow range. Then they released the few remaining raptors. The third line from one of the legions eliminated them with a few beams of blue light. The Darfarin that had herded the raptors quickly ran back to their lines. Marvin closed his eyes and looked down the hill with his magic. He saw the Darfarin had collected many of the buffalo and the antelope that had survived the encounter with the legions on the western side of the mountain. Only a few Mastodons had survived. A few magic arrows and they were dead.

Marvin walked near a trench with Dwarves and started to hum. The Dwarves took it up and soon were singing a battle song. The song spread as did their magic. Marvin remembered a story from his youth. For lack of a nail, a shoe was lost. For lack of a shoe, a horse was lost. For lack of a horse, a rider was lost. For lack of a rider, a message was lost. For lack of a message, a battle was lost. For lack of a battle, the war was lost.

A few percent of magic from Princess Amethyst had saved him from falling. He knew that even a few percent of magic could determine the outcome of this battle and this war.

Several Alfarins joined Marvin and gave him a status update. Before Marvin could thank them, they left. Marvin watched them and saw them head to the tent that held their provisions. He saw that their arrow quivers were empty. Marvin was sure there was a dead Darfarin for every missing arrow. They left the tent with full quivers. He wondered if they had caused enough disruption to delay the next attack. They had been doing what they could.

ATLANTIAN MAGIC

Marvin entered the command tent where King Vandian and the generals were talking. King Vandian looked at Marvin. Marvin said, "I have current status to report." Everyone immediately stopped talking.

Marvin said. "The Darfarins have collected the animals that survived the attack in the west. They are herding them up the mountain. They are magic fodder. They will use them to drain our magic reserves. Then they will send in the dire wolves and the ogres.

"The Darfarin have found a way to resist the arch magic and cast dark spells inside a bubble near themselves. It allows them some control of the animals. It might permit them to drain our magic at sword and shield range. The good news is the Alfarin scouts have reported the Darfarins have removed all troops and animals from the west. We should consider relocating those legions."

King Vandian said to Marvin, "King Baracian is at the western front. Report the information to him and request his presence here. Dismissed"

Marvin exited the tent and opened a portal through the arch to rejoin King Baracian.

After a few minutes, King Baracian returned with Marvin.

They entered the command tent. One of the depleted legions from the west had been sent back to guard the city of Atlantis. The fresh legion that had been guarding the city was on its way and should be arriving soon. The three legions from the eastern jewel had used their magical reserves to boost the magic reserves of the two freshest legions from the west. King Baracian would rather fight with two legions that had moderate magic reserves, than with five that were low on magic.

King Baracian left the command tent and disappeared through the portal. He returned with the two Atlantian legions from the west front. The depleted legions from the eastern jewel would rest and recover their energy reserves.

A large map was on a table spread out in front of them. Marvin advised one of the soldiers on the current position of the enemies. The soldier updated the map. King Vandian looked at Marvin and said, "Excellent work general. Keep us advised as you see fit."

Marvin said, "Yes my king." He bowed his head and left the tent.

Marvin received more scouting reports. He returned to the command tent where King Vandian asked Marvin to report.

Marvin said, "The Alfarin scouts report the Darfarins have brought all but token forces away from the northern cities. This is going to be their all or nothing assault. We need to get our newly arrived troops organized as soon as we can. And we need to conserve our magic until the end game. What's our current battle plan?"

King Vandian said. "The spearmen are to defend against assaulting animals, using their magic once the animals are away from the wards of the Darfarin. The bowmen are to restrict their fire and shoot non-magic arrows at the Darfarins if they come into range. The Dwarves are under control of King Feldspar. They are the second line of defense. Shandria is in charge of the knights, and she will use them at her judgment to fill in a breach if needed. Hopefully, she will get a chance to make a strategic charge like she did against the velociraptors and when she was defending the palace. She is also free to release them to the command of their captains if she thinks she is needed elsewhere."

Marvin said, "I need to add. The animals all move at different speeds and in their packs or herds. They are antagonistic to each other. That will force the Darfarins to send them in waves, first buffalo, then antelopes. Then the big battle begins, the dire wolves, the ogres, and Darfarin magic will commence after we are tired and low on magic."

Marvin saw the worried looks on everyone's faces. He said, "I have one more important thing to say to King Handrian before I go. The ladies and I decided you owe us a water fight when this is over."

It was so unexpected that everyone went quiet and then started laughing. Alandria yelled, "I chose Shandria for my team."

Handrian replied, "The ice-water queen and my baby sister verse the hot water general and his king. It doesn't seem fair since I know all your tactics."

Alandria jokingly replied, "You knew all my tactics."

Marvin laughed. The banter continued after Marvin excused himself. He saw an Alfarin scout waiting in the wings.

The Alfarin scout was looking at Handrian and Alandria joking. He asked, "Is everything alright?"

Marvin replied, "It's a crazy time for them. They are newlyweds and should be sharing their heat in bed. They were getting too worried and serious. I helped them laugh so they could bend with the wind before the battle."

The Alfarin smiled at Marvin's use of the Alfarin tree idiom, which meant to stand firm like a tree, but to bend and not break in a strong wind. He replied, "The battle is here. Bend with the wind."

Marvin recognized him as his friend Fraxinus, one of the Alfarin who had trained him. Marvin replied, "Bend with the wind, my friend."

Marvin felt and saw the portal open, and King Baracian arrive with his legions from the west.

As they arrived, the battle horns sounded. The buffaloes were coming. The animals were exhausted and pushed to their limits. But the compulsion of the Darfarins was too strong. They hurried uphill as fast as they could, which was a weak attempt at walking. They were little threat. The Dwarves went forward and dispatched them with their axes to conserve magic. Marvin was angry. Such beautiful animals were being twisted and used for an evil purpose. The Darfarins were forcing the Atlantians to kill the animals or to die.

Marvin thought of the slaughter of the American Buffalo from Earth's recent past and remembered Shandria having him pray over the dead wolf whose tooth he wore around his neck. Marvin walked to the front lines, intending to say a quiet prayer, but instead, he felt a strange stillness and felt compelled to speak loudly, "Forgive us great animals for we are forced to kill you to defend ourselves. We know that dark spells are enslaving you and causing you to attack us. May your death bring you freedom and peace, and may our Maker give us victory over the evil that enslaves you."

It had been spontaneous, and in the momentary quiet between battles. Marvin hadn't realized he was standing in the middle of the Atlantian legions. All had heard him. He heard weapons start to bang against shields. The noise spread and soon yelling joined it. Marvin turned around from the battlefield and began to walk away.

His magic was full, and his physical exhaustion was gone thanks to the war cake, but his emotional tank was empty. The cost of this war was already high, and the worst of it was yet to come. He fought to keep his head from hanging low from exhaustion. He noticed everyone was looking at him and raising their spears and swords as he walked past the trenches. Two Alfarin warriors came to him. They put their hands on his shoulder and then sped away.

Members of the royal party headed towards him. Queen Alandria reached him first. She bowed her head, then she put her hands on either side of his face and kissed his lips. Then King Handrian did the same thing.

Marvin was wondering what was going on. Why were kings, queens, and generals bowing to him? But he was too overcome to do anything. He was Atlantian; he was water. He was emotionally exhausted and went with the flow. Several more people bowed their heads to him then kissed him, followed by King Vandian and his wife, Queen Isaria, then King Baracian and last of all Shandria bowed her head and kissed him.

Everyone had returned to their duties. Shandria turned to walk away. Marvin touched her arm and asked her. "What just happened?"

Shandria smiled, took his arm and walked with him. She said, "In a brief moment of peace in the middle of the chaos of war, in sincerity and humility, you said a beautiful prayer that covered the thoughts that were in the hearts of all of us. It stated why we need to fight and gave us hope which firmed up our resolve and ended with a prayer to our Maker for our victory. We believe that our Father gave you your prayer on behalf of all of us. Since it came out of your lips, we bowed in respect to our Maker and Father, and kissed his lips through you."

Marvin replied, "But it was supposed to be a quiet personal prayer. I don't know why it came out so loud or what it meant."

Shandria replied, "That's one reason we believe it came from the Father. He gave you a prayer to pray for all of us. We trust He will answer it."

They came to where Shandria and Marvin had to split apart. Shandria dropped Marvin's hand, turned away, then turned back and said with an excited smile on her face, "Alandria and I are going to swamp you and Handrian." She smiled and hurried away to join her knights.

Marvin smiled, glad his mention of a water fight had worked as he hoped, but then he heard the trumpet of the battle horns. A minute later, the antelope attacked.

The antelopes were tired and exhausted from their forced, uphill march. To save magic, the Dwarven axmen dispatched them.

The Atlantian magic reserves were low, especially among the spearmen. Since they were the front line of attack, King Vandian ordered the septia to balance the magic between the soldiers. The front-line legions were intermixed with fresher legions that had arrived from the other islands. They shared their magic.

Suddenly the dire wolves attacked. Marvin heard the battle horns blow. He was surprised at the ferocity and the size of the wolves. They were twice the size of the one whose tooth was around his neck. Every TV special showed the persistent patience and coordination of a wolf pack in wearing down its prey. But dark spells had warped these wolves. They were fast. They were fearless. And they were out for blood and not food.

Marvin watched them for a few seconds to see how they moved and attacked.

Many leaped over the line of spears. Many of the spears broke leaving minor damage, rather than impaling the wolves. Their hides were either magically enhanced or naturally tough. Some wolves jumped over the trenches. Marvin pulled his sword, wove his speed magic, and ran to intercept the wolves.

His magic sword felt resistance but sliced deep into the first wolf. He doubted non-magical weapons would do any good. The Dwarves had left their trenches and were desperately carving through the wolves. The Atlantian were killing wolves, but the wolves were killing too many good soldiers. The soldiers were expending the last of their magic. That's when the Darfarins and ogres started to attack.

The Darfarin dark magic was still restricted inside their bubbles, but they had other magic they could use. Bolts of energy similar to ones from the archers came from their staffs. The Darfarin magical wards were stopping most of the Atlantian weaves, and only a few non-magical arrows were getting through. Marvin could see the Alfarin weaving magic from the woods on the flanks, collapsing the Darfarin's magic shields, as their arrows killed the Darfarins, but it was a small effect on the battle.

The third crafted counter weaves to protect against the Darfarin magical assault. The Darfarins had committed their ogres. They were approaching the front lines. They were faster than Atlantians or Dwarves on flat ground, but they were tired from their forced march up the hill.

Marvin saw King Baracian 100 feet from him. He raised his sword into the air and yelled to Marvin, "It's time." He jumped into the air and Marvin joined him. Their magic suspended Marvin and King Baracian between the earth and the sky. They started the movements and magic of the sky kata. The air, the water in the air, and the energy of the sky responded. A pair of opposite rotating whirlwinds formed around them.

Marvin felt something new about his relationship with the sky. It no longer resisted him but accepted him. And the earth no longer fought for his return. He felt freer than he ever had before. The pull of the earth on the molecules of his body, and the tides calling to the blood in his organs and veins no longer restricted him. The wind of earth no longer bound the breath in his lungs. He was part of the sky. He no longer had to expend a lot of magic fighting the forces of the earth. He felt balanced and focused. He listened and responded to the fluids about him, but they no longer constrained him.

The energy of the sky was his to control. And control it he did. Lightning and hail rained down upon the earth. It killed dire wolves, ogres, and Darfarins. The lighting killed, and the flash of the lightning blinded. The hail in the whirlwind caused confusion and fear. He could see the wolves running away from the battle. The lines of the Darfarin started to break from the onslaught.

The ionization in the air amplified his magic, but sky magic took a lot of energy. He could feel his magic reserves reaching critical just when the tide of battle was starting to turn. His magical energy was almost gone. He raised his sword into the air begging for more energy to control the energy about him. But everyone was engaged, and no one had any energy to spare.

King Baracian had stopped weaving lightning and was losing altitude. The king was falling. He was too far away for Marvin to do anything, and too far away for Marvin to share the few percent of magic he had left.

Marvin had found a place of balance between earth and sky, a place of harmony. He no longer needed to expend more than a trickle of magical energy to stay suspended in the sky. He had reached the place of peace and perfect balance of the grandmaster level. He was no longer in danger of falling, but he needed more energy to speak with and control the elements around him, and he had none. Marvin watched the battle reverse back the other way. The Ogres and wolves were once again attacking the legions.

Then Marvin felt the arch portal open. Giants in ornate armor came through the arch. They were twice the size of an Atlantian, and some were even taller. Others came in through their own portal. One carried a large battle hammer. He leaped into the air and joined the dance of the sky, but rather than use energy, he was generating it and giving it freely to the troops. Marvin's energy level shot higher than he had ever felt before. His sword was no longer taking energy from the magic swords below him. He was sending it down to the troops below.

Marvin heard the giant next to him yell and laugh. "Looks like you started the battle without us. It's time to see real lightning." Thor's hammer split the heavens with a bolt of lightning, which temporarily blinded everyone below. It traveled along the rain-soaked ground killing many Ogres and Darfarins. A dozen other giants joined them in the sky. And dozens more ran through the gate and engaged the wolves attacking the Atlantian troops. Several hundred more Asgardian warriors came through the portal.

One giant had a patch over an eye and wielded a large spear. He wasn't just using the energy of the sky to generate lightning but was generating his own. Some of the other giants ran into battle, past the trenches, and physically fought against the dire wolves and ogres.

Shandria ordered her knights to attack. They had supplied magic to everyone else, and the Asgardian's restored their magic reserves. They smashed into a wall of retreating ogres, their swords humming with magical energy.

Queen Isaria ordered the fresh legions from Atlantis and from the islands to charge. King Feldspar and the Dwarves ran down the hill and charged at the ogres. Their axes were glowing with magical energy, which they converted to fire.

Marvin closed his eyes and looked below. He saw the Darfarins and ogres trying to run away. They were in a complete rout. And next to him, he saw Shandria. She had released the knights into the command of their captain. She hadn't mastered the third level of the sky kata yet, but it didn't matter. Their armor was a bonded pair, and he assisted her. Her sky magic was less efficient, but there was an abundance of energy, so it didn't matter. He had his sky magic help steady and balance her between earth and sky. She would never have to worry about falling when she was with Marvin. They were united in their desire to free Atlantis from the Darfarins. It was time to press the attack while the enemy was in disarray.

The winds Marvin and Baracian had created were sweeping them north over the Island of Atlantis. Marvin adjusted them to take him where he needed to go. He felt drunk from the Asgardian magic. Asgardian magic wasn't just flowing through him. It had permeated every cell of his body. The Asgardians owned the lightning of the sky, so Marvin and Shandria shifted to water and wind magic. They formed hail the size and weight of cannon balls, but shaped like stalactites, and rained them down onto the invaders. They continued up the coast, blown by the winds they controlled. They attacked the ogres and Darfarin's, who were laying siege to the northern cities, with wind, hail, and lightning.

The battle continued past the first light of the morning, through the next day, and into the night. Marvin and Shandria had the magical energy supplied by the Asgardians, but their physical, emotional and magical exhaustion finally caught up with them, and their bodies were yelling for food. The Darfarin magic was so distinctive that they were convinced they had killed them all. All they had left was cleaning up the rogue animals they had missed, and maybe a few ogres. And that could wait a day.

ATLANTIAN MAGIC

Marvin realized he had long ago passed his physical limits. He created a portal in the sky, and they traveled back to the Atlantian arch. Marvin walked until he saw a crate to sit on and sat down. He was exhausted and breathing as if he had been running wind sprints, which magically he had. His adrenaline was winding down, and he needed a few minutes to rest.

Shandria said, "I need to get something to eat."

Marvin said, "I'll join you as soon as I catch my breath."

Chapter 73

Marvin watched Shandria leave, wondering where she got all her endurance. Then it hit him, she had been training all her life, and even with the magically enhanced routine of the forge and the Alfarin magic, he still had a long way to go. He admired her as he watched her walk away. Once Marvin caught his breath, he headed to the mess tent.

The Asgardians had supercharged Marvin's magic. But he had depleted his body's readily available reservoir of energy. His body was starting to starve. One of the mess attendants was quick to take his order. Marvin needed calories and water, and that's what they brought him. He didn't remember the meal afterward, only that it filled his stomach and took the edge off his hunger.

Marvin finished eating and saw that soldiers with injuries filled the back half of the tent. He hadn't realized they were using the mess tent to handle the soldiers with noncritical injuries.

Marvin felt the sugar from the meal give his body some relief from its exhaustion and starvation. Asgardian magical energy filled his body. He was exhausted yet wired by the excess magic. He felt like he had run a marathon and drank a whole pot of coffee.

He looked around. The army healers assisted by Alfarins were busy healing the most severe injuries in the medical tent. The mess tent was filled with soldiers that had fractures, torn ligaments, and deep lacerations in their muscles. It was an intermediate level of magic, serious and painful, but not immediately life-threatening. Most of the soldiers had learned basic healing weaves as part of their training or growing up and had treated the minor injuries.

Marvin knew the weaves to heal the troops. Being exhausted was no excuse to let them suffer. He had the magic, and the soldiers needed his help.

He saw an injured septian with a bandaged arm, waiting for magical healing. The wound was deep. Marvin walked over and asked, "I have been trained by the Alfarin to heal this type of injury. Would you like me to help you?"

The septian replied, "Yes general."

Marvin asked him to watch and learn the weave. Marvin showed him the weave and had him heal himself. It took several minutes but soon his arm was functional, and in a couple of days, he would be back to normal.

Marvin found a couple of other people with similar wounds, and he had the septian show them and try to teach them the weave. Only one of the soldiers knew enough healing magic to catch on.

Marvin got a show of hands and found several soldiers with some healing training. He taught each of them the weaves to heal their injuries and had them continue and help others.

Shandria showed up in the tent and saw what Marvin was doing. Marvin had trained half a dozen soldiers. Shandria smiled and started helping. A half-hour later Alandria showed up. Shandria was supposed to get Marvin. And Alandria volunteered to get both of them. Kings from more than one realm were asking for him.

They had treated many of the wounded, and the soldiers they had trained could heal the rest. Marvin was hungry again already. He grabbed a piece of fruit and left with the ladies.

Shandria had expected him to show up in the royal mess tent. Marvin didn't know there was a separate royal mess tent reserved for royalty and high-ranking officers. There was a third tent for lower-ranking officers. But after seeing the condition of some of the troops, Marvin was glad he had gone to the wrong tent.

On their way to the royal mess tent, Marvin saw a legion of weary soldiers exit through the arch to the area in front of the palace grounds. They were heading for their beds in the barracks. Marvin thought, "If I wasn't wired from Asgardian magic, that's where I would head."

Today, guests filled the royal mess tent. Half a dozen Asgardian gods, small 'g' thought Marvin, and several dozen Asgardian warriors were there. King Feldspar, his daughter, and many of their command staff were in the tent.

Food from the palace was arriving, as well as delicacies from Asgard, Crystal Mountain, and Alfamara. Asgardian mead, Dwarven mead, Atlantian mead, and spiced wine from Alfamara and Atlantis were arriving. There was also a keg of Ale from Asgard. Marvin wasn't sure whether it was from Asgard or the Palace, but Asgardian size chairs and furniture had been set up.

Marvin asked Shandria, "Where is King Baracian?"

Shandria suddenly looked sad. She said, "He hit the ground when he fell from the sky. Odin took him to Valhalla."

Marvin sat down in a chair and buried his head in his hands. He was too exhausted and emotionally drained to cry. He sat there sobbing, without the emotional energy to compose himself. He thought of all the killed and injured soldiers. The cost of their victory was high but far better than if they lost.

Shandria put her hand on his shoulder. He could feel the warmth of Shandria's hand, and her magic touching his. Somehow, it helped.

After a minute, Marvin looked up and asked, "Is the rest of the family okay?"

Shandria smiled, "Exhausted and beat up like everyone, but alright."

Marvin smiled. It was a half-smile since he was still thinking of King Baracian. Marvin wanted to drink and let go of all his stress. Hell, he wanted to get drunk and pass out. He didn't feel like celebrating the victory that had come at such a cost. But he knew the battle for Atlantis wasn't over yet. And the one time he had tried drinking away his troubles, all he did was get sick to his stomach and add a hangover to his problems.

Marvin did his rounds, thanking and greeting the guests. Entertainers from Atlantis showed up, and soon music filled the air.

Shandria asked Marvin how he had become friends with the Asgardians.

Marvin told her the story. "After we entered the portal back to Atlantis at Crystal Mountain, I found the portal had sent me to the Anastasi. The Anastasi sent me to Asgard. I spent several months in Asgard before the Anastasi brought me back to the same place and time I had left.

"As soon as I arrived at Asgard, Thor wanted to see how worthy I was. He challenged me to arm wrestle, to prove my worth to stay in Asgard. I felt like a child wrestling with a giant, which is what I was.

"I used every muscle in my arm to move Thor's arm. It didn't budge. Then I shifted in my seat and used every ounce of leverage I could while still keeping my elbow on the table. Thor's arm still didn't budge. Then I drew upon my magic, the strength of earth and metal, as well as the Alfarin nature magic to increase my strength. Finally, I harnessed the energy of fire magic and the forge. I put the force of the crashing waves and hurricane winds into my arm, and for a brief second, I put in the energy of sky magic. His arm still didn't budge.

"My magic was exhausted, and my physical strength gave out. Thor pinned my arm to end the contest. I stood up and said. 'You won against everything I had.' I held out my hand, and Thor shook it.

"Then Thor said, 'And you showed you have the heart of a warrior and the honor of a friend.'

"Thor's Asgardian magic then recharged mine.

"I ceaselessly practiced everything the Asgardians taught me. As you know, sky magic is very draining, but the Asgardians are masters of strength. Their magic generates magic energy, and they continually restored my magic. Normally my body could only grow enough magic for me to practice the powerful magic for a few minutes a day. But in Asgard, I had the magical energy to practice all day long. I practiced more in a day than I could have in a year, and I had several months of training.

"On the last day, Thor joined me in the sky. We laughed together and had a lightning bolt contest. His lightning bolt was larger than mine, but then I joked mine was larger than his when we took into account his size. We laughed and clinked together tankards of Asgardian mead. The next morning, I re-entered the portal. No one seemed to notice, but I was nursing the end of a hangover when we returned to Atlantis, and it wasn't from the Dwarven ball."

ATLANTIAN MAGIC

Halfway to morning, Marvin realized he was the only person from Atlantis who wasn't sleeping or passed out at their table. He had ended up with Thor, King Feldspar, the dwarven generals, and the Asgardian warriors that had joined them. They were laughing at the Atlantians, and partying loudly. They asked Marvin why he was the only Atlantian awake. He replied, "I learned an important rule of drinking at Crystal Mountain and relearned it at Asgard."

Thor asked, "What rule is that."

Marvin replied, "It's heavenly fun for an Atlantian to drink with Asgardians and Dwarves, but it's hell the next morning for any Atlantian who is foolish enough to try and keep up with their metabolism."

The Asgardians and Dwarves laughed.

The general from Alfamara joined them at the head table. There were still Darfarin in the realm of Atlantis, and they had the Atlantian arch stone. They needed to continue the attack as soon as possible to prevent reinforcements. They needed a plan to recover or destroy the arch stone. After some discussion, Marvin approved the mission as a scouting mission, since he felt he had the authority to organize a scouting mission.

But it was more than a scouting mission. Marvin knew he should discuss the plan with King Handrian and King Vandian who were sleeping at a nearby table. He needed to execute the plan as soon as possible. But it was dangerous. He didn't want his death on anyone's conscience. And he didn't want to delay the plan with court approval.

King Feldspar and the Dwarves lead the Asgardians back through the gate to continue the party at Crystal Mountain. Marvin looked around the tent. He saw an unopened cask of the finest Atlantian mead and ordered the quartermaster to deliver it to the Dwarven ambassador at his embassy in king Baracian's name. Marvin felt it proper that he could fulfill King Baracian's commitment.

Marvin Left a message with a scribe for King Vandian saying he had gone to Alfamara to organize a scouting mission. He took the portal to Alfamara. Queen Juniperia saw how exhausted he was, gave him a large meal to eat, and sent him to sleep in the tree he had shared with Shandria, along with a glass of sweet tasting liquid. Marvin fell right to sleep.

Chapter 74

Marvin slept through the day. They woke him up at sunset, and they served him a large meal. His whole body ached. Afterward, one of the queen's granddaughters escorted Marvin to her palace. She shared a glass of Alfarin wine with him and then asked him to take her arm and go for a walk.

They walked to a grove that was nearby. There were unusual flowers that had a delicate bioluminescent glow. The air was alive with fireflies, which added to the beauty. The queen said, "This is one of my favorite places to visit and nurture. The glow of the flowers attracts the fireflies. They provide nectar to the flies, and the flies carry the pollen to the next flower. Atlantis is under a full moon, but here we have a few hours before our moon rises. It allows us to see the beautiful glow better.

The queen said, "Just like Atlantis we are a peaceful people, we get along with everyone but the Darfarins. Our love and respect for nature and magic is the opposite of their abuse. They hate us for it, and we hate them in return. All the soldiers that trained with you and fought with you volunteered to go on this mission. It was tough selecting the handful to accompany you.

After the walk in the garden, the queen fed him another large meal, led him back to bed, and gave him another glass of the sweet drink. His body was still recovering from the physical and emotional stress of the battles. He slept peacefully and felt refreshed and alert when he woke at dawn. He ate a large breakfast provided by Queen Juniperia.

Marvin wrote a message detailing the plan and asked the queen to deliver it by a messenger after the mission was underway. By the time King Vandian received the message late in the morning, it would be too late for them to object.

It was a risky plan, but doable. Marvin didn't want his friends to feel responsible if he didn't survive. They could do without the guilt. Marvin didn't want to die, but if he did, it would be easier for Shandria to let go of him, and to find a prince to marry.

He changed his clothes, putting on an Alfarin chameleon suit. It worked with Alfarin concealment weaves and enhanced his ability to stay concealed.

Queen Juniperia had him wear a slatted wooden vest over his breastplate. Marvin looked at it. He was amazed at the complexities of the protection weaves on it. Reading the weaves was like reading a library, and many of the words he didn't understand.

King Feldspar had shown up and looked wide-awake. It was hard to believe he had fought all night, and then spent all day and night partying with the Asgardians. Marvin was glad he was there to see him off.

The queen handed Marvin a wooden talisman that was on a leather lanyard. He put it around his neck.

Marvin and eight Alfarin volunteers boarded a sleek Alfarin sailboat. Marvin opened a quiet portal, and they sailed the boat through to a spot south of the dark magic ward that surrounded the Darfarin arch.

Marvin looked at the sea around him. Further from the Darfarin ward was a ring of Atlantian warships. The magic on the boat hid it well. The warships made no change of direction or any other indication they had seen him.

Marvin felt the dark magic ward before he entered it. The sooner they sailed past the outer shell of the magic the better. Their vessel was near its top wind-powered speed, and she was sailing with the current when they entered the shell. He could feel the magical battle going on around him as the protection wards on their boat fought against the dark magic spells of the Darfarin arch. Ten minutes later, the battle between the dark magic and the Alfarin magic was over. Their ward had won. For now, they would be safe. They would get to the island in two hours.

Marvin closed his eyes and looked with his magic. Interesting, he could now look inside the shell but couldn't look outside it. He didn't like what he saw or felt inside the shell.

The Darfarins had a large fleet inside a natural harbor northwest of the volcano that was on the south end of the island. He could feel the arch crystal. It was crying and in pain, and its magic was hurting and angry, like a slave being whipped. Marvin opened his eyes and tried to control his anger. He tried to remember he was doing this for his love of Atlantis, his love of the Dwarves and the Alfarins, his love of the White family and the Atlantians, and his love of Shandria and her family. But he also knew he was doing it for his hatred of the Darfarins, the damage they had done to Atlantis, and to the innocent animals.

Back on Earth evil was more of a theoretical concept, but the Darfarins were pure evil. He hated them. But he refused to let his hatred rule his heart. He would do this for love, and because it was necessary.

If he had stayed on Earth, even if radiation and chemotherapy had extended his life, he would now be dead. But instead, he had gone on the most unbelievable adventure of all time. He had learned magic, sailed on a ship, fought in a war, and met some of the most remarkable people ever. And he had fallen in love, not just the love of need and desire, but love that was deep enough to let go for Shandria's needs. Marvin didn't want to die, but he realized he had a fuller life already than he would have on Earth. If he died, it would be what the Atlantians called a high tide death.

Fraxinus watched Marvin's face, seeing the internal struggle, but then saw a more peaceful look on Marvin's face. He knew Marvin was fighting with many emotions. He was happy his brother had won the battle and was bending with the wind.

Soon, Marvin saw the choppy water over the reef south of the island. Waves were breaking against the reef. He was afraid they would smash the boat into them. They had picked this location partly because the prevailing wind and current would allow them to approach without using magic, but also because the dangerous reefs would keep Darfarin ships away from the area. At the last minute, Marvin picked the boat up in a mound of water and allowed the waves and the wind to push the boat past the reef. He was sure the Darfarins wouldn't notice the brief, localized effect of the magic he used.

They sailed the boat and anchored it near the shore south of the volcanic mountain. Half the Alfarins scouted to the left around the volcano, and the rest scouted to the right. Marvin jogged around the volcano to the right but stayed higher up on the volcano. He wanted to scout out the area from the higher ground.

Marvin looked down at the encampment from halfway up the volcano. Between him and the arch were hundreds of ogre-sized tents. Several hundred Darfarin sized tents were located west of them, closer to the ocean. A makeshift pier jutted out into the water. There were a couple of boats at the pier. In the harbor were dozens of warships. The tent area was quiet, except for the snores of the ogres. The Arch was north of the tents.

He made a wide loop around the tents to the east.

He caught a glimpse of Fraxinus in the bushes and scattered trees to the east of the camp. Marvin saw him because he wanted Marvin to see him. Marvin now knew where his escape route was. Marvin waved a hand signal to let him know he understood. Fraxinus immediately waved back and disappeared.

Marvin snuck through the bushes near the cleared area by the camp. Soon he was near the base of the arch, which was north of the camp. Marvin looked around. As hoped, no one was guarding the arch. Marvin wouldn't need the Alfarins to create a distraction. Ogres hated daylight. They were nocturnal and asleep in their tents. It was just before noon, the middle of their sleep cycle.

Marvin looked closely at the arch. The Darfarins had constructed it of jagged volcanic rock, crudely fused together. Marvin needed to climb to the top where the arch crystal was. The crude construction gave him an abundance of hand and footholds. He started climbing.

He was halfway up when he saw a group of Darfarin walking on the pier. They were animated and seemed to be arguing about something. Marvin hid behind the back of the arch and watched them continue to a tent. Marvin knew if they saw him, he would look like part of the arch. But his training was to stay five times hidden, by magic, concealment, silence, stillness, and by being unexpected.

ATLANTIAN MAGIC

Marvin climbed the rest of the way to the top. The magical strength of the arch crystal was enormous. Marvin could feel it even through all the protective magic. His whole body was vibrating with the magical energy. He felt like ants were crawling all over his skin. It was an unnatural vibration, unlike the rhythmic heartbeat of the other portals. Marvin was sure the crystal's fight against the dark magic caused the vibration.

Marvin took off the talisman and touched it to the arch crystal. He wove magic to activate the talisman, and then more magic to assist the arch. Everything started to vibrate more. He held on tight to the arch. He was glad he was lying on top of the arch, or he might have fallen off. The talisman canceled out the dark magic that was controlling the crystal. And the arch crystal fought back.

The arch crystal was mad. They had ripped him from his rightful place, stolen his will, tortured him, enslaved him, and used him to hurt his family. He tore apart the dark magic that had held him captive and ended the dark magic weave that was enslaving him. He dropped the dark magic shell he was forced to generate.

The Darfarin magic was forcing him to steal magic and energy unnaturally from the reservoir of magma below the four volcanoes in the volcanic chain. The magma was becoming damaged and unstable. It would erupt in a few months. It would be easy to speed it up.

In its anger, the crystal took control of the deep magma, pulling up more energy from deeper in the earth, forcing the magma higher, and making it more violent. He had hurried up the eruption. Soon the whole island chain would blow-up and with it, his evil enslavers.

But then the crystal got its initial anger out and noticed the Atlantian that had set him free. He didn't want him to die. Until he was kidnapped and enslaved, he had never hurt or betrayed an Atlantian, and he swore he would never voluntarily hurt one ever again. He talked to Marvin.

Marvin felt the pain and angst of the crystal. Marvin told the crystal he was a friend. He remembered what Shandria had asked him on Earth and repeated it to the crystal. "Do you want to die with honor or do you want to live with honor? I'm hoping to rescue you, and I prefer you come home to the royal palace with me."

The Crystal thought for a second and said. "I want to go with you and help my family."

Marvin realized that in the crystal's mind he was an Atlantian. Marvin used earth magic to make the rock around the crystal soft and brittle. He flaked it away with his fingers and took out the arch crystal.

Marvin felt light headed. The crystal was too powerful for him to be directly touching. Even with climbing gloves on, it had too strong a magical presence for him to hold. He put it into a pocket on his cloak, which helped some. Then he climbed partway down the arch. The Darfarins were coming. He needed to move quickly. He jumped down the rest of the way.

Marvin knew he was visible. He had no cover, he was moving, and they were expecting to find something. He needed to get away fast. He started to run. The Darfarins had begun running towards the arch when the dark magic shell collapsed. They saw him, or at least they saw something moving. His magic concealed much of what they saw.

He felt their dark magic hitting him. The wooden vest blocked the magic. Another Darfarin blast knocked him to the ground. It must not have been dark magic. He leaped to his feet and started to zigzag. He saw Alfarin arrows fly by him and knew from screams behind him that they were finding their marks. Marvin was staggered once again by another magic blast. He did a shoulder roll and came up running, entering the tree line. Marvin quickly wove a portal, telling the Alfarins to go through first. He was about to run through when a spell hit his portal. It became unstable. He tried to hold it together as long as he could so the last Alfarin would make it home. Then the portal collapsed.

Marvin pulled out his sword, turned around, and sent a blast of lightning towards his attackers. There were screams, and they fell back. Marvin saw a portal open up behind the attackers. A woman with angry brown eyes and brown hair looked at him from under her hood. She was no Darfarin. Marvin was sure she was the woman he had encountered on Earth, the thief. She stepped through the portal. The Darfarins started to follow her.

Marvin felt the energy of the arch crystal. It was still supercharged. He tapped into it. It was the energy of the volcanic magma, the magic of fire and molten rock. Marvin's sword started to glow red-hot. He jumped into the air, balancing himself between earth and sky.

Marvin unleashed the fire from his sword directly into the Darfarin portal. He knew from his studies that it would go through but only for a few seconds. Predictably, the portal collapsed. The Darfarins turned around and started to attack. He swept the fire from his sword like a flamethrower through the Darfarins. The ogres were leaving their tents. He released it into the ogres and their tents. The fire energy was too intense for Marvin to control. He felt his body temperature rising. He released as much as he could, sending more fire towards the tents.

Marvin needed to protect the crystal from the Darfarins and get away from the island as fast as possible. He crafted a weave to blow him south and east. He then tried to craft a portal back to Atlantis, but there was magical interference in the sky which prevented him.

Marvin was still full of fire magic. As soon as he was over the ocean, he dropped down into the water, and then released the excess energy into the water around him. The water around him started to sizzle as it cooled him off and absorbed the residual energy.

He wove a current to transport him to the boat, rose out of the water, and stepped onto the deck. Rather than take the time to pull up the anchor, he cut the anchor line. The natural current flow ran north past the string of volcanoes.

He wove a current to carry him towards the east, directly away from the volcanic islands.

He tried opening another portal, but it failed. There was too much magical interference in the area. Smoke was coming from the volcanoes. He could see plumes of lava shooting into the air. Marvin talked to the crystal and found out it had caused the volcanos to build up energy. It would be no slow eruption. The volcanos would soon explode.

Marvin was sure the power of the eruption was causing the magical interference. He was hoping to generate another portal and get away. But none would form. Marvin pushed the boat eastward with wind and current as fast as he could. He hoped he could get far enough away before the volcanos blew, far enough away to generate a portal, or at least to survive the explosion.

Then he felt it. There was a difference in the feeling of the magic coming from the volcano. It was stronger, and the interference was growing. Marvin thought of volcanic eruptions, like Mount Saint Helens, which buried and destroyed property dozens of miles away, Mount Vesuvius, which buried Pompeii, or Mount Krakatoa, which created tidal waves, destroying scores of villages. And he had four volcanoes about to erupt.

He tried again to make a portal, but interference overwhelmed his magic. Even though he was sailing further from the volcano, the interference was increasing. He looked back at the volcano. The volcano looked as close as it did a few minutes ago. It was getting larger, rather than smaller as he sailed farther away. And it was starting to bulge. The once almost perfectly shaped cone was ballooning outward and getting fatter.

Marvin thought of abandoning the boat. Jumping into the sky and weaving a gale force wind would double or triple his speed, but the sky was in turmoil, and the intricate weave was unstable and fell apart before he could complete it. There was too much interference to talk to the Atlantian arch and get its help. He had left his Dwarven medallion behind, but he knew the interference was too disruptive for it to overcome.

Marvin could see the beginning of an eruption, with lava spitting high into the air. A cloud of smoke above the volcano was growing larger. It was forming not just above the southern volcano. More plumes were forming farther north, strung along the length of the volcanic chain. Marvin could hear the sound of the erupting volcanoes behind him.

Then he felt the boat drop as the water underneath him dropped in level. His boat banged off the side of a once submerged reef. He looked back towards the volcano, and all he saw was a giant wave approaching.

Marvin raced forward past the cockpit onto the foredeck. He was using the same wood magic the Darfarin's used to walk sideways up a tree to grip onto the jostling deck. He held onto the mast and lay down on the deck near the magic wards on the vessel.

Then the water level reversed. The water started to rise, lifting up the boat. Marvin doubted he would be able to hold onto the mast in the turbulence if the boat flipped over. He held his leg against the wooden deck and magically wove the fibers of the wood around his upper legs. The wood held him to the deck.

The front edge of the wave hit and lifted the boat up, rolling it over and over. Marvin was glad he had woven the wood around his leg. He was holding onto the mast to stabilize his upper body. The deck was holding onto his legs. The mast ripped from the vessel and pulled out of his arms.

The wood he wove held his leg to the boat. Every roll of the boat slapped Marvin against the deck of the ship like a rag doll. Marvin was totally disoriented. Then the boat ceased rolling over, and Marvin was under water, but only for a few seconds. The boat popped back above the water. The wave had moved past the boat, but there was heavy turbulence in its wake. The water was rough and choppy, but the boat had held together. Marvin lay there. His shoulders were sore but not dislocated. He was sure his nose was broken from banging against the deck. The wood had rubbed his lower leg raw. Bruises covered his elbows where they had repeatedly slammed into the deck of the ship as he tried to protect his head and face. But he was alive; he would recover. He wove some magic, and the bruises quickly healed.

He laid there and used his magic to look at the condition of the ship. There were several broken and smashed planks on the port side. Water was flooding the cabin area. Marvin lay and watched the weaves the Alfarins had put on the boat repair the broken planks and seal the ship. Magic was pumping water out of the bilge. Soon the water would be out of the boat.

But soon wasn't soon enough. Marvin didn't have any time left. He heard the loudest noise he had ever heard. The deep roaring pressure wave of the sound vibrated the deck and slammed his head against his arms, which he had put under his head. It was loud enough to make the water around him vibrate up and down like the head of a concert speaker. He looked back and saw the red glow of fire reflect off the smoke above the volcanic eruptions. There was so much magical static in the air that Marvin could barely detect the magic in his body. A dark rising cloud of volcanic ash darkened the glow of the erupting volcano.

Once again, he felt his boat dropping towards the floor of the ocean. This time Marvin wove magic to bind his wooden vest to the deck. Marvin started to hyperventilate to saturate his blood with oxygen. Then as quickly as the ocean had fallen, he felt it rise again. Marvin saw a wall of water towering high above the boat. It slammed into the boat, picked it up, and flipped it over and over. Then the boat started breaking apart. Marvin was dizzy and running out or air. He lost consciousness.

Chapter 75

Shandria woke up and saw Marvin was no longer at the party. She was surprised she didn't have a hangover, but then realized she hadn't fallen asleep from drinking too much. Her tiredness had overcome her. She was hungry and exhausted. She grabbed a bite to eat and took the portal back to the wharf by the palace, stopped by the war room, checked in, and then headed up to bed. She hoped Marvin was there, but she realized he must have headed back to the narrows.

She slept through most of the day and woke up starving. She grabbed a quick meal from the kitchen, that was still cooking around the clock, and checked in once more at the war room. Her mother told her she needed to catch up on her sleep. She went back to bed and slept through the night. She found out later that Alandria and her brother did the same thing. Whether it was the after effect of the speed magic, or being up for two days, she didn't know. But both were sufficient excuses.

The next morning, she returned to the war room no longer exhausted. She was surprised to hear that Marvin had left to organize a scouting mission at the same time the other realms had left. He must be exhausted, but she knew Queen Juniperia would take care of him.

She ate a less hurried breakfast and managed to get an hour to do her morning exercises, and bath before diving into her royal duties, which this morning was to help with the refugees. Many had already returned to their homes. It seemed like every carpenter in the realm was bringing in wood to repair or replace broken doors. Many, except for the ornately carved ones, the court paid for as part of refugee war assistance.

Alandria was touring the countryside, assessing the damage to crops and farms.

Handrian was commander of the Atlantian fleet and was documenting the damage to the fleet.

The palace was surprisingly quiet for all the things that needed to be done. Almost every court official was out on horseback assessing the damage. Most of the palace refugees had returned home. Legions from each of the northern cities were cleaning up the mainland. No Darfarins or ogres were found alive, only a few of their magic twisted animals. They were dangerous and quickly killed.

The council called Shandria to the war room. They had just received the communication with the details of Marvin's scouting mission, and it was already underway. They handed Shandria Marvin's report. They were too intelligent to consider it only a scouting mission.

Shandria paced, and waited, and paced. Then they received scattered communications that the anti-magic shell around the northwest islands had collapsed. Reports about volcanoes erupting arrived. The eruptions caused communication interference with the fleet.

The interference was interfering with communication to all the other islands. North Island reported a series of large waves had damaged their barrier island and caused damage to their western harbor.

Then they received word through the portal from Alfamara that the scouting party was under attack. Marvin had generated a portal, and everyone but Marvin and one Alfarin had made it back when his portal collapsed. Due to the magical interference, it was unlikely Marvin could have woven another portal. They got another report that the final Alfarin had come through the portal several miles away as it collapsed. Marvin hadn't come through.

Everyone but Shandria was convinced Marvin was dead. He had been through too much to die now. And if anyone were foolish enough to tell her it was a high tide death, she would hit them in the nose.

She ran down to the wharf and commandeered a fast rescue boat and crew. She was determined to search for Marvin herself. Shandria charted the tides and the wind and guessed at where Marvin could be. Three days later the crew was exhausted. Their magic was spent, and they were eating emergency provisions. The only thing not exhausted was Shandria's refusal to accept Marvin's death. He had survived wolves, waterfalls, cancer, dire wolves, velociraptors, Darfarins, ogres, falling from the sky, and insanity from the green goo. He would survive this. At least the magical interference from the volcanic eruption was starting to clear.

Then she got a brief direction from the dagger Marvin had given her. His magic tied her dagger to his. They set sail in that direction, pushed by current and the wind. They were too low on magic to use it to propel them. After an hour of sailing, the interference cleared enough to give her an updated direction. They adjusted course, and soon Shandria could easily detect the signature of Marvin's magic.

ATLANTIAN MAGIC

She saw Marvin's body bobbing up and down. It was attached to what was left of the wooden deck of a boat that still radiated Alfarin magic. The deck had stayed upright since the Alfarin boat magic kept it upright. She dove overboard and swam to the wreckage. Marvin's body was battered and bruised. His clothes were torn, but most of his body was covered by the wood of the deck that had grown around him.

She could detect no signs of life, but then the wood was bobbing up and down in the ocean. She feared Marvin was dead, and yelled, "No!" out of desperation. She had almost no magic, yet somehow, she found enough energy to talk to the Atlantian arch. A portal to Alfamara opened up. She swam Marvin's body through, still attached to the wooden deck.

Chapter 76

Marvin woke up in bed in the palace infirmary. He started to ask a bunch of questions. A couple of attendants came over and said, "First drink this medicine from Queen Juniperia." Marvin swallowed the liquid. It smelled like the palace gardens of Alfamara. He lay back down and dreamed of fields of flowers and the green vegetation of Alfamara.

The first attendant said to the second, "That's the last of the medicine. For two weeks he has been mumbling the same word."

The second attendant said, "We may want to make sure a physician is here tomorrow morning when he awakes. Maybe he knows what Krakatoa means."

The first attendant said. "It's not Atlantian. It doesn't sound like Alfarin. Maybe he heard it from the Dwarves."

Chapter 77

They kept Marvin at the infirmary for another two days. All the Royals were busy on court business. A court minister came by and a general from the battle. Marvin gave him a preliminary report; at least he thought he did. But Marvin was so out of it that the general didn't understand a word he spoke as he drifted back to sleep. The doctor's orders were to let Marvin rest and recover. The first day wasn't bad as the medication was getting out of his system. He found himself repeatedly dozing off.

Nothing from the boat trip had survived but his dagger, his breastplate, and his sword. The sheath of his sword was torn and needed replacing. Even Marvin's general necklace was missing. He jokingly wondered if they would take that out of his salary, or if they had demoted him and taken it off. Then he wondered how much a general's salary was and how long it would take him to replace a golden necklace.

He had rescued the arch crystal from the Darfarins only to lose it to the sea. At least the Darfarins no longer had its magic, and they no longer were a direct threat to Atlantis. Yet something in Marvin believed the crystal was still alive. And his gut told him he hadn't seen the last of the Darfarins.

The next morning, Mr. and Mrs. White brought him clothes for his release from the hospital. They had scheduled him for release the following morning. He was sure the Atlantians used the same designer as earth did for their less than modest hospital gowns. The mental image of riding a horse home in a hospital gown made Marvin chuckle.

Mrs. White said. "Our front yard was covered with blue and red waluia flowers after your victory on Mount Atlantis. White flowers of morning joined them when everyone thought you were dead. And now people are putting yellow flowers on our lawn. Those are well wishes for you. The yellow of the morning sun rising anew represents prayers for your recovery."

Marvin decided he liked the flower customs.

The last of their house guests had finally departed, having their homes repaired enough to move into. Marvin's bedroom and office kept shut, but the guests had full access to most of the estate. Marvin told the Whites he was proud of them, and hopefully, things would be back to normal soon. Marvin may have been unconscious for several weeks, but he still had a huge backlog of emotions to work through. Maybe the war council would give him a few days to recover before his next assignment. Or hopefully, they would give him time to visit Alfamara and Crystal Mountain.

Marvin was glad the Whites brought the kids. Marvin and the children had fun using magic to toss a ball of water around the room until a nurse came in and cleared her throat. His time with the Whites was up. He entertained himself for most of the afternoon trying semi-successfully to magically juggle three balls of water.

The following morning the doctor gave Marvin a check up and pronounced him ready to leave. Marvin dressed. It felt good to be wearing real clothes again. His sword and breastplate were excited to be with him again. His breastplate was bragging to Marvin about saving his life when multiple waves had slammed the boat into the bottom of the ocean repeatedly. Marvin thanked him.

A messenger arrived during his checkup with an official summons to appear before the court, which coincided with his official hospital release time. He thanked the doctor and nursing staff and exited the palace infirmary. Four members of the king's guard in full ceremonial dress escorted him to the courtroom. He had been under constant guard while he recovered.

Marvin reported to the Minister at the doors of the courtroom. The minister was in full ceremonial attire. It was different than when Shandria and Marvin had first arrived. It was something more formal. He was still surprised none of the royals had visited him while he was in the hospital. The guards around him seemed more serious than normal, if that was possible, and a little nervous. Marvin had expected to get a private talking to about his mission, but he was wondering if he was in deep trouble for violating a rule he didn't know existed.

The minister escorted him in. The king's guards on either side accompanied him to the line. The throne room was full. All three kings and their queens were on their thrones. King Feldspar, Queen Olivine, Queen Juniperia, and Prince Thor were sitting on thrones off to the side.

The guards had him kneel down. He looked up and realized King Baracian was among the kings sitting on a throne. He involuntarily jumped up and yelled, "King Baracian, you're alive!"

The guards quickly pushed him back down, then held his head, so it stayed bowed down. King Baracian smiled and waved at the guards to release their firm grip on Marvin's shoulders and head.

Marvin tried to keep his head respectfully bowed but was having trouble, being in disbelief that King Baracian was still alive. He was wondering why the kings and queens from the other realms were there. King Vandian signaled to the guards to have Marvin stand up.

King Vandian asked him. "Is Marvin your true name?"

ATLANTIAN MAGIC

Marvin thought for a second and realized he was on trial. He still didn't know what for. He said. "Marvin is the name my adopted Earth parents called me. I have always believed it was my name."

"What do you know about your birth?"

Marvin replied, "Nothing. A human family raised me. I always thought I was human. It was only after I left Earth that I learned I was Atlantian and not human, or that Atlantis even existed."

King Vandian said, "Let the court records show that Marvin has been examined and certified by this court as being Atlantian. Both by his blood and his magic."

He continued. "The courts of Alfamara, Asgard, and Iron Mountain have presented official documents before this court testifying to your birth. Queen Juniperia, Queen Olivine, King Feldspar and Prince Thor have entered official testimony into the records. Their word and reputation are beyond question in this courtroom. And with their blessings, we have entered their testimonies into the court records.

"The records and their testimonies all point to the same fact, and this court unanimously agrees on the findings.

"Marvin, you are the son of King Merlin and his wife Queen Morgania of Atlantis. You were born in Atlantis a thousand years ago. The Anastasi concealed you out of time on Earth to protect you and Atlantis. You are the prophesized lost prince of Atlantis. You have proven that by bloodline, by fulfilling prophecy, by magic, by your action in defending Atlantis, and by the testimony of King Feldspar, Queen Olivine, and Queen Juniperia. Both Queen Olivine and Queen Juniperia were present at your birth and knew you as soon as they saw you. And Prince Thor helped protect you soon after you were born.

"It is the honor and pleasure of this court to recognize your true name and title and to accept you into the royal family. Welcome home Prince Marvin of Atlantis. Come greet your family."

Marvin saw all the kings and queens of Atlantis stand up and smile. They stood with their arms held open. Marvin saw the king's guards on either side turn towards him, drop to their knees, and bow their heads. There was the sound of surprise and excitement and a rustle as the rest of the courtroom knelt down.

He slowly approached the stairs, in disbelief of what was happening around him. As he walked up the stairs, he saw king Vandian raise his hand. Trumpets blew. The courtroom stood back up and erupted in cheering and clapping. The kings and queens of Atlantis hugged and kissed Marvin. He was in disbelief. King Vandian placed a necklace signifying him as a prince of Atlantis around his neck.

King Vandian had Marvin face the court. After several minutes, the king raised his hand. Horns blew, and the people started clapping. After a few minutes, there were horn blasts, and the courtroom quieted down. The king dismissed the court. And they left for the blue room.

Marvin watched Thor walk into the blue room and finally understood why the halls, doorways, and room in the court area were as large as they were. Once inside the room, Marvin greeted the visiting kings and queens, who all addressed him as Prince Marvin. It would take some time to get used to his Atlantian title, and all the bowing he would receive.

Servants brought in spiced wine, mead, and delicacies. Marvin realized the only food he had eaten in several weeks was a liquid diet and some bland hospital food. He tried to eat without seeming like a pig.

Marvin asked Baracian, "What happened? I thought you were dead and taken to Valhalla."

Baracian replied. "My body hit the ground hard when I fell from the sky." He smiled and continued, "Unlike you, I missed all the trees. I was injured too severely to live. For all practical purposes, I was dead. The Alfarin general was there and wove powerful magic, which kept me alive. It balanced me at the edge. Oden took me back to Valhalla, thinking it was too late, but hoping just in case. In Valhalla, they healed my body and brought me back from the edge."

Marvin said, "I thought Valhalla was where they buried great warriors."

Thor laughed and said in his deep voice, "We do bury great warriors there, but it is also a place of great healing. King Baracian is a great friend and a great warrior. In his time, we would be honored to bury him there, but Atlantis has its customs, and after a much longer life, I am sure he would prefer to follow them."

Marvin said to Baracian, "I was emotionally exhausted from the battle. When I found out you were gone, I had no more tears to shed. All I could manage was a sob. I am relieved to see you alive and healthy."

Baracian said, "That's how most of Atlantis felt when we thought the hero of Atlantis was dead. But Shandria never gave up. She found your body adrift in the ocean and took you to Alfamara."

Almost on cue, a lady in waiting arrived with a message addressed to Prince Marvin. It was a blue Waluia flower and a card. Marvin read it out loud. "Princess Shandria of Atlantis and her parents, King Vandian and Queen Isaria, find you an acceptable suitor for their daughter, and request your reply for a formal introduction."

Marvin smiled and said. "You all know my answer is yes. How do I formally respond?"

Baracian smiled as everyone else laughed. He said, "Not so hasty. The court has appointed my wife and me as your official guardians and counsel. Since you still have much to learn, we have a say. Elantria, do you find Princess Shandria to be a suitable and proper lady for Prince Marvin's attention?

Elantria replied. "I'm not sure. She does come from a proper family, but she did flow around between realms with an Earthman. If he feels strongly about her, perhaps we can allow that one indiscretion as youthful exuberance. When I add her recent bravery in defense of Atlantis, I must conclude she has matured. I find her acceptable."

ATLANTIAN MAGIC

Baracian asked if any of the kings or queens had anything to say.

Feldspar said, "I think it is reckless for anyone so young and without a trade to contemplate marriage. He shows promise as a weaponsmith, but he still has several decades to get his journeyman license. I am sure I can use my influence and find him one of our masters for him to apprentice under."

Olivine said, "He is a general in the Atlantian Scout Corps, which in Atlantian society is as well respected as being a smith. They do things differently here, and it is proper for us to accept their customs."

Feldspar said, "Well, he did show valor on the battlefield, although he is a little reckless. But their armor has already chosen each other, and the armor has never been wrong. My wife is far wiser in areas of love and family. I yield to her wisdom."

Thor said, "I will never understand why anyone would rush in and marry someone they haven't enjoyed courting for a hundred springs and fought a hundred battles next to, but then again, worthy battles are hard to find. I know little about Atlantian customs, and all I know about love is that the heart knows what the heart knows. So, I find no objections."

Baracian said, "My queen is my expert advisor in the area of love and family. I agree with her judgment that princess Shandria is suitable."

He turned to Marvin and said, "The decision is yours. You can send her a white waluia if you aren't interested or a blue waluia if you agree to meet with her."

Alandria quickly said, "What about a red waluia?"

Elantria replied, "What? Become engaged right away and skip the introduction stage? They have barely known each other for the required six moons. If she refused the red flower, other prospective candidates might wonder why she rejected him. They would know he has a preference for her and not respond. I don't think he should rush into this."

King Baracian said, "Perhaps you are right, but then perhaps you are wrong. As Thor wisely said, 'The heart knows what the heart knows.' So, the decision is Prince Marvin's to make."

Marvin knew they were having fun at his expense. He replied, "You know Elantria, maybe you are right. Maybe I shouldn't rush into this. I have a drawer full of offers from some prominent women back at my residence in the narrows. I already have a few blue flowers and a few red invitations. Now that the court has recognized me as a prince, I'm sure there are other interested princesses. Besides, Shandria did spend that scandalous time with an Earthman, and you know how reckless they are."

Marvin started laughing, and laughter filled the blue room. The conclusion was already known. After the laughter reduced, he said, "My heart won't be denied. I'll take the risk. Please send her a red waluia."

King Baracian handed the lady in waiting a note that had already been prepared. His wife handed her a red waluia. The lady in waiting gave it to King

Pd MICHEL

Vandian. He opened the note, quietly read it and said, "Excuse us; we need to discuss this in private with our daughter." They left the room with the lady in waiting.

Baracian said, "So tell us what happened on the island, especially after the portal closed."

Marvin told them the story. He then asked, "So when can I see the records about myself, about my parents?"

Baracian smiled and replied, "Some we can view later today. But others are old and brittle. They will take our scholars time to preserve and restore. We asked for them to find original records. Now that they know who you are, I highly suspect that they will increase their search effort, as will the scholars at the university, especially when we encourage them to.

"Three of particular interest testified to the same thing. The court of King Merlin signed and officially sealed the documents a thousand years ago. King Feldspar, Thor, and Queen Juniperia received the documents from your father and hid them until the time was right to release them, which was right after the battle. It foretold the events that recently happened, and attributed them to Merlin's son, the lost prince. Your father and mother left you for adoption on Earth to protect you. It's humbling to hold a thousand-year-old scroll that names the current Atlantian Court.

"You once asked me what I knew about you but couldn't yet reveal. There are several prophecies about the lost prince of Atlantis.

"The lost prince would restore the arch of Atlantis. The lost prince will unite the sword and shield of Merlin. The lost prince will save Atlantis using water, sky, and fire. And the lost prince will rule the eighth Jewel of Atlantis.

"No one imagined the arch could be lost. I knew it had to be you when you restored it. Then you fulfilled the prophecies one by one. The last one says you will rule the eighth Jewel of Atlantis. There were only seven Jewel Islands, so at the time it made no sense. But the volcanic eruption joined the volcanic island chains into one. It's almost as large as Atlantis itself and is large enough to be a Jewel Island.

"It's a lifeless island now, but the soil is fertile. It will take decades, but it will be a beautiful island. It has two large natural harbors and several smaller ones. We need a prince to govern the island, and because of your lineage, tradition says you are that prince. It completes the prophecy."

Juniperia said. "Every few hundred years there is a grand conjunction. It becomes easy to move between the magical realms. At its peak, portals can open up in susceptible spots on their own. We are nearing that time again.

"You were born two major conjunctions ago. The Darfarins had perverted many Atlantians with their dark magic. They were spying and aiding the enemy. There was infighting in the streets. Even the palace wasn't safe. Your mother insisted you be born in Atlantis. We hid you in a building on the outskirts of

362

ATLANTIAN MAGIC

Atlantis during the war. A small team and I cloaked the building from their magic, and I delivered you. Queen Olivine was present at your birth.

"Your father generated a portal to Asgard, where Thor guarded us for a few days then took us back to Alfamara, while your father generated a false trail to Crystal Mountain, and several other realms to confuse the trail. We protected you at Alfamara until the Anastasi took you to Earth. Olivine and I held you in our arms many times. I knew you from the moment you stepped on my dock. I swore to your parents I wouldn't tell anyone who you were until you fulfilled the prophecies. As I said to you at Alfamara, blood doesn't lie.

"If you had grown up in Atlantis, you would have been assassinated before you were weaned. You could have stayed at Alfamara, but Atlantis needed your father and mother in the war. Eventually, you would have had to leave Alfamara, and you would still be a target for assassination. The Anastasi intervened and put you up for adoption on Earth."

Queen Olivine said, "When I held your hands I recognized you, even though you had grown tall and strong. It was all I could do to contain my excitement and keep my vow to your mother not to reveal your identity. King Feldspar wasn't as sure as me until the sword of Merlin chose you. Then he knew it was you.

"Your mother made Queen Juniperia and me your Godparents. Now come here so we can hug you like we have been resisting since you first showed up."

Marvin smiled, walked over to the queens, and returned the hugs they gave him. He couldn't wait to spend some time with them and find out all he could about his parents.

A few minutes later, Vandian returned without his wife, ignored Marvin, and started a discussion with Handrian about plans to restore the Atlantian fleet. It was less about restoring the fleet then about which shipyards on which islands to build the ships. The Atlantian flagship had been one of the oldest ships in the fleet, and they were discussing a complete new design.

Marvin listened to the discussion and heard the tsunami generated by the volcanoes had hit the North Jewel Island hard. It had all but destroyed their western barrier island and damaged many vessels in their western harbor. It would take the barrier island years to recover. Until then the port was at risk from a large storm surge. They wanted to give the island as much work as they could to compensate, but their shipyards would be busy for a while repairing its own fishing fleet. Most of the shipyards were on Eastern Island. But the trees that grew on Northern Island were used for much of the lumber.

Baracian asked Marvin about his time in Asgard. Marvin told him the story of learning sky magic from Thor and the Asgardians. Thor added his take on the story. He then said he saw a new maturity in Marvin during the battle. He offered to train Marvin for a few weeks in Asgard.

Marvin realized he now had offers from three other realms to train him in magic, and he still only knew half the beginning Atlantian weaves that every schoolchild knew.

Queen Isaria returned and sat down next to her husband. She whispered something in his ear. They both were smiling. Marvin saw they were holding hands.

A few minutes later, Shandria walked in, wearing full makeup and a gorgeous gown. It was obvious she had spent all morning getting ready for this. It explained why she hadn't visited him. His lineage was kept hidden until this morning, except for a few ministers, and he was sure Shandria knew and wouldn't be able to keep it secret.

Marvin hadn't seen her like this since the ball at Crystal Mountain. He stood up when he saw her enter. If anything, she looked more beautiful than ever. She had red flowers in her hair and carried a blue waluia. She walked towards Marvin and reached the blue waluia towards him. She saw the disappointed look on Marvin's face as he looked at the blue flower. She laughed, tossed the blue flower onto the table, pulled a red flower from her hair, and handed it to Marvin.

Marvin took the flower with a smile. Shandria reached behind his head and kissed him. Marvin put his arms around her and returned the kiss but then tried to back away. Shandria held him tight and continued the kiss. Soon Marvin realized he wasn't going to get shocked or burnt. The kiss continued for several more seconds before Shandria released the hold on the back of his neck and ended the kiss.

Marvin looked her in the eyes; then he saw anger flare up. Shandria yelled, "And don't you ever scare me like that again!" She hit him in the arm, then she smiled and kissed Marvin again.

Everyone laughed.

After the kiss, Marvin said, "I thought we only had five seconds for a kiss."

Shandria said, "We are now under an engagement weave. Now we have ten seconds. Everything else is the same."

The laughter continued. This time, Marvin initiated the kiss.

Chapter 78

King Handrian ordered a round of the best spiced-wine at the Broken Pier for Fletch, Bonzo, and Kippy, as well as the special, which was the fish of the day from the dock, for each of them. He handed the barmaid a ring-shaped coin and told her to cover today's expenses. She looked at the coin, having never seen a coin worth as much. The owner of the bar came over and sheepishly said, "My king, we won't have enough money to give you change for several hours."

King Handrian replied, "I guess all drinks are on the crown until the coin runs out."

A few hours earlier, King Handrian and Queen Alandria had shown up at the docks for a naval award ceremony. They took their seats. The Admiral called the names of several officers and captains of ships and presented them with awards for their action in the war. At the end of the ceremony, the admiral called up Fletch, Bonzo, and Kippy. They looked surprised, having complained before the ceremony that they did all the work, and the officers got all the glory.

The Admiral took his seat, and King Handrian and Queen Alandria stood up. King Handrian read out accommodations for selfless gallantry in the face of the enemy, and in risking their lives to save and protect a King of Atlantis. He awarded them the bronze shield. Alandria placed the medals around each of their necks and kissed each one of the men. She then handed each of them royal invitations for dinner at The Broken Pier for that evening. It was signed, Handy.

They ate dinner and swapped jokes about the crown, the navy, and the army. After dinner and a round of drinks, Handy said, "I almost forgot. The award comes with a gift from the crown." He pulled out three bags of money and handed one to each of the men. The bags held the equivalent of a year's pay.

Kippy had gotten married after surviving his time on the ogre ship. He and Bonzo started talking about house, home, and family. Fletch was quiet.

Bonzo asked Fletch what he was going to do with his money. Fletch said nothing for a few seconds, and then got up and left the table. Handy watched him walk over and talk to a serving woman. He saw them kissing in the corner and figured Fletch was going to spend some of his money in the back room with the woman.

But then Fletch walked back to the table. He was holding the barmaid's hand, and she was smiling. So was Fletch. He said. "Tondia and I are getting married and plan to use the money for a family. King Handrian and the rest of the table stood up, hugged and kissed Tondia.

Handrian realized he had misjudged the man who had saved his life. He was going to spend all the money on the woman, but not in the back room.

Fletch said, "She joked with me when I first started courting her. She said that she would marry me when I was good enough to sit down and eat with royalty. We have been talking about getting married for a while."

Just then, Prince Marvin, Princess Shandria, and Queen Alandria walked in. Everyone in the bar stood up and bowed their heads in respect. The place was silent. Prince Marvin yelled. "We heard the king was buying drinks and couldn't resist crashing the party. Please relax and carry on."

They walked over to Handy's table. Chairs appeared around the table, donated by people nearby. More spiced-wine was poured. Marvin and Shandria spent a few minutes at the table, then walked around the bar and talked to the customers. Most of the men and women in the bar either were in the Navy or associated with it. Marvin's wave had saved many of them or their friends from ogre ships. They were excited to shake hands and to share a few jokes.

They finished another round of drinks. Alandria stood up, grabbed Handrian's hand and had him get up. She said to Fletch. "Congratulations to you and Tondia. It was fun meeting you and joining you for a few drinks, but we have to go. I have to get Handy home before he gets in trouble with the misses."

Fletch laughed long and hard as the whole bar rose to their feet in respect as the Royals left the Broken Pier.

Epilog

She read the report the Darfarin ambassador had given her. "Damn it! Damn it! Damn it! How could you be so incompetent?"

She turned to the ambassador and said, "How could this have happened? How could you follow my plan so poorly?"

"I did everything I told you I would, and your troops and generals ruined it. When things started falling apart, you should have at least had the good sense to pull back and consult with me. But instead, you started the invasion moons late and lied to me that the invasion was going well until you lost everything. Then when you finally sent for me, it was too late to do anything.

"And now look at me." She pulled back her hood and shouted. "Look at me! The fire that he sent through the portal caught my robe on fire and did this to me. The same portal I wove to save your hive sisters after your foul-up. It will take another week for my magic to heal the scars, and several moons more for my hair to grow back.

"I killed the senior king and queen to prove my loyalty. Then I disabled the palace wards. I made sure Shandria got the cursed necklace. I stole the crystal and created your arch. I helped you seduce ministers in the court and enhanced your spy network. I even put in the backup plan that in another few weeks would have poisoned the royal court. And your constant delays and ineptitude ruined everything.

"You said the necklace we made her nanny give to the princess would disable her magic not destroy it and try to kill her. I want her alive and with her magic!

"If you followed my plan and my timing, all the royals but Princess Shandria would be dead, and I would be sitting on the throne of Atlantis right now. We would be reteaching the princess, and soon she would validate my rule at my side."

She turned her back on the Darfarin Ambassador, walked over, and looked out the window of her temporary palace at the workers with control collars tending the field below. She thought, "We harvest their magic, and they harvest the field. That's how to handle peasants. I will be invincible once I harvest the magic of Atlantis." She stayed looking out the window and ignored the ambassador until he walked away.

She knew her disrespecting the ambassador would make the Darfarin Hive Mother angry, forcing her to call her for an audience. The lost prince was the rock in the stream that caused the ripples that destroyed the flow of her plan. He needed to be eliminated, and Shandria was the key to him. And in the process, she would get Shandria.

ATLANTIAN MAGIC

About the author

Packs of Coyotes howled, snakes rattled, and Javelinas have run past the author as he hiked in the heat of the Sonoran Desert. He spent a cold night in a tent and woke to a half foot of new snow glistening in the early morning in the Tetons. The wings of wild finches dusted his outstretched hand as he shared his snack of potato chips the next morning.

He excitedly scuba dove among moray eels, barracudas, a nurse shark and a sea turtle. He watched the enchanted glow of dolphins gliding through phosphorescent waters from a sailboat in Florida.

He traded his half-finished snack, an apple, to a wild deer in a Florida swamp for a nuzzle and a chance to scratch behind its antlers. An alligator, he thought was a log until it moved, totally ignored his attempt to calmly snorkel away. It seemed not to care that it could out swim him, out run him, and out eat him. In case you were wondering, he didn't even consider feeding his dive partner, his younger brother to the gator. Although he did out swim him.

He crawled on his belly through a cave with a flashlight that worked well if you hit it in the right spot, admiring the sparkling reflection off the sand, his friends told him later was bat guano. And has fallen, repeatedly, several stories from cliffs, protected by a rope attached to a climbing harness.

As a volunteer fireman, he drove a fire engine and ambulance, pulled people from wrecked cars, performing first aid, and dumping gallons of water on residential and commercial fires.

In the Navy, he took a break from operating the nuclear reactor to steer the submarine with the chief of the watch "encouraging" him to keep the planes at zero degrees. He looked through and spun the periscope around as ocean swells caused the boat to rock back and forth. He Looked down from the top of the submarine's sail and watched the magic of the moon shining off midnight darkened water as the boat sliced through the ocean in a rare moment of peace at the end of a three-month patrol.

His moving around the country, courtesy of his job as an engineer, allowed him to collect northern friends who swap jabs about the weather during sub-zero northern winters and the 120-degree summer days of his adopted home in Phoenix Arizona. He lives with his beautiful wife and looks forward to college holiday visits from the Jedi knight son and Hufflepuff daughter his wife still thinks of as her younglings.

Pd MICHEL

Exert from: FOURTH SPACE

Time resisted change. Rich was in for the fight of his life. A time storm sprung up as soon as he tried going backward in time. It pushed him a half-hour downstream with the force of a riptide undertow. He moved to where energy swirls at the edge of the current were heading backward and made some headway. Then he found a break between time waves and fought to move backward against the time current. It took him almost an hour just to get back to when he had started. He was exhausted but refused to give up.

Then he found a rhythm in the waves. He held on to quantum level zero as the energy waves tried to force him forward in time. During the low part of the wave, he dropped to negative time and fought his way backward. He was at his limit, but the temporary rest between wave peaks allowed him to keep fighting.

Rich felt like he was ready to pass out at the end of a marathon when he looked at the clock on the wall. He had traveled an hour back in time. Rich slid back to normal time and rotated into fourth space. Time wouldn't affect him there. He climbed up to higher quantum level. Five dozen steps in the higher quantum level of fourth-space brought Rich to the stadium three states over. He now had the time to save his best friend.

Coming Fall of 2019

370

ATLANTIAN MAGIC

Excerpt from: ATLANTIAN MAGIC - PRINCE

Marvin grabbed a shield from the deck of the skyship. He was glad he did. Birds as large as eagles were attacking the ship. The edges of their wings were as sharp as a sword. He yelled, "Grab your shields." He saw Donnar fending off a bird with a shield. Marvin yelled, "I have your back if you have mine."

Marvin thought about what he could do with his magic. There were too few clouds to weave a hailstorm. And the birds, which he heard Donnar call razoras, were too fast for the ship to get away from.

Marvin wove a portal to the staging area directly in front of the ship. He ran towards the stern and yelled, "Everyone run forward." The captain saw his ship flying through the portal and repeated the command. Marvin wanted to be the last person through to ensure the portal stayed stable. The crew ran forward except for Donnar, who stayed behind to protected his back.

A long line of razoras sliced through the deck of the skyship just forward of where they were standing. They reminded Marvin of the many teeth of a chainsaw cutting through wood. Another line of razoras came through and widened the cut, and then another widened it more. Marvin felt the ship breaking up, and they were on the wrong side of the break. The forward section of the ship made it through, and the aft section started to fall to earth. Marvin let his portal close. The crew was safe except for Donnar and him. They were plunging to their death. If the fall didn't kill them, the vargren on the ground or the razoras in the sky would.

Marvin grabbed Donnar and tried to hold him in the sky with magic. But Donnar was too heavy for the weave Marvin had made. At least it had slowed their falling. Vicious vargren waited below them, and they were defenseless against the razoras whose attention was no longer focused on the skyship.

Marvin had expended most of his energy generating the large portal for the ship. Another standard portal would take too long to stabilize due to the magical static in the air. He saw a snow-covered mountain not too far in the distance that the vargren had gone around. It was clear of Vargren on the south side. Marvin grabbed a tighter hold on Donnar's armor. He had never opened a blink portal so large before. This would probably kill both of them. He was out of options. He said to Donnar, "Forgive me." A blink portal flashed around them, and they disappeared.

Made in the USA
Columbia, SC
19 February 2019